COPYRIGHT

Nowhere But Him by
June Prescott

This is a work of
fiction. Names,
characters, places,
and incidents either
are the product of
the author's
imagination or are
used fictitiously.
Any resemblance to
actual persons,
living or dead,
events, or locales is
entirely coincidental.

*Book design by June
Prescott*

*Editing by June
Prescott*

ISBN 979-8-9949713-0-7

NOWHERE BUT HIM

JUNE PRESCOTT

CONTENT WARNING

The following novel contains sensitive content, including:

Depictions of kidnapping/abduction.
Violence, threats, physical injury, and blood.
Trauma-related responses.
Fear and captivity.
Use of weapons.
Sexual content.
Strong language.

While this story is ultimately a romance novel, it includes suspense elements and explores heavy themes of survival, safety, and control.

Reader discretion is advised.

Prologue

Savannah

"It's snowing." Truthfully, I'm not even sure why I say it. It's the first thing I've offered up in days that isn't strictly necessary and the words fall flat in the endless silence of the cabin. I sigh softly as I watch the thick white flecks tumble lazily from the sky. I've always admired the shift of greys, purples, and indigos that the clouds take this time of year. The ground below is already buried beneath a soft, untouched blanket, and small beads of condensation drip from the edges of the window frame, carving slow paths down the glass. It should feel peaceful. Restful, even. Instead, it feels like everything we aren't saying.

"I know." His voice comes from behind me, deep and distant in that way it gets when he's been staring at nothing for too long. The way he's sounded since the fight. Since I found the notebook. Since the truth wedged itself into the space between us. I imagine his expression hasn't changed much either, wearing that same unreadable mask he refuses to peel away. Bulletproof, like the vest usually secured to his chest. "I used to love playing in the snow when I was little..." I trail off, lifting a finger to trace a line carved by a bead of sweat.

I watch my breath cloud the glass when I speak, pretending I'm closer to the outside world than I feel. "It always made everything look softer," I muse, trying to coax the conversation forward. "Even the ugly stuff." My heart constricts, the words wrapping a fist around it and squeezing. My gaze drops to the thin pool of moisture collecting on the windowsill. It's as shallow and miserable as the rest of the suffocating air of the cabinet.

No response. Just that same, distancing silence. I turn, chestnut waves falling over my shoulder as I face the man I can no longer describe as anything more than a stranger, even when the word tastes *wrong*. And far too complicated. He insists he's still keeping me safe and somewhere I've pushed far to the back of my mind, I know he is. But...It still doesn't dull the ache behind my ribs. Or the longing to be somewhere outside these four walls. "I'm going outside," I announce, standing from my chair. His boots halt behind me from their pace with a dull thud. "No, you're not." I flinch at the sharpness behind his voice.

Sebastian's eyes flicker when I move, finally landing on me when he's been avoiding my gaze for days. His eyes darken, muscle tightening in his jaw. "It wasn't a question," I raise my brow, crossing my arms defensively as I turn back toward the window.

"It isn't an option." His tone hardens, that subtle edge slipping in. A warning more than a threat, the voice he uses when he wants the conversation to end. The one that tells me pushing will only make things worse. The snow keeps falling outside, blissfully unaware of the tension that threatens to invade it from the inside out.

The still air stretches between us, thin as the frost gathering along the glass. I watch Sebastian's reflection instead of meeting his eyes. His broad frame, rigid posture, fingers flexing once at his sides like he's bracing for an argument that I'm too tired to start. I huff under my breath, too spent lately to care about sparing his nerves. "Relax. I'm not planning a dramatic morning run through the mountains. I just want air before I lose my mind. I'll be fine." Despite my attempt to keep my voice calm and cool, the words still bite at the edges.

He offers no outward reaction, but I can sense his irritation in the way his shoulders tighten and his posture further stiffens. "Savannah." He says my name like a statement of dismissal. His reflection shifts with observation. He takes one slow step closer, boots silent on the old wooden floor.

"It's snowing. It's cold. And you're not stepping onto that porch unless I'm next to you," his voice drops into that low, controlled register meant to keep me alive. I roll my eyes dramatically, throwing my head back with the motion.

"God forbid I inhale fresh air unsupervised," the sarcasm drips from each word muttered under my breath. But my traitorous heart...it swells with relief when he insists. Because after everything, the only time this all feels survivable is when he's standing beside me.

Sebastian isn't cruel. Not in the ways it would be easy to hate him for. And *God*—I wish I could. Things would be so much easier if I did. But he's immovable, an iron wall dressed in quiet gentleness, and sometimes that's worse. It makes the bars around my life feel like something I should apologize for. "It's just for a minute," My voice softens and I release a bated breath, offering him the first ounce of patience that I have in days. "Just to feel something real. Please." I ask more for his understanding than his permission. I would've gone anyway.

A beat passes between us. Two.

The snow keeps falling, as though the world is mocking the cages and warnings and the man hovering behind me like a shadow with a heartbeat. Finally, Sebastian exhales. One heavy, frustrated sound through his nose. Maybe I've crossed the line again unknowingly. The thought doesn't hurt the way it used to. In fact, I can't will myself to care at all. Because even if I did, I wouldn't expect him to explain. And If I did cross a line? At least that urges him to react rather than ignore my existence completely.

"You think I don't want to give you that? You think I wouldn't give you everything you've asked for if I could?" His voice isn't raised, but the words hit the air with more force than if it were, slamming into my chest like a train. "You think this is *easy* for me?" I turn to face him, catching the moment he looks away. His lips press together, damming words he can't admit behind them. His hands curl, then uncurl, as though he's holding tightly to something I can't see. He inhales a breath and releases it sharply before he speaks again.

"The people out there," he continues quietly, "want you gone." Heard that one before. My eyes narrow in his direction, blood rushing my cheeks.

"And you *don't*?" I whisper before I can stop myself. All I've been is a burden, a stupid girl he's been forced to babysit, secluded with no one coming to rescue *him* from *me*, either. I force myself to believe that's all this has been. It's easier that way, doesn't allow my heart to collapse in on itself.

His eyes snap back to mine, stormy and startlingly

alive for someone who tries so hard to stay unreadable. "Not even for a second." The warmth in his tone vanishes as quickly as it appeared, shuttered behind that steely resolve. My heart skips in my chest, memories of weeks past pushing to the front of my mind. There is no rewinding, no going back now that the walls he keeps around him have been rebuilt. He draws in closer until I can feel the heat radiating from his frame.

"Five minutes," he says at last. I almost squeal when I rush past him too eagerly and grab the oversized coat on the door to shrug over my shoulders. His steps behind me are calculated, his back straight, but he moves forward anyway.

"Not a step beyond the porch." His voice is stern again, but this time the threat is tempered with something else. Something that almost feels like hope. The smile that spreads wide across my features is involuntary but the giddiness that fills my chest with warmth is the first time I've felt excited for anything in the past week. "And if anything feels wrong," he warns, "We come back inside. Understood?" I nod, wide grin plastered in place, waving a dismissive hand. "Okay, yeah, I hear you," I hum.

Sebastian steps past me, reaching for the heavy latch on the door. For the first time in days, the world creaks open. Not fully, but enough that icy air slips in and kisses my cheeks, weaving itself into the cracks I've been trying to hold myself together with. I glide out onto the porch, close my eyes, and inhale sharply, breathing it in like a memory. Snowflakes drift through the gap, catching in my hair. For a single, fragile moment...I feel free. I take a step closer to the outside world, tilting my head back and letting the snow dance on my face.

And then a distant sound echoes through the trees

outside—sharp and metallic.

Sebastian freezes at the same instant I do, tension rolling off his body immediately. My head whips toward him, eyes wide, my breath catching in my throat. All the joy, the excitement, ripped away in one measly second. The blood drains from my face, my limbs going numb. I reach for him instinctively, my fingers curling into the fabric of his sleeve before I can think better of it. His arm shifts, guiding me behind him, shielding me with a precision that's almost muscle memory. My fingers tighten around his sleeve like a lifeline. "Sebastian...What was that?" My voice trembles despite my best effort.

The metallic noise rings out again. Slow, scraping, and deliberate. Not a branch. Not the wind. My stomach drops. My heart beats frantically in my ears, all our training time wasted. Everything—*everything*—he's taught me leaves my mind at the threat of real danger. Sebastian's entire body goes rigid. He moves before I can ask anything, one hand held upward in a silent command to keep still, the other closing around toward the knife tucked beneath his coat. Not the gun. The knife. The close quarters one. The one that means he's prepared for combat.

"Go back inside," he commands, voice pitched firm and lethal. "Wait—" My voice is unfamiliar as it hits my ears, desperate and squeamish just like the pit in my stomach. "Don't leave me alone," I plea, but the words mean nothing to him. All this time we've been secluded and the threat that Sebastian insists was going to return has never felt as real as this.

He's already stepping off the porch before I can mutter anything else, boots crunching softly in the fresh snow, leaving me standing in the door like a deer in headlights. My arms fold around my waist, pulling my coat together like a form of camouflage. He moves in carefully, like a predator hunting for prey, my eyes trailing each step. Cold air rushes over me in his absence, stinging my face with a sharp reminder of the world I've been begging to touch.

Past the tall pines that surround the cabin, I can make out a figure approaching the perimeter. Bundled in a dark jacket, moving with the easy confidence of someone who belongs to danger. The way Sebastian does when he performs his perimeter sweeps throughout the night. My eyes go wide and my hands curl in on themselves knowing I'm completely useless right now.

The gate groans as it swings fully open. Not forced or broken. *Opened.* My pulse rings through my ears, every extremity tingling. My eyes are tunnel visioned on the man who swears he won't let anything or anyone hurt me.

"Sebastian!" a foreign voice calls out, approaching too closely. "You better still be alive, you bastard!" My stomach tightens; the voice belongs to a male and exudes the same authority as Sebastian often does, though his tone is much lighter. Sebastian stops dead in his tracks. His jaw clenches so hard the muscles jump. Through the dim morning light and swirling snow, a tall, solid figure steps forward. My blood runs as cold as the wind that whips at my hair. *I've seen that face before.* On a photograph tucked inside the book. Younger, smiling beside a much different version of Sebastian. I catch the glimmer of the same silver chain dangling around his neck, tucked safely beneath his coat. Dog tags.

"...Jesse?" Sebastian's voice is rough as he grits through his teeth.

A short, relieved bark of a laugh answers. "You fall off the map for over a month and that's all you've got to say? I was ready to start digging through snow drifts for your corpse." Jesse steps into full view then. Snow clings to the sandy hair that peeks from underneath his hat, placed backwards on his head. His cheeks are flushed from the cold, eyes sharp and scanning in contrast. There's a looseness to him that Sebastian doesn't have, a warmth at odds with the weapon holstered openly at his hip and the same tactical gear that Sebastian adorns daily. And an old familiarity between them that carries both trust and ghosts. My pulse skitters at the exchange. Sebastian never talks about his past. Never slips up or mentions friends. No one should know where we are...but this man does.

Sebastian takes a single, measured step forward, posture loosening just a fraction. Unspoken trust passes between them, the kind of bond you can't manufacture. Even so, the muscles in his back remain tight through his coat. "What the *hell* are you doing here?" Sebastian bites out. I can feel the warning in it from the doorway, tight and maybe even protective. Jesse's smirk fades as he catches the tone. "You missed our check-ins. All of them. Sue me but I got worried, dude."

"I'm *fine*." Sebastian clips.

"You think that's the point?" Jesse snaps. Then his gaze sweeps the cabin, quick and tactical. Past Sebastian, toward me, left rooted in the doorway. He freezes instantly, his gaze locking onto me like a target. So does Sebastian, though I catch the guilty expression that flickers across his face momentarily.

"Well, I'll be damned," A slow grin spreads across Jesse's face as he whistles, "She's even prettier than the intel photos." The statement hangs in the air like a trigger half-pulled, feeling like more of a dig than a compliment. This stranger waltzes up to this hidden gate, secluded off the smallest gravel road I've ever laid eyes on, and *knows who I am*? The intel photos...like the ones I found. Pictures of me, of my family. It dawns on me uncomfortably that this operation is much larger than I could've imagined. And I'm left standing in suffocating darkness about the whole thing.

Sebastian moves subtly, blocking me from his full view with his frame like it's instinctual. Not aggressive, but possessive in the way he won't admit to. "She's not your concern," he snaps. I should be feeling defensive. Angry, even, at the secrets he continues to keep. But I can't. Not when beside Sebastian is the safest place I've ever been in my life.

Jesse's brows lift, amused by the exchange. "Are you forgetting who you're talking to?" The question carries the weight of authority, quickly replacing the jovial manner he held only minutes ago. "Everything you do is my concern, Bash. Especially when you disappear off grid with the one girl the entire east division is trying to hunt down." My breath stutters. He warned me that the danger wasn't gone. But hearing it from someone else? Someone who looks like he stepped straight out of Sebastian's past? It makes the threat feel real. I glance up at Sebastian, searching for reassurance or clarity; anything. But his eyes are locked on Jesse like his entire world just shifted. Like he's calculating or angry or...afraid. Not of Jesse or of what this means. But of losing control of a situation that he's barely been holding together.

Sebastian bristles and I swear the temperature drops ten more degrees. I swallow, stepping a little closer to the edge of the porch despite his silent command to stay put.

The snow is still falling, soft and gentle, completely unaware of the storm rolling across Sebastian's features. As it drifts silently around us, I'm painfully certain that there is so much more I still don't know.

1

Savannah

EIGHT WEEKS EARLIER

I slam the door to my room harder than I mean to, but the echo feels good. It feels final. Like something inside me has snapped and I'm not taping it back together this time. I'm twenty. Twenty years, five months, and six days old to be exact. And somehow, I'm still being treated like I'm made of glass, fragile and transparent.

The argument with my parents is still buzzing in my head. During dinner, it felt like all of us were trying to pretend the world wasn't about to split open. I could feel my father's anger boiling with every question I demanded an answer to, not that I got any. Nothing real, anyway. Every answer was clipped, every word sharp as a dagger meant to silence me. Every reason sounds ridiculous the longer I replay it.

You don't understand how the world works, it's not safe, you're too young.

But how am I supposed to understand the world if they won't even let me step into it? Maybe for them, everything will go back to normal tomorrow. But not for me. I'm done waiting for permission that will never come.

I flop back onto my bed and stare at the pattern of popcorn on the ceiling, my heartbeat still fast with anger and restlessness. Adrenaline courses through my veins like lava, my cheeks flushed crimson. I can feel the heat without reaching up to touch them.

Telluride is beautiful, sure. Postcards and snowcaps and tourists who think they've discovered some magical, untouched secret. But to me it's just... small. Predictable. The same faces every day, the same routines and gossip, the same mountains trapping you in like you're part of the scenery. I want more than this. I want to see more, experience more. My body craves adventure like oxygen needed to breathe. New York...the name alone feels electric. Busy streets, crowded subways, impossible skyscrapers that reach the clouds.

I want to know what it feels like to get lost in a place where no one knows who I am. Where no one looks at me like they know my life story before we even speak. Italy feels like a dream. Warm stone buildings, narrow streets full of color, art everywhere you look, history in every step. I want to taste food I can't pronounce and hear voices with accents that don't sound anything like home. Even *Florida* sounds appealing, at this point. Palm trees, humidity, beaches that go on forever. People say it's chaotic, but at least it's alive. I'd take chaos over routine any day.

But I've never gone anywhere aside from our curated

family vacations. Not without Mason trailing behind me like my personal guard dog. My older brother who acts like he's on some mission to keep me safe from whatever boogeyman my family thinks lurks in the dark. Nothing happens here. Ever. I've asked a hundred times, *why the rules, why the watchful eyes, why the constant caution*, and every time I get the same vague, patronizing answers. *It's better this way, Savannah. You'll understand when you're older.* I *am* older now. And I still don't understand anything.

All I know is I'm tired, down to my bones. Tired of being told the world is too big, too dangerous, too unknown for someone like me. Tired of being treated like some naive child when I'm old enough to want something different and to pursue those wants without being chastised. Tired of waking up every day and wondering if this is all my life is ever going to be.

When my eyes close, I can picture it. The airport, the boarding pass, the moment the plane lifts off and Telluride shrinks into nothing but memory. The idea alone makes my chest ache with longing. I want freedom. I want movement. I want *out*.

And this time...I'm going to take it for myself. Night can't fall fast enough.

I've been waiting in my room for hours for the house to shift into the quiet tension it holds during the night. My suitcase is open on the bed, half-filled with clothes I shove into it without folding. I don't care what they look like; I just need them gone, out of the closet and ready for my next move. My hands tremble as I pack. I can't tell if the way my heart thrashes at my chest is from excitement or fear. Maybe both. I'm stuffing my last sweater inside when the door clicks open without warning.

"Sav?" Mason's voice. I freeze, cursing internally. My eyes squeeze shut while my brain racks itself for some explanation that won't sound like a blatant lie. Of all the people in this house to catch me, he's probably the worst. He can see right through me. Consequence of spending too much time together.

I turn slowly. He's leaning in the doorway, arms crossed, expression unwavering, but his eyes go straight to the suitcase. Great. Perfect. Exactly what I needed. He steps inside, cautiously, as if he's approaching a rabid animal. "What are you doing?" he asks.

My chest tightens and I swallow thickly, puffing my chest out like the confidence I need in this moment will somehow manifest itself. "What does it look like?" I snap defensively. Mason isn't the subject of my frustration, but he's found himself standing in the line of fire. Guilt settles in my chest, but I push it down.

"Don't..." he says quietly. "Just... think about what you're doing." I laugh, the sound short and bitter. "Mason, this is all I've been able to think about for years. I'm done. I'm leaving. Nothing you say is going to change my mind so save your breath." His whole posture stiffens, and suddenly he looks older than twenty-four. He looks worn down, almost exhausted. My back turns to him as I continue to poke and prod my belongings inside the suitcase, anything that I can fit.

"Savannah, you can't just walk out in the middle of the

night." I roll my eyes and exhale an exasperated breath through my nose. Although Mason is the one person in this family that actually treats me like my brain works half the time, it's moments like these where it feels like he's still on *their* side. "Why not?" I snap. "I'm an *adult*! I can make my own decisions. I can't even live my own life here and you know that."

He shakes his head, lips pressing together in a thin line. "You're being ignorant, Savannah. This is why we treat you the way we do! You don't know what you're about to do. You have no idea what it's like out there."

"Maybe because no one has ever given me the chance!" I try to keep my voice down but even at a hush, my tone is tight with agitation.

"I'm serious," he says, voice rising as he takes a step deeper into my room. "You think Mom and Dad made these rules up for fun? You think I follow you around because I get some thrill out of it? Because I have nothing better to do with my time? You have no idea—*none*—what you're about to walk into."

"I know exactly what's out there," I fire back. "Life. Experiences! Places I'll never see if I stay locked up here."

"That's not what I meant and you know it. Think about what you're doing. You think sneaking out in the middle of the night sells the idea of your maturity?"

My palms face him, urging him to stop. "Mason, I don't care. I don't have time for this." The words spill out but I don't regret a single one. I can feel the sting in the corner of my eyes and hope that they don't betray me. Fighting with my parents feels normal, routine. Fighting with Mason feels like my heart being shredded and served up for display. Even through my anger and resentment, the bond I share with my brother is the only one that feels the way family is supposed to make you feel. Loved and cared for, instead of inconvenient or transactional. I turn to face him, eyes pleading as I speak. "I'm leaving. I've already made up my mind."

His eyes flare, hurt flickering through before he masks it. "Sav..." He steps closer, lowering his voice like that'll suddenly make me reasonable. "You're being naive. You don't understand how dangerous—"

I cut him off with a groan. "I don't understand because no one will tell me anything! Not even you! All my life all I've ever heard is *'it's dangerous,'* or *'you don't understand.'* Well, I'm tired of excuses! If no one will tell me what's going on, I'll just figure it out myself." I pause, hands braced on my hip. Mason is only four inches taller than my five-foot six frame but right now, as I stand my ground, I feel smaller than ever. "I don't want to live like this anymore and I'm not going to. Stop trying to change my mind!" I shout. This time I don't care who hears. "You all treat me like a child and then get mad when I act like one. This isn't fair." He opens his mouth, closes it, like he's contemplating some new reason that's supposed to compel me to stay.

"Some things are better not knowing," he settles. I huff a breath at his explanation and turn back to my suitcase, shoving and pushing more clothes before I flip the top closed and tug on the zipper. "That's not your choice to make for me." My voice is quiet now, laced with finality.

My decision presses down on both of us and closes in the walls of the room. For a fleeting moment, he looks like he might tell me everything. Whatever he's been hiding all these years. Whatever truth he thinks I can't manage. But then he swallows it down and shakes his head, stepping back. "You're making a mistake."

"Maybe. But it's *my* mistake to make."

He pauses, then, and I can see the defeat settle over him slowly in the gentle sag of his shoulders, the way his eyes soften as they scrape over me. "You're really going," he murmurs.

"Yes."

"And if I tell Mom and Dad?"

I shrug, heart pounding, praying that for once, he'll have my back and not theirs. Long enough for me to get a head start, at least. A taste of the freedom I crave. "Then tell them. I'm going either way." Something shifts in his expression...frustration, fear, maybe even resignation. He runs a hand through his hair and turns away like he can't stand to watch me tearing apart the life he's tried so hard to protect. "Sav..." His voice is softer now, almost despairing. "Please don't do this."

But I already have.

Dragging the suitcase off the bed, I brush past him and file down to the driveway. I hear him call my name after me but silence it with the thud of my suitcase skidding across the trunk of my car.

2

Sebastian

The garden is quiet tonight. Colder than usual, the kind of cold that bites at exposed skin and keeps most people sheltered inside. But not me. My post is the same as it's been for nine months: tucked in the shadows beside the old stone wall at the edge of the Monroe family's backyard, eyes locked on the house. Savannah's house. Most nights are uneventful. A light turns on, a curtain shifts, someone goes to bed too late. Nothing abnormal. Nothing that would justify how many resources are tied to protecting this girl who has no idea any of us exist.

But tonight is different. I hear the raised voices before I see them. Muffled at first, then sharper as the door that connects her bedroom to the back hallway swings open. Mason steps into view, shoulders tense, expression tight. Savannah follows, and she's practically vibrating with anger. *What the hell happened?*

I shift forward, eyes squinting just enough to see her face through the branches. Her cheeks are flushed, eyes blazing and movements jerky. Mason says something—too quiet for me to catch—but whatever it is, it pushes her over the edge. She shoves past him. That alone is enough to make me take a step forward, instincts prickling. My fingers flex at my side. If I've learned anything about her, it's that Savannah never pushes, she bends. She *yields*. She swallows irritation the way most people swallow air. But tonight, she barrels past her brother like she can't get away from him fast enough.

That's when I see it. The suitcase.

Not a duffel. Not an overnight bag. A suitcase, full and heavy dragging behind her, the kind people take when they're leaving for good. My throat tightens. I tap the mic at my collar, "We've got movement," I whisper, keeping my voice low. "Subject is packing. Repeat. She's packing." There's a crackle in my earpiece, then Jesse's voice, half-alert, half-bored. "Packing for what? A sleepover?"

"No," I snap, eyes glued to her as she storms down the drive. My steps follow the same direction, careful not to set off the motion sensor floodlights Mr. Monroe had installed six months ago. "You're not hearing me. She's leaving." Savannah throws open the back of her Bronco. Light green, older than she is, the kind of thing she loves because it has 'character' even though it barely runs on especially chilly days. I couldn't count the number of times she's had it in the shop for one reason or another over the past few months on both hands. The suitcase hits the metal floor of the trunk with a clunk that echoes across the yard. Shit. "She's actually doing it," I mutter.

"What's wrong?" another guy on the team asks. "We've

got her perimeter covered. If she stays local—"

"She's not staying local." I already know it. I can feel it. This isn't a tantrum. This is a breaking point. Panic creeps up the back of my neck. My fingers tremble with instinct. I don't know where she thinks she's going, but she can't just vanish off grid. Not without ruining months of containment. Not without walking straight into dangers she doesn't even know exist. We know that her family has tried to warn her without explicit detail, but like any other twenty-year-old, she thinks it's all bullshit. In Savannah's mind, the world is full of wonder, not full of threat. Not like I know it to be.

Mason steps into the yard, calling her name. She doesn't even look back. Savannah slams the Bronco's door shut, climbs in, and the engine groans to life. "Hayes," Jesse's voice comes through, now sharp, fully awake and focused on the mission as he drops my last name into the comm. "Don't let her out of range."

"I'm already on it."

I move before the taillights hit the street, slipping through the back gate and cutting across the service easement behind the garage. The Charger is parked where it always is, blacked out, invisible unless you know where to look. I climb in, turn the engine, and pull out just far enough to keep her in view. No headlights. No sudden movements. Far enough back that she won't notice; she probably wouldn't, anyway. She's being reckless, irrational. I keep myself close enough that nothing else, no one else, can get to her first.

"I've got eyes," I say into the comm. "On her tail. I'll figure out what's going on."

Because something *is* wrong.

Savannah doesn't run.

Savannah doesn't fight.

Savannah doesn't *leave*.

Not unless she's been pushed into a corner so tight she can't breathe. And whatever made her desperate enough to grab a suitcase in the middle of the night? I'm going to find out.

Savannah's taillights weave ahead of me, a dim red glow dipping and rising with the curves of the back roads outside Telluride. Two hours. Two hours of her driving aimlessly—small loops, sudden turns, doubling back like she's lost in her own thoughts or trying to outrun them. Even from here, I can tell she hasn't planned a damn thing. She's not thinking. She's reacting. Something happened that broke her and this was her solution. To run, with nowhere to go.

And I'm hoping, *praying*, she'll eventually realize that running in circles at midnight isn't the great escape she imagined. In my earpiece, Jesse's voice cuts through the quiet hum of my engine. "Two hours, Bash. At this rate she's gonna hit the Utah border before deciding she left her toothbrush behind."

I grit my teeth, white knuckling the wheel through my impatience. "Shut up, Pierce. She doesn't know what she's doing."

"Ooh, touchy." He's lucky he's on the other side of the comms and not standing in front of me. Higher rank or not, the more he teases, the more my fist twitches.

"Something feels off" I snap. "This isn't normal, not even for her."

The comms go quiet as the truth hangs there, heavy and cold. Jesse and I have both been trained to know in our gut when something has gone awry without having the facts to prove it. And that's when it happens. A flash, white and violent, ruptures in the tree line ahead. A split second later, a sound cracks through the night. A gunshot.

My body reacts before my brain catches up. Everything inside me goes still, sharp, focused, muscle memory honed years ago in Afghanistan. "Contact!" I bark into the comms. Savannah's Bronco slams to a sudden stop, brake lights flaring, her scream ripping through the air.

Before I can hit my own brakes, a black SUV bursts out of the dark, fishtailing across the road and cutting me off. Tires spit gravel across my windshield as they slam to a stop. Three men spill out like they've been waiting for this moment. Just like I have. I don't think, I move, my body working on intuition alone. I slam the car into park, kill the engine, and I'm out the door with my pistol up before the dome light even flickers. "Hayes—wait for backup!" someone shouts over comms. Muted noise in the back of my mind. "There's no time!" I clip back.

The first man reaches Savannah's door. I fire. Clean and controlled. He drops. The other two instantly return fire. Bullets rip through the air, slamming into metal. I duck behind my open door, the impact vibrating through it. "Hayes—talk to us!" Jesse's voice hits my ear like a punch. "How many—"

"Three," I bark. "One down." A round whistles past my head. I feel it slice the air. They're organized, came prepared. I lean out, fire again. It forces one back, making him take cover behind Savannah's Bronco. But when I pop up for another shot, aimed and focused on where theirs came from, my stomach plummets.

Savannah isn't in the driver's seat anymore, her figure

gone as quickly as the SUV appeared. It's already peeling out before I can scramble back into the driver's seat.

"Savannah!" I shout, even though I know she can't hear me, wouldn't recognize my voice if she could. "Fuck!" I curse, knuckles connecting with the bulletproof glass of the driver's side window. Where the hell did she go? My pulse spikes, chest heaving with struggled breath. Adrenaline burns cold through my veins. She was just there. Two seconds ago, she was right there. Jesse's voice is frantic now. "Hayes—status? Where's the subject?" I scan the dark, every instinct screaming.

She's gone. I've lost her.

3

Savannah

The world tilts violently as hands grab my arms and rip me from the comfort of my Bronco. Shouts, grunts, and the boom of doors slamming fill the air around me. I hit the ground on my back, scrambling to stand. I don't have time to run. I barely have time to scream before they shove me into the back of the black SUV. At the front of my mind, I know no one can hear me. Not out here. I try to struggle, claw at them, remember any self-defense that my brother taught me; but they're strong. Too strong. My fight-or-flight kicks into overdrive. My hands press against either side of the door where it waits for me ajar. "No!" I yell, using what strength I have to keep myself in the open.

I hear it again, the loud bang that ricocheted off the tree line before my world came crashing in. My breath catches in my throat and I whip my head toward the sound but I see nothing. Nothing but the SUV they're trying to force me into, never ending darkness, and one of the men dropping to the ground. "*What—*" I can't gather my thoughts quick enough to form a sentence before I hear the sound again, a flash of white coming from behind the vehicle.

I feel one of them press something cold and hard into my side and I stiffen with immediate recognition.

"Get in the fucking car, now, Savannah!" he spits, my name too familiar on his foreign lips. "Don't fight it." A chill runs down my spine, bumps ghosting up my arms. My throat burns. *How do they know my name?* I don't know these men. I've never seen them before in my life. Panic wells up, hot and fast, burning through my chest. My mind flails, searching for a way out, for anything familiar. I'm yanked into the back seat, my arms aching from the force. And then I hear it.

My name. Soft, urgent, calling me from somewhere far away, somewhere my gut tells me I *should* recognize. "*Savannah!*" It's coming from outside. Someone is there, someone sees what's happening! My chest hammers. My stomach lurches. My mind clings to hope like a lifeline. "Help me!" I scream hopelessly again as the door slams shut and the barrel is jarred tighter against my ribs. I wince, trying to pull away from the pressure. My heart prays it's Mason—*please let it be Mason.* But the voice... it isn't him. It's calm and strangely confident. It's lower, something I don't recognize, but it carries an unfamiliar sense of authority.

"Who—what—" My voice trembles. "Quiet!" A hand clamps over my mouth. My pulse explodes in my ears, the ringing deafening. The SUV lurches forward and my body is cemented to the backseat. The world outside is a blur of headlights and trees in my frantic gaze, the road disappearing behind us. The men string together sentences in another language, Italian I think, and I wished I paid more attention in class.

I cling to the seat, knuckles white, and fight not to

panic entirely. I try to make sense of what's happening, of *why* they know my name. My thoughts spin faster than the wheels beneath us. *I'm going to vomit.* Instincts take over as I bite the hand clamped over my mouth but I'm immediately met with a sharp, hard jab against my side. I cry out in pain and he digs the barrel into my ribs again, "Behave yourself if you want to see tomorrow," he threatens through clenched teeth. I blink rapidly, my eyes stinging with that familiar burn. My arms wrap around my waist, as if I have any capability of shielding myself from this nightmare.

My teeth tug my lower lip inward, chest rising and falling furiously. I remain silent, swallowing the bile that rises in my throat. Something I'm certain of is the voice I heard yelling my name knows more than I do. That voice *owns* this moment in a way that terrifies me more than the men holding me ever could. I close my eyes, trying to anchor myself, trying to imagine Mason's face, hear his real voice, feel something solid and safe. But the world around me has vanished and I realize... I'm truly alone.

Completely, utterly alone.

4

Sebastian

I hit the ground behind my Charger's door, chest heaving, adrenaline burning through every vein. My fist pounds the ground before me. Savannah's gone. These men are organized, precise, and they have her. They're moving fast. Faster than I anticipated. Every instinct I have screams that they know exactly what they're doing. This was planned. "Pierce," I hiss into my comm, voice tight with rage, barely above the wind whipping past as my vision tunnels. "She's been taken. SUV, black, heading east on County 12. Eyes on her. Move. NOW."

Static crackles, then Jesse's voice, sharp and controlled. At least one of us is calm right now. "Copy that. I'm on it. Units prepped."

I slam my hand against the roof of the car when I stand, trying to calm my nerves, trying to steady my breathing enough to think. *Think*, Sebastian. Every second counts. Every second she's in their hands, the danger multiplies. I punch the accelerator. Tires squeal against asphalt as I peel out, keeping a careful distance behind the

SUV. They can't spot me, not yet. Not if I have any hope of getting her out safely.

The road twists and narrows, the Bronco a tiny green blip in my rearview mirror. I track the SUV obsessively, memorizing every turn, every flicker of brake light. My mind races with questions. *Where are they taking her? How many are involved? What's the motive? How long have they been watching?* The fear I felt earlier, the panic for her safety, hardens into a cold, sharp focus. This isn't just about stopping a runaway girl anymore. This is extraction. Containment. Survival. I glance at the dark horizon. There's no time to hesitate, no time to plan the perfect approach. I know the way these men operate. They've waited. They've set this trap. And right now, Savannah is the bait.

I grip the steering wheel tight, knuckles paling with force. "Don't lose her," Jesse's voice comes again, a low rumble in my ear. "We're coordinating intercept points, we've got your twenty. You have eyes, Hayes. Keep visual. Don't engage until she's clear—"

I cut him off, voice sharp with warning, "I'm not waiting. Not this time." No room for negotiation. Shit like this is why I was pulled into the special operations unit in the first place. Nothing gets between me and my target. Until now.

The SUV darts into a narrow stretch of road flanked by thick forest. Shadows swallow it whole. I follow behind, keeping my distance, every nerve buzzing with danger. Every instinct sharpened on foreign soil, every late-night patrol, every scenario I've ever prepared for—All of it is screaming one thing: she's mine to protect. I tighten my grip, load my pistol, and mutter under my breath, barely audible, "Not today. Not her. Not on my watch."

The SUV's taillights vanish around a bend, then reappear, brief and flickering, before they turn sharply up a hidden drive I never noticed before. It climbs steeply, weaving between trees so dense I would've missed it even in daylight. I ditch the Charger at the bottom of the drive. Thankfully, the winter storm that was supposed to hit this weekend has held off and the ground, although frozen enough to pack the gravel, is free of slick ice or snow as I climb it on foot. A tiny house sits at the top, old and remote. The cover of the porch sags and the walls look like they could cave in at any gust of wind.

Perfectly placed for someone who doesn't want to be found. My stomach drops. They didn't pick this place at random. They've been watching her. Studying her every move. Just like we were.

So how the hell did we miss *them*? Which one of my men failed their post? Which perimeter went dark? How long had they been closing in while we babysat the wrong shadows? It doesn't matter. Not right now. They won't have a job after tonight, but that's tomorrow's problem. Right now, Savannah is all that matters. I close in behind a line of dense pines and lift my comm.

"Target is stopped and in reach," I whisper. My voice sounds like it's coming from somewhere distant to my own ears, laced with urgency. "Confirm visual." My voice is confident unlike every other part of me. Jesse answers instantly, "Copy. Units in route." My blood boils, knuckles curling at my sides. She doesn't have the time to wait. I'm in this alone. I don't contemplate before I begin to maneuver between the trees, keeping low and out of sight. My eyes stay fixed on the shell of a house as the SUV doors open.

Two of the men drag Savannah out, one on each side

of her, their grips firm on her arms. She stumbles, almost falling, and their grip tightens. Too tight. I watch her face pinch in the dim porch light as she cries out and one of the men juts her forward. I can see him spitting something evil at her, just out of earshot. A hot, controlled rage burns through me. They put hands on her like she's nothing. They think they can make her disappear. They think no one's watching.

I have to force myself not to break cover. The urge to rush them, to put myself between her and everything else, is overwhelming. But that'll get her killed. Or me. Or both of us. Patience. Timing. Precision. That's what I've trained for.

I crouch behind an old stack of firewood as the men shove her through the door. She cries out again—small, sharp, swallowed quickly. It slices through me. My hand finds the weapon holstered at my side reactively. The door slams shut behind them. Now it's just me, the night, and the pounding of my heart. I take a breath, then another. *Think, Bash. Think.*

My eyes sweep the perimeter quickly. Only one vehicle, no external patrol. No motion sensors that I can see. Two men inside, maybe three if I missed one. Doubtful. They may have planned this attack, but my unit must have slipped by them just as they did us. There's no outer protection.

The SUV's trunk is still open. Good. They were confident. Sloppy with their work. Jesse crackles into my ear, voice low and tense. "Hayes, do not go in alone." A warning, like he can read my thoughts. The result of too much time together spent in a warzone. I ignore his warning, I have to if I want to keep this girl alive.

"Too late," I shake my head to no one but the listening forest. "There's no time." I slip closer, sticking to shadows, mapping every window, every exit. One in the back is

cracked open, just an inch, but enough. I spot the faint glow
of a lamp inside, moving shadows of the men pacing. Two
shadows.

I hear her wail before I see her and my eyes scan the
room. They land on her, tied to a rickety wooden chair in the
middle of the otherwise empty room, her eyes trailing the
men as they cross back and forth in front of her. There's a
thin gash on her forehead and duct tape sealing her mouth
but she appears otherwise unharmed. Even from here, I can
see the panic hiding in her features.

I freeze, everything in me narrowing to a single point.
Get her out. No more mistakes. I ease up beside the window,
pulling the half-mask bundled around my neck up to cover
my nose and mouth. I won't be clumsy, no risk of a revealed
identity. I listen to their hushed voices with strained ears.
"...boss will want her alive," a man says.

Alive. Brief, fleeting relief punches through me.
Followed by a foreign drive of fear. Why alive? Who is their
boss? I shake my head quickly, pushing away the thoughts
beginning to consume my mind away. I can't think about that
now. Their footsteps move away from the window, deeper
into the room. This is my opening. I tap my comm once. Not
for permission, just for record.

"Going in," I whisper. Before Jesse can argue, I
untangle the small clear piece from my ear and let it drop
over my shoulder. I slide my pistol free, steady my breath,
and move. Every step is deliberate, every thought razor-
sharp. Savannah is inside. Scared, alone, and in pain.

And I'm getting her out. No matter what waits behind
that door.

5

Savannah

Two hands on either arm grab me before I even comprehend the vehicle coming to a stop. Fingers like iron clamp around my arms, dragging me onto the porch, and I know that if I live to see tomorrow, I'll have fingerprint shaped bruises. The cabin has an overwhelming aroma of dust and smoke, a single lamp flickering in the corner providing dim light despite the endless night outside the door. It must be after midnight now; I know I was driving for hours before this happened. Surely, someone is looking for me by now...Right? My family wouldn't go through all the trouble to keep me locked away for all this time just to not notice I'm gone. That's what I tell myself—to ease the nausea that refuses to subside.

The door slams, dragging me out of my thoughts as I flinch in reaction, and a chair scrapes across the floorboards. "Sit," one of the men commands. I barely have time to gasp before they shove me into it, a quiet yelp escaping my lips as my back slams into the old, dense wood of the chair. "Fuck you!" I snap at them, eyes dark with rage. A flash of silver shines in my peripheral and then I feel a sharp sting above my eyes as the butt of the gun connects with my forehead. I shriek in response but I'm quickly silenced by a wide piece of tape being slapped over my mouth.

Before I can reach to claw myself free of it, rope is wound around my wrists, tight enough to burn. My ankles follow, securing me in place despite my protests. I pull once, hard, but the knots don't budge. The two men step back, shapes moving in the dim light, voices low but unmistakably muttering about me. "Don't mess her up," one of them snaps, "she's more valuable alive." "Yeah. Let's keep her that way," the other fires back.

My heart sinks thinking of the alternative. Valuable? *What could they mean by that? Am I being held for ransom? What would they want with my family? Is this what Mason wouldn't tell me before I left?* My thoughts drown me as my eyes swim back and forth between the two strangers. They're both tall, broad; no way could I overpower them even with all the self-defense in the book. My mouth goes dry. Panic presses up my throat, begging to spill out, but I force my face still. If I looked scared, they'd enjoy it. I won't give them that.

One of them steps forward until his shadow swallows everything else. He crouches, bringing his face level with mine. His breath is warm and sour against my cheek, just like the crooked grin spread across his features. "You're lucky," he says, dragging his fingers slowly across my skin. I want to recoil but I try to remain stoic. I'm sure my pupils are the size of saucers. "Girls like you usually don't get this kind of consideration." His voice drips with his Italian accent and disgust crashes through me so fast I don't think. I just react.

I rock myself forward, my head cracking against the bridge of his nose before the back legs of the chair slam back onto the old floor. I feel a sharp burn across my cheek, his palm connecting with my skin. My mouth fills with the taste of iron at the impact. "*Puttana—*" He curses in his native tongue, face twisting with detestation.

The lights cut out and I inhale sharply through my nose as my head whips, eyes searching for anything to land on. But I'm blind. Totally, completely blind. A deep darkness washes over the room. For one second, there's no movement. Then everything happens at once. A body slams into a wall. Someone grunts. Something metallic clatters across the floor. Footsteps, fast and purposeful. A struggle. A curse. Then...two gunshots, sharp and deafening in the small room. Two flashes of light just quick enough to see their bodies slump to the floor, landing with a hard thud each.

I jerk back against the chair, screaming against the tape over my mouth, heart pounding so violently it hurts. Silence follows, interrupted only by my gasping for air once the tape is ripped off and the creaking of the chair in my desperate attempt to escape. Then hands are on me again. I thrash immediately, kicking, twisting, trying to get away even though the rope is still holding me down, burning my wrists with each jerk of my arms.

"Don't—don't touch me!" My wrists suddenly fall free. The rope is loosened and dropped, and I tear at it, fighting even harder now that I can move. My hands fly up, connecting with anything in their path, nails clawing at the figure in front of me that I can feel but not see. My body shakes with adrenaline as I try to stand but I'm held steady by two strong hands. "Get off of me!" My voice is shrill with desperation as it leaves me. I writhe and flail, elbows, knees, all the hardest parts of my body that Mason taught me would hurt the worst.

"*Savannah.*" A voice grinds out. Male. Steady, not filled with desperation or fear or anger. "Let me go!" I yell, clawing at the arms that hold me steady. One of the hands moves from my arm and clamps over my mouth, the other wrapping tight around my waist when I'm pulled to stand, holding me in place despite my attempts to break free. Whoever this is, their torso feels much larger than the men from before, strong and stable. I can feel their heartbeat thumping against my back as I try to free myself from his grip.

"Shut up and stop fighting if you want to get out of here alive," he barks. My heart drops into my stomach but I'm exhausted. I turn my head to face the owner of the voice, my eyes adjusting to the darkness. His face is half covered in black fabric and the less I try to fight free, the looser his grip around me falls. Not like the other men, whose forceful grip left aching marks on my upper arms. "What do you want from me?" I plea, my voice cracking on the last word.

"Cooperation," he commands immediately.

I don't know if it's the rhythm of his heart pressed to my back that's soothing or if it's the absence of the ties around my joints, but something in my gut tells me to listen, a sense of foreign safety washing over me as I stop thrashing. My hands rise to grip the strong arm around me to keep myself on my feet, knees buckling from exertion. My throat burns and my heart still beats erratically against my ribs. The tears that have been threatening all night finally spill over as I give in to realization. The stranger supporting my weight might be my only chance.

6

Sebastian

Savannah's movements slow, then stop entirely. I can feel the tremor still running through her, but she's no longer trying to claw my face off. Good. I need her head clear for what comes next. I can hear her heavy breaths as her tears fall against the hand I had clamped over her mouth and anger buzzes in my head that she's hurt, but we have no time for that now.

"Savannah," I repeat quietly when I lower my hand. "Listen to me. You're going to do exactly what I tell you. No hesitation. No questions. Understood?" She swallows hard and I can feel the hesitation in her slow nod. I take her arm, gently this time, and guide her toward the front door. The house is pitch black except for the faint outline of the exit, washed in moonlight.

But the second I crack the door open, my blood goes cold. There's a second SUV parked ten yards out. Black. Engine off. Lights off. They must have pulled up during the commotion. But whoever's in it isn't here to help the men I just put down. They would've stormed in already. They're waiting. Watching for movement.

My comms crackle where the earpiece dangles over my chest. "Status update?" Jesse's voice filters through, casual and unaware. I don't answer. My eyes are locked on the silhouette sitting perfectly still in the SUV, head turned toward the porch. No movement. No attempt at backup. No attempt at communication. Every nerve ending within me is on fire, telling me this is all wrong.

I lean close to Savannah's ear. "Go to the back porch. Now. Wait for me there." She's terrified, I can feel it, but she listens without protesting. She slips into the darkness behind the cabin, footsteps clumsy but soft. The moment she's clear, I melt into the shadows of the living room beside the window, gun drawn. The lights snap back on when I flip the breaker back the other way.

I look back through the window, quick and low. Enough for one glimpse. The figure in the SUV turns his head slightly, leaning forward just enough that his face is illuminated for a fraction of a second. My stomach drops to my feet, pulse kicking faster against my ribcage. He's one of mine, one of my own team.

My fingers flex around the trigger. No one screwed up the op. No one was sloppy. We've got a mole. He's not here for the other men at all; he's here for me. For her. I'll be dead before I let that happen.

Silently, I move out the back door, ripping the comms from where they're secured at my waist, quiet as I can, and drop it into the shadows. I can't trust who might be on the other side. Jesse is safe, this I know, but I can't trust anyone else who might be listening. I curse myself that it slipped past me so easily. I never make mistakes like this and never trust others for good reasons. My men have been screened;

trained and background checked. I make a mental note that if we make it out of this alive, I'll have every one of them skinned to get to the bottom of this.

Creeping around the exterior corner of the house, I'm careful of any leaves that may crunch under my boots. Savannah is waiting where I told her. She's a tight, shaking silhouette against the faint light bleeding from the porch door. I raise my finger to where my lips sit under my mask, signaling the need for stealth. Then a hand, waving her forward. Signaling her to follow me, stay on my heels. Her wide eyes lock onto mine but she nods again in understanding. We move. Very carefully. Very quietly. And I know one thing with uncomfortable certainty: I have to get her out of here before my own unit finishes what they've started.

The cold hits with the impact of a fist the second we clear the protection of the porch. Midnight winter air, sharp enough to bite straight through clothing. And Savannah is wearing practically none. Just a crewneck sweater reading "Telluride" in baby pink letters and a thin pair of black leggings suctioned to her frame. At least she had enough sense to wear sneakers.

She gasps, a tiny sound, curling inward instinctively. I turn my head toward her with warning eyes to stay silent, my hand swiping once in front of my neck. I can already see the shake starting in her shoulders. Not good. Not for what we need to do.

Once we've cleared the perimeter into the tree line I whisper "Eyes on me," barely audible, shifting her waist so she stands slightly behind me. "Don't break from my steps." She nods, but when we start down the steep slope behind the cabin, I hear her foot slip on ice-crusted leaves. I react fast, catching her elbow before she tumbles. She yelps quietly.

She's freezing, her arm an ice block under my touch. "We don't have time for noise," I bark quietly, unintentionally harsh, but following my direction is necessary right now. "Slow but controlled," I steady her with my grip on her elbow, "Focus on where I place my feet." She's trying. I can feel the effort radiating off her, but the cold is brutal. Her breath is coming in shaky bursts, each exhale a cloud in the dark. The forest around us is dead quiet, except for the distant hum of the SUV's engine kicking over. He's moving. I tighten my grip on her elbow with urgency. "We have to pick up the pace."

"I—" Her voice cracks. "I'm trying," she mutters through a locked jaw. This is the kind of cold that chatters more than your teeth. The kind that you feel in your bones. She is trying; I know she is. I release an exasperated breath, reminding myself to be patient. She's terrified, exhausted, freezing, and barely steady on her feet. Her legs drag, catching on roots. Every few steps she stumbles, and I reposition her without stopping, without speaking, guiding her weight forward. The tree line thickens, branches weaving overhead, blotting out even the faint moonlight. She's shivering violently now; I can hear her teeth clacking.

"We'll stop soon," I lie, shrugging off my tactical vest. Without missing a step, I secure my thick jacket around her shoulders before snapping the vest back over my shoulders, careful not to disturb my mask. I can't risk her seeing my face. Not until I can think of a plan that extends farther than these woods.

"Just need distance." I watch from my peripheral as she hugs the jacket around her, swallowing her frame as we continue to move through the forest. Behind us, a car door thuds shut and I freeze. Savannah bumps into my back, soft and startled. I turn slowly, signaling her again to stay quiet.

Through the forest, I can hear the leaves crunching down the same path we've left behind us. Slow footsteps moving around the house, then toward the woods. He knows and he's on the hunt. Being that he's from my own team, he'll be able to predict my movements. I have to think, *now*.

I catch Savannah's hand and pull her into motion. "We have to move." We whip through the trees faster now than we were before. Her breath turns rapid, but she keeps up as best she can, tripping once, twice, each time catching herself on my arms. "We're almost to the ridge," I whisper. "Once we're over it, he won't have line of sight," my words are brisk through my labored breath. She doesn't answer, I don't know that she can, but her grip tightens on my arm.

The forest starts to slope upward. Savannah stumbles on the incline, knees buckling. I slide an arm around her waist to support her weight, keep her moving. "Just a little more," I breathe. "Don't stop. Not here." The footsteps behind us pause and there's a brief moment of silence. He's scanning, searching. He knows that we couldn't have gotten that much distance between us yet.

I haul Savannah the last few feet up the ridge, her legs shaking beneath her. When we crest the top, I pull her down behind a fallen pine, covering her with my torso to shield her from sightlines. She's trembling violently beneath me, breaths coming too fast, bordering on hyperventilation. I tip her chin up with a gentle grip, hoping that some of the heat from my body weight will transfer to her. The fallen leaves work to shield us from the wind, a moment of relief. "Savannah. Look at me." Olive toned eyes dart to mine.

"We're not safe yet. But you're doing good. Really good." I know that she's still terrified, confused, even, but I need her to stay with me now more than ever.

There's a beat of stillness as I listen. Then I hear it—another car door, another engine. More than one. He's not alone anymore. The mole isn't tracking us. A team is. "Fuck, *fuck*.." I whisper, squeezing my eyes shut and pinching the bridge of my nose before I release a slow breath. I have to stay controlled to dull the fear I know she's engulfed in. I shift my hand to the small of Savannah's back, lifting her with me as I stand. "We have to keep moving," I whisper. "Right now. And you don't let go of me for anything." She nods, terrified but determined. Taking her hand, I pull her deeper into the woods.

7

Savannah

Branches whip against my arms as we push deeper into the trees, faster now, not careful the way we were before. He's no longer placing each step with perfect precision. He's rushing. Urgent. And I'm trying, I really am, but my legs feel disconnected from my body. The frigid wind is burning my cheeks with each breeze, burning my chapped lips, numbing my fingertips.

I try my best to keep up but my steps get sloppy. I'm slipping on snow crust, stumbling over roots I swear weren't there a second ago. Each time I falter, his hand clamps around my wrist and pulls me forward before I can fall. Whoever he is... he moves like he's done this a thousand times. A ghost cutting through the trees. Efficient and unshakeable.

Maybe that's why I keep following him. Even though I don't know his name, or maybe I do, maybe I heard it, everything is a blur. I can feel the control in his movements. The purpose. And right now, purpose is the only thing keeping me upright. The cold gnaws at me, sharper with every step. I can't stop shaking, even swimming in the thick coat he offered. My hands have gone numb, my toes too, and I'm terrified that at some point my legs will just stop cooperating and I'll fold into the frozen leaves. My lungs burn with the bite of the air, chest heaving with every step, and underneath it all is an overwhelming sense of dread I refuse to acknowledge.

Behind us, somewhere far but not far enough, a whistle cuts through the trees. Then another. I force myself not to look back when I hear the hiss of tires chewing through ice. I don't know who they belong to. I don't know if they're the kidnappers, or someone worse. I only know they're looking for me. Tears threaten to brim again, and I can feel bile rising higher in my throat with every move we make.

My breath catches, my pulse relentless in my neck. He notices and tightens his grip on my wrist just enough to steady me without slowing down. I have to be strong if I want to survive, that much is obvious. Minutes blur together. Or maybe hours... I don't know anymore. Time feels stretched too thin, like it might tear at any second. The wind slices across our faces, the trees thinning out just enough that I can see the sky bleeding starlight over the ridgeline.

The mountains look like shadows, threatening to expose our position. The same ones I used to stare at from my bedroom window, night after night. The ones I used to imagine escaping into when everything felt too heavy to hold. Like my future was just on the other side of them. Funny. I always thought they'd feel... freer than this.

We crest another slope, breathless. He slows, just slightly, scanning the darkness below us. I take advantage of the change in pace, trying to fill my lungs with a deep inhale. I follow his gaze, but all I see is black and more black. Maybe shadows are moving but maybe my eyes are just playing tricks on me from exhaustion.

My chest tightens with all the possibilities running through my mind, the potential outcome of tonight, if we ever make it through.

He turns to me, just for a moment, and in the faint moonlight I see the grounding impulsion behind his eyes. He's not relaxed. Not confident, not anymore. For a second he looks just as shaken as I am. I try not to let that sink into me, realizing that the only chance I have with this man may not be a chance at all. If he's scared, I don't think I want to know what, or who, is behind us. "We keep moving," he whispers. And I nod, because right now... I don't have anyone else. I don't have *anything* else.

Just a stranger pulling me through the dark, the frigid air chipping at my lungs and the mountain that used to feel like freedom now feeling like the edge of something much more terrifying. I keep following him, as quickly as my legs will allow.

We break through a line of trees so suddenly that I almost crash into his back, hands steadying myself across his shoulders. The forest drops away into a narrow strip of open space. A road. Or what *used* to be one. The gravel is so old and patchy it's more suggestion than path, twisted and uneven, with weeds pushing through every crack. No one in town ever talked about a road up here. No one local would even attempt something this forgotten. And yet he walks onto it like he's been expecting it. I'm not sure if that comforts me...or scares me more.

Does he really know where we're going? Or is he just moving, trusting his instincts, and training and whatever map he has carved into his head?

For all I know, we could be walking in circles. But he doesn't hesitate once, not a single misstep. He seems to know where to turn, where to slow, where to pick up speed. I wish I felt that sure. Or felt anything at all besides the cold sense of despondence that hasn't left my body in hours.

The wind threads through the tall Ponderosa pines overhead, their branches bare and skeletal. It's the only sound left. "Please..." The word slips out before I can stop it. I hardly recognize my own voice. My fingers curl around his hand, squeezing, more for balance than anything, but he steadies me instantly, like he was waiting for it. I duck under the reach of moonlight and sink onto a rotted, hollow log. It groans under my weight, flakes of old bark breaking away beneath my legs.

My arms ache both from fatigue and the harsh grip of the men earlier. My lungs are sore from my heaving breath. My head pounds beneath the gash on my forehead. I've never felt this much defeat in my life. I want so desperately to give up, to give in to whatever threat we're running from. But I can't. I force myself to stay upright.

He stops a few steps ahead, turning toward me with a sharp exhale. Frustrated, surely due to me slowing him down, but restrained. His silhouette is rigid, like he's calculating how much time I'm wasting by sitting down. I lift my gaze to his, eyes too wide as they connect with piercing blue ones above the black fabric that shields the remainder of his face, and everything inside me feels like it's trembling all at once. "Please tell me we're going to get out of here," I beg, voice breaking on the edges. "Please."

I need something. Anything. A sliver of hope. A sign he has a plan and I'm not just blindly trailing behind the first stranger who grabbed me that *wasn't* trying to kill me. I need to believe this isn't for nothing. For a moment he doesn't move. Then he steps closer, kneeling in front of me, his crystalline eyes meeting my own. "I'm not going to let anyone hurt you," he says, and it feels like a promise. His voice is low, roughened by exhaustion and tension, but steady. Steady in a way nothing else tonight has been.

And I believe him.

The relief hits so hard it nearly knocks me back against the log. My chest loosens just enough for a full breath, the first I've had since I was in my car. For the first time all night, I don't feel like I'm running toward a cliff edge with my eyes closed. I feel like someone's actually fighting to keep me alive. Even if I still don't know why.

8

Sebastian

Savannah walks beside me along the edge of the gravel road, her steps uneven, dragging no matter how hard she tries to hide it. I keep her close but not in the middle of the path. She'd be too exposed. Even out here, even on a road that hasn't seen a car in a decade, I can't let myself relax.

I glance down at my watch that's smeared with dirt, half-frozen against my wrist. Ten past two. We've been moving for hours. Through the cold. Through the dark. Through every damn thing I should've been able to stop before it ever touched her. Exhaustion crawls up my legs and knots in my lower back. A slow, heavy ache that tells me I've been running on adrenaline for too long. And if I feel like this, Savannah has to be on the edge of collapse.

She hasn't complained once, at least not in the way I would've expected. That, somehow, makes the guilt worse. A sharp, hot twist in my chest. I failed. My only assignment was to keep her safe and now I've found myself miles deep into the forest with her in the dead of Colorado winter. I failed to catch the mole before he got anywhere near her. Failed to keep her out of this nightmare. Failed to see what someone on my own unit was planning right under my nose. It eats at me with every step.

The road curves and the trees peel back enough to reveal the outline of the gate. A rusted metal square, aged by weather and time. Most people would think it leads to an abandoned property or nothing at all. To me, it's the closest thing to home I've had in years. I push it open, the hinges screaming in protest, and guide her through, making sure to take the time to latch it back behind us. It looks as unbothered as it did just moments ago. Savannah doesn't ask where we are, doesn't hesitate, she just follows the same way she has all night. Her shoulders slump, her breathing ragged, and I'm pretty sure she's too tired to form a question even if she wanted to.

The ghost of a driveway stretches out ahead, a long tunnel of dark pines, covered now by a beaten path of grass, dusted with frost. My cabin sits at the end, barely visible, a faint outline swallowed by the night. It sinks into the shadows of the tree line without a trace, just the way I like it. I hear her breath stutter slightly behind me, knowing that it's come into her view, too. Still, she follows my lead. When we finally reach it, I step up onto the small porch and reach above the doorframe. The key is still there, wedged against the old wood. No one's been here since I left. Good.

I unlock the door, push it open, and head inside. The familiar smell—pine, freezing air, old coffee—wraps around me like a heavy blanket. I flick on the small lamp by the door, the soft amber light filling the space. Savannah hesitates in the doorway, hugging her arms to her chest, shaking so hard the lamp's glow flickers across her skin. "What is this place?"

Her voice is meek when she speaks.

"My home," I give her the simplest answer I can right now. I don't look directly at her, not yet. If I do, I'll see everything I failed to protect her from. "There's a shower at the end of the hall," I mutter, voice low and rough. I gesture toward the narrow hallway to the left and move past her, pretending to busy myself with the light switch near the door. "It'll knock the chill off." Her breath catches in a tiny, grateful sound. She hesitates again but finally steps inside, the old wood creaking beneath her light steps. I push the door shut behind her and finally gain the confidence to look her way. And I think she looks like she believes she's safe. Even if I'm not sure we are. Even if I know this is just the first step in keeping her alive.

She moves quietly down the hallway, peering around the room with an intense curiosity like she still thinks she's in enemy territory. I turn every lock, securing each latch with precision.

9

Savannah

The old cabin is small and quaint, like something you'd see in a magazine selling cottage furniture. It smells of woodsmoke and dust and I assume it's been vacant for a long time, considering the way the floors creak under each step. In the living room, there's a couch and a worn armchair that looks like it sags under the weight of the air. It connects to the kitchen, cast iron pots hung on the walls of the otherwise empty room, aside from the small table that sits in the center. When I shuffle to the bathroom, I make note that it's the only door to the left, one shut door across the hall.

I pause before stepping into the shower, half-expecting the door to swing open behind me or the lights to cut out like they did in the other house. Every sound, the groan of old pipes, the soft thump of a branch hitting the tiny window near the ceiling, shoots straight through me like a warning. My nerves are shredded, twitching at everything, causing my body to jolt every time I hear a noise.

I brave a glance in the mirror while the water warms

after shedding my clothes. My eyes linger on my battered skin. The crust of blood beneath my hairline, the bruises that mark my upper arms, my wrists. The fiery shade of my chapped lips. A stranger stares back at me through the reflection. A memory of the girl who left home tonight.

I shudder at the thought and turn to step in. The water is hot when it washes over me. Hot enough to melt the ice from my skin. To thaw me out of the exhausted, zombie state I was in for hours running through the tall Colorado pines. Hot enough to make me close my eyes and exhale for what feels like the first time in hours.

I stand there too long. The heat burns my shoulders, my back, but I don't move. I'm not sure that I can anymore. The steam fogs the mirror, the tiles, the air around me. My thoughts scatter and collide, spinning faster than I can keep up with. *Am I safe here? Is this really a rescue...or just another trap with a different face? A face I haven't seen...Did he bring me here because he wants to protect me? Or because the others will know exactly where to find us?*

It's too much. All of it. My body is too tired to process any of it. I lean a hand against the wall and bow my head, feeling the sting of water on the back of my neck. I wanted to get away. To start a new life for myself. To taste freedom, finally, instead of constantly being watched over like I'm fragile. I'm not. I'm stronger than my family ever thought I could be. I had to be to put up with the constant nagging, the judgment I faced from every direction, every person I came into contact with.

I always caught the stares and the whispers, the neighborhood veering away from my family, especially my father. I never understood it, blamed it on jealousy. Because we looked so happy from the outside. Because of his success.

Now I realize I had it all wrong. I'm still not sure the reason behind all of this; especially tonight's events. But I will get answers. I have to, now more than ever.

I'm numb. Fully, terrifyingly numb. Maybe from fear. Maybe from the cold. The water cools before I shut it off, my skin prickling when I step out into the cold air that rushes past the shower curtain.

A small pile of clothes is folded neatly on the edge of the counter, like they were placed there quietly, respectfully, without any intention of startling me. A long-sleeved henley shirt that practically swallows me whole, dropping almost to my knees when I shrug it on. And sweatpants that are far too big. They're soft, worn, the kind of fabric someone reaches for after long days or late nights. I have to roll the waistband twice to get them to stay on.

My legs still feel like concrete. My hands shake as I rough dry my hair with the towel and take a moment to breathe before stepping out of the bathroom, eyes squeezing shut like I can will the night away. The hallway looks darker now that the adrenaline is wearing off. My footsteps are soft on the wood, and each board creaks in a way that makes my heart leap into my throat. But it's warm now, more so than when I came in.

I force myself to keep moving. The smell of woodsmoke reaches me before the fireplace comes into view, warm and crackling, a welcomed contrast to the freezing air still clinging to my skin. I make my way down the hallway toward the dim lamp glow bleeding from the main room. I'm still not sure what waits for me there. My pulse ticks loudly in my ears, each beat feeling like it vibrates through my whole body. The cabin is silent otherwise and for a moment, it feels like I might be alone.

But when I step into the room, I see him and I come to a quick stop. The mask is off. The vest, too. It's the first time I've really looked at the man who rescued me. At least...I think he rescued me. Unless all of this is some long, elaborate ploy, and I'm just too exhausted to see the strings being pulled. He looks... more human, now. He sits in the armchair that looks like it's seen better days, far too small for his broad frame. His elbows braced on his knees, head bowed like he's miles deep in whatever thoughts are tearing at him.

I study his profile before I take another step. The firelight flickers against his caramel-colored hair, catching the strands that fall across his brow. His eyebrows pinch together, a tight line, like whatever he's thinking about is something he'd rather not face. The flame dances against the ripples of muscle visible through his shirt without his armor.

I clear my throat, soft, hesitant, and finally step closer. "Thank you," I murmur, folding onto the edge of the worn couch and tucking my knees to my chest. I pull my sleeves down over my bruised wrists like it's something to hide. The fabric smells like sandalwood and something bold. The space between us feels thick with tension, or maybe that's just me, tied into knots I can't unravel. There are a million questions I want—no, *need*—to ask. None of them make it out.

He lifts his head. His eyes read exhaustion but they meet mine without hesitation. For a fleeting second, I catch the ghost of a grin tugging at his mouth. Maybe relief that we're both still breathing. "Don't mention it," he says back with a short nod. His shoulders sag a fraction, releasing whatever has been driving him for hours.

I stare down at my hands, picking at a jagged nail, trying, and failing, to steady my breathing despite the ragged beating that remains in my chest. "What do we do now?" The question sits like a stone in my stomach. My pulse throbs unevenly behind the words that I'm not even sure I want to know the answer to.

Do we have a next move? Does he expect me to keep up the pace we've been sprinting at? Is he planning to leave me here? Are we sitting ducks waiting for the others to find us? Or worse—*is he waiting for them, too?* Possibilities slam into me all at once, making my head pound. I squeeze my knees tighter and brace for whatever comes next.

10

Sebastian

I release a long breath, slow and controlled, hoping the exhale will buy me a few more seconds before I have to actually answer her. I drag a hand over my jaw, feeling the grit of the day still clinging to my skin, and shake my head slowly. I'm not sure I have the answer she's looking for.

"You're safe now," I try to keep my voice low and steady, offering her some sort of reassurance. I mean it. Or at least...I can hope our position isn't compromised. The only other person in existence that knows about this place is Jesse. My most trusted friend. My brother. Nowhere in my mind is the possibility that he could be in on this. No. Jesse wouldn't betray me that way.

Savannah's brows pull together and she shifts on the couch, pulling her knees closer like she's trying to disappear into herself. "How do you know?" I can sense the worry hiding behind her words. I lean back into the old armchair, the cushion drooped with time and allow my legs to stretch in front of me, letting the fire paint my features in flickers of gold and shadow.

"Because I'm going to make sure of it." I pause, my gaze moving briefly to the heavy locks on the door, the reinforced window frames, the layers of quiet precautions only I would notice. I placed them all deliberately. I draw in a breath. "And because this place has been my safe house for a long time.

"Safe house?" she echoes, her head tilting with an innocent curiosity like she doesn't understand the words. Of course she doesn't know any of this. She *shouldn't*. Her world, until tonight, was one where danger looked like bad dreams and horror played out on a screen, safely contained behind glass. She's never seen what real monsters look like, the kind that don't hide under beds but walk the streets in plain sight. The kind that smile while they ruin lives. The kind I've made it my business to hunt.

My chest tightens at the realization of what those men exposed her to. What I've exposed her to. I drift my eyes over her wrists, hints of bruising blooming across her skin in shades of purple and yellow that match the point on her temple. It's more violence than she's ever been witness to, I'm sure. I offer a small, clipped nod, keeping the explanation as thin as possible. The less she knows, the safer she is. At least for now.

"I'm sorry..." she begins, voice cracking with the weight of everything she's been holding in. She runs an unsteady hand through her hair, staring at me with wide, overwhelmed eyes. "This is all—God, it's *a lot*. Did you know those men? How did you know where I was? And—sorry, but... *who are you?*" She doesn't breathe between them, the questions I've been running from since the moment they stopped her in the street.

The muscles in my jaw throb from clenching for hours with strain and I can feel the sting behind my eyes, the burn deep in my lungs, the exhaustion that's been stalking me since I found her. Savannah deserves answers...but every truth I give her is a thread leading back to things I've kept buried for years.

I meet her gaze, steady but reluctant. For a moment, I let the silence stretch, weighing every possible version of the truth in my mind. Each one feels like a loaded weapon left on the table between us. I scrub a tired hand over the back of my neck and exhale slowly.

I have to start somewhere, give her something. So, I choose the simplest explanation, one that doesn't include my past or too many details about my job.

"How much do you know about your father?" I lift a brow as I study her, waiting for her reaction. The question hangs heavily in the warm air, louder than the crackle of the fire. Savannah's face shifts instantly. Confusion, then disbelief, then something sharper, more defensive. She recoils slightly at the question, her eyes narrowing as if the very suggestion is an insult. "My father? You...you know my father?"

I keep my posture guarded, mind racing through the history I shouldn't say aloud. The months of surveillance. The meetings in back rooms and border towns. The cartel connections threaded through her father's pristine reputation like rot beneath the wallpaper. The way I had been assigned—ordered, really—to keep an eye on her as a contingency plan should everything go to hell. Exactly as it had tonight. I watch her carefully, unsure how much truth she can shoulder, unsure how much I'm even allowed to give her. Every detail is a risk. Every omission is one too. But she's staring at me now, wide awake despite the dark circles beneath her eyes, her breath caught in her throat.

Waiting for words I'm not sure I have the courage to give her.

"Better than you think…" I begin, settling back with a crushing feeling in my chest that wasn't there an hour ago when branches battered my shoulders and ice sliced through my skin. My eyes flick briefly toward the kitchen cabinet and I wonder if there's any scotch left from the last time I ducked out here. *God*, I could use it right now.

But Savannah deserves some level of truth. Even if it's the trimmed, sanitized version. "I've been watching your father for a long time," I keep my voice calm and speak slowly, confidently and without any room for confusion as I choose each careful word. "He's involved in things you don't know about…things you were never *meant* to know about." My lips press together in a thin line before I continue. "And I'm not going to go into detail. The less you know, the safer you are."

She sinks further into the couch like it can swallow her, watching me intently as I speak, but I push forward. "Your father is a dangerous man, Savannah. That's why I know who you are. To answer your question, my name is Sebastian. My job is to keep you safe. I—" I pause, shame flickering across my face, hesitant with just how much information I should share. "I don't make mistakes in my work. Ever. Until now." My throat works around the admission, fingers flexing in my lap. "But it won't happen again. I promise you that." If there's anything I've said tonight that needs to land, it's that.

Savannah shakes her head, her hands lifting, palms facing me like she's warding off the tide of information.

"Whoa. Whoa, whoa—*wait*." Her voice trembles, rises two octaves, but she's trying to hold herself steady, blinking as if to physically clear her vision. "Your *job* is to keep *me* safe? What does that even *mean*? I've never seen you before." She scoffs at the mere idea, damp hair clinging to her cheeks. "No, seriously—what are you saying right now? That my dad is some kind of... *criminal*? That you, what, follow me around for a living?"

She laughs louder this time, a broken, disbelieving sound. "This sounds insane. Completely insane. You have to be joking. Right? This is a prank?" Her voice becomes more frantic the longer that she speaks. She pauses, then her eyes go wide with discovery, "Mason put you up to this, didn't he? Well, he made his freaking point." Her arms cross over her chest, expression shifting from shock to disbelief to anger, then repeating the pattern all over again. "You can take me back home now."

I watch as she unravels in small, subtle ways. The way she grips the edge of the couch cushion, the way her eyes dart to the door, then to me, to the fire, like every shadow suddenly has teeth. Like every instinct she has is telling her to run and all I can do is pray that she stays. She has to. Savannah stands, hands placed on her hips as she pads back and forth, in front of me, to the fire, across the room, and back.

I lean forward, forearms resting on my knees, but my eyes stay trained on her. "No. This isn't a prank or some twisted joke. I would never let someone hurt you for humor," I admit. "I'm telling you what you need to know to survive. You don't have to trust me. But tonight proved why the assignment exists."

Savannah stops, shooting me a narrowed glare. Her

breathing is shallow. "What *assignment*? Why do you keep saying that?" she asks, voice barely more than a whisper as my name graces her lips for the first time. I hesitate. Too long because she notices. "Tell me." She presses, her voice urgent, pleading. She stiffens in front of me the longer I hold my silence, turning to face me. "*Sebastian*," she grits my name, "What assignment?" she insists again, this time with more force.

I meet her eyes fully and allow a sliver of the truth to settle between us, heavy and real. "You," I breathe. "Keeping you alive. That's the assignment."

11

Savannah

For a moment, I don't move. I don't breathe. I don't even blink.

You. Keeping you alive. That's the assignment. The words through my head like they were dropped down a cavern, hitting every wall on the way down. I stare at him, waiting for the punchline, the smirk, the reveal that he's joking or lying. Anything other than what it sounds like. But he just holds my gaze, steady and unflinching. And that's somehow worse.

My mouth feels dry when I try to speak. "Me?" I repeat, as if saying it again will make it make sense. It doesn't. It only sends a cold sting up my spine. "I—I don't understand." My head shakes in disbelief as I reach up and run a hand through stringy, damp knots. My father...dangerous? Me...a target? This man—*Sebastian*—assigned to me like some sort of government-issued babysitter?

Everything in my body tells me to run. To move. But my legs are heavy, plastered in place in the middle of the room. I drag myself to slink back on the edge of the couch, letting my body melt into it. Despite everything I've just been told, my gut continues to tell me that this is the best chance I have right now. Here. With him. What other option do I have, anyway, given what he's told me?

My heart beats a frantic, uneven rhythm inside my ribs with something tangled and electric and nauseating. Shock, maybe. *Boss wants her alive,* the man's voice from earlier rings through my head. Could they have been referring to my own father? Did they want to take me home? No... My dad wouldn't have let them hurt me, even if this is all true.

"This is insane," I whisper, dropping my head into my hands. I scrub them both over my face as if it'll wake me up and drag me out of this living nightmare. "I mean—my dad...he's a lot of things, but dangerous?" The word tastes strange in my mouth. Wrong. Like I'm saying it about a stranger. But then again...how much do I really know about him? A hollow ache opens in my chest, spreading slowly as I drop back onto the couch.

"My whole life," I murmur, more to myself than to him, "he's been traveling, and taking calls behind closed doors, and disappearing for days at a time. I thought it was business. Normal, stressful business. I never thought..." I trail off, unable to finish the sentence, hand closing over my mouth.

The longer Sebastian watches me the more unsettled I feel. "I don't even know what's real," I admit with a long sigh, resting my hands under my chin. My palms are still warm from the shower, but the rest of me feels cold. Empty. "Men drag me from my car. You show up out of nowhere. My dad is apparently some kind of criminal?" My voice cracks. "And you've just been... following me? Watching me? For what—

months? Years?" The last word wobbles. I lock my fingers together to hide their trembling.

I don't want to cry. Not here. Not now. Not in front of someone who might not even be on my side. I drop my gaze to the threadbare rug, blinking hard. "Why me?" I ask softly, barely loud enough to carry. "What did I do to deserve this?" It's not an accusation. It's a genuine, aching question. Sebastian doesn't answer right away, the only sound the soft pop of sap burning in the fireplace and the faint rattle of wind against the windowpanes.

A shiver runs down my spine like the cold is still lingering from the hours past. I can feel him thinking. Feel the weight of whatever he's choosing not to tell me. When he finally exhales, it's slow and full of patience that I don't feel like I deserve. "You didn't do anything wrong," he says quietly. I almost laugh but the gentleness in his tone catches me off guard, different from the intensity he's carried all night.

When I look at him, his elbows rest on his knees, hands dangling between them, shoulders bowed under invisible weight. "This isn't about you screwing up, or choosing wrong, or being in the way." He shakes his head once, jaw tight. "You were born into a situation that should've never touched you. But it did. And I'm here because when things get ugly with men like your father, their families become collateral."

Collateral.

The word lands like ice water in my stomach. My throat closes around the next breath, rough and shaky. "So that's it? I'm just—some piece on a chessboard my dad screwed up? And now, what? This is my life?" His eyes flick up sharply, and for a moment, I see something fierce behind them. "No," he says, firm enough that it roots me in place. "Not a piece. Not disposable. That's why you were assigned protection. And I'm going to fix this. It's what I do."

"Protection," I repeat, hollow, still not sure exactly what all of this means. But that's more information that I'm not sure I could handle right now. "Is that what this is?" I fire at him too pointedly. Sebastian's neck flares with heat like he's still fighting his thoughts.

"It's what it was supposed to be," he mutters, gaze dropping to the floor. "Until tonight." The guilt in his voice coils through the room like smoke. I should be angry, should be terrified, but instead I'm just... numb. Too full of questions to feel anything else. I rub my hands over my thighs, over the soft fabric of the borrowed sweats, grounding and useless all at once. "So what happens now?" I ask, barely above a whisper. "If this wasn't supposed to happen and my dad isn't who I thought he was and I'm some kind of target or something...what do we do?" Sebastian leans back, scrubbing a hand over the stubble on his chin.

Then he meets my eyes again. "Now," he says, voice low and certain, "we stay alive." Everything in me feels like it's collapsing inward. "Starting with you getting some rest," he adds, softer. "You're exhausted. And we're not doing anything until daylight, at the least." I want to argue. To demand more answers. To say there's no universe where I can sleep right now. But my body disagrees. My bones feel like they're made of wet sand.

I swallow hard, nodding once. "Okay," I whisper. I hesitate, but the sickly feeling in my gut pushes out my next words, "Just... don't leave. Please."

Through it all, the last thing I want is to be alone. Even if I'm not sure that I can trust him yet. Even when he's sitting across from me and I still feel lost in complete solitude. I catch a glimpse of something like surprise in his expression but it disappears as quickly as it came. "I'm not going anywhere," he assures me. A warm, flickering ember in the middle of all this cold chaos sparks in my chest at that. For now, I let myself believe him.

12

Sebastian

The conversation went...better than it should have. Better than I deserved. I watch her for a beat, the way she hugs her knees and keeps stealing glances at me like I might dissolve or snap or tell her another truth that shatters the world under her feet. And hell, part of me wishes I could undo some of what I said. She was never meant to know about any of this. About me, about the assignment, the shadows her father walks in. We were supposed to be ghosts in her periphery. Shields she would never see.

Three more months, that was the plan. Ninety days until her father would be in handcuffs, and she would go back to her quiet life and I would go back to mine. Everything was set in motion. She would never know how close danger had brushed against her. But tonight blew the whole damn plan apart and now I'm stuck with a target who knows my face. A girl who was never supposed to be part of the equation. A mole that's buried somewhere in my unit and a year's worth of intel that might already be compromised. I exhale through my nose, overwhelmed by it all and clueless about how the hell I'm supposed to back pedal this.

"Come on," I sigh, standing from the chair and offering my hand. She hesitates for a moment before slipping her fingers into mine gingerly and rising from her perch on the couch. Her hand is still trembling faintly and I hold it carefully, enough that it seems like I'm afraid she'll break. Maybe I am. I guide her down the hallway and the wooden floors creak under our steps. The cabin is quiet, untouched, like it spent years waiting for something to happen inside it and is startled that it finally did.

The bedroom is the only other door at the end of the hallway aside the bathroom. When I push open the door and flick the light switch, she stops short. Her cheeks flush with something between embarrassment and nerves. "Oh..." she mutters, shifting her weight awkwardly. Her hand crosses her chest to rub her upper arm, eyes darting to the floor.

I let out a bemused laugh. It's genuine and the first sliver of relief I've felt since I kicked in that door hours ago.

"Don't worry," I tell her, lifting a hand in reassurance. "You'll have your privacy. I'll sleep on the couch." She turns toward me, brows pulled together. "But—you need rest too. You haven't stopped since..."

"I'm fine," I cut in, firmer than I mean to be. "It's not like I could sleep right now anyway," I offer, softer this time, hoping she'll let it go. Her lips part like she wants to argue again, but she stops herself. Maybe she sees the truth in my face. Maybe she feels the tension buzzing under my skin, the adrenaline that hasn't let go of me since the moment I realized she was being taken.

After a moment, she nods. "Thank you," she whispers. And the way she says it with quiet earnest hits deeper than it should. I clear my throat and step back, "Try to get some rest." She slips into the room, closing the door with a soft click. My instincts come alive with the door separating us, her out of my sightline.

The cabin settles into night slowly, like it's holding its breath, waiting for the next pin to drop. After Savannah shuts the bedroom door, I stay there for a moment in the hallway, listening. No footsteps. No crying. No whispered panic spiraling into the dark. She's either desperately trying to calm herself or she's too exhausted to do anything but collapse. I stand there too long, staring at the wood grain like it might tell me what comes next, wishing for the hundredth time tonight that things had gone according to plan. But nothing about this night has. And something tells me nothing about her will either.

Either way, she's safe. For now. I return to the main room, kill the lamp, and stand in the dim glow of the fireplace. My eyes adjust instantly, my body shifting into the familiar hum of vigilance. The adrenaline hasn't worn off completely and probably won't for hours. I drag a knuckle across my brow, exhaling sharply. This wasn't supposed to happen. Any of this.

Savannah wasn't supposed to be *in play* tonight. She wasn't even supposed to be home. She had a late-night shift at the bookstore she normally stays for. I did my job well. I always do. I intercepted the call from her boss, knowing her shift had been cancelled, that she'd be home unexpectedly. I waited outside her window for her room to be swept into the same darkness that shadowed my figure against the stone wall of her yard. Just like it did every night before.

Except tonight she'd made one unpredictable choice. She left. She walked out of the house two hours after their show of a family dinner. No routine. No pattern. A complete break from everything we'd mapped out. The men who grabbed her...they couldn't have known that. No one could have known that. Hell, I never saw it coming.

I sink down onto the couch, lean forward, and pull my field notebook from the cargo pocket of the tactical pants that still cling to my legs. I flip through the worn pages of scribbled observations. Her typical routes, timestamps, behavior patterns. Everything precise. Everything consistent. Until tonight.

My eyes squeeze shut as I huff a harsh breath into the quiet room. If she broke routine...then the ambush wasn't based on surveillance. It wasn't chance. It was information. Which means someone fed them intel. Which concretes that someone on my team isn't just sloppy, they're compromised. They had to have communicated with these other men that she had left, which way she was heading. Feeding them every direction that I commanded into our comm system.

The knot in my gut draws tight, a slow-burning coil of dread. I pull my encrypted satellite pager from the opposite pocket. It's dark, no incoming signals from the last hour. Nothing from Jesse. Nothing from command. I scroll through the earlier messages from today, from before everything went to hell.

One stands out.

A ping marked **CONFIDENTIAL – PRIORITY 2** from 19:04.

It's short. Too short.

UPDATE: PRIMARY SUBJECT WILL BE ALONE
TONIGHT.
 -M

My stomach drops. Not "Savannah." Not "the daughter." *Primary subject.*

And "*Alone.*" Tonight.

Except she wasn't *supposed* to be alone. Not unless someone knew she'd been called off her shift. I reread it, pulse thudding savagely in my throat. The timestamp is minutes after Savannah made her spontaneous decision to leave her house...meaning whoever sent this message was talking about her schedule as it *happened.*

They weren't predicting movements at all. They were watching. Listening. My blood goes cold and the color drains from my face, a wave of nausea washing over me.

This wasn't about opportunity. This was a coordinated extraction attempt. And Savannah, the person I've spent almost a year protecting without her ever knowing, was the target all along. I sit back, spine rigid, notebook slack in my hand. A heavy, sick truth settles in my chest.

Savannah wasn't taken to pressure her father. Or as collateral. Or as a mistake. She was the objective from the very start.

A tired hand runs over my face, forcing my breath steady. Part of me wants to storm into the bedroom right now, shake her awake, and tell her everything. About the intel, about the mole, the threat. But she's been through enough for one night, and she needs rest more than she needs another nightmare.

And I need to think. Need to get ahead of whoever's

already three steps in front of me. The fire crackles low in the corner of the room. Outside, wind claws through the pines. I stand, step quietly to the window, and scan the tree line. No movement. But that means nothing. Not anymore.

Savannah had no idea she'd walked straight into a trap tonight. No idea that her impulsive decision to leave her house almost ended her life with the catastrophic events that followed. And she definitely has no idea that someone on *my* team is the reason those men found her at all. I tuck the pager away, set my back toward the hall, and force myself into stillness. I'll keep watch. All night if I have to, just like I always do. Because the truth is a wildfire. And eventually, it's going to reach her. But not tonight. Tonight, I keep her alive. I won't make another mistake.

Not again.

13

Savannah

The bedroom is dark when I flick off the light. Dark and eerily quiet. No streetlights. No cars passing. No hum of distant traffic. Just a single-paned window, the pale outline of the mountains beyond it, and the faint whisper of knocking branches against the roof. I slip beneath the blanket, pulling it up to my chin. It's musty, like no one has laid here in ages, and smells faintly of sandalwood and musk. Sebastian's footsteps fade down the hall, slow and measured, and then there's nothing but silence.

Deep, consuming silence.

I lie there staring at the ceiling, my mind a carousel of every impossible thing that has happened tonight. Every truth that's made itself known, if I believe him. The strangers. The gunshots. The woods. My father. Sebastian.

Assignment.

Protection detail.

Keeping you alive.

None of it fits into the world I thought I lived in. It feels like someone cut my life open and stuffed a different story inside my skin. I've never done any explicit drugs before but I imagine this is how it would feel. Like you're walking through life but looking at it from the outside, as if I'm watching a movie through someone else's eyes.

I turn over and face the window. Then again, my eyes drifting toward the slim sheen of light peeking from beneath the door. I curl into myself, then stretch out. Push the blanket off and then tug it back over me. Nothing helps. The thoughts are too loud, colliding over and over again in my head, trying to make sense of the details I know I'm not being told. Eventually, the exhaustion hits me like a wave, dragging me under mid-blink.

I wake with a violent gasp. My hand flies to my chest, pressing hard against the ruthless pound of my heart. The other rakes up into my hair, gripping, shaking. My breath comes in sharp little bursts, hot, uneven, and drowning. I press a hand over my mouth and release a hushed wail, squeezing my eyes shut as I attempt to calm my ragged breathing.

The nightmare clings to me like wet fabric, heavy and weighing down all of my limbs. The house again. The hands again, gripping me too tight. The bruises that linger on my arms ache in memory. The all-consuming darkness again. But this time, when the lights snapped back on, Sebastian wasn't the one standing there. It was my father. And he wasn't there to save me. I force myself to breathe through it. One inhale. One exhale. Again.

When I finally pull myself upright, my pulse still skipping, I hear a voice. A low one, floating down the hallway. Sweat beads my palm as my ears strain to hear the words clearly. It's no use, the voice too muffled to understand from here. My eyes stay trained on the door, half expecting it to come nearer. To rip me away again, pull me back into the hell of the night's events. My breath shakes with every inhale.

I slip from the bed slowly, bare feet silent on the floor that's gone cold with time as I creep toward the door. It's cracked just enough for a thin line of dim orange light from the fireplace to spill down the hall. I recognize Sebastian's voice, hushed and gravelly, like he's trying not to wake me. I inch closer, pulling the door as silently as I can. I wince when it creaks softly. Holding my breath, I step into the hallway. I peek around the corner, praying as I steal a glance that we're still alone. To my relief, I only see one shadow, the closer I get. And when I reach the end of the hall, he's not on the phone. There's no device in his hand. He's talking to himself.

"...three weeks," he mutters, quiet but tense. "At least. No comms. No extraction. No backup." He scrubs a hand through his hair, pacing once across the living room and I duck into the darkness of the hallway, pressing my back to the wall, careful not to be seen. The firelight paints sharp lines across his face—jaw set, eyes haunted. "No mistakes," he whispers to the empty room. "Not again. Not with her."

My chest pulls tight. A mix of anxiousness and acceptance that maybe he's being honest. Maybe he is here to keep me safe. He stops by the window, staring out into the black silhouette of trees. "If they find the cabin..." he says under his breath, "then we're already dead." My chest caves, breath leaving me all in an instant. I lean back further from the doorframe before he can turn and see me, heart rattling against my ribs. The nightmare still clings to me, but now it tangles with something more real. Because if Sebastian is this worried...do we even stand a chance?

Three weeks. No backup. No help. And *dead* if we're found. I slip silently back into the bedroom, easing the door shut. The darkness feels different now. It suffocates me with whatever secrets it hides. I move to the bed, pulling the blanket around my shoulders like a shield, staring at the slice of moonlight across the floor. Unable to move, unable to blink. I sit there and try to process my new reality. I don't know what half of it means but it unsettles me enough that I don't sleep again, even when my eyes burn and my back aches.

By the time morning comes, soft gold light showers the bedroom ceiling, warming the wooden beams above me. Dawn. I must have drifted off at some point, though I don't remember when. My muscles are tight like I've run a marathon in my sleep. My mind feels as bruised as my arms and wrists. I push the blanket aside and sit up slowly. The room is small in the daylight, simple. The bed remains unmade, dust floats across the dresser, a lone lamp on the nightstand, and a narrow mirror hangs slightly crooked on the wall. Free of anything that would resemble decor. Didn't Sebastian say this was his home?

I move toward the dresser, hoping for...something. Anything that fits me better than the oversized henley clinging awkwardly to my body. I ease open the first drawer.

Empty. In the second, I find a few shirts, all too big, worn soft at the seams. I pluck a navy tee out, holding it up to assess it. It's just as baggy as the henley, but maybe less tent-like. I change quickly, goosebumps rising on my arms as the cold morning air brushes my skin. It hangs shapelessly around me and I huff a breath of discomforted frustration, wishing more than anything my suitcase had been saved, too. To wear my own clothes would be to have a sense of security in the moment. Something familiar, comforting.

The third drawer holds nothing but an old pair of socks and a flashlight that flickers pathetically when I test it. I sigh and rummage a bit deeper. My fingers brush something small and stretchy, a rubber band.

It will have to do. I gather a handful of fabric at the back of the shirt and tie it off, cinching it enough to feel like I'm wearing something that actually belongs to me. When I nudge the drawer closed again, something catches—a corner of manila yellow. A folder, thin but stuffed full. My brows stitch as curiosity flickers, followed by an uneasy wave of dread. I slide it out slowly, glancing up toward the door to make sure it's still shut. Stuffed in the back of the bottom drawer, whatever it contains wasn't meant to be discovered.

I open it with caution. The first page is a photo. Of me. Walking to my car outside the bookstore, head down, bag over my shoulder, completely oblivious. The next is my father, shaking hands with someone I don't recognize. Then my brother at a football game. My mother leaving the grocery store. My brother's girlfriend laughing on our porch. My best friend leaning against her car, waving at someone off camera.

A sick, sour pit forms deep in my stomach. He wasn't lying. Sebastian really has been watching us. *All of us.* For how long? Weeks? Months? There are no time stamps, but I can tell by the changing of the colors in the background that the photos coincide with the changing of the seasons. Does that mean the rest of it is true, too?

My hands tremble as I flip through the photos, some of them notated with places and numbered days, but when the tears prick at the corners of my eyes, I blink them back fiercely. Crying won't help. Falling apart won't help. I inhale shallowly, then shove the folder back into the drawer with force, like it burns my fingers. I smooth the drawer closed like it was never disturbed.

If he wants me to know more, he'll tell me. And if he doesn't...maybe that tells me something too. I swallow hard and step into the hallway. The cabin is quiet except for the faint hum of the refrigerator and the low pop of cooling embers in the fireplace. My bare feet make almost no sound on the cool wooden floor as I move toward the living area. He's easy to find once I grace the end of the hall.

Sebastian stands at the back door, posture stiff but balanced, his shoulders rising and falling slowly with each breath. He's holding a mug with both hands, fingers wrapped around it like he needs the warmth more than the drink itself.

Even from behind, I can sense the exhaustion in the angle of his shoulders, in the slight slump of fatigue he can't quite hide. He couldn't have slept. A part of me feels guilty. His hair is tousled like he's run his hands through it a dozen times. The muscles along his back are tight beneath the thin tee shirt he must've changed into sometime during the night. His stance is alert but weary. The look of someone willing himself not to collapse.

He hasn't noticed me yet. For a moment, I just stand there, watching him stare out into the trees like the answers are somewhere between the branches. A chill runs through me. Not from fear, but from the quiet realization that whatever storm we stepped into...he's been standing in it far longer than I have and I might've just caught the eye passing over.

I hover in the doorway longer than I mean to, unsure how to announce myself in the thin morning light. Sebastian hasn't moved since I appeared, his shoulders still squared. His gaze is pinned to the forest beyond the glass that remains frosted, telling me that it's still early.

For a strange moment, I feel like I'm intruding. Like this is *his* world and I've stumbled into it barefoot and uninvited. Finally, I clear my throat. He flinches, just barely, and turns his head enough to see me. His expression softens for a fraction of a second, then rearranges itself into something neutral. His eyes are dark, riddled with worry and sleeplessness. "Morning," he says, voice low and rough.

"Morning." I tuck my hands into my sides, carefully stepping further into the kitchen. "Did you, um...get any sleep?"

His jaw flexes tight and his gaze returns to the back window. "No." *Right.* I figured that much. I step closer, drawn by the warmth of the fire and the smell of coffee drifting from his mug. "Is there...more coffee?"

He juts his chin toward the counter without turning toward me again, "Help yourself."

I pour a cup, even though my hands shake around the mug. I'm not sure if it's nerves or exhaustion or the folder still burning in my mind like a lit match. I lower myself to sit at the small kitchen table, eyes wandering the room again in new light. It doesn't look much different than last night. There's a small bookshelf tucked into the corner of the living room I didn't notice last night and what looks like a shotgun hangs above the door. Other than that, the only things that feel the room are the scarce pieces of furniture.

Sebastian stays by the door when I sit, doesn't turn to face me or mutter a word. I drink in the silence of the room until it's uncomfortable. "So..." I start cautiously, feigning confidence by straightening my posture and tilting my chin upward slightly. "Can I ask you something?"

He exhales through his nose, like he already regrets what's coming. "You can ask."

"But you won't answer," I mutter under my breath.

He hears it, his eyes narrowing in the reflection. "Depends on the question."

That feels like a challenge. Maybe it is. I sip my coffee and go for it, one brow perking in his direction. "What exactly *is* your job? You said you're part of some protection detail but that could mean anything. So are you military? Intelligence? Government? Private security? Something else?"

"Something else," he says shortly and I already feel a defeat settle into my chest. I wait for him to elaborate. He doesn't.

"*Okay...*" I press on, tapping my fingertips across the side of the mug cradled in my hands, "Then what's your title? What do people call you?" Give me *something*.

"Sebastian."

I roll my eyes as the rest of my features flatline. "Very funny."

"Wasn't meant to be."

God, he's frustrating. "Fine. Then how long have you been doing... whatever this is?"

"A while."

My eyes narrow at his back and I push down the audible groan of frustration that threatens. "Define a while."

"No."

I stare at him, mouth agape. "No?"

"No," he repeats, flatly, final. The irritation flares faster than I expect. Hot, sharp, impossibly out of place considering he literally saved my life. But every clipped answer feels like a door slammed in my face and it reminds me too much of home. Of my father's cold avoidance. My mother's half-truths. Mason telling me where I can go, who I can see, what I shouldn't ask. It all presses against my ribs until my temper snaps.

"You're joking, right? I'm stuck in some cabin in the middle of nowhere with a man who won't tell me *anything* about himself and hardly about what's going on, besides the fact that apparently my dad is a criminal and my whole life is a lie. And you expect me to, what, sit quietly and not ask questions?" I scoff, a bitter sound. "Go along with whatever little plan you have mapped out in your head? Forget it! It's not happening. That's *not* fair. I expect answers."

Despite my efforts to sound assertive, my temper tantrum is exactly that. Even to my own ears, I sound like a bratty little girl, fully anticipating things to go her way. Annoyance bubbles in my stomach at the sound of my own voice.

The rude truth is that Sebastian owes me nothing. He's already done more than enough, and I shudder thinking of what could have been the outcome of last night without him. He finally turns fully to face me, mug braced in his hands like he's holding back the urge to shatter it. I instantly feel small under his gaze but I square my shoulders anyway. "I expect you," he says evenly, remaining calm even with my brief outburst "to stay alive. That's it."

My jaw drops for a moment, lips parted in disbelief before I snap it shut. "Great. And I'm supposed to do that by blindly following your orders? Right? No freedom. No explanations. Just 'do what I say,' because that worked out so well with every other controlling person in my life." I push my mug forward, arms crossing over my chest.

His stare sharpens. He clearly isn't the type to back down and internally, I'm already preparing to lose this battle. Maybe because everything was supposed to be different now. I was supposed to be making my own decisions instead of continuing to follow someone else's direction.

"This isn't about control, Savannah." His words remain tight. Shrugging, I'm sure my expression reads the same stubbornness I used to show my family every time I heard the word 'no'.

"Sure feels like it."

"It's *not*." His voice drops, suddenly colder, free of all gentle, consoling hints I swore I felt last night. "It's about survival."

"Same thing," I mutter, annoyed and tired and fed up with everyone dictating my entire existence. He steps closer, the exhaustion cracking through his stern mask.

"You want freedom?" he asks, leaning down and bracing his palms on the table. "Freedom gets you killed right now. That's the difference."

I swallow hard, blinking twice. I know he's right. And what choice do I have? I have no idea where we are. No clue which direction I'd go if I ran. No phone, no one to call if I had one, and no idea who I could trust at this point. No one but the man standing in front of me. Nowhere to go but with him. Wherever it may lead.

He continues, voice firm but not unkind, "You have no freedom *because* your life is on the line. Because people are hunting you. Because I'm the only one on your side, whether you believe that or not." The words hang heavily between us. My throat tightens, irritation deflating into something smaller, more vulnerable.

I lower my eyes, fingers tightening around the warm ceramic. He exhales, softer this time, and runs a hand through his hair. "You don't have to like it," he adds, voice continuing to soften. "But you do have to listen to me." I want to argue. God, I *want* to. But I can't. Not when I know he's right. Not when I remember the look on his face last night. The fear, the determination, the guilt, all whispered into an empty room because he thought I was asleep. I take a shaky breath and nod slowly.

"Okay," I sigh a breath of defeat. "Fine."

His shoulders relax by a millimeter.

14

Sebastian

I turn back to the window, more to steady myself than to continue my so-called vigilance. Dawn slowly washes the pines in pale gold, quiet and deceptively peaceful. On the opposite end of the counter, the coffee machine beeps signaling the second pot I've brewed this morning has finished.

I need to get control of this situation. Of her questions and expectations. Of myself. The more she knows, the more vulnerable she is. The more I risk screwing up again. But she's watching me now, from the table with legs tucked up, oversized shirt cinched around her waist, trying to look smaller than she is. Trying to make sense of the ruins of her life. I rub a hand over my beard and force my voice steady.

"We need to establish some ground rules." I state firmly. Her eyebrows pinch in my direction and the freckles on her nose dance when it's crinkled. "*Of course* we do." The sarcasm is soft, but it hits. I deserve it. "First," I continue with an exhale, ignoring the roll of her eyes, "you don't leave the cabin. Not for any reason. Not the porch, not the road. If you're not in my line of sight, you're in danger."

She mutters something under her breath along the lines of *always in danger apparently*, but I proceed without acknowledgment. "Second, no communication with anyone outside this cabin. No phone calls. No messages. No attempts to reach out. No...smoke signals. Nothing."

Savannah deflates a little, lips tightening. "First of all, I lost my phone. And I wouldn't know who to call or message, anyway. So, I guess I have no choice but to be a prisoner."

I close my eyes briefly, pinching the bridge of my nose. "You're not a fucking prisoner. You're *alive*," I mutter through clenched teeth, my frustration surfacing, and catch her flinching. A sudden guilt shoots sharply through me. I shouldn't have said it like that.

I move closer, resting a hand on the back of the chair opposite her, knuckles closing around it to ground myself. "Third... you listen when I tell you something. Immediately. This isn't negotiable."

Her eyes narrow by a fraction, the defiance simmering just beneath exhaustion. "And if I don't?"

I meet her eyes, piercing through her gaze. "Then I can't keep you safe." She breaks eye contact first. Her shoulders curl inward, anger giving way to fear. I hate that I put that there and I hate that it's true, but there's no side stepping around the facts that we now face.

I clear my throat, regaining her attention. "Next few days we stay put. You rest. I'll secure the property, ration supplies, monitor the perimeter—"

"So this is really happening," she whispers. "This isn't just...a stop over." Her voice is small. Too small. And it twists something sharp inside of me. More guilt, for letting her get

here in the first place. Shame at the face of my failures. "No,"
I admit quietly, feeling as defeated in the moment as she
appears with the way she curls around herself. "It's not."

She nods, a slow, resigned motion, a brief pause
slipping between us before she speaks again.

"At least you're here. If I have to be trapped in a cabin
with someone for...however long, I guess I'm glad it's you.
Someone that doesn't want to hurt me and hasn't lied to me
for years." The words are innocent, her eyes fixed on her
mug. Completely harmless and almost absent, even. Like they
slipped through without a thought. And I'm clueless as to why
she's grateful for the inconvenience of my company, but
relieved she's pushed aside her stubbornness to listen.

The words still crash into me with force. Because no
one's ever said something like that to me. Not with that
sincerity. Not looking at me like I'm not just a weapon, a
shield, a name on a file. But a person. A person she's choosing
to trust. An unfamiliar comfortableness pours over me, warm
and dangerous. I swallow hard, tearing my gaze away before
she can see it and lay the truth between us. "Savannah, you
don't know me."

"Then tell me something about you," she chimes, like
it's the simplest request she could've made. Not pressing like
she was earlier. Genuine. "Anything," she adds when I remain
silent.

No. No, that's exactly the line I can't cross. I shake my
head abruptly, raking a hand through my hair. "The less you
know, the better. We're not—this isn't..." I force myself to
take a breath. "You need to see me as one thing. The person
keeping you alive. Nothing more." Her expression falters,
hurt flickering behind her eyes before she hides it. And damn
it, I feel that too.

I turn my back to her, gripping the counter until the wood bites into my palms. I can't afford to see her as anything other than an assignment. I already slipped once. No bond. No softness. No mistakes. Behind me, her voice is quiet, barely above a whisper. "You keep saying you're the only one on my side, Sebastian. But it doesn't feel like that if you won't even look at me." The words cut deep, uncomfortably accurate.

I shut my eyes, tongue running over my teeth. When I finally turn around, I keep my expression neutral, professional. But inside...the line between assignment and *Savannah* is already blurring. Maybe because I've studied her from afar for months. But having her *close*, interacting...she shouldn't feel this familiar. I remind myself that she's still a stranger, even when I already know all the skeletons in her closet.

The drive to keep her safe is already beginning to feel like more than my job alone. It feels guttural, instinctive. And that terrifies me more than anything outside these walls.

Her words hang in the air. Soft, pained, and too honest for either of us. For a long moment, the only sound is the faint crackle of dying embers in the fireplace. "You're right," I sigh. Her eyebrows lift slightly, surprised at the inch I choose to give her. Maybe she didn't expect me to admit it. Maybe I didn't expect it either. "This is...new to me," I say, my voice faltering. "Or at least, this part of it. I'm good at the security side. The logistics. The planning and observation. But anything beyond that...especially making things feel *normal*?" My chest tightens as I shake my head slowly, my insecurities besting me. Most of the time, all I have to be is Sebastian Hayes, the leader. The protector. The shadow. Not...Sebastian, the *person*. "That's not something I've done in a long time." I rub a hand across the back of my neck. "But I'll try. For you. Okay? I'll try to make this as easy for you as I can. I know this has to be hard for you. Your life turned upside down overnight and I'm sorry for that."

Her lips part like she wants to say something but stops, something soft washing across her expression. Gratitude, maybe. Relief. Something that magnetizes me toward her in a way that can't happen. I clear my throat quickly and nod toward the small kitchenette, desperate for a distraction.

"Let's have breakfast. It's not much, but it's something." She follows me to the cupboard and the cabin suddenly feels smaller. Opening the cabinet, it's as bleak as I expected. There's oatmeal packets lined in a row and a jar of instant coffee. I pause, then check the fridge to find a carton of eggs that—*thank God*—aren't expired. "Gourmet it is," I deadpan.

Savannah lets out a small laugh, quiet, breathy, and genuine. "I mean...compared to being kidnapped? Yeah. Pretty gourmet." It's the first real humor I've heard from her, and it settles somewhere in my chest I didn't know was vulnerable. I pull a skillet from under the stove and set it on the burner. "Scrambled okay?"

"Anything's okay," she says softly, sliding onto the small wooden stool by the counter. "I'm just grateful for a taste of normal." I feel a softening behind my ribs, deep and unwelcome. I crack the eggs into the pan, stirring slowly. She watches me with a curious sort of attentiveness, like she's trying to piece together the man behind the job.

"You cook?" she asks.

"I survive," I correct.

"Those are different," she murmurs. I don't respond. I

can't. Not when the distinction hits closer to the truth than I like. A few quiet minutes pass before the eggs finish. I divide them into mismatched plates and slide one toward her. She takes it with both hands, like it's something precious. "Thank you," she says. Two simple words. But the sincerity behind them almost undoes me.

We eat in a silence that's different than it was earlier in the morning. It's not tense or strained, but almost companionable. The kind you share with someone you trust, even if trust is too strong a word for what this is. Halfway through her plate, Savannah pauses, studying me. "Did you really mean it? About trying to make this feel normal?"

I meet her eyes and take a beat before I respond, carefully chewing over my words. "I don't know how to do normal anymore," I admit. "But I'll try to figure it out. For the next few days, at least." I don't add *or weeks*, though the thought lingers like a shadow in the back of my mind. There are many things I remain uncertain of but the minimum length of time we will have to stay off grid is not one of them. It's a truth I choose to omit for her sanity.

She nods slowly. "Okay. We'll figure it out together, then." She adds a soft smile that feels undeserving. *Together.* The word echoes louder than it should.

I look away before she notices the way it unsettles me. She's the assignment, I tell myself over and over until the words don't feel real anymore. But sitting here, eating eggs in a quiet cabin in the morning, like a routine that most people share regularly...it's getting harder to pretend that's all she is. Worse than that, it's getting exceptionally harder to ignore the way her smile causes my pulse to jump involuntarily.

15

Savannah

After breakfast, Sebastian clears his plate with the same quiet efficiency I've noticed he does most things. No wasted movements. No softness left over from our shared meal. When he finally speaks, his voice is all business again. "You need to learn a few things if you're going to stay alive here."

I blink at him. This man's mood swings like a pendulum. "Wow, I really enjoyed breakfast, too." He ignores the sarcasm. Or refuses to take the bait. "Finish your coffee. Then meet me outside." His command is stern, leaving no room for questions or remarks.

Outside. My stomach tightens at the thought. The woods still feel like they're full of ghosts waiting on me to fall to tug me back into darkness. But I nod in compliance anyway. By the time I step out onto the porch, the sun has risen enough to melt the frost on the railing and warms my cheeks with a comfortable tingle.

Sebastian stands a few feet away in the clearing beside the cabin, sleeves pushed up, hands braced at his hips like he's preparing to coach a toddler through tying their shoes. "Okay," he says, "first lesson. Awareness." I arch a brow, eyes darting left to right like I'm missing something hiding in the tree line. The problem is, I wouldn't know what to look for even if it jumped out at me. "Awareness of what?"

"Everything." He says it so flatly, so seriously, that I laugh. It earns a stern glare in reply. Schooling my features, I try to follow his instructions as he teaches me how to stand with my weight balanced, how to look and listen without being obvious, how to move silently without tripping over every pinecone in the forest.

Except I *do* trip. Repeatedly. On pinecones, on roots, on flat ground that somehow betrays me. Sebastian exhales through his nose in a way that tells me he's restraining judgment. "You're putting your weight in your toes. It needs to be in the ball of your foot."

"I can't help my toes!" I snap.

"Everyone can help their toes."

"That sounds ridiculous," I mutter.

He drags a hand down his face. "You're making this harder than it needs to be."

"Maybe you're *making* it harder," I shoot back. "Not all of us grew up in a combat boot commercial, throwing knives as soon as we could walk and shouting commands instead of saying 'mama'."

His eyebrows lift at my defiance and he folds his arms over his chest. He looks bigger that way. Like a statue, carved straight out of camouflage and discipline. "I didn't '*grow up*' in anything like this," he corrects me.

"Oh? So you just woke up one day magically able to

glide across the forest floor like a woodland ninja?" My arms cross back at him, my smirk almost mocking in nature.

He stares at me for two full seconds before shaking his head, a faint and exhausted almost-laugh escaping him, "God help me."

"See?" I say, a satisfied grin tugging at my lips. "Even you know that this is ridiculous."

He steps toward me, close enough that I feel his presence like a rush of heat in the cold air. "Savannah," His voice is steady and stubbornly patient. And I can't ignore the rush of waves through my stomach at the sound of my name rolling off his tongue that way. "You're tired. You've been through hell. And I'm pushing you because if something happens, I need your body to know what to do before your mind has time to panic." *My body can think of several things it wants to do,* I think to myself. And then, *get it together. Not the time.*

I exhale a long, defeated breath through my nose, my fingers finding my hair and running through it absentmindedly. "I just...don't want to be useless."

His expression softens. Barely, but I see it. "You're not useless," he says quietly, assuredly. "You survived last night. Not everyone in your situation would." Heat creeps into my face—and not from the sun. I nod slowly in understanding.

We move into the next part of training, basic self-defense. He teaches me how to break a hold, where to strike if I need to, how to use my weight even though I barely have any. Except every time he demonstrates something, he has to touch me. Guiding my arm, shifting my stance, pressing a hand lightly against my back or shoulder. Each contact sends a shiver through me that has nothing to do with fear. He must sense it, because after the third correction, he steps back abruptly, clearing his throat. I already feel vacant when he moves away. "Good," he says, even though it definitely was not good. "Let's stop there."

"I can keep going," I offer, breathless, and ridiculously desperate for his approval. He shakes his head. "You need rest. And food. Training on fumes will get you hurt." His tone is firm, the way it gets when he doesn't want any disagreement. But then something flickers across his face. Hesitation, maybe, or guilt. Maybe something I don't have a name for yet.

"Hey," I blurt before I can stop myself, not wanting the conversation to end. "For what it's worth...you're actually not bad at teaching."

His mouth quirks. Not a full smile, but close. "Don't spread that around."

"Right...people might think you care or something. I'll ruin your reputation," I say solemnly.

"You already are," he mutters under his breath. But there's no malice in it. Instead, it's soft and dangerously warm.

Something eases inside me a fraction. Because maybe I can exist in this place without unraveling. Sebastian gathers the water bottles we'd brought out and gestures toward the cabin. "Let's go," he says, quieter this time. "Let me get you inside before the temperature drops." I follow, a strange flutter in my chest. I convince myself that he's only doing his job. Nothing more, nothing deeper, as hard as that is to swallow, considering I don't think anyone has ever cared this much for my wellbeing.

The temperature drops fast once the sun dips behind the ridge, shadows swallowing the cabin like an inhale. For dinner, we managed to find and share a gourmet meal of cheez-itz and instant noodles. I'm rinsing our dishes in the tiny sink when I hear the front door click open. I glance over my shoulder just in time to see Sebastian slip outside, silent as ever. Interest tugs at me, disguised as curiosity. I wipe my hands on a towel and drift toward the front window, easing two fingers between the curtains and peeking out.

He moves like he did in the woods. Fluid, intentional, and every step placed with purpose. He checks the tree line first, scanning it the way someone trained to notice the smallest anomaly would. His posture shifts, listening, reading the wind, assessing shadows. It's all second nature to him. Like breathing. He circles the cabin perimeter with practiced precision, pausing at the corners, testing the sturdiness of the fence line. He even glances upward, like danger could come from the sky if it really wanted to. And maybe for people like him...it could.

I watch him for longer than I intend to, eyes tracing the efficient lines of his movements. The way he crouches to inspect the soft ground. The way he touches the latch on the back gate, testing its give. The way he stays low, aware of angles and visibility. Each practiced movement secures the fact that I know I'll be safe here. And it further fuels my lingering curiosity about his past. About who he really is. Where did he learn this?

I know he wasn't telling the truth earlier. *Something else* is a lie so thin it practically evaporates. People aren't born knowing how to clear a perimeter. They don't just pick up evasion techniques or seamless hand-to-hand combat. Or the ability to listen to the forest like a conversation.

These things are taught. Drilled into someone until they're instinct. Military. Government. Something covert and intentionally shadowed. It's almost frightening, trusting a man that could make me disappear without a trace. But then again…something deep inside me knows he won't hurt me. Or let anyone else, for that matter. And for my own sanity, I have to believe that.

He stops at the edge of the trees and stands still for a long moment, staring into the dark like it's speaking to him. His shoulders sink just a little. Not with weakness, but weight. Weariness. The kind that seeps deep into his bones and still bleeds on the outside. This life, whatever this is to him, has carved him into the shape he is. Rigid and unwavering, sharp enough to cut but worn enough to ache. He's not the type of man who ends up protecting some stranger's daughter by accident. He's the type of man someone assigns to something impossible. And somehow, that impossible thing became me.

The hair rises at the back of my neck with the strange awareness that he's more than a shield in my mind. He's becoming someone real. Someone with a past I'll never fully understand. Someone whose boundaries aren't as solid as he wants them to be.

In the time I've let my mind wander, Sebastian finishes his circuit, touches the porch rail like he's grounding himself, then turns toward the door. I step back from the window before he can catch me staring, pretending to finger through the slim choice of literature on the bookshelf near it. When he walks inside, shaking the cold from his hands, my eyes find him and he looks up at me through the dim room. My stomach flutters in response. The door clicks softly behind him as he steps inside. He doesn't say anything at first, just hangs his coat on a hook by the door and exhales through his nose, slow and tired. I can't force myself to look away, my mind firing question after question at myself.

He glances up, my features filling with heat in the shame of staring, hands curled nervously together. "You okay?" he asks, his tone somewhere between concern and confusion. I nod, teeth capturing my lower lip, the truth tangled somewhere behind my ribs.

He walks past me to the counter, my eyes still following him as he refills the same mug of coffee that I'm fairly sure he's been nursing since dawn. His movements are deliberate but weighted. He must be running on fumes. Fumes powered entirely by duty and fear and whatever else he's refusing to tell me.

I study him for another moment, trying to hush my mind. His back is to me, shoulders strong but tense, faint bruise-colored shadows under his eyes. I watch the way he checks the window even while standing inside, like danger could appear at any second. I can't stop my thoughts from circling the way he moved outside. Professional and efficient. A protector and a weapon all at once. A mystery.

Before I can talk myself out of it, the question slips out. Soft, careful, but too honest to swallow back. "Sebastian...where did you learn all of that?" His hand freezes halfway between the coffee pot and the counter. He doesn't turn around immediately. Instead, he sets the pot down with a quiet clink and braces both palms on the countertop, head bowed slightly like the question itself pains him. I almost feel a fraction of guilt for asking.

The old clock by the door clicks loud enough to fill the space of the room, the same sound I imagine his mind is making while he deliberates how he's going to avoid my question this time. When he finally turns, his expression is shuttered, but with a faint crack running through it. Not annoyance or anger, but like what he wants to say is too heavy for me to bear.

"Why do you ask?" his voice is guarded and he looks past me instead of meeting my gaze. I swallow, losing any courage I might have had moments ago. The photos I found in the drawer earlier flash to the front of my mind. "Because, like I said when we were outside...people don't...just *know* how to do what you do. All the things you showed me today. The way you move, the way you—" I gesture helplessly toward the window. "—handle danger. It's not normal."

He watches me, jaw tense, and I'm sure he's tossing bullshit answers through his mind even as I speak, debating which will satisfy me the most. I take a breath before I continue. "You said your job was 'something else.' But it's not. And I'm not stupid. So...I guess I'm just trying to understand who's protecting me." Another silence. He drags a hand through his hair, gaze shifting to the floor for the first time since I met him. "It's not a life you want details about," he finally says.

"That's not an answer," I retort back.

"It's the only one you're getting." His tone isn't cruel, but tells me enough to know he's building a wall not to push me away, but to keep himself from unraveling. I still feel the crash of disappointment. Sebastian may not give me the answers that I want, but from what I can tell, he hasn't lied to me, either. That in itself is refreshing. I step a little closer, my voice softening. "I just want to know something that proves I can trust you."

Something resembling vulnerability, if he's capable of such a thing. Maybe fear that he's failing again. "You can," he says quietly. "I promise." The words hit deeper than I expect. It's nothing that I was looking for but the gravity behind them assures me enough. I study him, searching for the truth in his face, and I can see it there. He believes what he's saying. He means it.

But there's more he isn't telling me. A lot more. And I can't decide if that scares me or makes me feel safe. He clears his throat and looks away, like the moment went too far. "Get some rest," he speaks to his mug instead of me. "It'll be a long day tomorrow."

"I can take the couch tonight if you want," I offer, my gaze lingering on the dark circles beneath his eyes and the clear exhaustion in his stance.

He breathes an unamused laugh, "Not happening."

"Come on," I murmur, edging myself closer cautiously, like he might reach out and bite if I step too close. "I can tell that you're tired. I really doubt anything is gonna happen because I decided to sleep on the couch."

"I said no, Savannah." His words are razor-sharp and final, carving a pit in my chest. He straightens his posture, facing me again. "We have a long day tomorrow and I don't need you tired and dragging."

I feel a pang at the shift, exhaling sharply. "*Fine.* Whatever." I cross my arms over my chest, hiding the wince at the bitterness dripping from my own words. "Can you at least tell me what we're doing tomorrow, then?"

"Staying alive." His voice drops even lower. "And pretending this is easier than it is." My brows come together at his words, eyes narrowing a fraction. He turns toward the window again, shoulders drawn tight. The end of the conversation and no room for protest. Again. And maybe I'm just fooling myself, but I get a sense that he feels the charge in the room when we stand too close, too.

I stand there for a moment too long, hoping that if I

don't retreat automatically, he'll change his mind. Guilt gnaws at me, knowing I'm the reason for his exhaustion, knowing that I'll be awake for hours, anyway. With an exasperated sigh, I give in. "Goodnight, Sebastian." I hesitate a moment longer, waiting. He doesn't say it back. I don't know why I expected him to.

With disappointment in my chest and a thousand unanswered questions crowding my thoughts, I finally turn away and withdraw into the bedroom.

16

Sebastian

The cabin settles into a quiet I would normally welcome. But tonight, it feels tight around the edges, like the walls are listening. Like the night itself is waiting. Savannah disappeared into the bedroom twenty minutes ago, maybe thirty. I'm starting to lose track. My sense of time has been slipping since yesterday, blurred by adrenaline and fear and whatever the hell else I'm pretending not to feel.

I should be doing another perimeter check. Should be reviewing intel. Should be reinforcing the back window lock that sticks or checking the satellite pager for any communication from base. Instead, all I can think about is whether she's sleeping. Whether she's okay. Whether she *feels* whatever this dangerous pull is that I can't shake, too.

A stupid thought. Irrational. Undisciplined. Feelings make mistakes, I know that.

But exhaustion makes even the sharpest instincts dull. Before I can talk myself out of it, I slip down the hallway. The floor creaks beneath my weight and I wince. Ridiculous, because there's no danger inside the cabin—at least not the kind I'm trained for. The bedroom door is cracked open an inch, just enough for a whisper of moonlight to cut across the frame. I hover in the doorway, careful not to step inside as I let my weight lean against it.

She's curled beneath the blanket, hair spilling across the pillow in a dark tangle, one hand tucked under her cheek. Her breathing is soft and even, peaceful in a way I haven't seen since before everything went wrong. A way I'm envious of. I tell myself I'm checking to make sure she's safe. That she hasn't had another nightmare. That she's still breathing.

But the truth is...I just want to see her with the weight of the situation lifted, even if only in sleep.

She looks younger like this. Softer. Not the girl who cracked a captor's face or stands her ground against me. Not the girl who snapped back with sarcasm during training or asked questions she shouldn't have the courage to ask. She looks like someone who deserved a normal life. A real life. A life untouched by men like her father...*or me*. Guilt gnaws at my throat and my chest tightens uncomfortably, the sensation unfamiliar and unwelcome. People don't get under my skin. Not ever. Distance is survival, attachment a liability. These are things I learned early and hard.

But standing here, watching her...I can feel my walls beginning to crack, each carefully placed brick slipping out of place. I force myself to step back and feel my hands curl at my sides. *Turn around. Leave. Let her sleep.* When I reach the living room, the exhaustion hits all at once, heavy and unavoidable, like I've been running from something that only I can see. My body feels too heavy, my thoughts too slow.

I tell myself I'll sit for only a minute, just long enough to clear my head. The couch isn't comfortable, not in the slightest, but I've slept on worse. I lower myself onto it, lean my head back, and close my eyes only to blink the burn out. My arms cross over my chest, as if protecting myself from the threatening vacancy of the cabin.

I'm just resting. Not sleeping. I can't sleep. Not when…

My breath drags unevenly.

Not when she's here. Not when I'm responsible. Not when the world outside this cabin is still moving against us and the gravity of uncertainty constricts every thought.

But the cushions sink beneath my weight, the warmth of the freshly lit fire grazes my face, and the last of the adrenaline finally drains from my bloodstream. My muscles start to loosen despite my best effort. My eyelids grow heavy. *Damn it.* Not now.

Sleep captures me before the thought finishes. Not the deep, peaceful kind she managed to find. But the kind born from collapse. Unwanted and unprepared. The last thing I'm aware of is the soft crackle of the fire and the lingering image of her asleep, safe, burned behind my eyes like a brand.

17

Savannah

Something drags me out of sleep. Not a sound at first—just a feeling. A prickle along my arms. The kind of instinct that comes before consciousness. I'm half asleep when I hear it. A ragged breath. A low, rough murmur. A sound that doesn't belong in the dark. Not here, when it's only Sebastian and I in the cabin. My eyes snap open.

For one terrifying second, I'm back in the woods, in the nightmare I thought I'd left behind. I sit up quickly, scanning the small bedroom with nothing but moonlight to guide me. Nothing moves. Nothing's wrong. But the noise continues. A strained exhale, a broken whisper I can't make out. Footsteps? No...shifting fabric. Weight on the couch or the chair, the creak of the worn wooden frame whispering behind the tattered gasping.

My heart hammers against my ribs. I reach blindly for something, anything, I can use for protection. My fingers close around the fragile base of the brass bedside lamp. The same lamp that didn't work when I tried to turn it on last night. *Perfect.* Right now, it's a weapon. A terrible weapon, but a weapon, nonetheless. Clutching it tightly between clammy palms, I creep down the hallway, each step soft but trembling. My fingers curl tighter around the cold metal with every breath. The muddied words grow clearer the closer I get.

A sharp inhale. A whispered "No—" Then another sound...pained, choked, like he's trapped somewhere far away. Panic sets deeper into my chest. I round the corner into the living room and freeze. Sebastian is alone on the couch, tangled awkwardly in a thin blanket, head thrown back, jaw clenched. The fire has burned low, painting him in a weak orange glow. His chest rises and falls in uneven bursts, his fists tightening and releasing. He's asleep, but not peacefully.

I lower the lamp, placing it on the floor beside me, shame prickling my cheeks at catching him in a vulnerable moment. But the fear doesn't fade completely. Not when his breathing spikes, not when he flinches like someone's hitting him in this nightmare he's trapped in. I hover for a moment, unsure, then inch closer. "Sebastian," I whisper. He doesn't respond. I swallow hard and hesitate for a heartbeat before bending beside him, reaching out to gently shake his shoulder. "Sebastian?" I try again. Nothing.

My teeth gnaw at the inside of my lower lip as he grunts in his sleep, gasping sharply, head lulling to the side. Even like this, his brows are stitched together with a firmness that never really fades. I suck in a sharp breath and settle both hands on his shoulders this time, my face mere inches from his. "Sebastian!"

The reaction is instant.

He jerks upright with a violent inhale, his hand

shooting up to grab my wrist, tight. Too tight. The other goes immediately to his side, reaching for a holster that isn't there, fingers curling around empty space. "Sebastian! Hey, it's just me," My voice quivers, breath catching in my throat. "It's Savannah." I try to tug my wrist free, but his grip is a vise.

His storm-colored eyes are wild for a moment, unfocused, searching the dark, not seeing *me* at all. Then they land on my face, recognition breaking through the fog. He freezes. He releases my wrist like it the touch scalds him and sits up too fast, too rigid. He pushes himself back into the couch, immediately putting space between us. I take a step back, rubbing my wrist gingerly, my pulse still racing frantically.

His chest heaves once, twice. "Fuck—" he whispers. His eyes drag from the bruises lingering on my upper arms down to my wrist where he released his lethal grasp. He grimaces as he folds forward, elbows on his knees, head falling into his palms. "I'm sorry," he mutters, voice raw and unguarded as he shakes his head. "I'm—*dammit*. I didn't mean to—" He stops himself short. The guilt is written in every line of his posture, in the slight tremble of his fingers threaded through his hair. "You shouldn't have seen that."

I rub my wrist carefully, shaking my head. "It's okay. I'm fine," I try to assure him. But seeing *him* like *this*...that takes the breath from me. Sebastian, the man who fought off an armed group alone. Who navigates the woods like he was born in them. Who never flinches, never hesitates, never relaxes. I watch as he unravels in front of me, feeling completely helpless.

For a second, I think it must be the exhaustion. Then I wonder what terrible thing he could have been dreaming of to have him reacting this way. Of what he's gone through. Before I can think too hard about it, I step around the coffee table and lower myself onto the couch beside him.

Not too close. But close enough. "Do you want to talk about it? I ask, my voice as timid as it is firm. "No," he replies immediately.

I pause for half a second, then lay a hesitant hand between his shoulder blades and rub small, steady circles. The same way my mother used to do to me when I needed comforting. He doesn't move right away, doesn't breathe, doesn't push me away. Then slowly, unbelievably, his shoulders ease beneath my touch. His muscles soften, tension bleeding out of him like he's been holding himself rigid for years and only now remembered how to let go. He almost leans into it, into *me*, before catching himself. When my fingers find the hair at the back of his head, his head tilts back into my touch.

The shift is small, but I feel it. A quiet surrender. He reaches over gingerly, grasping my opposite wrist and brushing his thumb across the fingertip shaped bruise that remains there. His features twist as if it physically pains him to look at what those other men did to me. Just as quickly, he pulls his hand away from mine. A moment of trust he probably never meant to give. After several long breaths, he straightens abruptly, retreating back into himself, the familiar armor sliding over his expression.

"You should go back to bed," he croaks without looking at me. His voice is calmer now but his eyes remain haunted. "Okay," I whisper, though I don't move right away. He still won't look at me. And that may sting...but for the first time since meeting him, I saw the man beneath all the steel. I don't think he knows how much that means. And so, I retreat back to bed.

The morning greets me with an empty kitchen. A cup of coffee sits on the table beside a plate of eggs, still steaming. I move to the back door, peering out of the small window at its center and find him. He's there. Gaze fixed on the vast, barren trees, like he's contemplating a deep truth neither of us can name.

18

Sebastian

I've already circled the property twice since the sun began to crest over the mountain tops, both sweeps taking longer than necessary. The forest is quiet. Eerie almost, save for the rustle of raccoons and squirrels moving somewhere beyond the tree line. Even the wildlife seems to be keeping its distance this morning, as if the turmoil inside me bleeds outward.

The lingering chill of the night cuts across my face when I step onto the porch for the third time, and I welcome it. Anything to keep my mind from circling back to last night. To the way she tried to comfort me even after I grabbed her like that. The way her fingers felt as they pushed through my hair and I enjoyed it too much. Anything to ground me here. I didn't mean to fall asleep. And I sure as hell didn't mean to go back there when I did.

The streets are dry as bone, cracked and hollow, with memories of homes burning on either side of me. Thick, black smoke clogs the air. It smells of tar and ash and despair.

Somewhere in the distance, people are screaming. The kind of screams that never leave you. The kind that lodge themselves into your bones.

Jesse's voice cuts through it all, shouting that we have to go. That there's no time. That she's gone, they're all gone. Still, I search. I dig through rubble, through what's left of the city, no longer able to tell if I'm clawing through brick or bone. Hands grab my arms before I can process what's happening. Too many of them, too strong to fight. My unit drags me back despite my protests, despite the way I fight against them until my throat burns and my chest aches.

And deep inside of me, the truth burns like acid. I failed her. Failed all of them. I warned her not to come back while we were gone. Told her it was too dangerous, that she needed to leave while she could still get out. She never listened. She never would.

I turn back toward the cabin, exhaling sharply through my nose as I bring myself back to the present. I feel her eyes on me before I see her, that familiar weight pressing between my shoulders. When my gaze finally lands on the window, it confirms what I already know.

Savannah stands just inside the back door, arms crossed over her chest, watching me through the small pane of glass like she's afraid I might vanish if she looks away. After last night, part of me wishes I would.

"Morning," I mutter when I step back inside, heading straight for the pot of coffee that's long since gone stale. The warmth from the fireplace feels suffocating. Or maybe it's my own thoughts. I shrug out of my jacket and drape it over the back of a chair.

"Morning," she replies, her voice brighter than her

expression. She watches me carefully, like I'm something unpredictable that she doesn't know how to approach. "How'd, um...how'd you sleep?" Even as she asks it, I can feel the regret in the question. Last night, she saw too much. I crossed a line I shouldn't have. The memory of her hand on my back burns through me, sharp and unwanted, leaving behind a starved sense of want. Something that men like me don't get to have. I take a sip of the cold coffee, swallowing the bitterness. "I didn't. Not really."

Her gaze drops, fingers twisting together the way they always do when she's nervous. *Do I make her nervous?* The weight of it settles painfully in my chest. I want her to feel safe here. I just don't know how to give her that without hovering, without smothering her, and still holding onto my sanity. "I'm sorry to hear that," she mumbles, still not looking at me.

I drag a hand down my face, scrubbing over the stubble beginning to appear at my jawline. I don't remember how many days have passed since I last shaved. I take the seat across from her. "I wanted to apologize again for last night. You really shouldn't have had to see that." My voice is clipped, deliberately controlled and free of the liability of emotion.

"Everyone has bad dreams, Sebastian." Her comfort is as warm as it is unsettling. I don't deserve it. "It's not like you can control that."

I shake my head, running my tongue over my lips before answering. "No." A breath escapes me, frustration aimed inward, where it belongs. "I didn't mean to scare you. I shouldn't have grabbed you like that. It won't happen again."

She doesn't argue. Instead, she stands and moves to the sink, rinsing the breakfast dishes like nothing is wrong.

Like the air between us isn't still charged. "Okay," she says simply, cheer returning to her voice as if she can will the tension away, "what are we doing today?

"Training," I reply dryly. "Meet me outside when you're ready." I don't wait for her answer. I pull my jacket back on and step out through the back door, filling my lungs with cool, hollow air. For a moment, while I'm alone, I let myself breathe.

19

Savannah

The air in the kitchen is palpable after our excuse of a breakfast. The contrast between the raw, shaken man I woke from a nightmare last night and the rigid, untouchable version of Sebastian standing across from me this morning makes my head spin. How one person can feel like two entirely different men is something I still haven't learned how to digest. His answers are clipped and cold. My heart sinks despite knowing what to expect.

Outside, I tug on the jacket that's too big over the shirt that's too big, rolling the sleeves back so I can actually use my hands. When I join him in the clearing, he's fully returned to the same immovable man as usual. His shoulders are squared, jaw locked tight. Today isn't going to be easy. Not for my body and definitely not for my heart.

"Okay," I inhale deeply through my nose, "I'm ready." I don't even have time to set my feet shoulder-width apart like he's drilled into me before they're swept out from under me. "Hey!" I yelp, tipping backward, but his arm catches me before I hit the ground. He sets me back on my feet, already retreating, arms crossing over his chest. "You said you were ready," disappointment drips from every syllable.

"You didn't even give me time!" I shoot back, narrowing my eyes. "Try it again," I challenge. This time I place my feet properly, bracing myself. Except instead of his ankle hooking behind mine like usual, it slides behind my knee and suddenly I'm glaring up at him from the grass. "That's not fair!" I protest, sounding embarrassingly childish.

"Nothing in this life is fair, Savannah," he says evenly, his voice strikingly cold, free of emotion. "And certainly not someone trying to hurt you. Run it again." I groan, rolling my eyes with exaggerated drama. Fine. Two can play his game.

Instead of scrambling up, I lunge from the ground and grab his ankle, yanking hard enough to surprise him. He goes down with a grunt, landing beside me. "Ha!" I shout triumphantly, a smile stretching across my features. For half a second, I swear I see the corner of his lips twitch. Just as quickly, he's all business again.

"Well played," he muses, already sitting upright and dusting off his hands. I take advantage of the angle and crawl toward him as quickly as my legs let me. But before I can spin around behind him to grab his arms the way he's shown me before, I'm tackled flat onto my back. I huff out a breath, defeated. His arms pin mine above my head, his weight solid and immovable. My eyes lock with his. "Never let them know your next move," he says. Behind the seriousness in his voice, there's a hint of a smirk on his lips.

Grinding my molars together, I plant my feet and thrust my waist upward, using everything I've got. His weight shifts and suddenly he's beside me instead of on top of me. I flip onto my knees, straddling him before he can recover. My hands land on his biceps, pressing them into the ground. "Never let them know your next move," I mock, sticking my tongue out. *Very mature, Savannah.* Still, pride swells in my chest. I won this round.

I flip my hair over my shoulder, sitting up in place. The awareness crashes in quickly and alarmingly, lighting my senses ablaze. The way my weight settles in his lap. The heat of his torso radiating beneath me. The sudden stillness. My cheeks burn, heart stuttering rapidly. I try to move but my legs don't cooperate. He doesn't move, either.

His crystalline eyes, piercing and intense, lock onto mine. They're the kind of eyes you could drown in if you weren't careful, pale blue in the center and framed by a dark halo that deepens the color at the edges. A storm that disturbs the air before it ever comes near.

He props himself up on his elbows, brow lifting slightly. "Good. What do you do from here?" I know he means the training. I do. But my thoughts drift anyway. To the warmth of his chest, the hard muscle beneath my thighs. The rustling sounds of the forest are muted by the pounding of my heart and the soft curve of his lips.

"I—" I shake my head, my breath hitching unsteadily. The words disappear. "Remember your training," his voice drops an octave as his gaze drops to my lips. "Sebastian..." His name slips out as a whisper, fragile and reckless.

Before I can second guess myself, my lips crash against his and everything becomes an intoxicating blur. His lips taste like coffee, the bitterness burning sweetly on my tongue. I feel a rush in my chest, the heat of his mouth, the groan that slips from him when my fingers curl into the hair at the side of his neck. He kisses me back like he's been starving, like control is something he's already lost.

His hand grips my hip, holding me there. My arms wind around his neck and my knees tighten against his sides. His fingers crawl up my back, lifting my shirt in their path, warm against the winter chill that bites at my skin. When his tongue parts my lips, I let him. I crave it. I push closer, whimpering softly, needing the contact.

The sound seems to snap him back into reality. He pulls away abruptly, eyes squeezed shut, regret etched across his face. "*Shit—*" He lifts me by the waist carefully, like I'm breakable, and sets me beside him. "I'm sorry..." He lifts a hand, pinching the bridge of his nose, and I'm left speechless. "I—" He exhales harshly and I can physically feel the wall separating us sliding back into place.

"It's okay," I reassure him quickly, reaching out to rest a hand on his arm. He recoils from my touch and the rejection hits like a physical blow.

My chest caves, something inside me shattering quietly. He stands, turning away from me like he can't bear to look at the wreckage. "I need to..." He trails off, a hand rubbing across the back of his neck, swallowing thickly. "I need to do another check."

And then he's gone, storming around the side of the cabin and leaving me sitting alone on the grass. I bring my fingers to my lips, tracing the ghost of his touch still burned there. I sit like that for a long moment, forcing the tears not to fall. Feeling empty and foolish and like I just crossed a line I don't know how to draw back from.

20

Sebastian

I don't trust myself to look back at her. If I do, I know what will happen. I'll pull her into my arms and kiss her again and my body will refuse to let go. I round the corner of the cabin and pause when I reach the pile of firewood settled at the far end of the tree line. Every step away feels wrong, like I'm betraying something fragile, something that won't wait for me to decide who I'm allowed to be.

Her kiss still burns on my mouth. It wasn't rushed or desperate, but soft...almost careful. Like she was testing the ground between us, seeing if it would hold. I should've pulled away. But when I tasted her lips, for one reckless second, my world fell to a single point. Her.

None of it mattered anymore. Not the assignment, not the men that took her, not bruises that battered her skin. Nothing but the sweet sound she made when I pushed my tongue into her mouth.

That's the part I can't forgive myself for. I flex my hands at my sides, trying to ground myself in something solid. The Earth beneath my boots, the familiar weight of the axe in my hands when I lift it from the stump to chop another log in half. Anything but the memory of her lips, the way her breath caught when she pulled back, eyes wide like she hadn't meant to hope—and did anyway.

I wanted to stay there. To let my hands explore every inch of her smooth skin, to taste every corner of her mouth, to breathe her in like the first bloom of flowers in the spring. The truth settles heavy in my chest as I drop the axe and move farther into the trees. I wanted to turn back, cup her face, take what she offered and pretend it wouldn't change anything. Pretend that wanting her wasn't already costing me sleep, focus, discipline. Pretend that I could touch her without ruining her.

I've spent years learning how to live without the things I want. But she's different.

And it dawns on me, harsh and unsettling. This isn't a fleeting thought or a moment of weakness, at all. It's a slow, brutal realization unfurling in my gut. I don't just want her. I want a life where I don't have to walk away from her. And that's the one thing I can't have.

Because wanting her means risking her. It means letting my guard down in ways I swear I never would again. It means admitting that I can't control the outcome anymore.

I stop at the edge of the clearing, forcing myself to breathe through the ache pressing behind my ribs. The trees sway in the wind, mocking me with nature's quiet laughter, while I try to stand still in the unforgiving reality I've let myself imagine that I'll never be able to reach.

She kissed me like she trusted me not to break her. And the cruelest part is knowing I already have. I keep walking.

Not because I don't want her—but because I *do*.

21

Savannah

The days begin to blur together in a strange, quiet rhythm. By the end of the first week, I know the creak of every floorboard in the cabin. I know which windows whistle when the wind pushes too hard. I know that Sebastian wakes before sunrise every morning, no matter how little sleep he gets. I know he pretends not to be exhausted and he checks the perimeter at least three times a day. Once at dawn, once at mid-afternoon, once right before dark. I know that every time he returns inside, his eyes scan the room automatically, but they land on me before anything else.

I know he doesn't like letting me out of his sight for long. And I know I pretend not to notice. Still, he doesn't let himself get too close. Like there's an invisible force around me that keeps him at arms-length distance.

Training continues, too. Some days I'm better. Some days I'm terrible. On the terrible days, I snap at him. Sometimes he snaps at himself. He never lets his touch linger for too long when he corrects my posture and I pretend my heart doesn't crack a little further every time he pulls away.

Our conversations stay cautious. We avoid topics that are too intimate, too personal. Avoid the inevitable discussion about leaving this place. I know he's thought of the next steps, keeping me in the dark. I pretend it doesn't bother me, like it never crosses my mind. I've surrendered myself to completely trusting him and try not to ask too many questions. Sometimes I get a glance of the man beneath the armor and I relish in those moments. The occasional spark of humor breaks the tension, but never for long. We orbit around each other. Close, but always aware of the invisible line neither of us fully understands.

The nightmares haven't returned. For him, at least, not when I've been awake to hear them. For me, they've changed. Less about being taken. More about losing him in the dark. Or waking up without him here. It's ridiculous, I know that. But I also know that every time I close my eyes, I still feel the memory of his hands on my skin. Of his lips. Not painful. Just...real. Real enough to haunt me in my sleep.

22

Sebastian

The first week crawls by slower than I expected. Savannah adapts faster than she realizes. She listens, she learns, she pushes through every miserable drill I put her through. She's clumsy, sure. She trips over roots and rugs and her own feet, but she's trying. Harder than most recruits I've trained. Harder than I ever thought she would or was capable of. Not that I'd tell her that.

I keep our conversations guarded. Every word measured like we're both afraid of stepping on a landmine buried somewhere in the space between us that we both tactically avoid. But somehow, she keeps managing to chip away at the silence I've lived in for years. I hate how much it's working. I tell myself it's the isolation. The stress. The responsibility. Anyone would start to crack under it. Anyone would start to...notice things. That's what I tell myself. But the truth is, I notice *her*.

More than I should.

I notice the way she chews her lip when she's concentrating and how I want to tug it free with mine. The way she rolls her eyes when she's trying not to smile. The way she mutters under her breath when she's annoyed at me. The way her breathing steadies when she finally gives way to sleep, her dark eyelashes a stark contrast to the light freckles that dot her nose. And the way I feel inclined to check on her every night before I allow myself rest. Hell, sometimes I'm doing something completely routine—checking windows, loading firewood, securing the locks—and I catch myself listening for her footsteps in the hall or waiting for her soft, hesitant "goodnight" before she shuts her door. I don't know when I started looking forward to it and I don't remember the first time I said it back. Probably the moment I realized I shouldn't.

I notice the way she waits for me in the mornings. I plate her food before I perform my perimeter check and yet, when I return, it's untouched. And she sits at the table, expecting me to join her. Sometimes I do, but most of the time, I keep my distance at the counter. I notice the way that she asks me how I've slept, even when the answer is always the same. "Barely."

And then there's her laugh.

God help me, her laugh. Light and warm and so out of place here that it knocks something loose in my chest every damn time I hear it. I don't know what to do with that. I shouldn't be doing anything with that. Because she's not here *for* me, she's here *because* of me. She's here because of the danger I failed to stop. Because of what her father did. Because of the mole I should've caught a year ago. And no matter how many times her companionship comforts me, I remind myself:

> *She is not mine to get comfortable with.*
> *She is not mine to want anything from.*
> *I am here to protect her. Nothing more, nothing less.*

So I stay distant. Cold, when I'm afraid I'm getting too close. Even when it's difficult to maintain that line. I can see the hurt settle across her entire being when I give her a moment of closeness just to retreat back into myself. I tell myself the space is necessary. But the truth that I'm avoiding is that it's getting harder every day to see her as just the assignment.

And that realization scares me more than anything waiting for us outside these cabin walls. Feelings are reckless and lead only down a path of distraction. It's a risk I can't take. Not when her safety is at stake. Not when so many variables are still questionable.

23

Savannah

I wake before the sun, unusually early. Something feels...off. It's subtle at first, a twist in my stomach, a prickle on the back of my neck. It's wrong in a way I can't name. My eyes open slowly, adjusting to the faintest gray light creeping through the curtains. The first sign of daylight breaking over the cap of the mountains.

The cabin is silent. I lie still, straining to listen for his footsteps in the hallway, the soft creak of floorboards, the click of the front door from his usual dawn perimeter sweep. Anything. But I hear nothing. A pit grows deeper in my stomach by the second. I push the blanket back and slip out of bed, careful not to make a sound as I cross the small room. The air is chilly against my bare legs beneath the hem of the navy tee I now claim as my own, goosebumps rising instantly. I hold my breath as I crack the bedroom door open.

The living room is empty. The couch, though rumpled

from his failed attempt at sleep, is vacant. I can smell the coffee from his mug that sits abandoned half-full at the end of the counter. The fire is down to a faint glow, barely alive. "Sebastian?" I whisper into the quiet, barely loud enough to hear. No answer. My pulse spikes, filling my ears as I move deeper into the room. Each step feels heavier than the last, dread anchoring to my ribs. I tell myself he must be outside. He's always up first. He's probably sweeping the perimeter like he always does.

But the nagging feeling that something isn't right follows behind me like a shadow.

I cross the room to the window and peek out through the curtain, looking left, looking right. The way he taught me. Nothing but the woods stare back. Silent and still, free of any movement. No familiar broad-shouldered figure pacing the tree line. No shadow where he usually stands, scanning for threats only he knows how to see. I swallow hard and try again, looking left, looking right.

He's out of view.
He's checking the back of the cabin.
He's fine.
He wouldn't leave you alone.

But the silence is deafening. My stomach twists into knots as I move to the front door, fingers trembling as I reach for the latch. My breath catches in my throat, my whole body hesitating. *You don't go outside without me,* his voice echoes in my head. My heart thumps relentlessly against my chest as I unravel the locks. I crack it open by an inch, the cold morning air rushing in against my cheeks and bare legs. "Sebastian?" Barely a breath. The sound dissolves into the trees. I open the door wider, pulse thudding painfully against my neck. "Sebastian?" This time it comes out sharper, laced with panic, echoing into the dim woods.

Still nothing.

My breaths shorten, coming fast and uneven. He wouldn't leave. Not after everything he's drilled into me. Not when I'm the one person he's promised to keep safe. Unless something happened. My grip tightens on the doorframe, knuckles white. The color drains from my face. "Sebastian!" I call, louder now, my voice cracking on the last syllable. "This isn't funny!"

The wind absorbs the sound. No answering footsteps, no irritated sigh, no deep voice telling me to get back inside. Just birds, somewhere in the distance, the wind howling through the trees, and cold, unforgivingly deep silence filling the space between it all.

Fear fills every space inside me, thick and suffocating. My throat closes in on itself as I take one shaky step onto the porch carefully to avoid the center board that I know moans under my weight. I search the shadows like he taught me, scanning edges and corners and movement, waiting for my eye to catch any sign of life. The hair lifts at the back of my neck just before I hear a rustle at the corner of the yard. I nearly jump out of my skin, hand flying to my chest. A rabbit hops across the yard, unbothered by my presence. "*Sebastian,*" I whisper again, and this time there's no strength behind it at all. Just a plea.

Please be here.
Please be okay.
Please don't be gone.

The quiet stretches too long. He's not here.

For the first time since the night I was taken, I feel truly, terrifyingly alone. My breath stutters. I slam the door shut and twist the locks—top, middle, bottom—hands shaking so violently I almost miss the latch. I pull the half-cracked curtains, every last one, until the cabin sinks into a smothering dim blue, both from the rising sun outside and the dying fire popping quietly in the fireplace. I move like he taught me, heel to toe, staying in the shadows, staying low. Avoid the windows, stay in the corners, stay out of sight. My ears ring, blood roaring through my veins so loudly it drowns out every thought.

In the kitchen, I fumble through drawers and grab the sharpest knife I can find. My grip is slippery with sweat and I almost drop it, my breath coming in gulps.

What do I do now? What would he want me to do? All he prepared me for was, "Savannah, *if anything happens to me, you fight your ass off."*

Fight what? Fight *who?*

I drop to the floor, sinking against the cabinets, and staying clear of the windows. I curl into myself, tucking my elbows tight to my sides as a sob rips out of me, raw and broken. I clap my hand over my mouth to muffle the sound, but the tears come anyway. They shake me so hard my ribs hurt. I don't know how long I sit there, knife trembling in my grip. I wait, and I wait, and I wait. For him to come back through the door. To wake me from this nightmare. To tell me he was just checking the perimeter, and it hasn't been as long as it feels.

But then...a creak. The porch. I flinch at the sound and my heart stops beating, head whipping toward the door. Another creak. My breath hitches as the doorknob turns.

Everything inside me goes electric. I launch myself across the kitchen floor, positioning behind the door just like he taught me. Body coiled, ready, and terrified all at once.

The door swings open.

I jump, literally leap, onto the intruder, more instinct than skill, the knife shaking wildly in my grip. I land across broad, solid shoulders, momentum carrying us both off balance. I nearly slide off from the force alone. My weapon is raised, but my aim is wild and chaotic. Before I can bring the knife down, I'm grabbed firmly by the arms and shaken loose.

I slam into the floor, breath knocked out of me as I double over. My head spins as I attempt to regain my breath. I blink up at the intruder. And the moment I see him standing over me, breathless and wide-eyed, everything inside me erupts. *Sebastian.* Alive. Breathing. Staring down at me in startled disbelief.

Rage detonates inside me in an instant.

24

Sebastian

The door creaks as I push it open, the freezing morning air following me into the cabin when I place the duffle of supplies beside me. I'm halfway through kicking off the snow from my boots when a blur of motion slams into me. A body, small and trembling. There's a choked sound. And—what the hell—is that a *knife*? Something clatters against my shoulder, momentum knocking me back a step.

Before I can process it, instinct takes over. I grab the arm coming at me, twist, and shake the attacker loose. The knife hits the floor first, skidding across the room, and the body follows with a thud I feel in my spine. I whip my head down, ready to subdue, and freeze. Savannah stares up at me, cheeks streaked with tears, hair wild, shirt hanging off one shoulder and ghosting over bare legs, breath coming in sharp, panicked bursts.

My chest collapses inward. *Shit.* "Savannah, what—?"

is all I manage before she scrambles to her feet, fury erupting like she's detonating from the inside out.

"You *asshole!*" The words hit harder than the tackle. She shoves me full force, panic fueling every muscle. I let the impact rock me back. She shoves again, smaller this time, shoulders shaking violently. I can't do anything but watch and listen as she unravels before me, my insides feeling like they're doing the same.

"Where did you go!" she screams, voice breaking in half. "Where the hell did you go?" Her voice is shrill but I can feel the ferocity behind it. I raise my hands instinctively, palms outward in a surrender, a plea, I don't even know which. "Savannah—"

"No!" She cuts me off, pounding a fist weakly against my chest. "Don't *Savannah* me! Don't—don't you *dare!*" Another shove. Another hit. Her tears are falling too fast for her to wipe away. I take it. Every push. Every punch. I deserve each one. Guilt riddles inside as she yells, continuing to smack and swat at my chest. My chest that feels like it's collapsing in on itself the more she continues, knowing that this reaction is all my fault.

"I woke up and you were *gone!*" she cries. "Do you have any idea— *any* idea what that felt like? After everything? After—after you—" My hands hover in the air, my brows coming together in concern, blinking rapidly and unsure how to fix what I've caused. I've broken her and I didn't even see it coming. "I went out for supplies. I didn't think you'd be awake..."

How could I have been so stupid? So careless? Savannah's emerald eyes are rimmed red, hair sticking to her cheeks as she berates me and I choke down every single word. I feel myself crumbling from the inside out. I'm supposed to make her feel safe, supposed to be protecting her. And I made the biggest mistake I could have. Leaving her alone. The protectiveness I feel for her is unwarranted because I'm the one that caused her to shatter

Her voice breaks and her legs buckle. She falters and I catch her on instinct.

My arms wrap around her before she hits the ground and she collapses into me like a storm hitting land. Shaking, choking on sobs, clutching my shirt with cold fingers. She presses her face into my chest, gasping like she's been holding her breath for a lifetime. "Savannah..." My heart is about to jump through my chest, hands clinging to her back, holding her flush. I lower my head, my voice as gentle in her ear as I can manage, begging to offer some sort of comfort, "I would never leave you."

I feel her head turn to look at me and her expression breaks me all over again. Full of devastation. Of broken trust, slipping like sand through my fingertips. "But you did!" Her voice is defeated. "Listen to me," I keep my voice steady, even when everything in me is yelling at me to stop. To pull away. That this is too much, too close. My brain knows I'm making a mistake. My body won't let me move.

"I would *never* leave you." I mean the words with everything in me, my gaze holding hers firmly. Her arms slide around my waist like they've always belonged there.

I hold her tight. Tighter than I've allowed myself to hold anything in years. Her body trembles against mine, and it destroys me. Absolutely destroys me. I look down and my stomach twists into a knot of shame. She's barefoot and clutch marks redden her wrist from where she must've been gripping the knife. She's still shaking with leftover adrenaline. Or fear. Or panic. Maybe all three, twisted into a messy, intricate knot.

All because of me. "Savannah," I whisper into her hair, voice raw, "I'm sorry. I'm so damn sorry."

She sobs harder, digging her fingers into the fabric of my shirt like I'm the only solid thing left in her world. "I thought someone took you," she gasps. "Or killed you. Or— you were just gone. Forever." Each word slices deeper. God. I never should've left without telling her. I never should've let her think, even for a moment, that she was alone.

I tighten my arms around her, one hand cradling the back of her head, the other locking around her waist, pulling her fully against me. "I will never do this to you again," I say, and my voice cracks on it. I don't care. She needs to hear it. "Do you understand?" She cries into my chest, shaking harder, and I lower my forehead to her hair, eyes squeezing shut.

"I'm sorry I scared you like that," I murmur, guilt choking me as I speak. "You shouldn't have been out here hiding, armed with—God, Savannah—I—" My throat closes in on itself before I can finish. I glance at the knife on the floor, my stomach turning with nausea at the aftermath of my actions. "You followed everything I taught you because you thought you were on your own," I whisper, mostly to myself.

She lifts her head enough to look at me, eyes swollen and breath shaky. But still, admittedly, breathtakingly gorgeous. "I'm not built for this," she whispers. "I don't know how to do this."

The raw honesty of that nearly folds me in half around her. "You did exactly what you were supposed to do," I tell her, gently brushing a tear from her cheek with my thumb and tucking her hair away from her face. It's the first time I've touched her like this. Soft, deliberate, not out of necessity. I let my fingers linger too long against the delicate skin of her neck, pulse still thumping rapidly against my touch.

"You stayed quiet. You armed yourself. You hid. You fought. Savannah...you *survived*. Again." She swallows hard, looking up at me with something between fear and pride. Slowly, unsteadily, she wraps her arms around my waist again. And this time, I feel her *choose* to hold on. I rest my chin on her head, one hand rubbing slow, grounding circles on her back. The same way she did for me the night she woke me from the nightmare.

For a long moment, we stay like that, and despite every nerve ending in my body yelling at me, I allow it. Breathing the same uneven breath. Standing in the dim cabin doorway as the early morning chill curls around us. Her shaking finally slows. Her breathing evens...not completely, but enough that I can feel the trembling settle into something softer, something exhausted. She's still folded against me, fingers knotted in the fabric of my shirt like she doesn't trust her own legs to keep her upright. Truth is, I'm not sure I trust mine either.

Not after what I just felt. Not after what I'm still feeling. I run a steadying hand down her back, slow and careful. "I'm right here," I whisper without thinking. And that's when it hits me. Hard. Earth-shatteringly deep. In the center of my chest and I allow myself to feel it, even if it's only for this moment.

I *care* about her. Not the way the assignment said I should. Not the distant, professional kind of care that keeps a person alive because they're a job, a responsibility, a target. This is different. Raw and vulnerable and different.

Because the moment I stepped back into this cabin and saw the terror on her face...saw the knife in her hand, the tears on her cheeks, the sheer panic she'd swallowed all on her own? Something inside me tore open. Protective instinct I can explain. Mission-driven focus I can justify. But this? This hollow, twisting ache when she cries? This fury at myself for leaving her alone? This overwhelming need to keep her pressed against me until I can breathe again? This is not part of the job.

I hold her a little tighter, just for a second, needing the contact more than I should. She fits against me in a way that feels wrong. And *right*. Like she belongs there. Like my body has been missing her this whole time, even when my mind wouldn't let me. Her fingers curl into my shirt again, hesitant but deliberate, like she's making sure that I'm really there. I shouldn't let her hold me like this. I shouldn't want her to. Shouldn't *need* her to. But I do.

God help me, I do.

She sniffles quietly, the sound soft against my chest and I tilt my head down, my chin brushing her hair, and let the truth hit me full force:

I don't just want to protect her.

I want her to be safe. Calm. I want to hear her laughing again. I want her to look at me the way she did that morning at breakfast with eyes warm and hopeful and trusting. I want her safe because she's *Savannah*. Not because she's my assignment.

And that realization petrifies me. Because caring this much? It's a weakness. A crack in the armor I've spent years reinforcing. And yet, as she finally eases her grip, her hands sliding down but lingering on my arms like she's reluctant to let go...I know I wouldn't trade this feeling for bulletproof armor if I tried. I inhale a shaky breath I hope she doesn't feel. She looks up at me with eyes still wet, rimmed red, somehow still full of trust I haven't earned.

And I think *God, I'm in trouble.* Because she's beautiful. Because caring about her isn't optional anymore. It's instinct, automatic. And it makes my stomach twist uncomfortably.

And now the only thing more terrifying than losing the mission...is losing her.

25

Savannah

My breathing finally begins to slow and the shaking gradually eases. We're still wrapped in each other's arms, which takes me a moment to realize as I sober. Another to realize he hasn't moved. This...this isn't his speed. It isn't right. Not this closeness or this vulnerability. Not the way he's holding me like I'm something fragile that's going to break any second. It dawns on me that I've crossed the very line that he's drawn deepest in the sand.

Guilt pricks at me, followed by shame, insecurity. My cheeks flame scarlet, eyes casting downward. I know he doesn't want this. It's just to calm me down, nothing more. My fingers loosen from his shirt, and I start to pull away. But then his arms tighten.

"Don't," he whispers. "Just..." he doesn't finish the thought. I feel his chin move against the top of my head. It's soft. Not a command, not clipped or sharp like usual. Gentle.

I go still. Slowly, I tilt my head back to look at him. His eyes meet mine, and the confusion hits me first, followed by something warmer, deeper. Something I've never been familiar with but can recognize immediately. I feel it in the way my heart stutters over itself and my stomach turns backflips. Sebastian doesn't look away or loosen his arms around me. And maybe...Maybe I can admit that I don't want the moment to end either.

He finally breathes out a long, steady exhale, and guides me backward, releasing me from his grip. His hand moves to the small of my back. The touch is barely there, but it sends a quiet tremor through me, my skin fire where he touches. I let him guide me down onto the couch and I melt into it, body shaken and emotionally spent. To my surprise, he stays beside me. Close enough that my knees brush the outside of his thigh when I tuck my legs up in front of me. It feels embarrassingly intimate, like we've bypassed several steps of normal human interaction and landed...here.

I feel the heat crawl up my throat and my eyes drop to my lap. My voice is small when it comes out, "Where the hell did you go, Sebastian?" I deserve answers. Answers that he might not have been willing to give before, but I'm not leaving him any room to avoid my anymore.

His hand reaches for mine and his fingers brush across my own that I didn't realize were still trembling before gently folding around them, warm and solid against my skin. Too steady for someone who just watched me unravel completely in his arms. But that's Sebastian. A steel fixture, even in a tornado.

When he speaks, his voice is soft, as if giving me something precious. "I went to a supply cache," he says, and I'm struck by the easy honesty. The fact that I didn't have to pry or beg this time or throw a fit of frustration.

"A couple miles into the woods. We were running low

on rations. If something happens here..." He pauses, thumb brushing across my knuckles. "I needed to be prepared." I lift my gaze, sweeping his features. He's watching our hands, like the truth is easier to confess if he's not looking directly into my eyes. But he looks different now. Or maybe I'm just seeing him differently. Not as the man who barged into that dark room to rescue me. Not as the stoic soldier shadowing every move I make. But as someone who's more human than I ever expected him to be. Real, exposed, and unfiltered for the first time.

"This isn't the first time I've been stuck here," he adds quietly. "But... it's the first time it's happened with someone else." My breath catches. He continues, his voice unfamiliarly soft for someone like him. I can feel his walls lowering as he speaks. Not breaking entirely but at least thinning where I can start to see over the edge.

"I didn't wake you," he admits, "because you were finally sleeping. Really sleeping and so calm. You looked peaceful. And I didn't want to take that from you unless I had to." Warmth blooms somewhere deep in my chest at his admission and my stomach flips at the way he caresses my hand so gingerly when he speaks.

He swallows, jaw flexing with the next truth, like he doesn't want to speak it out loud. "But it's still dangerous, Savannah. Even if it feels calm right now. If they find us—" His grip tightens slightly, fingers threading through my own. "I *need* you safe." He says it like a vow. Like a promise he intends to carve into stone. He inhales shakily, forcing himself to keep going.

"I'm going to figure out a plan," he says. "A real one. I just...haven't had one yet. Not beyond getting you here.

Everything's been reactive. Improvised. And I'm sorry about that. You deserve better." He looks up then, his gaze bare and exposing his soul as he meets my own. Unguarded. Not like the hard, calculated man who dragged me through the woods that first night.

Even with his confession, his lack of a plan and his uncertainty, I'm not afraid. Not panicking like I should be. Not now and not of what comes next. Because he's here, because he's holding my hand like it's anchoring him. Because for all his stern orders and sharp edges, I trust him more than I've trusted anyone before in my life. Since the first night, dragging behind him through the mountains, I've trusted him. Blindly, maybe. But I'm still alive. And I know with absolute certainty one thing: Sebastian will not let anyone hurt me. Ever.

I squeeze his hand gently, the smallest smile tugging at my lips. "It's okay," I whisper, offering him the same reassurance. "We'll figure it out. I trust you." He exhales, like those words lift something impossibly heavy off his shoulders. And even though neither of us says it aloud, we let the truth simmer between us. We're not surviving this alone anymore. We're surviving it *together*.

26

Sebastian

The remainder of the day follows the quiet routine we've established. Breakfast, training, my perimeter sweeps, dinner, quiet. Except...nothing feels routine anymore. It feels like the whole world has been broken open and everything is much heavier now. It charges through me every time I look at her and every time she looks back. And *Christ*—I never noticed how much she looks back at me. Not in a way that makes me feel uncomfortable or watched. But in a way that tightens my chest unbearably with the need to be close to her again.

At breakfast, she moves around the kitchen with this soft, effortless grace. I shouldn't be watching her this closely. I keep reminding myself of that, to no avail. The sleeves of my old sweatshirt are rolled to her elbows as she quietly washes off our plates, her hair tied messily on top of her head with wisps falling along her neck. When she catches me staring, she blushes and looks away. But I notice the grin that she hides behind her shoulder.

I notice the way she straightens her posture and the way the sweatshirt that's basically a dress on her skims the top of her bare thighs. My body notices that more than my mind and I have to shift my weight to tame the heat that coils at the bottom of my abdomen when my imagination betrays me.

A week ago, I wouldn't have noticed any of it. Or I would have forced myself not to, anyway. Today, it dives into my thoughts without interruption. "Thanks," she almost beams when I hand her a plate and my fingers brush against hers, rough where hers are silk. She pulls in a sharp breath and I remind myself that it's just routine, but the word feels so meaningless now.

In the afternoon, we continue her training. She continues to improve. Mostly because she refuses to quit. Maybe because I've stopped trying to keep distance between us. Her steps grow more confident and every victory earns her a rare, small smile from me. And each time I give her one, her cheeks warm and her eyes soften like she's hearing a compliment no one has ever given her before. "You're getting better," I tell her after she executes a perfect breakaway move that almost lands me on my ass. Her entire being seems to respond. Her shoulders lift, lips pressing together in a shy but pleased smile. She looks...proud of herself. And delicate. And small. I'm over half a foot taller than she is. I was aware of that before, but now I feel it each time I'm near her.

When I adjust her stance, my hands practically engulf her waist. My fingers curl carefully around her wrist and it feels breakable in my grip. Her pulse thumps against the touch of my thumb rapidly and I know she feels it, too. The electricity that seems to pass through us like a current.

Every touch feels like I'm handling something precious. Every breath draws me closer, leaves me wanting more. My eyes wander, watching the way her waist sits perfectly against my groin when her back is to me. The way my shirt collar is so loose around her neck that when she bends, my eyes follow the slender line of her neck, down to her chest. I watch the way the water lingers on her lips after she takes a break, and I refuse to acknowledge the way I want to wipe it away with my own. I shouldn't think like this. I'm failing miserably.

When I do my perimeter checks, I can feel her watching me through the window. I tell myself that she's just doing it to learn. She thinks I don't notice, but her gaze pierces my back so intense that it almost stings. I can feel her eyes on me with every step I take around the tree line. And instead of feeling exposed, annoyed, distracted...I feel steady. Confident. I don't know when that started either.

When I return, she pretends to be busy with the blanket on the couch or turning the page of a book I know she isn't actually reading. I catch the faint flush of her cheeks again and I feel a smile stretching across my own.

At dinner, she sits next to me instead of across from me. Her presence is warm and her knee bumps mine. "Sorry," she murmurs, but neither of us move away. Instead, I shift closer until my leg rests against the outside of hers. Her smiles are small, quiet and earned. I shouldn't let myself get this close. But she already is and some traitorous part of me has given up entirely on pushing her back.

When we finish our meal, we sit on the rug in front of the fireplace, legs stretched out and basking in the heat radiating from the flames. Her shoulder brushes my arm with every breath she takes. The fire pops softly, casting golden light across her face. Her muted green eyes catch the light like early morning fog rolling over the sea, soft yet impossible to look away from.

She looks almost serene. And beautiful in a way that steals the breath from my throat. Savannah draws her knees up in front of her, gaze lost in the flames. "I don't really miss home," she says suddenly. My head turns with curiosity. "No?"

She shakes her head, eyes locked on the fire instead of turning toward me. "It's strange. I thought I would. I thought I'd ache for it." She hesitates, chewing over her words, then continues, quieter. "But being stuck here, even with all the danger, I feel more free than I ever did there." My chest aches for her at the admission because I understand it all too well.

"Why?" I ask. "What exactly made home feel...not free?" It's foreign to me. The concept of home, all together, but even more so, it being a place that you don't miss. I guess it's easier for me. I never had a place to call home in the first place.

She exhales slowly, her brows stitching together as she ponders the question. "I don't know. Expectations. Pressure. My family was always deciding things for me. Where I should go, what I should want, who I should be." Her voice goes soft with honest vulnerability. "And now it's just...me." She glances up at me, a slight shrug of her shoulders. "And you."

I should look away but I don't. I hold her gaze, reading the emotions behind it. She swallows then starts again. "I know this isn't normal. I'm not crazy or naive, even though I'm young. I know that it's not permanent and I'm not fooling myself into thinking that it is...I know it's dangerous and unpredictable and probably stupid. But—" She shifts closer, her knee brushing my thigh again but this time she doesn't pull it away. "I feel like I can breathe here."

The fire crackles, filling the room with gentle pops and occasional sizzles. My hand twitches with the instinct to reach for hers. And maybe I shouldn't. But she's looking at me like I'm the first safe thing she's ever known and I'm failing spectacularly at keeping my walls up. I clear my throat. "I'm glad you feel that way."

Her eyes flicker with something warm. Something I'm starting to crave and something I don't think I'm able to walk away from anymore. "I want to show you something." The words leave my mouth before I fully consider them. Before I remind myself that showing her pieces of me, real pieces, is the last thing I should be doing. But she looks at me with those wide eyes that are as green as spring itself, and I'm tired of pretending that I don't feel like everything in me collapses when she does. I stand and offer my hand.

She doesn't hesitate before she takes it. I feel her small palm in mine and I guide her. On the way out, I reach for the blanket draped over the couch and settle it around her shoulders, letting my hands smooth down her arms longer than necessary. I grab my coat, shrugging it on and ushering her toward the back door. The night air is sobering but she steps into it without complaint.

I lead her past the porch, past the dwindling pile of firewood, and past the tree line she's never crossed on her own. From day one, she's treated the border to the yard like a warning. Like stepping beyond it means losing sight of everything familiar and stepping into the line of action. I'm glad for that. It's easier to keep her safe when she's always in my line of sight.

"Where are we going?" she asks, but it isn't wary or impatient. It's curious, almost excited. I feel myself loosen at the sound. "Wait for it," I flash her a lazy smile and I feel a childish giddiness building inside that I'm not even sure I felt when I *was* a child. She follows behind me without protesting, the worn blanket brushing against my knuckles now and then. Her footsteps crunch softly in the frost, close enough that I feel her warmth even in the winter air.

The trees thin and then open altogether. The hill drops off into the small dock that sits off the half-frozen pond, stretching like silver glass beneath the moonlight. The reflection makes it appear endless, shining like it's full of hope and possibilities. Her breath catches as she drinks it in and that alone makes bringing her here worth it.

When we reach the end of the dock, I lower myself to sit at the end, legs dangling above the ice that crests the edge of the pond. I glance up at her, silently inviting her to sit. She settles beside me, her knee brushing against mine, and I feel it again. That familiar tug in my stomach, the pull that urges me to stay near her. "This place," I pause, my eyes drifting out to the reflective ripple of moonlight, "is the only place I've ever felt safe." Her head turns toward me, I feel it, but I keep my eyes forward. It's easier to talk to the water than face the way she listens so intently.

"Away from the world," I continue. "No expectations. No guards. No people waiting for my next move." No one to disappoint. No mistakes to be made. No one to care about so deeply that it hurts. Nothing but...quiet. And now, her. She pulls the blanket tighter around her shoulders and sits in the silence with me. After a moment, she lets her head tip against my arm. Light, tentative, but there. A warmth spreads through me that has nothing to do with the coat I'm wearing.

"Why show me?" She asks softly after a moment. I swallow hard, glancing down at the way her head fits perfectly against my shoulder. *Because you're the only person I've ever wanted to share this with. Because you make this place, me, feel less empty. Because the idea of you not knowing this part of me feels wrong now.* "Because you deserve a place like this," I settle with a long breath, omitting the deeper truth. "Somewhere you don't have to be afraid."

She shifts closer, just slightly, and her voice is barely more than a whisper. "I feel safe with you." My heart staggers. I close my eyes for a moment, trying to breathe around the feeling rising in my throat. Because the truth—the one I can't admit to her—is that she makes me feel something I've never had. *Home.* The truth that I can't even admit to myself...is that I think she's every piece of me that's always been missing.

27

Savannah

Sebastian and I sit there in silence for a long time. Listening to the wind whisper to the mountains that cradle us on all sides, the faint rustle of nocturnal creatures moving through the underbrush. Listening to the stillness between our breaths, warm and alive as it fogs the cold air between us. And even though we're out in the open, exposed under the moonlight, surrounded by nothing but darkness and pine...I've never felt safer than I do right now. My heart blooms with every inhale, every shared heartbeat.

The air bites at my nose and the tips of my ears, but my cheeks burn with heat. The kind that has nothing to do with the weather. It's the closeness—his closeness. The way his coat feels rough against my cheek as I lean into him and he doesn't pull away. The way his body radiates warmth I pretend I'm not chasing. The way his calloused palm finds mine in the dark, fingers weaving between my own like it's instinct. Like he was always meant to reach for me.

He doesn't look at me when he does it. He just...does. As if it's the most natural thing in the world. And I don't let myself feel foolish for settling into his touch.

Moonlight washes over the pond, painting everything silver and blue and soft, the reflection shimmering across our hands. I could sit here forever, suspended in this moment where everything complicated is held at bay by the simple fact that Sebastian is beside me. The man who dragged me out of hell. The man who carries guilt like armor and tenderness like a secret. The man who, without knowing it, has become a place of safety in a world that stopped feeling safe a long time ago.

He's taught me so much while we've been stuck here. How to listen for danger, to move quietly through the shadows. How to stand my ground and breathe through fear. How to defend myself, physically and emotionally. But the most important thing, that I never expected to learn...that I'm valuable. Not as a pawn, or a negotiating piece. Just being Savannah. Not because of my father, or because of what I know, or what I can offer. Not even because of what others expect me to be. But because when he looks at me, when he really looks at me, it's like I'm worth choosing.

I turn my head up toward him, the moonlight catching the sharp lines of his profile. He's staring out across the water, brows furrowed like he's thinking too hard again. Like he's fighting himself the way he always does. I squeeze his hand gently and his thumb answers by dragging across mine. Even when he's far away, he's paying attention.

I don't know what is becoming between us. But sitting

here with the mountains guarding our backs, the pond glimmering before us, and his fingers interlaced with mine, I'm not afraid of it. Even when I know that it will shatter my world when it ends. And I'm sure, inevitably, it will. Sebastian will return me home and we'll go our separate ways. He'll go back to fighting demons he doesn't talk about and I'll go back to...whatever dread awaits me. The truth of it haunts me.

I tip my head just a little, "Thank you for bringing me here." My voice is nothing more than a whisper into the night. And I hope that he hears what I mean but can't bring myself to say—*thank you for making me feel like I matter*. I'm not sure if he understands or not what he means to me, yet, but his hand tightens around mine. And for right now, that's enough.

We stay on the dock until the cold starts to invade my lungs, stinging the tips of my fingers and creeping through the blanket around my shoulders. Sebastian seems to sense it before I do. Without a word, he gives my hand a small squeeze and rises, offering the other one to help me up. The walk back to the cabin is quiet but comfortable. Warm in spite of the frost in the air and blanketing the grass. Our footsteps crunch on the ground beneath us and our joined hands swing gently between us. Ever so often, my shoulder brushes his arm. He doesn't move away. Instead, drapes an arm around me and pulls me into his side.

The dim moonlight breaks through the branches overhead, casting shadows across his face, sharpening the line of his jaw, softening the rest. I can't stop staring at him and I know that he can feel it. He looks...peaceful. It's foreign, on him, but beautiful.

By the time we reach the cabin porch, my heart feels like it's too full for my chest. My body is filled with so much warmth that I swear we took the fireplace with us. He holds the door open for me and the air from inside slips over my skin like the blanket still draped from my shoulders. The door shuts behind us and suddenly, the cabin feels smaller. Quieter. Full of everything we didn't say out there on the dock.

Sebastian shrugs off his coat and hangs it on the designated hook by the door. I clutch the blanket tighter around myself as I watch him, nerves fluttering deep in my stomach. He turns toward me and it feels like my world stops. He looks…softer, in the golden light of the lamp. Like the night peeled back layers of distance he's kept between us.

My throat tightens at the realization that I don't want this moment to end. I don't want to wake up and pretend that tonight didn't happen. I don't want the space between us to grow again once the day resets. So before I can overthink it, before fear can tangle my tongue, I speak. "Sebastian?"

He turns toward me then, "Yeah?" I swallow, hesitating. Because the question about to leave my lips makes me feel small. Exposed. "Do you think…you could stay with me tonight?" His expression shifts. Not in shock, not really. His gaze remains safe, unguarded the way it has been all night. I feel the pressure of relief washing over me. His eyes search my face as if he's trying to make sure that I mean it.

"I just—" I fumble, heat rising to my face and I avert my gaze, landing on the grain of the wood floor. "I sleep better when you're close. And I…I don't want to wake up and not know where you are. Not again." He doesn't answer, not immediately. I pull the blanket closer around my shoulders but I feel him step closer, slowly. Every inch he closes feels like a question he's silently asking and every breath I take feels like an answer.

When he stops in front of me, the blanket still around my shoulders, he lifts a hand and tucks one of the fallen strands of hair behind my ear. His fingers linger against my neck. "Yeah," he mutters, nodding, voice deep, and something I've never heard from him before. "I'll stay."

My breath catches and my grin spreads embarrassingly wide as I lift my gaze to him again.

He lets his hand drop, but only to rest lightly on my arm, guiding me gently toward the bedroom that I suddenly can't walk to fast enough. The room is shrouded in darkness but with him beside me, it doesn't feel so empty. I crawl into the bed, maybe too eagerly, and Sebastian doesn't hesitate, or pause, or question. He simply takes the place beside me and I feel the mattress shift under his weight.

The bed is small, barely made for one person, but I don't mind my frame being pressed against his. And if he does...he doesn't show it. I nestle into his side, the blanket cocooning us both, and drape my arm across his chest. His body heat is immediate, comforting, a steady anchor that calms the frantic rhythm of my heartbeat. I breathe him in, sandalwood and something bold, a scent that I've grown familiar with—maybe dependent on.

My hand brushes over his chest, meaning only to settle there, but instead my fingertips find two small ovals beneath the fabric of his shirt. Warm from his skin, hanging from a thin chain that I never took notice of before. It takes only a second for the realization to hit. *Dog tags. Military.* Of course, I was right. Everything he's shown me, everything he's done, every instinct, every movement. It all finally makes perfect sense. All the pieces snap together in the dark, clear as daylight.

A hundred questions ignite in my mind, but I don't ask

any of them. Not tonight. Not when he's lying beside me like this, letting me hold onto him and pulling me closer. Instead, I flatten my palm against his chest, feeling the rise and fall of his breathing beneath my fingertips. Strong, steady, and present. His arm wraps around my waist, pulling me in until my forehead rests beneath his chin, my breath soft against his collarbone. His hand settles on my hip, not gripping, just...there. Holding. Protecting me.

I exhale, my breath trembling in a way I hope he doesn't notice. I let my eyes flutter shut, basking in his warmth. The truth is simple and terrifying...I don't care what the dog tags mean.

I don't care what secrets he's still keeping. I don't care that he's something dangerous, something disciplined, something honed by a world I've never touched. None of it matters. Not when he's here and when his heartbeat matches mine. And I don't let the truth take this moment away from me.

I shift even closer, letting the steady drum of his heartbeat drown out the last shadows of fear from earlier. Letting the truth settle into the quiet between us. Because the truth? The truth is much bigger than any secret he might hold. Because the truth is that this man, this protector, this soldier, this *stranger*...My stupid, stupid heart is falling in love with him. Even when I know that when this is all over, it will be my ruin.

I swallow the feelings and, in the darkness, I whisper so quietly I'm not sure he hears "Sebastian...thank you." For staying. For holding me. For letting me feel like I belong somewhere. Even if it's only here, in this cold cabin, with him.

His grip tightens on my hip, just a fraction. "I'm not going anywhere."

28

Sebastian

Savannah drifts to sleep faster than I expect. One moment she's curled into my side, breathing soft and uneven and the next her hand loosens on my chest, her body melting against mine like every muscle finally surrendered. My body doesn't budge. Not when she's warm and small and giving me all the trust I don't deserve. Not when her breath whispers gently across my collarbone, slow and steady. Not when her leg brushes across my thigh under the blanket, electrifying my every nerve ending. I lie there, staring at the ceiling, every sense in me alive.

Her hair smells like the cheap cedar shampoo from the cabin bathroom. Her fingers twitch occasionally, brushing the fabric of my shirt. Every place her body contacts mine shoots lightning through my veins. Her thigh shifts against me again and I have to inhale sharply, forcing my body to stay still. This is dangerous. *She* is dangerous. Not because she's a threat. She couldn't hurt me if she tried. But because she's everything I've pushed away for years. Untrained territory. Savannah is soft and trusting and all-consuming, like the first breath of air after you've been underwater for too long.

Her frame fits against mine too easily, too perfectly, her head tucked beneath my chin and her arm draped across my chest, rising and falling with the rhythm of my breath. Like our bodies have always been missing each other without knowing. And *God*—it feels so right.

My hand tightens where it rests on her hip and she answers, her body gravitating into my touch like she recognizes it even in her sleep. I squeeze my eyes shut and try not to focus on how her skin is satin beneath my calloused palm. I shouldn't want this. I shouldn't entertain it at all. She's the assignment. The daughter of a man who put a target on her back. The girl I was supposed to protect from a distance. Never touch, never know, never hold. Never *need*.

But reality crashes against me like a tidal wave sent to destroy entire cities as she's pressed against my ribs, trusting me completely in a way no one ever has. I can feel myself cracking. And what's worse...I can feel myself wanting to.

Her fingers curl sleepily and slowly into the fabric of my shirt, right over my heart. Like she's anchoring herself. Like she knows, somehow, that I'd move the earth to keep her safe. And now? To keep her happy.

I exhale deeply through my nose, quiet and rough. I can feel myself falling into whatever this is, my body accepting that she means more to me than I'm willing to admit despite my instincts fighting back against that. And I know, if I care too much, I'll make mistakes. Mistakes that get people killed.

But then she nestles closer and my whole argument collapses. Because in this bed that's too small, in this tiny room, in the dark warmth of her sleeping weight against my side? None of it matters. Not the mission, or the assignment, the rules, the protocol. There's just *Savannah*. And then I'm losing the battle I've been fighting since the night I pulled her out of that hell.

My thumb brushes her hip in a slow, unconscious arc. She doesn't stir; just breathes deeper and relaxes like she's finally at peace. And for the first time in years...maybe I am, too. Here, with her.

I stay awake for most of the night, listening to her breathing, memorizing the feeling of her against me, and wishing I could freeze this moment and keep it safe from the world that's already stolen too much from us. I lay there, dreading morning light and what I know will come with it. The truth settles in slowly, quietly, and undeniably. I will never be able to walk away from her. Not now, not after this.

And I'm not sure that I want to.

When the morning light drifts through the dusty window, I'm hit with the weight on my chest that already feels too familiar. Savannah is still draped across me, calm in a way I've never seen from her outside of sleep. Her breath keeps brushing the hollow of my throat and every time it happens, I feel a shiver run down my spine in spite of the body heat radiating between us.

She shifted closer in the night somehow, until her leg sandwiched between mine and one of her hands ended up tangled in my hair, like she's afraid I'd disappear in the night. And I must have shifted, too, my arm wrapped securely around her waist because she's practically on top of me now. My hand remains on her hip, where it was from the moment she fell asleep, my thumb resting against the curve of her bone. I should move it before she wakes, allow us some distance. I tell myself that twice. My body doesn't move.

The sunlight filters through the thin curtains and brushes against her face, turning the tips of her lashes bright, making her hair glow where it spills across my chest. Her lips slightly pout and her cheeks have a hint of a flush. My heart explodes inside my chest at the sight.

I let my fingers drift, just barely, over the blanket where it covers her waist. Memorizing the shape of her, the curve of her hip, the weight of her thigh on top of mine. My body notices that too and I pray she doesn't shift upward any more than she already has. My self-control is already hanging on by a delicate thread.

She mumbles something unintelligible in her sleep that almost sounds like my name and pulls even closer, pressing herself fully into my side. My heart reacts before my mind does, each thump louder than the last. *I'm in so much trouble.* Savannah's body against mine feels like when you find a missing puzzle piece after you've almost entirely given up on finishing it. The thought hits me hard, violently. Forbidden and unacceptable.

I exhale slowly, trying to force logic through the fog of want swirling in my chest. Everything in me is telling me to bolt, that this is the assignment, and I'm breaking protocol with every lingering second. But last night, when she asked me to stay with her trembling voice and her eyes begging for something she couldn't put into words? I didn't even consider saying no. I should have. I hesitated. But the part of me that's still human, still capable of feeling *something*, answered for me.

She stirs again, head tilting under my chin. Her lips brush my collarbone with the movement, unintentional but enough to make my pulse jump. I clamp my jaw tight. I need to get myself under control before she wakes. Before she looks at me the way she did last night—wanting something from me that I'm not sure I'm capable of giving her, no matter how badly I want to. And when she makes a soft little sound in her throat, like she's clinging to whatever dream she's in, my fingers clutch her hip without permission, protective and drawing me in when I have no right. When my mind tells me I shouldn't feel that way.

But I do. More than I want to admit. More than I can manage. More than is remotely safe or fair for either of us. The sunlight creeps higher, warming the quilt, warming her hair. She shifts again, her cheek brushing my chest. I crave to tilt her chin higher, press my lips to hers, and stay in this bed with her all day.

I know she's going to wake up soon. And I have no idea how to pretend this night didn't change something inside me. No idea how to lie when every part of me is screaming to keep her close. Or how to keep my walls standing when she's already infiltrated my every thought. But I force a slow inhale, a steady exhale, unintentionally matching my breathing to hers.

My mind wanders as I watch the rise and fall of her chest. My lips remember the tingling sensation that was tattooed into them the moment she kissed me during training. My heart thuds recklessly against my ribs as my body recalls the weight of her straddling me, how easily I could've let it turn into something more, could've taken her right there in the grass, given in to a pleasure I haven't allowed myself in years. The woodsy smell of her hair invades my senses and when my mind takes me where it really wants to, it's with the thought of her body intertwined with mine in intimate, irrevocable ways. Ways we could never come back from.

29

Savannah

Daylight warms the back of my eyelids before I have the courage to open them. Because I can feel his frame still secured beneath my weight. At some point in the night, I realize I must've moved, shifted or stretched, reaching for him in my sleep. And somehow, I ended up half on top of him, my cheek against his chest, my arm draped across his torso, my leg curled tightly between his. And the most shocking part? He's still there. He hasn't moved or tensed or created space like he usually does. And I'm acutely aware that he doesn't feel as rigid as he always seems. For once, it feels like he's as relaxed as I am. I don't dare move. I beg the minutes to stretch, to relish in the moment, for the morning to linger.

I keep myself still, barely breathing, afraid that if I shift even an inch the moment will crack open and vanish. I know that this can't last. Even when admitting it to myself plummets my heart into my stomach. So I breathe him in instead and try to quiet the flutter rising in my stomach. I let myself feel it, to burn this moment into my mind, every detail.

My palm is splayed across his abdomen, over the soft cotton of his shirt, and I can trace each line of the muscle beneath my fingers. His breathing lifts and falls beneath my hand, steady and controlled even in sleep. Or...not sleep. Because now that I'm paying attention, I can feel the subtle tension hiding under the stillness. Not fear or discomfort, I don't think. Aware, in the way that he always is. His hand is still resting on my hip, warm and solid, his thumb curved slightly inward like he tightened his hold in the night. And the heat of his grip makes something inside me melt.

With a deep breath, I brave enough to crack my eyes open.

The room glows in morning light flooding the floorboards, catching dust motes drifting lazily in the air. Everything feels softer in this light. Safer. Like the world outside the cabin doesn't exist and can't touch us here.

I tilt my head up just enough to see him. Sebastian's eyes are already open. Not wide or startled, just watching me quietly, like he's been awake for a long time and chose to stay that way. His gaze softens when our eyes meet, warmth flickering behind the usual guarded steel.

He doesn't pull away when he meets my eyes. Doesn't clear his throat or pretend nothing is happening. He just looks at me. And suddenly, under his gaze, my heart is beating far too loud in the stillness. "Good morning, Sebastian," I whisper, because it's the only thing my brain can manage. I feel the involuntary lift of my lips and pray it doesn't spread across my whole face, leaving me looking as dumbfounded as I feel.

His chest lifts beneath me with a slow inhale. "Morning." His voice is low and rough, sleep-deepened in a way that sends heat crawling up my neck. I allow my fingers to inch upward, but hesitate before they grace his cheek, itching to feel him beneath my palms. Instead, I let them curl back into the fabric of his shirt.

"Sorry for, um, using you as a pillow," I hide my grin by capturing my lip with my teeth. His lips twitch—barely, but I see it. A ghost of a smile.

"You slept," he says quietly. "That's all that matters." Something warm and helpless blooms in my chest, and I have to look down again, suddenly aware of just how intimately we're tangled together. His hand tightens on my hip, and I melt into his touch. A wordless reassurance. A wordless *stay.* And I do. Because here, in the delicate hours of the morning, pressed against him like I belong there...I don't want to be anywhere else.

I turn myself enough to lift my head from his chest and look at him fully. His eyes trace my face like he's memorizing something he's forbidden to keep. "Did you sleep at all?" I whisper. His jaw tightens and he offers a subtle shake of his head. "Not really." I open my mouth to apologize again, but he beats me to it. "But I didn't mind." The words hit low in my stomach, warm and startling. His voice is too soft for the hour, too honest for the man who's spent days dodging every truth about himself.

"You could have moved me," I admit, reluctantly. His eyes flick down to where my hand rests over his ribs, then back up to mine. "I didn't want to." My breath stutters; honesty, again. It would be so easy to pretend I didn't hear that. To laugh it off or bury it under nerves. But something in me refuses to hide anymore. Especially not from him.

"Sebastian..." I whisper, and his name feels different on my tongue this morning. Softer, more personal. Like it belongs there. His hand slides a little firmer around my waist, guiding me closer until my chest presses fully into his, lighting every inch of my skin on fire and swirling every feeling in my stomach. The blanket shifts with us, but the warmth between our bodies is enough on its own. He swallows, throat working as he searches my face. "You should be careful saying my name like that."

"Why?" My voice comes out breathier than intended. The subtle tilt of my head brushes my cheek against his chin. His gaze drops to my lips. *Oh.* My heart thuds so loudly he must feel it against his chest. Heat creeps up my chest, my neck, my cheeks, under his gaze.

"Because..." He pauses, exhaling, fighting demons I can practically feel radiating off him. "Because I won't have the strength to pretend anymore."

Something in me snaps in all the best ways, like he's just granted me permission that I didn't have the courage to ask for. I lift a hand and brush my fingers along his jaw, tentative at first, his untrimmed stubble rough beneath my touch. He closes his eyes, just for a second, breathing in sharply like the touch steals something from him. When he opens them, the look in them is heated. Unmistakable. Undeniable. Everything that's been simmering, building, tightening between us since the night he rescued me...it's all right there.

"*Sebastian?*" I whisper again, testing the warning, too curious of what comes next. His breath shudders and I feel his core tighten beneath my leg. That's all it takes. He lifts his hand from my hip, sliding it up my spine, cupping the back of my neck with a gentleness that contradicts the strength in his grip.

"Savannah..." His voice breaks, quiet and raw. "I can't."
I don't speak. I can't. Instead, I lean in. My nose brushes his
softly, his breath landing on my lips. A moment suspended so
carefully it feels like the entire world might exhale with us.
"I'm asking you to." A whisper of a challenge, my lips inching
closer to his.

His restraint snaps as he closes the distance. His lips
are soft against mine at first—hesitant, docile, almost
disbelieving. They move like he's terrified and desperate all at
once. I tighten my hand in his shirt, pulling myself closer. I
can feel his armor slipping. It's slow, hungry, and consuming.
His thumb strokes the back of my neck, guiding me,
grounding me, and everything inside me sways. It's
intoxicating, fierce and gentle all at once.

When we finally break apart, our foreheads rest
together, breaths mingling in the warm space between us.
He's the first to speak, voice cracked open and vulnerable in a
way I've never heard. "I shouldn't have..." he murmurs.

"I wanted you to," I whisper. His lips are still inches
from mine. His chest is rising too fast beneath my palm and I
can feel the way his heart ticks strongly like it's going to
come through his chest altogether. And in spite of his words,
I can see the truth in his eyes—he wanted it, too.

Sebastian's breath is still unsteady against my lips.
Mine is worse. He's staring at me like he's terrified and
craving and unraveling all at once. Something inside me pulls
tight, hot and aching. I don't know who leans in first, maybe
we both do. But the moment our mouths connect again,
everything shifts. His lips don't move softly against mine like
before. It's anguished, immediate, wanton, and filled with the
sense that we've both been waiting too long.

His hand moves from my neck to my waist, gripping, pulling me closer until there's no space left between us. The blanket falls away from my shoulders. The air hits my skin, cool and sharp, but his hands are warm and everywhere I want them to be. A small sound escapes me, involuntary and embarrassingly needy.

It ruins him. His other arm wraps around my back, lifting me with effortless strength until I'm straddling his lap. My knees sink into the mattress on either side of him, and his hands slide down, anchoring my hips in place. The shift in position sends a shock right through me, heat coiling low in my stomach. I can feel him through the thin fabric of the worn sweats still trapping my lower half. He's as needy as I am, his body responding to my weight on top of him, the bulge I feel between my legs undeniable. Another soft whimper sounds against his lips.

I can't think. I can't breathe. My mind is inebriated, swimming through thoughts of his taste and my own selfish desire. The moment I even consider pulling back, his tongue drags along my bottom lip, slow and devastating, and my resolve shatters. I press closer and I can feel the way his body reacts. The tension in his thighs, the way he inhales sharply against my mouth, the low sound in his throat he doesn't manage to swallow. "Savannah..." he breathes, but it's not a warning. It's a confession. A breaking point.

His hands slide up my back beneath the fabric of my shirt, flaring wide between my shoulder blades as if he's fighting to hold himself together. My skin is a trail of sparks and embers behind the path of his touch. I thread my fingers into his hair, guiding his mouth back to mine, kissing him with every ounce of pent-up fear and longing and want I've been holding in for weeks. Nothing else matters. Not the stuffy cabin that we're trapped in, the danger that's so far out of mind it's forgotten, or the fact that all of this is temporary. Nothing matters but the taste of his tongue weaving dangerously with my own.

Sebastian kisses me back like he's been starving. There's nothing careful about it now. No restraint. No hesitation. Just heat and need tangled twisting together in an intricate dance. I roll my hips without meaning to, a small, instinctive movement and the groan he releases against my mouth nearly undoes me. He answers with an involuntary rise of his hips, pressuring exactly where I need to feel him between my thighs.

He drops his forehead to my shoulder like he's trying to breathe, his grip tightening on my waist as if anchoring me there will save him from crossing some invisible line again. "*Jesus...*" he exhales, voice rough, strained. "I—Savannah, I don't—" he stutters.

I don't let him finish. I take his face in my hands and bring his lips back to mine. This kiss is softer, but no less desperate, a quiet answer to his fear. Permission he didn't have to ask for. His hands slide to my waist, fingers flexing against my skin, and for a moment we're both suspended. Trapped between what we want and what we're terrified to admit.

I pull back only enough to see his eyes, breath shaking. "You don't have to stop," I whisper. His jaw tightens, holding the truth behind it. His chest rises unevenly beneath mine. And the look in his eyes...hungry, torn and overwhelmed, sends me spiraling.

"You don't know what you're doing to me..." he rumbles, voice low and breaking apart. But I do. Because I feel it too. "Please.." I murmur against his lips and when my hips roll again, it's purposeful. Begging. I lower my torso until my breasts pressing against his chest, aching for his touch, causing my hips to settle further into his grip. "I need this."

30

Sebastian

I've dreamed about moments like this without ever letting myself admit it. Savannah in my lap, warm and breathless, her fingers tangled in my hair, her mouth on mine like she's trying to pull the air from my lungs. Her body pressed against me in a way that threatens every ounce of self-control I've spent years building. But nothing—*nothing*— prepared me for the reality of it. Her soft gasp against my lips. The way she moves without thinking, seeking me. The trust in her hands, her body, her breath. The absolute certainty that she wants me.

And *God...* I want her. More than I've wanted anything in years. When she whispers, "I *need this,*" every thread I've been holding together with frayed wire and denial since the night I found her comes undone. "Savannah..." I sigh against her mouth, but the warning in my voice collapses before it's even formed. Because she's looking at me like I'm something safe. Something wanted. Something chosen.

No one has ever looked at me like that.

I feel her full breasts lower against my chest and her hips settle into my hands, pulling me closer, and I lose the fight I've been waging with myself since the moment I carried her out of that cabin. The groan I release against her lips is guttural, harsh, as I press my hips up into her where she's placed on my lap, my cock straining the thin fabric that separates us.

I tighten my grip on her waist and flip my weight, guiding her onto her back, bracing myself above her. For a heartbeat, I force myself to look at her, really look, to be sure. Her eyes are wide, shining with something tender and fierce all at once. Her breath catches in her throat. Her fingers trace my jaw, feather-light, and I know she feels my restraint crumbling.

"I want this," she whispers, sensing my need for reassurance. My chest tightens, and I swear the world tilts. That's all it takes. All the walls I've built, all the discipline, every line I swore I wouldn't cross...they fall away like they were never there.

I kiss her again, deeper this time, and she opens for me with a soft sound that nearly unravels me. My hands move with slow certainty, mapping the line of her waist, the curve of her hip, learning her by touch alone. My hands are rough on her smooth skin, ghosting up her ribcage beneath her shirt, landing just beneath the curve of her breast.

She arches into me, trusting, searching, wanting. I'm painfully careful, because she deserves gentleness, not the storm clawing at my ribs. But she's pulling me closer, urging me on with every breath, every touch. Her heartbeat races beneath my palm as she whispers my name like it's something sacred.

I murmur something, maybe a warning, maybe a

prayer that I didn't know I believed in until now, but she silences it with her lips against mine, her fingers tugging the back of my shirt. I comply with her silent request and rise only enough to shrug it off over my head. Impatience gets the best of my senses and hers follows quickly after, dropping them both to the floor.

My lips trail down her neck, painstakingly slow, nipping and sucking, leaving my mark. The tags that dangle from around my neck follow, coiling against her skin. She answers with a quiet moan and her leg lifts to wrap around the back of my thigh, pulling me into her. My mouth finds the sensitive peak of her breast, closing around it as my opposite hand gives attention to her other, worshiping every inch of her. "Sebastian—" she breathes, arching into me again. My name sounds divine leaving her lips.

Her fingers tighten in my hair and my teeth clamp gently onto her nipple in response, causing her to cry out again. I swear it's the sweetest sound I've ever heard. I'll replay it in my dreams. "Tell me what you need," I brush my nose against her sternum, my hand trailing teasingly slow down the middle of her abdomen, fingertips pausing just above her waistband as my hungry eyes meet hers.

"Please—" Her voice is laced with intoxicating saccharine as she begs. I tick my tongue against the roof of my mouth, shaking my head. "Use your words." My lips ghost up the side of her neck, pressing a kiss to the soft skin beneath her ear. "Please touch me," she squirms beneath my touch.

Her permission finalizes the deconstruction of my invisible armor. This girl is mine and I belong to her just as deeply. We're far past the point of no return and I have no interest in pretending none of this is happening.

"*Good girl*," I praise quietly into her ear. My self-control loses the battle entirely as I lock my fingers into her waistband, freeing her of any clothing that still shields her from me.

My fingers find her core and she's already slick with need for me. "*Fuck—*" I groan, my lips crashing against hers again. I spread her heat with my hand, finding her clit and working it with expertise circles. I can feel her hips writhing beneath me as she moans breathlessly into my ear. Her body jerks as my lips find her neck again and I push two fingers inside her. "You're so tight for me," my cock aches against my sweats and I press my waist against her thigh, my own body begging for friction. I don't stop until she completely comes apart from my touch.

I watch as her body arches from the mattress, her thighs tighten around my arm but her hands find mine, cementing it in place where I continue to stroke her heat until she rides the wave of her orgasm entirely. She's breathless as she peers up at me through dark lashes, lips swollen from our kissing, cheeks flushed with aftermath.

The mattress shifts when I lift myself to tug off my sweats, my cock springing free, and the cold air of the room is welcoming and sobering. "Tell me what you want," I breathe, positioning myself between her knees. Her chest still heaves, eyes wild as they meet mine and she reaches forward, grasping my waist and pulling me toward her. "I want *you*," she whines and I fall apart at the sound of those sweet words.

I lower my head and watch the way her pussy spreads around me as I push into her, slowly at first, my lower stomach yearning with need that's finally being released. I groan at the feeling of her slick warmth around me. My hands hook around the back of her knees, hinging her legs as I bury myself in her, completely.

I keep my movements slow at first, careful not to hurt her and because I know that if I move any faster, all of this will end too soon. I won't be able to hold out. But the more she cries out in pleasure, the more my thrusts pick up in reply, burying myself as deep as her body will allow.

I can feel her edging closer, her muscles tightening around me and I know I'm on the verge myself. "That's right," my hands travel to the outside of her thighs and my grip is so tight I know it will leave bruises. My mark to admire for days to come when we finish, just like the one my teeth left on her neck. "That's my good fucking girl," I growl. Vicious, white heat dims my peripheral as I feel her convulse around me, all the tension of the last weeks melting around us.

She cries out my name and her eyes meet mine, her delicate hands wrapping around my wrists. My thrusts become messier, needier, feeling my own climax building. I start to retreat and she tightens her grip. "Sebastian—" she moans my name breathlessly, "I want to feel it." If I was in trouble before, I'm fucked now. Because with her looking up at me with glassy eyes, skin glistening from light beads of sweat across her forehead, and begging for me the way she is…I don't stand a chance.

I feel myself spill inside of her and I groan in pleasure, my breath trembling as I lose control, lowering my forehead to hers. I wrap an arm around her waist and hold her tighter than I ever have before, throbbing deep inside her. And I know with utmost certainty this is where I'm meant to be. And I will never have the control to walk away from this. From her.

31

Savannah

I'm plastered to the bed, comfortable under Sebastian's weight, my insides performing gymnastics. My earth shattered and my mind whirling. The world feels...different, now. Like something inside of me that had been wound tight for years finally loosened its grip and let me breathe. He moves before I can even gather my thoughts, lifting me effortlessly from the bed as if I weigh nothing. His movements are slow and reverent in a way that makes my chest ache.

Cradled in his arms, I let my head fall against his chest, looping my arms around his neck. He doesn't speak. He doesn't need to. The way he holds me tells me everything. I've never felt so delicate. So cared for or so seen. So...chosen.

Sebastian carries me to the bathroom and turns on the shower, steam surrounding us in slow clouds. When he sets me down, he's even more careful, as if he's afraid to disturb whatever fragile, holy things just happened between us. I can feel his remnants drip down the inside of my thigh and it makes me feel almost...giddy. Special. He kisses my forehead, tender and lingering, and steps out to give me privacy. I hesitate, not wanting to wash away our shared moment, but the water is hot and refreshing on my newly bruised skin. I admire the oval shapes on my thighs. Tender, but not painful. Full of more meaning than words.

The memory of his hands floods me. His voice breaking when he said my name. The way he looked at me like I was something precious. His dog tags dangling over me that I didn't ask about. By the time I wrap myself in a towel and return to the hallway, my legs feel steadier, but my heart...my heart feels unrecognizable.

I step into the living area and pause, leaning against the doorway. He's at the stove. Cooking. For me. For us. I watch him from across the room before he takes notice. He moves with ease rather than urgency. He remains shirtless, but the muscles in his back aren't wound as tight as they have been since we arrived here. His sweats hover at his toned waist and small, red streaks run down his back, left from my nails. The sight alone is enough to pool heat in my stomach all over again.

And when he turns to me, something in his expression softens in a way I've never seen. Not even last night. The walls he always keeps so tightly constructed...they aren't just lowered. They're gone.

"Feel better?," he asks quietly, as if the words themselves are too loud for whatever ethereal magic lingers between us. Even his voice sounds different now. It's unshielded, his real voice for the first time, maybe. "I don't think I could get any better," I whisper back, shy in a way I haven't felt since I was a teenager with a crush. I move forward and wrap my arms around his waist from behind as he plates our breakfast. Eggs, oatmeal, and toast, the same staples as always, but now it feels...more intimate. Like he's making sure I'm taken care of because he wants to. Because he chooses to.

We eat together in serene silence, different from my first meal here. Our knees brush under the table, and every time our eyes meet, he gives me a small, soft smile that makes my pulse trip over itself. Everything has changed. And it keeps changing.

Our routine settles into something new. Something undeniably *us*. We share a bed now without me having to ask. It happens naturally, as if there was never any other way. At night, I curl into his chest and sink into the deepest sleep I think I've had my entire life, knowing that I'm untouchable here. He wraps his arm around my waist like it's instinct. Sometimes he presses soft kisses to my shoulder when he thinks I've drifted to sleep. Sometimes he pulls me closer in the middle of the night, half-asleep and unaware.

But always, we wake up as close as we started, a tangle of legs, arms, and the blanket shielding us from the outside world. We don't talk about titles or what this makes us—we don't need to. We simply flow through our routine with an ease now that doesn't seem so heavy or suffocating.

During the day, we continue my training, and I think I'm actually getting better. Except now, when he adjusts my stance, his hands linger on my hips. When he praises me, his voice goes soft and low, and I feel it everywhere. When I stumble, he catches me with reflexes that are so instant it makes my heart somersault. And sometimes, when we least expect it, we end up pressed against a wall or tangled on the couch, kissing like we can't remember we need oxygen. His hands in my hair, my fingers gripping his shirt, breaths mingling between rushed, desperate kisses that never fail to leave me dizzy before they turn into something more. We've christened almost every room of the house. *Almost.* Sebastian swears the kitchen is sacred. But he can't keep his hands off me. And I don't want him to. Because now it feels like we're a couple. We move through our days together, living in our own small world where danger doesn't exist and time doesn't matter.

I barely think about the outside anymore. Or rather, I choose not to. The idea of this ending, of leaving this cabin and this man, makes something cold wash over me that I push to the back of my mind every time. I've noticed that when he thinks I'm not looking, he watches me with a look so full of emotion it steals my breath. It's tender. Protective. Something dangerously close to love, if either of us would ever name it. And sometimes...I catch myself looking at him the same way.

There are still questions I don't ask. About his past, the scars on his shoulders that illuminate a silver reflection in the moonlight after we're left breathless and naked, tangled together. The dog tags that dangle from his neck when he hovers above me. The shadows behind his eyes that tell secrets his mouth will never admit. I avoid them, because I don't want to risk this fragile, beautiful thing we've built.

I don't want to say something that pushes him back behind those walls he's worked so hard to keep between us. So I let the questions sit in the back of my mind, quiet and unspoken, trailing circles around my thoughts at night until they finally lull me to sleep.

For the first time in my life, I'm choosing happiness over answers. Because even though I crave to know this man more deeply, to see all of his skeletons and still choose him...I know he's already showing me the parts that matter. The parts he's never bared to anyone else. And I know he's giving me his deepest secret already.

His heart.

After Sebastian finishes the last perimeter check of the evening, we settle onto a blanket spread in front of the fireplace, my back against the couch and his head resting in my lap. My fingers trace absent paths through his hair as I thumb through the pages of *Jane Eyre*, one of the few books tucked into the cabin's tiny collection. Everything feels easier now. Sebastian still retreats into his thoughts sometimes. Except now, when he does, I know that he'll come back to me.

"Do you ever think about it?" I ask, setting the book on the cushion behind me. My gaze drifts to the way the glow of the fire reflects off of his mahogany-colored hair. "What it would be like, I mean. Away from here." Sebastian doesn't answer right away. He shifts, turning onto his back where he's facing me now. His eyes seem to search mine for what feels like an eternity before he speaks. "All the time," but there's pain in his words, like the thought itself is overwhelming and impossible.

I know that it's complicated. That there's no guarantees past this place, that neither of us wants to admit how temporary this all is. Still, my heart cracks at the trepidation behind his eyes, even when I feel it too. "What does it look like to you?" I tilt my head at him curiously, my fingers still combing through his hair. His gaze drifts from mine but his lips curl into a slow, soft smile.

"I think it would be..." he pauses, chest rising as he inhales a deep breath, eyes still fixed on the ceiling. "Complicated. And messy. You'd see parts of me that you shouldn't have to carry. And it would be hard not to worry about you every time I leave a room. But," he exhales then, his endless blue eyes finding mine again. "I would spend every day making sure you knew you were worth the trouble." I swallow at that, my lips parting a fraction when my heart stumbles over itself.

"I think it would be beautiful," I admit. "And free. And I'd want you to know that I choose you, even with all the weight you carry." My lips mimic his, turning upward at the edges. "I could help you carry it, you know," my thumb brushes over the stubble along his jaw, slipping beneath his lower lip. "I can handle that."

Sebastian lifts his hand, resting it over mine, and presses a kiss to my palm, "I know you can. But you don't have to." He sits up then, wrapping his arms around my waist and pulling me into his lap. My knees straddle his hips, arms snaking around his neck.

"Don't get me wrong," I hum, leaning down to ghost my lips over his neck. "I could stay here forever. Although..." I sit back up, glancing down at the way his shirt hangs off my shoulders before I lift my gaze back to him. "I do miss having my own clothes sometimes."

He arches a brow, head tilting to the side in faux confusion. "Who said you need those?" He asks, hands running up my sides and lifting my shirt with them. I shiver under his touch, my arms rising as he pulls my shirt over my head, discarding it to the floor beside us. The fire is warm against my bare back, my hands trailing down Sebastian's chest.

"Guess I don't as long as you'll keep me warm," I hum as his hands palm my breasts, feeling his lips ghost against my collarbone when he dips his chin.

His lips trail down my sternum and I arch my back into his touch when he rolls my nipple between his thumb and index finger. "I think I can do that," he murmurs against my skin. I press my hips into his, reaching to tug at his shirt from the hem. He meets my silent request by shedding it over his head, the fabric dropping to the floor beside mine.

My eyes wander over his body, each muscle appearing as if they were carved straight from stone and molded to fit perfectly against my body. Tilting his head up, he presses two fingers to my lips. "Open."

My breath stammers at the request but I obey, parting my lips and taking his fingers into my mouth, my tongue swirling around them, eyes locked on his. The way his lips pull into a smirk that plays on arrogance makes my thighs clench around his waist.

"Good girl," he praises when he pulls his fingers from my mouth and replaces their absence with his lips, his teeth grazing across my lower lip and tugging it into his mouth. My moan is hushed against the kiss when I feel his palm press between my legs, two fingers slipping beneath my panties and sliding up my heat. I roll my hips into his touch and feel them push inside me, my fingers curling against his shoulders.

His thumb presses against my clit, fingers pulsing

slowly, too slowly, as my tongue swipes across his lower lip. "More," I breathe against his mouth.

I whine when he pulls his hand away, pulling back slightly to look down at him, my brows knit together. "What—"

"Shhh," he hushes me by pressing a finger to my lips momentarily, pulling it away only to shove at his pants, his cock smacking against my thigh once it's free. His hand finds my waist, lowering my weight as his other pushes my panties to the side and out of the way.

I sink down onto him, lips parting as he stretches me open, a shaky breath leaving me. "*Sebastian*," I groan, lowering myself until my hips meet his. I dip my head forward, forehead falling to his shoulder, my core burning sweetly around him. I devour the feeling as I rise on my knees and bring myself down again, slow enough to feel every inch of him sink deeper. His hands grab my ass, guiding my movements, teeth nipping at my earlobe as he groans against it. "Holy shit," he breathes.

His pleasure is enough to push my movements faster, rocking my hips against him again, coming down with more force each time. My hips slam onto his and the room fills with sounds of skin smacking skin, tangling deliciously with heavy breaths and soft moans.

I wrap my fingers around the chain that hangs from his neck, leaning back to brace the other on his thigh, my head thrown back toward the warm glow of the fireplace. I feel his hands smooth up my thighs and close around my waist, holding me in place as he lifts his hips and drives into me.

His hips thrust against mine with enough force to bounce me upward each time and my nails dig into his thigh, my vision darkening around the edges as he leads me toward my climax.

A low, breathy groan leaves him when I feel him release inside me, the warmth sending me over the edge. My hips roll into the feeling, his cock throbbing mercilessly as my muscles clench around him. I lean forward, resting my forehead against his as I savor my orgasm on top of him, fingers tangling into his hair. And when my breath evens out, my muscles slowly calming, and the sensation fading, my lips stretch into a smile.

My eyes flutter shut and I hum softly, brushing my nose against his. "Like I said, I could stay here forever," I mutter, followed by a quiet giggle.

He chuckles softly at that, pressing a soft kiss to the corner of my lips and folding his arms around me to pull my chest against his. "I wouldn't complain."

32

Sebastian

I didn't mean for this to happen. Any of it. Not with her, not with anyone. Not ever again. I keep my emotions locked away for a reason. I can't allow people to get close to me without expecting them to get hurt. In my line of work, it's the only outcome. But the more days pass, the more nights I spend with her curled into me, the more I feel the foundation of my life cracking beneath my feet. Whatever rigid discipline I've lived by... it's slipping. Breaking. Because of her. Because of the way she looks at me like I'm worth more than the blood on my hands. Because when she touches me, it feels like the first moment of peace in a life built on violence. I never intended to fall in love with her when I brought her here. But I did. And that...that scares the hell out of me.

Even more terrifying than merely the idea of love is the thought of breaking her heart. And the conversation about what happens next that's inevitable. She's making the bed when I return from my dawn perimeter check. She must've stirred awake after I'd left. Flat sheet snapped into place, hair falling loose around her shoulders, wearing one of my shirts that hangs off her frame like it was meant for her. She looks...comfortable. Safe. At home. Which is exactly why this will hurt.

"Savannah," I say. My voice comes out more reluctant than I intend. She looks up, all soft, tender eyes and admiration and I almost lose my nerve when she offers that gentle smile that I know is reserved only for me. She doesn't speak, she waits for my words. I force them out around my throat that feels like it's collapsing.

"I need to go out again. For supplies." The light in her expression dims immediately, features falling flat. "Again?" she asks quietly. "You're leaving me again?"

I swallow, a short nod of my head. "I'm telling you this time. It'll be quick. And I wouldn't leave if I didn't know you'd be okay here."

"Is that supposed to make it sound better?" Her voice cracks just slightly, and something sharp twists beneath my ribs. She turns away, fussing with the blanket edge to keep her hands busy. She pauses like she's giving up, dropping the blanket and turning to face me with arms crossed. "I'll come with you." she states matter-of-factly, trying for steady but failing. "We've been training. I'm getting better. You said so."

"You are getting better," I sigh, brows pinching together in the middle.

She takes a step forward, "Then let me help."

I reluctantly take a step back. "You can't."

Her chin lifts, that stubborn streak I've come to know—and adore—flashing through her eyes. "Why *not*, Sebastian? What's the point of all the training if you're just going to keep treating me like I'm a helpless little girl?" Her lips press into a thin line and the fire I've grown so familiar with washes over her.

I lift a hand, pinching the bridge of my nose. Now isn't the time for her to be defiant. "The training is last resort preparation. You being out there increases the risk tenfold."

"That doesn't mean—"

"It means I won't chance it," I snap roughly, in an effort to end the conversation. I catch the faintest flinch before she goes still. And I hate myself for it instantly. I step closer, taking a breath and softening my tone. "Savannah...if something happened to you out there, I—" My voice falters. I swallow hard, shaking my head. "I wouldn't recover from it."

Her breath catches, eyes widening just enough to show she heard the truth buried in what I said. But she's still hurting. And angry. Still feeling small and useless.

"So what, I just sit here?" she scoffs. "And do what? Wash dishes? Read a book? Wait for you to get back?" She shakes her head, reaching for the sweatshirt draped over the dresser and pulling it over her head. "No. I'm coming with you."

"No." My eyes darken in warning and I reach for her wrist, pulling her to face me. "You'll sit here, and wait, *alive*. You're not coming with me. End of story. It's too unpredictable and your safety is not something I'm willing to risk."

She flinches again like I struck her, yanking her wrist from my grip, the truth that we've been avoiding thickening the air. Because even though I know we've both been dwelling in this fairytale we've created, the danger has not been evaded. I watch as her defense builds, piece by piece, the way she tucks herself inward and curls her arms around her middle.

The warmth in her expression dims, replaced by something wounded. I've seen her sad. I've seen her scared. But I haven't seen *this* since before we shared a bed, before she trusted me with her body and her heart. "*Fine*," she spits through her teeth, her gaze dropping to the floor between us. "Go, then."

It crushes me immediately. "Savannah..." I reach out, but she steps back.

"No. It's fine," she says too quickly, shaking her head and holding a hand up between us, the distance as physical as it is emotional, now. "I get it." But she doesn't. And just as quickly as our growth sprouted, I've ruined everything, even if out of necessity.

She turns away, pretending she's suddenly fascinated by the dresser drawer, and I feel the guilt sink like a weight in my stomach. I want to tell her everything. That I'm terrified. That losing her would destroy me. That I'm not strong enough to let her come with me and risk watching her die in my arms.

But protecting her matters more than her feelings. More than my guilt. More than the fragile peace we've built between us. Even more than the truth—that I'm in love with her. So, I swallow it and clear my throat, forcing my voice steady. Free of any emotion that might give way to the turmoil building in every part of my body.

"I'll be back before dark." She doesn't look at me when I speak. Doesn't answer. Just nods once, tight and distant, in a way that's too familiar for comfort.

And the space between us feels colder than the dead of winter outside. I pause in the doorway, wishing I could take it back. The tone, the bluntness, the distance...but knowing I can't. Knowing softness with her is dangerous. Knowing caring makes my work sloppy. And I can't let that happen. Not when someone out there still wants her dead. Not when someone on my own team sold us out.

I close the door behind me and brace a hand against the exterior wall, eyes shut, breathing through the shard of regret lodged in my chest. I'm doing the right thing. I *know* that. But leaving her like that…It feels like tearing out a piece of myself and leaving it on the floor to be swept away.

I make it to the supply cache in half the usual time, fueled by anger and frustration, guilt that I can't shake. Leaving Savannah, hurting her when every part of me wants to protect her…it tears at me from the inside. But I can't have distractions. That's exactly why she couldn't come with me. I can only pray that she'll come to understand and I'll find forgiveness when I return.

The forest is too quiet as I move down the familiar path. The wrong kind of quiet that makes my hair stand and my senses go high alert in an instant. My hand goes to the weapon at my belt before my brain even catches the instinct, muscle memory engraved deep. The cache is carved into a hollow beneath an old fallen pine, covered with branches and snow. Only someone trained would know it was here. And someone trained has definitely been here.

Tracks are carved into the otherwise undisturbed blanket of snow that surrounds the trunk of the tree. My pulse spikes, ringing in my ears. I circle silently, scanning the tree line, every sense sharpening. I duck into the covert of the hanging limbs, hyperaware of my own heartbeat—then I hear it. The faint shift of weight, a breath too loud for deer, the metallic click of a weapon being steadied.

I turn just as a figure bursts through the trees and recognition hits like ice, steeling my frame. Mathers. One of the men from my unit. Or...what *used* to be mine. He lunges at me, no hesitation, no attempt to question or confirm identity. An act of violent, intentional betrayal.

I catch his arm, twist, and the fight devolves into hand-to-hand immediately. He's faster than I remember, fueled by something ugly and full of desperation. Or orders, and I don't know which is worse. He swings first, wild and sloppy, connecting with my temple. I stumble slightly but recover, landing a shot to his ribs and another to his jaw.

He doubles over for a moment, glaring up at me, "You know they'll find her. Can't run forever, Hayes." He grins, bloody and unhinged, before he spits at my boots. He lunges for me again and I fist his collar with one hand, the other closing around his neck, my thumb pressing his jugular. He swings his head forward, cracking my nose with a sharp crunch. My vision goes red and I close my grip tighter around his neck.

"Tell me who sent you," I seethe. It's useless. He meets my eye but his gaze is guarded, cold. "They're coming for you both—" He tries to muster but my fist connects with his jaw again before he even finishes the sentence and I release his collar, pushing him to the ground.

He drops hard, breathing but unconscious. I stand over him, chest heaving, knuckles throbbing, unbothered by the blood gushing from my nose. My boot lands on his throat and his eyes bulge at the sudden lack of air. "Who the fuck sent you, Mathers?" I bark at him. The same twisted grin graces his features and he attempts a maniacal laugh, one that's hard to achieve with no air supply.

I curse under my breath; his intel is worthless, anyway. Betrayal fuels me as my heel connects to his temple, his body going limp. Irate with red vision, I pull his motionless body down the bank and roll him to the bottom of the incline. I leave him there for whoever will come looking. They're close. Much closer than I thought. "*Dammit!*" I curse into the wind, knuckles chipping away at the bark of a barren tree when my fist slams into it.

My heartbeat screams in my ears, my entire being vibrating with resentment. Savannah is nowhere near safe. And I left her there alone. I shove extra supplies into my pack with shaking hands and bolt through the trees, adrenaline burning through the cold.

I don't feel it when a branch whips across my cheek. I barely notice the swelling around my eye. I just need to get back to her.

Now.

33

Savannah

The cabin feels too quiet, the tick of the old clock by the door the only sound. The old clock that my eyes can't seem to break away from and the drumming of my pulse in my ears. Every creak sounds like a warning. Every gust of wind through the chimney makes my heart jump. The conversation replays over and over in my head. The stern tone, the clipped command, the coldness I thought we'd left behind. Part of me wants to stay angry. Wants to cling to the stubborn part of me that hates being told no. But something else is happening too. My mind starts drifting to the dark corners I've avoided: *What if it would be easier to leave?*

A clean break. Slip out while he's gone, walk until I hit a road. Flag down help and go home like none of this ever happened. What's left to be afraid of anyway? We've been holed up in this cabin for days, weeks...I don't know anymore, with nothing except the walls closing in and the knowledge that I'm falling in love with a man who refuses to let me stand beside him. Maybe leaving would hurt less than staying. Maybe it's time.

I shove clothes that don't belong to me into a duffle that doesn't belong to me, hands trembling the whole time. His scent lingers on all of it, suffocating me and deepening the ache of my own actions in my chest.

Every zipper, every folded shirt feels like a betrayal, but staying feels like drowning. Like waiting for the moment he realizes he doesn't need me the way I need him. I picture him walking back into the cabin and finding me gone. Something jars in my chest, sharp, painful, and almost unbearable. I swallow hard, trying to shake the feeling of regret already working in my throat. "Maybe it's better this way," I whisper to no one but myself, even though the words feel like ash in the back of my throat.

I pace the length of the cabin a dozen times, rehearsing what I'll say when he returns. No, not what I'll say. What I'll scream. That I'm done waiting. Done being benched. Done feeling like a fragile thing he has to guard instead of someone who could help him fight. That he doesn't have to do this alone. Or shut me out every time he starts to feel something. But the longer he's gone, the more something icy creeps up my spine. Worry, fear, a longing I don't give a name to. I peer out the curtains into the horizon. The sun has long set and the endless dark of night swallows the cabin whole. He said he'd be back by dark.

What if something happened to him? What if he doesn't come back? The same worries from the last time he left cloud my mind. I press my hands over my face and shake my head hard. *Stop. Stop thinking like that.*

I hear the heavy, familiar thud of boots on the porch and my heart lurches into my throat. I spin toward the door, ready to start the fight I've been building like a dam inside my chest. But when the door swings open, the whole argument caves in on itself. My stomach falls to the floor at the sight of him.

Sebastian stumbles in, bruised knuckles split open, a blackening eye, dirt streaked across his coat, and dried blood smudged across his face. He wears the same stoic look on his face as the night we met. He looks like he crawled through hell and back. "*Sebastian!*" The scream rips out of me before I can stop it. I crash into him, hands skimming over his arms, his shoulders, his face. Checking for injuries, needing to feel him solid under my palms. "What happened? *Oh my god—* who did this? Why didn't you take me? I could've helped! I could've been your back up, that's the whole point of all the training—"

He exhales a shaky breath, somewhere between relief and agony, and grabs my wrists gently, but he doesn't move them away. And he doesn't meet my eye. "Savannah...slow down." His voice is hoarse. But I can't. Not when he's standing in front of me, solid yet bruised and battered.

Tears blur my vision, anger and fear and love twisting together until I'm shaking. "You can't just leave me here and then come back looking like *this!*" I shout, my hands framing his jaw and my thumb brushing his bruised cheek with gentle, desperate care. "You can't expect me not to worry—" He leans into my touch like he's starving for it

"I'm fine," he grumbles

"You are *not* fine."

His lips twitch into a weak, pained half-smile, like he's trying to make this all seem lighter than it is. "No," he admits, "But I'm here." My knees nearly give out. I exhale a shaky breath and press my forehead to his chest, gripping the fabric of his shirt like it's my lifeline. His arms slip around me, pulling me in tight, tighter than before, like he never left at all. "I'm sorry. I'm so damn sorry," he mutters quietly.

But sorry doesn't explain anything. Sorry doesn't account for the injuries marking his body or ease the cold fear spiraling down my spine. I pull back just enough to see him clearly, my heart dropping into my stomach. His eye is swelling shut, the bruising blooming deeper into his features with every passing breath. I lift his hand and his knuckles are torn open. There's dirt smeared across his jaw, a cut just below his brow, another across the bridge of his nose.

"Sebastian..." My voice trembles. "What happened to you?"

He tears his eyes away, brows furrowing together. "Nothing you need to worry about," that stern tone returns to his voice, stripping it of any gentleness that was there moments ago.

"Don't do that." My throat tightens. "Don't shut me out. Not after—" I stop before the word *everything* slips out. He closes his eyes briefly, fighting something inside himself. When he looks at me again, the truth is there, heavy and unavoidable.

"There was someone at the cache," he says, voice quiet like he's hoping I won't hear. "Someone who shouldn't have been there."

My blood runs cold as I tighten my fingers around his hand to avoid the threatening quiver of panic that threatens to wash over me. "Who?"

He hesitates before he answers, like I won't be able to handle the truth, or maybe he can't. "One of mine." A hard, painful beat passes between us as I try to digest that.

"One of yours?" My eyes narrow and my head shakes

slowly. "What do you mean?"

He doesn't elaborate, but the implication slices clean through me. Sebastian has never given me the full story about his background. Only hints, the edges of a life shaped by discipline and danger. The dog tags around his neck that I curl my fingers around at night, the way he moves, the training he's given me. All of it has whispered *military* or something close to it. But none of that explains *this*. None of that explains why someone from his past would be out here now, trying to hurt him. Why they'd be involved at all.

"I thought this was because of my dad," I whisper, voice barely steady. "I thought I was in danger because of him...not because of you."

A muscle ticks in his cheek. He still won't meet my eyes. "They were looking for us," he adds without explanation. "For you." I feel the air leave my lungs.

"And you fought them?" My voice rises, thin and cracking. "*Alone?*" I see that same, protective armor brace itself over his features and it's answer enough. I glance at his knuckles again, the deep bruises spreading across his cheekbone. He looks like he walked out of a war zone

"You could have been killed," I whisper. "Sebastian, you—

"But I *wasn't*." His tone sharpens, steady and unyielding. "I'm fine. I handled it.

"Stop saying you're fine!" I gesture helplessly toward his injuries, my own tone cutting like a knife through the air. "Nothing about this is fine.

His hands close around my wrists, lowering them gently. "It's over.

My head shakes again, silently begging him to meet my eye. "You can't know that."

He exhales through his bruised nose, lips pressing together in a thin line before he speaks, shoulders tensing. "I said it's over." The snap in his voice makes me flinch. Not because he's harsh. But because the lie is so painfully obvious. He drags a hand through his hair, chest rising and falling unsteadily. "I'm telling you what I can," he says, softer but strained. "Trying not to scare the hell out of you."

"You're too late for that," I whisper, a humorless scoff filling the space between us. Something in his expression softens, slightly cracks. Only long enough for him to step closer, gently cupping my chin with his battered hand, thumb brushing across my cheekbone. The contrast between his roughness and my trembling breath makes my throat tighten. "Baby, I'm here," he murmurs, his expression strained even as he speaks. "I came back. Nothing is going to touch you. Not while I'm breathing. That's all I can give you right now." *Baby...*The word escapes him so easily and a flush immediately creeps onto my features.

I swallow hard, exhaling a breath and turning a little too quickly toward the kitchen. "Sit down," I call over my shoulder.

"What?" He trails me with his eyes, I feel them on my back like I always do.

"Sit," I insist, already pulling open the cabinet door beneath the sink for the first aid kit. "You're hurt. Let me help, please. At least let me do this for you." He grumbles something unintelligible, a sound somewhere between surrender and exhaustion, and lowers himself onto the couch. I kneel in front of him when I return, dropping the first aid kit beside me and pulling his hand into my lap. His skin is hot, swollen under my shuddering fingers. "This looks bad."

"It's nothing." He has the nerve to shrug, as if I'm not surveying all his bruises and scrapes, cleaning his wounds for him. My eyes dart up at him and I resist the urge to roll them into my skull at his apathy.

"It's *not* nothing. Stop saying that." I dab antiseptic onto the torn skin. He barely reacts but I do. My stomach twists, a mix of nausea and anger that someone did this to him. Gently, I smear ointment over the wounds and wind a roll of gauze around his knuckles. His breathing shifts, a quiet tell. He sees it. He sees *everything* I'm trying to hide. "Look at me," he says softly.

"I'm fine," I mutter, focusing too intently on wrapping the gauze. I finish with one hand and move to the other, this one scarred even worse. I pull my lower lip between my teeth, anguish smothering me and constricting my throat.

"Try again," he calls my bluff easily.

I swallow hard, keeping my eyes focused on nursing his wounds. He tilts my chin up gently, forcing my gaze to meet his. "What's going on in that head of yours?"

I shake my head, placing the spare gauze back in the kit and letting my hands fall against his. "Nothing," I whisper.

"Savannah. Talk to me." The way he says my name, firm and warm, breaks something in me. My voice slips out, frail. "You could have died. And I wouldn't have known. I would've been here, just...*waiting*. And what if you didn't come back this time?"

His hard expression falters, cracks enough for me to see what he tries so desperately to hide underneath. The understanding, the guilt, the part of him that wants to pull me close again and swear he'll never leave me like that. And then... something shifts. I watch it, *feel it*, happening in real time, like someone flipped a switch.

The softening behind his cloudy eyes vanishes, swallowed by something colder. A flicker of restraint tightens his jaw. The apology dies on his tongue before it even hits the air. His eyes harden in a way that feels like a door being shut right in front of me. I feel my heart not just crack, but shatter, watching the last of our relationship slip between my fingers like a rope that I can't grab fast enough.

He leans back slightly. Not far, but enough that I feel the difference. "Savannah," he says again, but the tone is different now. Less warm. Less open. More...practiced. Like the militant man that I met, not my protector who's softened for me. "That's never going to happen. I'm here. That's what matters." It should comfort me. It doesn't. Not with the way he says it, the finality free of emotion.

It feels like he's retreating. Rebuilding the distance we'd torn down together. The man who held me through the night, who whispered my name like it meant something, is suddenly buried under that steel mask again. And I don't understand why, or what I've done wrong. I shake my head slowly and feel that sting at the corner of my eyes, the betrayal of the lump growing in my throat. "I'm sorry. I was worried."

He leans back further on the couch, putting physical space between us, shoulders squaring in a way that looks deliberate. Like he's reminded himself of something he wishes he could forget. The mission. His duty. Why we're really here. His voice drops to something almost clinical and I can feel myself starting to spiral. "You don't need to worry about what happened. I took care of it."

The words slice through me. *Took care of it.* As if he hadn't come home bleeding. As if he hadn't scared me more than anyone ever has. As if I don't have every right to feel like the Earth was falling from underneath me. I try to swallow the hurt, but it tastes bitter. "That's not what I meant," I whisper, weak. He doesn't flinch but I see his eyes flicker, the tiniest crack in the armor he's trying so desperately to put back on. "I need you to trust me," his voice is quieter but still guarded.

"I *do* trust you," I retort, the sharpness of my tone accidental. "That's the problem." I hear the hitch of his breath, so fast, so subtle I almost miss it. I catch the slight flex of his fingers. For a second, I see the softness again, the man I shared a bed with, the man who touched me like he'd fall apart if he didn't. The man who kissed me like he'd been waiting years to do it. But then he shutters himself off again just as quickly. He pulls his hand from mine to adjust the bandage on his knuckles. An excuse more than a necessity. A retreat disguised as practicality.

I can feel the space widening by inches, painfully slow, like a crack spreading through glass. My hand automatically feels empty, small, in the absence of his. *He's pulling away.* I can feel it. I can feel him slipping behind the defensive walls I thought we'd destroyed together and right now, I don't see anything I can do to stop it. All I know is that the warmth between us has shifted into something teetering on the edge of disappearing if I breathe too hard, so quickly that it feels like it's given me whiplash. And I'm suddenly terrified of losing him in a way I didn't know was possible anymore.

He studies the floor instead of me, jaw tight, breath steady and controlled. His eyes are absent, years away, not here with me. Not soft or warm or caring. He's controlled in the way that I've learned he gets when he's forcing himself not to feel something. I can't stand the silence.

"So," I start, voice small, too thin, "you... should

probably rest." I try to sound casual. Normal. The way I would any other night. He doesn't respond. I force a breath and keep going, locking my fingers together as if it'll calm my trembling hands or the shake in my voice. "Your injuries will heal faster if you get some sleep. You always say recovering is half the fight, right?"

My heart pounds louder and louder, the longer he doesn't answer, avoiding looking my way entirely. This isn't like him...not with me. Not anymore. I stand slowly, awkwardly brushing my palms against my thighs. "Come on." I stretch my arm out toward him, offering my hand the way I have every night since we started sharing a bed.

"Let's...go to bed." It's not just an invitation. It's a plea. One that I know he can hear behind my words. A bandage I'm trying desperately to place over whatever this is. But he doesn't take my hand. He doesn't even look at it.

Instead, he shakes his head once—slow, deliberate, lethal. "I can't tonight," he says quietly. "I need...time to think." His words are softer now but they hit like a physical blow.

"*Oh.*" It's all I manage. Just that one syllable. Fragile. Stupid. Bare. I pull my hand back, folding it into the other to hide how badly they're shaking. He still won't look at me.

I force a smile that's thin, brittle, and a little painful at the edges. I can feel myself crumbling inwardly with every ticking second of the clock that had me trapped earlier in the evening. The one I wish I could turn back to before it all fell apart. "Well," I try to joke, though my voice cracks in the middle of it, "I'll, um...keep your spot warm." He doesn't laugh or soften. He doesn't say anything. He doesn't bristle or crack. And that hurts more than anything he could have said.

I wait. For a second. And then another. Then a few

more. Long enough that hope flickers desperately, embarrassingly—stupidly, inside my chest. He stays rooted in the same place, shoulders squared, eyes fixed somewhere far away from me. Finally, I nod, more to myself than him.

"Okay," I whisper. "Goodnight, Sebastian." I turn toward the hallway before my face can betray me, before he can see the way my heart is disintegrating in my chest. With each step the distance stretches wider, heavier, until the doorway feels like the threshold of a world where he isn't fully mine anymore.

Before closing the bedroom door behind me, I glance back one last time. He still hasn't looked up. His gaze remains locked on something miles away. The latch clicks softly, sealing the quiet between us. I stand there for a moment, my back pressed to the door, thoughts spinning so fast they blur together and I feel lightheaded. The first tear slips down my cheek before I even feel it coming. Another follows. And another. Finally, I force myself toward the bed. Cold, untouched, and far too big without him. I crawl beneath the covers and curl into myself, listening to nothing but the vicious wind clawing at the window and the slow, painful cracking of my own heart as it keeps me company through the night.

34

Sebastian

The night falls silent after she disappears behind the bedroom door except for the hushed sobs I can hear filtering down the hallway. My chest caves inward each time a new one sounds and I have to force myself to remain on the couch with my elbows on my knees. Staring at nothing, listening to everything. Every crack of the cabin's frame, the pop of the fireplace. Every groan of the wind that feels alive. Every guilt-ridden beat of my own heart. I sit there and I replay the ambush again, and again.

Each punch. Each breath. Each realization that the betrayal runs deeper than I thought. Mathers' sick face when I confronted him. The overwhelming rush of anger, desperate need to get back to her. That someone once close to me is willing to break rank, break oath, to get to Savannah. And then, just as relentlessly, I replay *her* face. The way her eyes widened when she saw my injuries and how she shouldered that fear to nurse them. The way her voice shook when she said I could have died. The way she held out her hand in a gesture that was small, and hopeful, and trusting. And I turned her away.

I tell myself that it's necessary, the only way to keep her alive. I tell myself that she can't know how much she matters or the choices I'll make because of that. But no rationalization keeps the images from burning behind my eyelids of her standing in the dim cabin light, trying to be brave while her heart broke right in front of me.

I shove a hand through my hair and stand, pacing the length of the living room. I check the window, the front door. The back, the tree line. I watch for shadows, movement. Listen for any sound that doesn't belong. Not because I think someone's actually there but because movement keeps me from thinking about her.

Except it doesn't, not really.

But it keeps me locked in the living room, keeps me from rushing to her, apologizing, laying every truth out between us. Truth that will hurt her more than I already have. Every time I circle the cabin, every time the boards creak under my boots, I think about whether she's awake, whether she's crying, whether she's staring at the wall wondering what she did wrong. *Nothing.* She did nothing wrong. But I can't tell her that. Not without risking everything. Again.

I pause outside her door only when I'm certain her breathing has gone soft and even, peek inside and crumble all over again when I see her there, curled in on herself. Her cheeks reflect the light of the stars that glisten through the curtains, tear-stained even in sleep. I tell myself I'm verifying her safety, nothing more. Even when I know it's a lie. I check on her twice more before dawn, keeping my distance at the doorframe, watching the rise and fall of her chest. Asleep and safe, but free of the gentle peace she found in her dreams before tonight. Before the pressure of the damage I've caused came in like a hurricane and wrecked it all.

By the time sunlight bleeds through the trees, my body feels like lead. I haven't slept. Couldn't. My knuckles scream in protest with each flex, my cheek throbs with a deep, bitter ache. My ribs pull tight with every breath, souvenirs from the ambush.

But it's all easy to handle compared to the quiet pain waiting in Savannah's eyes when she greets me. She emerges from the bedroom cautiously, like she's not sure which version of me she's going to get. The one who touched her gently in the dark or the one who shut her out the moment she needed comfort. I don't let myself look long enough to find out.

"Morning," I say shortly, already at the stove. I dish portions into two bowls without turning around, keeping my face neutral, unreadable. She stays away a few feet uncertain. Hopeful but hurt. I place her bowl at the end of the table, but I don't sit. I can't leave any room for misinterpretation. I eat standing by the counter, shoveling food into my mouth like its fuel and not something we used to share in soft, quiet moments. My ribs burn with each breath.

My knuckles sting when I grip the fork. Every swallow feels tight in my throat. But seeing her tuck into herself, trying to pretend this shift doesn't cut as deep as it does, it burns worse than any wound I've ever had. She clears her throat softly. "Are you...feeling any better?"

"Fine." One word. Sharp. Concise.

She tries again. "Last night, when you—"

"Drop it," I snap and continue to try to convince myself that this is the only way to keep her safe. Her shoulders sink beneath the weight of my tone and I loathe myself for it. But I don't retract it, I can't. Talking about the ambush leads to talking about the betrayal. Talking about the betrayal leads to talking about the target. Talking about the target leads to the truth: Someone from my own unit wants her dead. Or worse.

And if Savannah knows everything I know, she'll stop being cautious. She'll volunteer to help. She'll put herself at even greater risk. I can't let that happen. Even if it means losing her trust. Even when I know if it means breaking this thing between us that was fragile to begin with.

After breakfast, we train. I push her harder than usual. Hard enough that she shoots me confused glances between drills. I need her to be ready for whatever might come next. Because the threat is more real now than it has been since the night she was taken. "Again," I tell her, voice flat. She lunges, missteps, and nearly falls. I catch her instinctively but release her just as quickly. Her breath stutters, her eyes pleading. "Sebastian—"

"Keep your guard up." My tone is all bite, no warmth. She listens, but the light in her eyes dims a little more each time. Her touch when our hands brush during a correction is a live wire under my skin. But I force myself not to react. I push away any reminders of the nights I let myself have her, hold her, feel her. I keep every movement strictly professional. Even when the distance slices straight through me.

The day passes with minimal words. She asks a question; I shut it down. She attempts a smile; I look away before it reaches me. She tries to touch my arm when I pass her, I move too quickly for it to land. It hurts. *God*, it hurts. But losing her would kill me and the only way to prevent that is to pretend I don't feel the pull between us. Straining. Begging to be repaired. So, I pretend it all meant less than it did. Pretend I'm only her protector, not a man who's falling for her so hard I know I'll never recover from this. Tonight, I do an extra perimeter sweep before dusk. Pain flares through me with every step.

Savannah thinks I'm pushing her away because I'm angry. But the truth is something I don't think she'll ever fully understand. I'm doing it because I love her. Because I have to.

I can't pinpoint when the change starts. But I notice it in the way she moves quietly through the cabin now, steps light, almost hesitant like she's trying not to take up too much space. I notice it in the way her eyes flick toward me during breakfast. Not in warmth, or expectation, but as if she's bracing for the version of me that she knows is here now. I notice the way she doesn't say good morning or goodnight anymore. The way she doesn't expect me to follow her to bed or offer her hand any longer. Every goddamn second of it. I created this distance, but she's the one stretching it now. And it's killing me, festering from the inside out, like a rotting wound that never stood a chance.

She used to approach the table with a soft smile, shy and sweet tugging at her mouth. Now, she hardly acknowledges me at all. I put her breakfast down. "Thanks," her voice is barely above a whisper and she doesn't meet my eyes. She used to wait for me to sit beside her. Now she doesn't look surprised when I stand. She eats slowly, mechanically, while I shovel my food like it's the last supper. Her shoulders curl inward, sagging like she's shrinking, protecting herself. And every time I catch her glancing toward me, I see her look away just as fast. I pretend not to notice. But I do. I notice it all.

I notice the way she follows every command during training. Every movement, every correction, without argument. But the spark is gone. The eagerness she used to show. The way she used to glow when I praised her progress is dimmed to nothing more than some form of obedience. When I reposition her stance, I feel her stiffen under my touch. Not because she's afraid, but because I've taught her not to expect softness anymore.

Savannah doesn't ask questions anymore. Doesn't beg for answers she knows I won't give. And when I say, "Again," she doesn't roll her eyes or huff or tease me like she used to. She just nods and repeats. Like a soldier, like someone resigned. Like someone I've failed. I try to convince myself that this is good, safe, necessary. But it's a lie that tastes like sour regret.

After my afternoon perimeter check that I added into the schedule, she sits on the couch reading, something she plucked from my tiny shelf of books. Her knees curl to her chest, her hair falling forward in soft waves around her. My heart stops because she looks peaceful in a way she hasn't in days. She doesn't look up when I pass. Not the way she used to track me with her eyes, soft and curious, waiting for any scrap of attention. Now she keeps her gaze focused on the page, even when I note that she hasn't turned it in ten minutes. When I walk outside to perform another obsessive sweep, needing the physical space to keep myself sane, she doesn't linger at the window to watch me like she used to. The glass stays as empty as I feel.

She makes dinner before I get the chance. The sight stops me cold in the doorway. Savannah stands at the stove, stirring something quietly, taking up space in the cabin we've shared but keeping a distance as though unsure she belongs here anymore. I force a breath. "You didn't have to do that," I say.

She shrugs, still not looking at me. "I was hungry." Her voice is free of any of the light-heartedness I'd grown to adore. And then she plates her food and sits at the far end of the table. I eat standing up again. She no longer waits for me, watches me, or lights up when I enter the room. She no longer looks up at all. And watching her pull away feels like bleeding out slowly.

After dinner, I hear her bedroom door close earlier than usual. No checking to see if I'm coming with her. No hesitating in the doorway. Just the quiet click of a lock I've never heard her use before. And I stand there in the dark cabin, exhaustion weighing on me, injuries throbbing, heart twisting in ways I swore I'd never let happen. I feel her slipping away from me, further with every minute that passes. Because I pushed her to. Because I made her think I don't want her. And because every time I imagine crawling into that bed beside her, wrapping my arms around her, feeling her breathe against me and taking it all back...I force myself to stay rooted to the cold wooden floor instead. Distance keeps her safe, I know that. So why does it feel like I'm losing something I can't survive without?

35

Savannah

Sebastian barely looks at me, barely speaks to me. Touches me only when necessary, during training, and even then, his hands are cold and his actions are detached. It's like we never shared a bed. Like he never kissed me breathless and his fingers never traced my spine, memorizing every curve of my body. Like his body never curled around mine in the dark. And pretending otherwise feels like a knife carving its way through me.

I can't sit here any longer and ignore the growing ache in my chest. I need an explanation. I need something, any sign that I didn't imagine this, that it wasn't all just something I wanted too badly. I listen for his return in the morning the way I used to. When the front door finally creaks open, my pulse thuds recklessly against my neck. I don't give myself time to overthink it before I move.

I stand from the bed, inhaling a deep breath, and

smooth my palms down the pale blue button up that matches the shade of his eyes. It's big, too long in the torso, like everything else I wear here. But I choose to ditch my leggings, the only clothing that belongs to me, and saunter into the living room bare-legged. I sweep my hair over one shoulder, exposing the open buttons at my collar.

Sebastian sits in the worn armchair, back to me, eyes fixated on the window. I hesitate, only for a second. Then I move behind him. Slowly, I slide my hands over his shoulders and down his chest. His muscles stiffen beneath my fingertips, the tension immediate and rough, but I don't pull away. "Hi," I purr near his ear, my lips brushing his neck. I need to know this was real. "Everything clear this morning?" I ask softly, even when I already know the answer. If it wasn't, he wouldn't be here.

Sebastian clears his throat and for one fragile, fleeting moment, he leans into my touch. His hands graze over mine and ghost up my arms, like his muscle memory betrays him. I let my lips find his neck again, tracing slowly up to his jaw. "Do you want some breakfast?" I ask, brushing my nose against his bruised cheek, my voice light.

"Savannah..." he breathes, fingers tightening just slightly on my arms. Not pulling me closer, but not pushing me away, either. The conflict behind the way he says my name tells me everything. He wants this too, he just won't let himself have it.

Circling the chair, I lower myself onto his lap, my knees bracketing his thighs. My hands trail back up his chest, winding around his neck. "I'm just asking if you're hungry," I feign innocence, tilting my head, my mouth curving into a soft pout. His body is rigid beneath mine. He doesn't speak but his eyes say everything his mouth won't admit to. "I miss you," I admit quietly, braver than I feel. And that's when he cracks.

He exhales like the fight finally leaves him. His grip tightens, pulling me an inch closer. Just enough that his forehead brushes my chest, his breath warm against my skin. "*God, this isn't fair...*" He whispers, so quietly I almost miss it. He lifts one of my hands, the motion careful. His thumb brushes over my knuckles before he turns my palm upward and presses his mouth to it, slow and lingering.

"Don't you miss me, too?" I whisper.

For a heartbeat, he doesn't answer. Striking blue eyes pierce into mine with a ferocity I'd forgotten they can hold. Then, all at once, he tilts his head and his mouth finds mine like it's been searching for it this whole time, slow and careful and devastating in its tenderness. My hands slide into his hair, lacing behind his head, and our tongues dance together long enough to lift an ounce of weight off my chest, hope blooming bright and reckless. Long enough for me to believe that this time, he's choosing me.

The kiss feels like a confession. Like an apology.

But when he pulls back, the absence is immediate and cold. His forehead rests against mine, breathing unsteady, his hands planted on my thighs like letting go would hurt too much. And then they slide to my waist, my skin burning under his touch, before he gently moves me off his lap.

He stands, putting space between us like it's the only thing keeping him upright. "I can't." The words come out broken, almost hollow as they drive straight through my chest. The lips still taste like him when he steps away, my fingers brushing against them gently before anger erupts inside of me, curling its way ruthlessly up my spine.

"No!" My hands curl at my sides as I rise to my feet,

turning on my heels to face him, "You don't get to do that," I snap sharply. "You don't get to touch me like you want me," My voice shakes but I press forward. "And then look at me like this is some terrible mistake!"

He doesn't turn but his head tilts back like he's praying this moment will end. "I didn't imagine this, Sebastian. And you don't get to keep proving that it's real and then pretending it's not!" My throat burns the longer he keeps his back to me.

His shoulders remain tight, unwavering, and I step closer, fueled by anger and hurt. "If you can't do this..." I press, my chest aching. "Then stop looking at me like you want me. Stop letting me touch you just to pull away. Stop making me feel like I'm asking for something wrong when all I want is *you*..." One lone tear slides down my cheek, uninvited, and I quickly swipe it away. "I can handle you, and this, and whatever it means for what comes next," my voice breaks, "But what I can't handle is you breaking my heart and calling it protection."

When I finish, the silence lingers for a long moment, thin and brittle. Weighted with everything I can't take back.

"I'm sorry," is all he mutters before he's gone again, the front door clicking shut behind him.

I stay where I am long after he's gone, the echo of the door closing ringing in my ears. I wipe my face with the back of my hand and cross the room to the window. He's gone. Again. *Fine.* I've spent days waiting for him to come back to me, choose me, to acknowledge me at all. So I'm done waiting. If Sebastian won't give me answers, I'll find them myself.

I start my search in the bedroom. The dresser drawers first, empty except for the shirt I borrowed and the excuse of a flashlight I found before. Nothing else. Nothing personal. Even the manilla folder I once discovered has been moved. Under the bed—dust, nothing more. The closet—bare, except for a duffel whose contents are weapons and spare clothes. Nothing that tells me who he is. Nothing that explains why he's suddenly a stranger again. It makes my chest burn with defeat disguised as misplaced rage.

I tear through the choice of books next, stacked lazily on top of each other on the slim bookshelf in the corner of the living room. I glance over every worn cover. Flip through every dog-eared page. Every hollow crease between spines. My breath hitches when I see it. A book that isn't a book at all. A small, worn box, carefully placed to blend in. I pull it from the shelf and hesitate, hands trembling. When I gain the courage to flip open the lid, my world tilts violently and I feel all my blood rush to my feet. This is it. *This* is what I've been looking for and it was right in front of me this whole time.

Inside is a neatly folded map, worn in the way it's easy to tell it's been opened and folded back again and again. Several strong red lines cover the page, drawn through the mountains. Arrows, coordinates. And all of them lead here. A red circle off center of the page. This cabin. *Me*. Beneath it, I find another folded paper.

A photo, tinged with age, the creases solid white lines that cross in the middle like it's been hidden long before any of this. A group of soldiers stand in desert gear, the sand bright behind them. My stomach turns with instant recognition. Sebastian stands near the center, younger, sunburnt, smiling like someone who hasn't learned to shut the world out yet. Someone who hasn't been hardened into the man pacing the woods outside.

He looks...*happy*. Happier than I've ever had the chance to see him. The ache that hits me is sharp, sudden, and intruding. My eyes catch on a thick red circle around the face of another man in the photo, drawn in the same marker from the map. And above all their heads, written in blunt letters: UNIT BREACH SUSPECTED. My hand covers my mouth, my breath going shallow despite the adrenaline pounding through me.

But it's the notebook that reads Field Notes on the cover that breaks me. Page after page detailing nights at the cabin. At first they're cold, detached, like a log kept for work.

Subject secured.
Threat level manageable.
Training progress: minimal.

The words turn over in my head. *Subject*. Not Savannah. Not a person. Not someone he touched like she mattered. Just...subject. But then...the notes change. Small shifts at first. A line about my determination. Another about my stubbornness.

Then the more recent ones—

She's improving faster than anticipated.
She's trusting me more than she should.
Her safety is becoming difficult to detach from.

My heart hammers so hard it hurts. And then my eyes drift to the last line.

Emotional compromise confirmed.

I stop breathing entirely. He knew. He knew how much I care. He could see it. And maybe this was him admitting that he does, too. He wrote it down like a tactical failure. Like caring about me, touching me, wanting me, was all a mistake. The hurt is so sharp I clap my hand over my mouth, silencing the wail I feel escaping. The truth that's so sobering I can't gather my thoughts. But suddenly, everything makes sense.

I thought I wanted answers...until I found them.

The forced distance, the coldness, the refusal to come to bed. His sharp tongue and clipped answers. The way he shut down the second danger escalated. He wasn't pulling away because he didn't care. He's pulling away because he *does*. But knowing that doesn't soothe the wound. Not when he shut me out. Not when I gave him the most vulnerable parts of me only for him to discard them like they never mattered. Not when he let me fall apart without explanation while he watched. Not when he acted like I was something to avoid.

The front door creaks and I whip my head toward the noise. *Shit*—I didn't hear him returning this time. I barely have time to close the notebook before he steps inside, cold air clinging to him, jaw set in that hard, emotionless line. His eyes go straight to the open box. Then to the photo in my hands. And his face twists in a way that's foreign even after all this time.

"Savannah," he says, his voice low and as pointed as

knives. "What the hell do you think you're doing?" I flinch at his words. He's never spoken to me like that before. My voice shakes, my hands trembling around the photo that remains in my hands. "What you refuse to let me do. Trying to understand what the hell is going on."

He strides forward, quick and lethal. "Put that down. Now."

"No!" The word comes out broken and raw in spite of the alarm at his sudden defensiveness. I've seen Sebastian worried. I've seen him in what I imagine is the closest thing to fear for him and I've seen him agitated. I've even seen him happy. But I've never seen him angry. Is that what this is?

"Why would I do that?" I press myself forward, my own hostility outweighing any caution to his tone, "You won't tell me anything. You don't answer my questions. You keep secrets. You never let me *all the way* in. You made me think I meant something and then you—" My voice cracks and I inhale a shaky breath to steady myself. "You acted like it was nothing." I can't look weak. Not now. Not when I finally know something. I can't prove that he was right, that the truth might just be more than I can handle.

He flinches like my words struck him, jaw slackening before he speaks. His expression softens, a flash of hurt flickering behind his eyes. "It wasn't nothing." The words are gravel when he speaks, clawing their way out of his throat as he takes a step further into the room.

"*Really?*" I snap. "Because it feels a lot like I was an assignment. A responsibility. Your '*subject*'", I throw finger quotations at him, flailing the notebook at his chest. "Something you had to *handle*. Something for..." I pause, scrambling for words. "For fun. Until you realized you'd made a mistake. Until you realized this meant more to me than you thought it would."

His eyes flick to the notebook that lands with a loud slap on the floor after it collides with his chest and darken with something dangerous. Fear, maybe. Or regret. I can't place it. I'm not sure that I want to. "You went through my notes," he says, voice tightening but eerily calm. "You don't trust me." I catch his fingers flexing at his sides.

"How could I, Sebastian?" My voice breaks. I rise from my place on the floor, facing him fully and standing as tall as my frame will stretch, just as he's taught me. "How could I, when everything I know about you, I had to find written in a notebook instead of hearing it from you?" He steps closer. Too close. The tension rolls off of him in waves but it's not enough to bridge what's between us. What used to be between us.

"I never meant to hurt you." The words cut straight through my chest, a dagger meant to finish a job, not just injure. It feels like a lie when he says it.

My eyes slip shut only for a moment, a feeble attempt to gather myself. "Then why does it feel like you've done nothing but hurt me for days?" I force myself not to waiver, my gaze locked on his, searching for...I don't know. An apology. Some sign that this is tearing him apart the same way it's doing to me. His breath shudders. He looks at me like he's standing on a cliff edge and one wrong word will send both of us over it.

He shakes his head, voice fracture-thin, and turns toward the window. The silence stretches into minutes as he turns into that fixture that seems to be miles away again. "You were never supposed to matter this much."

Everything inside me goes quiet, my ears ringing with a deafening silence only interrupted by the shattering of my heart, a million tiny shards scattering across the floor. Because maybe I finally understand. His walls weren't about indifference. They were about fear. And fear doesn't protect you from heartbreak, it delivers it. Straight to your ribs like a clean, merciless blow. I set the photo down with trembling fingers, my breath unsteady. I offer him the most pathetic excuse of a smile that I can manage, nodding just once.

"Looks like I don't, anymore." The surrender barely makes it past my lips, no louder than a whisper. "You win, Sebastian."

This time, I'm the one who walks away. I leave him standing in the wreckage of everything unsaid and I leave whatever pieces of my heart are still intact on the floor between us. My feet are concrete blocks when I retreat down the hall, feeling each step like it's detached from my body. For the second time since arriving here, I turn the lock on the bedroom door.

36

Savannah

The argument keeps replaying in my head, over and over, until the words dig into my ribs like splinters, stealing any possibility of sleep from me. Every time I close my eyes, I see his face when he said it: *You were never supposed to matter this much.*

I wish I could decide which part hurt more. That I mattered, or that he regretted it. When the sun crests over the mountain tops and fills the room with a thin sheen of light, the cabin is quiet and none of my hurt has eased. My face feels swollen, my chest aching, but I refuse to let myself lie in bed like a wounded animal.

I force myself to move. If I don't, I'll drown in the four walls closing in around me. Sebastian is already awake, boots on, coat half-zipped, heading for the door without a glance in my direction. His eyes flicker once, enough to confirm I'm alive, and then he's gone, the latch clicking behind him. A few weeks ago, that would've gutted me. Today, I let it roll off my shoulders like I'm practicing the art of letting go. I don't let him see me falter.

I make breakfast myself. I read while I eat, forcing my eyes to stay on the page even when I feel his presence taking up space in the room. I train on my own before he returns. Clumsy, imperfect drills, but mine. I don't join him in the yard at our usual time. I wash the dishes slowly, methodically, grounding myself in the small tasks I can control. And when the panic tries to rise, that familiar tightness that squeezes my lungs when I think of danger or isolation or Sebastian's coldness, I breathe through it. I didn't survive the night I was taken by being helpless. I didn't make it through the woods by being weak. Maybe he saved my life, but I've kept myself alive too.

The days grow colder and shorter when the snow starts. Small flakes at first. Gentle and forgettable. *Relatable.* Sebastian retreats deeper into himself, moving like a shadow through the cabin. He doesn't tell me where he's going before he leaves. He doesn't ask how I slept and I've made sure he can't check on me at night anymore by securing the lock on the door out of spite.

He doesn't sit near me at breakfast and eventually, he stops asking about training, too. Fine. If he needs the space, I'll give it to him. But I won't let myself crumble because of it. I pull one of his oversized coats from the closet, ignoring the pang I feel when his scent hits my senses, and start doing the work he used to do. Tidying, reorganizing supplies, counting the canned food, sweeping the floors. Not because it's required but because I can.

Because I want to reclaim some sort of the control that I'd so willingly relinquished to him.

I continue to go over the training steps he taught me, memorizing the motions until they feel like mine instead of borrowed pieces of his world. If he looks in my direction at all, it's brief. But I catch the surprise when he notices I'm not curled in bed or watching the window for him. I'm moving. Breathing. *Surviving.* With or without him.

The quiet between us changes shape. It's not jagged anymore. Not sharp with the remnants of our forgotten touches or our last fight. It's flatter now, wider. A space too large to stitch back together. He barely speaks and I don't try anymore. But I'm not allowing myself to drown, not the way I thought I would. I've stopped trying so hard to read every shadow on his face. Stopped waiting for him to break first. Instead, I create my own rhythm.

Even when it blends together painfully, I push forward. I cook and I read. I practice my drills, I clean, and I breathe. I listen to the wind whisper through the trees and I watch the snow stack quietly outside the window. It's not freedom but maybe...maybe it's strength. And when I catch a glimpse of myself in the mirror that night, messy hair, cheeks flushed from exertion, eyes tired but determined, my reflection has changed.

I'm not the same girl who first walked into this cabin. I'm not even the same girl who fell apart in his arms. Somewhere in the tension, the heartbreak, the betrayal, I found something steadier inside myself. Maybe it's survival, or growth. I'm not sure the name of it. But whatever it is... it keeps me going without needing him to breathe.

That night, as I curl under the blankets alone, the world is quiet except for the faint hiss of snowfall piling up on the roof. And when morning comes, I pull open the curtains and breathe a soft gasp. The world outside is transformed, blanketed in white. Something inside of me cracks.

A softness, a memory, a longing I haven't let myself feel in days. I try to hold on to the peace that seems to transfer into me from the undisturbed outdoors as I move to the living room, choosing to stay there and watch the snow fall through the frosted glass of the window, unbothered by his company.

37

Sebastian

I hear her before I see her. Her footsteps glide across the creaking floorboards quietly, like she's trying not to disturb me, before she settles in front of the window. For days now, she's moved like a ghost. Silent, careful not to brush against me or linger too close. And I deserve it. Hell, I *earned* it. But this morning, her voice graces the room like the breath of air I didn't know I needed.

"It's snowing." The words are soft. Like she's testing whether her voice still matters in this space. The sound settles something within me that's been on edge for days. I stay leaning against the counter, arms crossed over my chest, but my eyes are glued to her. "I know."

She tries again, trying to bridge the gap I put between us. Trying to talk like we used to, easy and open. "Snow always makes everything look softer," she murmurs. "Even the ugly stuff." I want to say something back. Anything to let her know that I'm listening. That I want to hear what she has to say, that her voice settles every buzzing nerve under my skin, that my arms ache to hold her again and my heart calls out for her in the silence.

But if I give her an inch, I'll give her everything. So, I bite my tongue. She lets out a faint exhale, fogging the window. I see her shoulders slumped in her reflection, her gaze downcast. She moves like her limbs are heavy. I can tell she's frustrated, lonely even in my company. And still trying. Then, she glances back at me and my heart stutters in response. I don't have time to process it before she announces "I'm going outside."

Every muscle in my body locks, my spine going rigid as alarms sound in my head. "No, you're not," I scoff at her. She turns to me fully, one brow arched. "That wasn't a question." My brow furrows as I meet her eye. "It wasn't an option," I shoot back, my tone hardening.

The laugh she returns is full of disbelief, unphased completely by the finality I tried to convey. "*Relax*, Sebastian. I'm not planning a dramatic morning run through the mountains. I just want air before I lose my mind. I'll be fine."

The jab lands harder than she realizes. Because I know I'm the reason she feels trapped. I'm the reason she feels caged. And I hate myself for it every second of the day. I'd do anything to take it back. To go back to holding her like she's the only thing that keeps me afloat and kissing her until it felt like my lungs were collapsing. Anything but let her in.

I can't let her outside alone, not when she'd be so exposed. Not after I was ambushed. "Savannah." I straighten, taking a slow step toward her, like she might bite if I move too fast. My voice comes out steadier than I feel. "It's snowing. It's cold. You're not stepping out there unless I'm beside you." She rolls her eyes like it's the stupidest thing she's ever heard—dramatic, exaggerated, absolutely intentional. And somehow, despite everything, it's the most alive she's looked in days. There's fire in her again, sparking behind her eyes and on the tip of her tongue when she speaks. *God*, I missed seeing her like this.

"God forbid I inhale fresh air unsupervised," She snaps back, her tone razor-edged and purposeful. It lands exactly where she wants it to, square in the center of my chest. My heart plummets. For a split second, the hurt must show because I blink it away, forcing my expression back into something neutral, something safe.

"It's just for a minute," She sighs, the venom softening into something weary. "Just to feel something real. Something that isn't these four walls. Please."

Something real. The words echo through me like a hollow shell. Like she honestly believes everything we shared, everything I'm still fighting myself not to reach for, was nothing. That I imagined it. That *she* imagined it. She isn't asking permission. But she doesn't want my refusal either. She just wants...something. Anything that doesn't feel like the prison I've built around her.

I pause, jaw tight and grinding, breath burning in my lungs. *Fuck.* I know she needs this, but every instinct I have screams at me to stop her. To keep her inside these walls where I can shield her. Where no one can touch her. Where I don't have to fear losing her with every minute that passes. I exhale sharply through my nose, fingers curling absently into fists at my sides. "You think I don't want to give you that? You think I wouldn't give you everything you've asked for if I could?" The defeat bleeds into my voice before I can swallow it. "You think this is *easy* for me?"

I wish she understood what I meant. That I wasn't only talking about her misery here. Nothing about this is easy. Not ignoring her. Not moving through our days separately. Not pretending what happened between us wasn't the closest thing I've had to peace in years. Not watching her slip away because I told myself I had to let her. "The people that are out there," I force out, the words as sharp as blades on my tongue, "They want you gone."

Her gaze snaps to mine, accusation and pain swimming in her eyes. "And you don't?"

My lips part, closing again into a hard line before I finally find words. My eyes lock onto hers, desperate and raw. "Not for a second." I can't blame her. I've given her every reason to think I'm pushing her away for good. That she's a burden. That she shouldn't trust me. I step toward her again, scanning the world outside the window, checking shadows, counting risks. "Five minutes." Before I even finish the words, she's already glowing and reaching for my spare coat like she's been waiting days to breathe. "Not a step beyond the porch," I warn, but I'm not sure that she hears me.

And then she *smiles*. A real one.

It hits me so hard I forget how to breathe. I follow her toward the door, pulse kicking against my ribs. I sober myself quickly as I grab my own coat. "And if anything feels wrong, we come back inside. Understood?" Her grin doesn't falter, not even a little, as she nods. And for one impossible moment, I let myself believe this could be enough. These fleeting moments of her happiness. Allowing her these small freedoms to feel like she has some sort of control.

Cold air invades the room when I pull the door open, carrying fine flakes of snow that contrast her dark hair. She closes her eyes, breathing it in like she's starving for it. For a split, cruel second, I wish things were different. That she could have this moment without fear hanging over it. That I could give her everything she wants just to see her smile again.

It's short lived before my thoughts are interrupted. A scrape cuts through the quiet, metal on metal. I tense instantly, arm snapping back to move her behind me. She goes willingly. Too willingly. Even now, she trusts me more than she should.

"Sebastian—" Her voice trembles, and I curse myself for letting things get this far. My hand finds the knife inside my coat. If it's close quarters, the knife is faster. Cleaner. The noise comes again, misplaced in our quiet, sheltered world. I feel her fingers grip my coat sleeve and it nearly undoes me. Even after everything, she still reaches for me. Still believes I can keep her safe. "Go back inside," I command as I take a cautious step forward. "Wait," her voice is desperate and it rips me wide open, but I'm already moving. "Don't leave me alone—" she pleads from behind me.

A voice booms through the trees, familiar enough to break years of instinct and stop me in my tracks. "Sebastian!" I freeze with recognition. *No. Not now.* The gate swings open. A broad figure emerges through the snow, sandy hair dusted white from the weather, moving with that same cockiness he always has. "You better still be alive, you bastard!" he calls, grinning like this is a reunion at a bar instead of a goddamn compromised safety zone. I step out onto the porch, jaw tight. "...*Jesse?*"

He barks a relieved laugh. "I swear to God, man—you fall off the map for over a month and that's all you've got to say? I was ready to start digging through snow drifts for your corpse." He steps fully into view, posture loose and easy, so painfully opposite the rigid tension locking up my shoulders.

"What the *hell* are you doing here?" I snap.

His smirk fades, replaced by something more serious. "You missed our check-ins. All of them. I got worried, dude." I pinch the bridge of my nose, a frustrated breath clouding the air. Our check-ins. Of course. How the hell did I let that slip? How could I have been so careless? So reckless? "I'm *fine*," I mutter, clipped and unconvincing.

"You think that's the point? You know the deal. One of us goes dark and the other responds." he fires back, irritation sharpening his words. My throat tightens in agitation, but I press my lips into a thin line, respecting his rank before I speak.

His gaze sweeps over the cabin before landing on Savannah and locking in place, his expression falling almost dumbfounded. I feel her shift behind me and instantly, guilt floods my chest. My whole body tenses, instinct roaring to life. "Well, I'll be damned," Jesse whistles, and the asshole beams. "She's even prettier than the intel photos." Immediate, territorial heat surges through me. I step forward before I even breathe, positioning myself between them, blocking his view of her completely. "She's not your concern," I seethe.

"Are you forgetting who you're talking to?" He asks, brows forming a crease as he squares his shoulders, taking another step closer to the porch. "Everything you do is my concern, Bash. Especially when you disappear off grid with the one girl the entire east division is trying to hunt down." His words hit like a crack of thunder. And behind me, I feel Savannah go still.

38

Savannah

The tension between the two of them dissolves into the snow as quickly as it appeared. Jesse steps under the porch roof like he owns the place, arms crossed, shoulders relaxed, wearing a smug little smirk that practically expels familiarity. I know instantly he and Sebastian go way back.

I recognize him from the photograph of his unit. Younger, but smiling beside a much different version of Sebastian. "I've gotta say, Bash...you drop off the map and go dark and it turns out you're holed up in the woods with a girl?" Jesse clicks his tongue, chuckling. "Didn't picture you as the romantic-getaway type."

My head tilts curiously at the nickname—*Bash*. I feel Sebastian stiffen in front of me, muscles coiling tight. A small smile threatens to rise on my features. "It's not like that," he growls. "You know that." And just like that, whatever flicker of humor I felt snuffs out.

"Uh-huh." Jesse hums, like he doesn't believe a word. His attention slides to me then, openly assessing me like I'm a classified file he wasn't cleared for. "She *is* pretty. Never did

263

get a good look at her before." I shift behind Sebastian's shoulder awkwardly, torn between shrinking away and standing my ground. I hug my arms around my core, unsure if I'm supposed to feel flattered or intimidated.

I don't know if this is normal banter between the two of them or if he's purposefully aiming to get a rise out of Sebastian—but it *works*. His entire body goes rigid and I swear I can see steam rising off of him. Before I can take another breath, he steps half a pace in front of me, shielding me completely. A barrier, a form of warning. I should be annoyed, but the wave of protectiveness radiating off him is too fierce to ignore. It courses through me into hopeful places I'd laid to rest days ago.

Jesse's grin widens at the display, absolutely thrilled to get a reaction. "Oh *wow*. Look at you, lover boy," He muses when Sebastian steps in front of me. I edge a little closer to Sebastian's arm without meaning to, looking for comfort, survival, something deeper I refuse to name. But I lift my chin all the same. "Thank you," I say, cutting into the conversation and letting a sweet smile slide into place. It's for Jesse, technically. But the sting behind it? That's for Sebastian and he knows it. I can practically hear the hostility crackle through him.

"*Savannah*." My name leaves him through clenched teeth, full of warning, almost pained. I shouldn't enjoy the reaction. But after days of silence? After feeling invisible? I'm proud to have earned it. More than I'd admit aloud.

Jesse snorts in amusement at the exchange. "Holy shit, there's tension already. This is better than cable." Sebastian snaps his glare toward him, sharp enough to cut steel.

"What exactly are you doing here?" He asks, defensive

than curious. Jesse shrugs easily, still smirking. "Well. Since you decided to play Houdini and I drove through two counties of wilderness to get here, I figured I'd check whether you were dead."

"Funny," Sebastian mutters.

Jesse gestures between the two of us, brows lifting. "So, you wanna explain why you're breaking protocol? Or why *she's* here? Because I know you, Bash, and you follow rules like religion." My stomach sinks. *Protocol? Rules?* There are pieces of this puzzle I still don't have and both men know it. My annoyance from earlier resurfaces, flushing my cheeks and tightening my throat.

All this time and I'm still left in the dark. Sebastian exhales harshly, a misty cloud puffing into the air in front of him and a heavy weight settling between his shoulders. Jesse watches him too closely with eyes that are bright and curious, prying despite the banter.

I feel exposed, caught in the crossfire of secrets I was never supposed to know. Jesse's posture shifts, amusement dimming with impatience. "You gonna tell me what's going on? Or do I have to guess?" Sebastian shakes his head once. "I'm not explaining it."

Jesse blinks, stunned at the direct denial. "You're kidding, right? I was on that mission too."

My head jerks up toward Sebastian. My voice feels small when I speak despite all the emotions bubbling inside fighting for attention. "*Mission...?*"

Jealousy sparks at the fact that this man knows more about what's going on than I do and I'm the one living it. My heart beats too hard in my chest, the air thinning more with each passing exchange.

I knew there were things I didn't understand and I was

still aware that I don't have any of the details. But hearing it said like this, so casually, makes it feel like there was an entire world underneath my feet I didn't know I was walking on. "No. Not now," Sebastian snaps before I can say more.

A flicker of confusion crosses Jesse's face, quick, but real. The strain between them shifts, pulling more taut, like some invisible line of trust has been broken. Jesse runs a hand through his hair, sighing. "Alright. Look. If you're in something serious, I can help. That's why we do the check-ins. That's why I came out here."

"I don't *need* help," Sebastian cuts in.

"Maybe not," Jesse retorts before he can say anything else, eyes narrowing. "But you sure as hell need *something* because you look like you've slept maybe an hour since I saw you last. Not to add, last time you acted like this? We were in Helmand Province and you were bleeding through your gear." My breath catches so sharp in my throat that I nearly choke, sputtering a cough. *Helmand.* A place I only recognize because of the photo. A younger Sebastian, the reflection of a different life, an entirely different world. I look up at him now and he looks like a man being peeled open.

"I'm handling it, Pierce." Sebastian says, but his voice...it cracks. Only a little, but enough that I notice and for Jesse's expression to soften with reluctant understanding. Jesse studies him then sighs, long and resigned, when he nods.

"Whatever, *Hayes*," He drops and it dawns on me that I'm just now learning Sebastian's last name. Another small piece of his life that's been left in the dark. "Keep your secrets. Just know I'm not leaving until you stop acting like a cornered animal," Jesse adds.

A shiver slithers down my spine at his declaration that

he's staying. My heart sinks and I feel...violated. Like Sebastian and I's private little world that we've created is being invaded. Logic fights with emotion, telling me I have no right to feel this defensive. It's not like this could ever be permanent, anyway. The woods feel too open, too quiet. I can tell Sebastian feels it too by the way his shoulders lock up again.

Before either of them can speak or I can think any better of it, the words tumble out of me, "Come in." I'm not sure what expression I'm wearing based on the confusion written on both of their faces when they turn my way. Frightened? Steady? Determined? Maybe all three. My hands curl into the sleeves of Sebastian's coat, grounding me before I can regret it. "Both of you," I say, quieter this time.

Jesse tilts his head, eyes flicking to Sebastian, like he's seeking approval. "Thought you didn't want company."

"I *don't*," Sebastian snaps, though the edge softens as his warm hand hovers at my back, guiding me toward the door. I relish in the first lingering touch I've felt since our fight. "But we're staying out here too long," he adds. I glance up at him, hope stirring recklessly around the ache in my chest. He won't look at me directly, but he doesn't move away either.

Jesse must notice the unease in his voice, because the amusement fades quickly, replaced by something more earnest. "Sebastian," he levels, "what are you worried about?" Sebastian doesn't answer. He shakes his head, gets us both inside, and locks the door—every bolt, every latch, sealing us in tight.

The moment the locks click into place, the cabin feels smaller than it ever has. Warmer in a way that has nothing to do with the fire crackling across the room. I tug off the oversized coat and hang it in its natural place by the door, suddenly feeling too exposed without it. Sebastian steps back from the door first, shoulders rigid, posture guarded like he's waiting for something to go wrong.

Jesse stands in the middle of the room absolutely unbothered, hands on his hips, snow melting into droplets at his boots as he scans the space with the casual confidence of someone who's walked into danger enough times to stop flinching. And then there's me, suspended somewhere between them. Or maybe pulled in both directions at once. Jesse's eyes land on me again, curious and too knowing at the same time—and I have to force my spine straight under his gaze.

"So," he says, loud enough to fill the entire living room with his voice alone and I stop myself from flinching. He claps his hands with a loud boom before rubbing his palms together. "This is where you've been hiding. Cozy." He lifts the edge of the blanket thrown across the couch, inspecting it before he drops it again. "Didn't realize you went domestic, Bash."

Sebastian's jaw ticks so sharply I swear I hear it. "It's not—" Sebastian starts.

"—*like that*," I finish for him under my breath, bitterness curling at the edge of my tongue. He glances at me at the same moment Jesse does and the weight of both stares makes my skin prickle. I drop my gaze too quickly. Jesse huffs a laugh, head tipping back. "Could've fooled me."

My insides twist, tired, raw, and worn thin from weeks of holding onto too many secrets. Sebastian steps closer to me, subtly, like he's not even aware he's doing it. A quiet instinct. A silent claim. I pretend not to notice. Or...I pretend it doesn't make my stomach flutter.

But at the same time, I feel the irritation lingering beneath it all. Irritation that he acts like he has the right to claim at all after pushing me away. Irritation that he has the nerve to step closer when he's let me feel so alone. Jesse raises his brows at the move, and suddenly I feel like I've been dropped into the middle of a conversation they've been having long before I existed in a language that only belongs to them. A world I'm still on the outside of.

"Well," Jesse starts again, crossing his arms as his attention fixes fully, directly, disarmingly on me. "*Savannah.* Did Bash over here happen to mention me at all?" My lips part when he calls me by name, catching me off guard the way he says it like we've known each other for a lifetime already. I clear my throat as if it will muster up an ounce of courage, facing this man who's a stranger to me but clearly someone important to Sebastian. "No," I say honestly. "He doesn't tell me much at all." I feel Sebastian stiffen beside me and I can read his expression without having to look at him.

Jesse's smile falters. Not out of pity, but some sort of understanding. A flicker of something softer slips through his expression, just for a moment. "Yeah," he glances at Sebastian with a knowing look, "he's always been a real open book." The sarcasm is thick as molasses.

Sebastian exhales through his nose, rolling his eyes at the exchange. I step a little farther into the room, no longer content to hover behind Sebastian like a shadow. I feel Jesse's gaze follow the movement, thoughtful, weighing me the same way Sebastian does, but with no hesitation behind it. If Sebastian looks at me like I'm breakable, Jesse looks at me like I'm capable.

It's jarring, maybe a little intoxicating, and dangerously refreshing. "So this is the girl," Jesse says, leaning back against the arm of the couch with too much familiarity as hazel eyes drift back to Sebastian. "The one you've been off grid for. The reason command's been losing their damn minds."

Sebastian snaps, "Jesse." He attempts to close the door on the conversation like he so skillfully does with me. But Jesse...he's unphased. "What?" Jesse lifts his hands in surrender. "Not like she doesn't deserve to know somebody's going insane on her behalf." My heart thuds hard enough to hurt.

Sebastian shifts and takes another small step forward, like he's trying to put out a fire with his own body. "Enough," he says, voice low, controlled, but fraying around the edges. Jesse looks between us and I can see the realization slowly clicking into place. As if he's finally, truly piecing this all together.

"Oh," he says quietly. A smirk spreads, slow and pleased, brows waggling. "*Oh*, I see." Sebastian stills like he's been shot right there in the middle of the room. I feel warmth climb into my cheeks, stupid and embarrassing, and I hate that Jesse sees it. I hate that anyone sees anything when my entire world has been crumbling at the edges since the night Sebastian pulled away from me. I hate that my stupid face reveals everything I'm thinking before I'm ready to speak it aloud. But Jesse's smirk only grows. "Come on, Bash. I'm not blind." He gestures between the two of us. "Anyone with a pulse could tell there's something going on here."

"There isn't." Sebastian bites out. The denial, again. The crack of my heart, again, sharp enough to puncture. Jesse's smirk fades with a curious tilt of his head, brows puckered feigning confusion. His gaze shifts to me. Sharper now, more perceptive. "Is that true, Savannah?"

My lips part and I pause before I speak. My name feels foreign leaving his lips and I don't know what answer I'm supposed to give. What answer I *want* to give. So, I just stand there. My eyes land on Sebastian, who's looking at me the way he did the day he shut the door in my face. Regret boiling beneath the surface, pain he refuses to acknowledge, a fortress locking itself tight again.

And Jesse sees all of it. He whistles low. "Man," he mutters, half-amused and half-sympathetic, "you really must've screwed this one up." The words slice straight through the room. Sebastian's gaze snaps to him, lethal and daring. But I almost laugh. Because it is true. There is nothing going on. And I was so, so foolish to think there ever was, or could ever be, anything real between us. The air in the room pulls tight, like a rope fraying knot by knot.

I clear my throat, reaching blindly for something to anchor myself to. To distract myself before either of them see the truth that burns behind my eyes. "Um—would you...like some coffee?" I manage, forcing my voice steady as I turn toward Jesse. I offer a tight grin, my hands clamped together in front of me.

His grin brightens like I just handed him ammunition. "Sure, darlin', that'd be great." *Darlin'?* The word lands like a spark in my stomach. Sebastian tenses so violently the air seems to thicken. I pretend not to notice and slip into the kitchen before the heat in my face betrays me. I focus on the motions. Pour, settle the mug, breathe. But I still feel two gazes on me: Jesse's openly curious, Sebastian's storming behind me like thunderclouds rolling in over a tumultuous sea.

Ignoring the sting of blue eyes burning into my back, I bring the cup back and hand it to Jesse. His fingers brush mine in an intentional, featherlight tease. I feel it everywhere, my body betraying me, and I swallow thickly, the corner of my lips twitching.

"Aren't you sweet," he says, giving me a wink beneath his lashes. My grin spreads unwillingly and I take a seat on the couch, pulling my legs up beneath me. My face floods with warmth just as Sebastian moves. He sits beside me on the couch—no, *into* me. Squishing himself between Jesse and I. His thigh presses firmly against mine, the pressure warm and unyielding, staking a silent claim he won't speak aloud. I stop myself from glaring in his direction at the audacity of only acknowledging me now that we have an audience—even when my heart skips a ridiculous beat at the contact.

Jesse's brows lift in amusement over the rim of his mug. "So," I start, clearing my throat again and fixing my gaze on him, "how long have you two known each other?"

He leans back, stretching an arm along the couch behind him. "'Bout ten years. Since the academy. He was grumpy back then too."

I bite back a laugh. "Always been like this?" I ask innocently, "Any tips for how to handle his mood swings?"

Sebastian cuts me a warning glare so sharp I almost feel it on my skin. It does nothing to stifle the giggle clearing my throat. Jesse ticks his tongue against the roof of his mouth. "Mood swings? Oh darlin', that's generous. Bash here used to glare at his own shadow." I snort—an involuntary, poorly concealed snort.

Sebastian bristles beside me, grumbling quietly. "That's a tad dramatic."

Ignoring him completely, Jesse grins wider. "But he's softened up a little, I guess." He nods toward me, "clearly."

Sebastian inhales sharply, jaw ticking. "Jesse. Knock it

off."

"What?" Jesse asks, shrugging with a playful innocence that fools no one. "I'm just makin' conversation."

"Exactly, *Bash*." I muse, drawing out the nickname intentionally, taking the opportunity to twist the knife just a little more. I turn my attention back to Jesse. "He never answers anything when I ask. Guess it takes having an audience." Sebastian's head snaps toward me, narrowing his eyes in a way that promises a conversation we are absolutely not having in front of company.

Jesse leans forward, elbows on his knees. "Well then, Savannah..." The way he says my name is warm, teasing. "Any other questions I can answer? Since Bash here likes to keep secrets. Some things never change."

"That's enough," Sebastian growls under his breath, hands curling in his lap.

"Okay," I say quickly, before this erupts into a testosterone-fueled showdown in the living room. My palms clap loudly against my thighs before I stand, shooting Jesse an apologetic smile. "Excuse us one second."

I grab Sebastian's wrist, ignoring his startled resistance, and drag him down the hallway. His boots scrape against the floor as he follows reluctantly. As soon as we're out of sight of the living room, I whirl on him, my finger lifting to jab accusingly at his chest. "You don't *get* to be jealous, you don't get to be annoyed, and you certainly don't get to control my conversations," I hiss, keeping my voice low. "*You* broke up with *me*, in case you forgot."

His eyes flare, lips parting in shock. "We weren't—Savannah, that's not—"

"You *did*," I whisper harshly. "You ended us before we even got to *be* anything. So if I want to have a conversation with someone that actually answers my questions? That's *my* choice, not yours." He steps closer, towering, frustration hiding behind his eyes. I stand my ground, straightening my shoulders and lifting my chin to steady my gaze on his.

"I was protecting you. You know that," he speaks through clenched teeth.

My arms cross defensively over my chest and I shake my head at him, barking a laugh full of disbelief. "From what? Getting hurt?" My voice cracks before I can shield it. "Yeah, good fucking job, Sebastian." Silence fills the space between us, heavy, trembling, and blistering with everything neither of us has said out loud. His jaw clamps so tight that the muscle jumps in his cheek.

Behind us, down the hallway, a muffled snicker sounds. Jesse. He heard—*all of it.* My heart sinks at the noise, cheeks flaming with realization. Sebastian's face drains of color, then flushes with fury. He exhales hard through his nose, shutting his eyes like he's trying to force oxygen back into a drowning set of lungs. "I need to do a perimeter sweep."

Of course he does. He turns, shoulders tight, and stalks toward the back door. And just like that...Sebastian disappears into the snow. Again.

39

Sebastian

The cold hits me like a vise around my lungs the second I step off the porch. I need it. Need something sharp to remind me that I'm alive and keep me from unraveling completely. My boots sink into fresh snow, already covering the tracks from the three of us on the porch. My head pounds as I breathe in the crisp air. I force my senses outward. I scan the tree line, shadows, watch the wind direction, listen to the sound of distant branches. Anything but the echo of Savannah's voice in my head. *You broke up with me.* I grit my teeth and start the perimeter sweep, but my focus scatters. I can't get it out of my mind. Not this time. The hurt in her eyes. The accusation. The goddamn truth behind it.

I didn't break up with her. I tried to distance myself. For her safety, for my sanity. But the result was the same, wasn't it? She felt abandoned, cast aside like none of it ever mattered. And Jesse hearing that entire argument...Perfect. Exactly what I needed. I circle around the back of the cabin. Everything's clear. No tracks but mine and the faint, older ones from earlier in the evening. I run a gloved hand down my face and exhale a curse into the frozen air.

Why did she ask Jesse if I was always like this? Why did she smile at him like that? Why did it *bother* me so much? I know why. I've always known why. I just keep trying to kill the truth before it reaches the surface. Deny myself before it does any more damage than it already has. I loop back to the front porch. Jesse is standing there now, leaning against the support beam, breath fogging in the cold, watching me like I'm some rabid animal he's deciding whether to approach. "Thought you were gonna keep walking 'til spring," he says lightly. I stomp snow off my boots but I don't answer, keeping my gaze cast downward.

"You good?" His tone drops, still casual, but probing. I pause again, and despite the frigid winter air, my blood runs hot all the way through to my fingertips.

"No," I finally muster an ounce of honesty. He nods once, like he expected that.

"You wanna talk about it?" He asks.

I scoff, throwing him a brief scowl, "No."

He snorts in response. "Terrific. This is going well already." I shoulder past him into the cabin. Jesse follows, shutting the door behind us. Savannah is nowhere in sight, probably hiding in the bedroom, avoiding round two of our disaster. Good. Safer that way. At least, safer for my health at the moment. Jesse plants himself by the table, arms folded, studying me through narrowed eyes. "Like I said earlier," he starts, "you really screwed this one up."

I glare at him, but he just raises a brow. "What would you know about it?" I snap.

"Come on, man," he says, "I've seen you take a bullet to the vest and react less dramatically than you did when she said you broke up with her."

"Jesse—"

"And the way you looked at me when I called her pretty?" He clicks his tongue with a shake of his head. "Bash, if looks could kill, I'd be six feet under."

My chest tightens and I shrug off my jacket, busying my hands, trying to do the same with my mind, "Drop it."

He ignores that entirely. "You're in love with her," he states like it's fact, etched into stone and unable to be erased. Is it really that obvious? The words hit harder than the cold ever could. I glance up at him and pray that he can't see everything I'm not saying written across my face. "I'm not—"

He cuts me short, "You are."

"No," I repeat, sharper. "This isn't—"

"Spare me," he mutters. "I've watched you bleed in sandstorms. I've watched you crawl out of blown-out buildings. I've watched you haul me halfway across a hillside when my leg was full of shrapnel. I know you better than anyone." He leans forward. "And I've *never* seen you like this."

I look away. My hands curl at my sides. My pulse spikes, ringing in my ears, thumping against my chest so hard I'm not sure it won't jump out. Because he's right. And I can't admit it. Not when loving her endangers her. Not when the mission, the threat, the entire reason I'm here is because she's already a target.

Jesse sighs heavily, rubbing the bridge of his nose. "Look," he says, quieter now, "I get it. You're scared."

My jaw locks together. "I'm not scared."

"You're terrified." He gestures around the room. "At what's out there. At what's in here," He taps his chest. "And especially at what's in you. What's in both of us. That darkness. That drive."

I freeze, my breath heavy between us. Jesse softens, just slightly. "You think keeping her at arm's length is protecting her, right? But from what I've seen already, you're hurting her worse than anything outside this cabin ever could." Guilt breaks through my ribs gnawing and dull, like a bruise that won't heal. I know that he's right. I know what I've done to her. I see it on her face every time she looks at me. I see it in her movements; soft, sluggish, quiet. I see it in the way she doesn't try to joke or tease anymore. I see it in the way she...*exists*. Instead of living.

"I can't lose her," I admit in a low, brutal whisper. "Not after everything." My throat works around the vulnerable admission. One that I'd never have the courage to tell anyone else. "Not like this."

Jesse studies me for a long moment, his expression softer now, serious in a way only a handful of people alive have ever seen. He exhales, slow and steady. "Talk to me, Bash," he murmurs. "There's clearly more going on than what command briefed us on. A hell of a lot more." A muscle in my cheek jumps. My throat goes tight. I release a tense breath and finally take a seat at the table next to him.

"There's a lot you don't know," I start. Jesse's brows lift, but he nods. Not pushing. Just waiting. And for the first time since this mission went sideways, I let some of the truth crack through.

I drag a hand over my face. "The night she left home...nothing that happened was a coincidence." Jesse's posture sharpens, instantly alert. I continue. "Her father's people were already there. They were waiting. Took her to a secluded house off some hidden road up the mountain." I shake my head. "By the time I realized there was a breach in surveillance, it was already too late."

"That's when you went dark," Jesse mutters. I nod, shoulders sagging, "Yeah." He whistles low, but waits for more. And there's more. *Too much more.* I rest my hands on the edge of the table, grounding myself. "When I infiltrated the house, two operators were inside. I took them out but when I secured her, there was another waiting outside." I hesitate before I continue. Before I let the truth detonate. "One of ours."

Jesse's eyes widen, brows shooting upward as he leans up, losing the last bit of casualty in his posture. "You're sure?"

"I'm sure." That image, his face, still imprinted behind my eyes. "It confirmed the breach. They weren't after her father. They were after her." Jesse mutters something under his breath, standing and pacing once across the kitchen. "Jesus, Bash. Why the hell didn't you call it in?"

I bark a humorless laugh. "And tell command one of us flipped? That someone in our unit has been selling intel for months? They're watching for a weak link, Jesse. If I called it in without proof, I'd put her straight into a body bag." Jesse nods, eyes heavy. Understanding. But that's only half the truth. The easier half.

"Alright. And you've been hiding out here since...?" I return the nod before I continue. The memory of the ambush hits like a shove to the chest.

"It's been quiet until last week. I was ambushed at my supply cache. Tracked," I say. "They followed my trail north. One was waiting in the trees, watching for movement. It was Mathers." I look up at him. "He wasn't there for supplies. He was there for information. For her. He's the mole, but I don't think he's been working alone.

"You neutralize the threat?

"Didn't have a choice."

Jesse sighs, scrubbing a hand down his face. The reality settles over us both like a fresh layer of ice. "This is worse than command thinks," he shakes his head, "Worse than any of us thought."

I nod. Because that's the part that keeps me awake every night. And then the part I didn't mean to say surfaces. The part I didn't want to say. "But that's not the entire problem," I force out, voice low. "There's...more."

Jesse straightens, turning toward me and waiting for me to continue. "Go on."

I swallow. Hard. My chest tightens, my lungs refusing to expand. "I've been training her," I say. "Teaching her the basics. Situational awareness. Defense. How to move quietly. How to run."

Jesse's brows climb. "You trained her? Sebastian—You know that's against protocol."

I scoff, as if the rest of this hasn't been. "I had to!" My hand curls into a fist. "She was vulnerable. She had no chance out here on her own if something happened or if I went dark. Someone had to give her a fighting shot."

"And that someone was you," Jesse says. I don't answer. Because we both know it's true. Finally, he asks, quiet but cutting straight through me, "What else, Bash?" The question lands like a pressure point. My breath catches. "There's guilt," I admit, the words scraping out of me like gravel. "A hell of a lot of guilt."

"Because you disappeared with her?" Jesse asks.

"No," I whisper. The knife twists deeper as I finally let the truth hit the air for the first time. "Because you're right. I'm falling for her." Jesse goes completely still. The air between us shifts, like even the walls lean in. He already knew. But saying it out loud, admitting it...that makes it real.

"I shouldn't have let it happen," I say, forcing the words out even as they tear at the inside of my ribs. "I should've kept the line clear. Kept the mission clean. But...the nights here, the training, the fear—*her* fear—she trusted me. And I—" My voice cracks. I clamp my jaw shut before it can break any further. "She depended on me," I finish. "And I failed her by letting it get personal."

Jesse blows out a long, slow breath. "Bash... you didn't fail her."

I laugh, brittle. "Didn't I? I pulled away when things got dangerous. I shut her out. And she—" I shake my head. "She thinks I don't care.

"But you do," he says and it feels more like he's testing my confession than making a statement.

The answer comes easier than breathing. Terrifyingly easy. "Yes," I whisper, "More than I should." Jesse studies me, his expression lost between admiration and disbelief.

"Jesus Christ," he mutters. "You really love her."

I rub a hand over my face, ashamed of the truth but powerless to deny it. "I can't. I can't put that on her. Not with everything going on."

Jesse shifts closer, leaning over the table slightly. "You're not putting anything on her," he says quietly. "You're giving her a choice. She deserves that much. You need to tell her. I could tell from the minute I walked up there was something going on between y'all. And she's clearly feeling the same way."

My gaze drifts toward the hall, mind picturing Savannah, hidden behind the bedroom door. Shielding herself there because of me, again. I know he's right. And it scares me more than anything outside these walls.

"So what now?" He asks, clapping a hand on my

shoulder. I steady my breath, every instinct sharpening.

"We need a plan," I say flatly.

Jesse straightens immediately, the soldier in him displaying front and center, "We'll hit first." My pulse steadies and I nod, purpose returning. Grounding me. "We use her as bait," he continues. I nearly choke, eyes flaring in his direction. "Absolutely not. I'm not risking her."

"It's the only way we draw them out," he argues. I curse under my breath. He's right. They won't come anywhere near her with us around. I scrape a hand over the stubble at my jaw, weighing the risk. The reality. The fact that whether or not I stand still, this doesn't disappear without taking action.

And beneath all of it, Savannah's voice echoing. *You broke up with me.* I didn't. I just didn't know how to hold her and protect her at the same time. Jesse lowers his voice. "If she's willing...we can finish this." My stomach twists. Because I already know she'll be willing. She'd walk into fire if it meant reclaiming her life.

But I'll be damned before I let her burn.

40

Savannah

The cabin is still dim with early morning light when I pad into the kitchen, arms wrapped around myself for warmth. Hoping, praying, that maybe this time Sebastian had stayed. Maybe he'd be sitting at the table with that stoic look softening just a little when he saw me. Maybe he'd offer coffee. Maybe he'd try. But the kitchen is empty and his boots are gone from beside the door. "Of course," I mutter under my breath, rolling my eyes at no one in particular and blinking back the sting I refuse to admit feels like disappointment.

"Damn. Rough morning?" I release a sharp gasp, hand flying to my chest as I whirl in the direction of the voice. Jesse's head pops up over the back of the couch, hair sticking up in every direction, blanket half-draped over him like a man who lost a fight with sleep. He grins, bright and unbothered, rubbing a hand over his jaw. "Good morning, sunshine," he muses. My heart slows, just barely, and despite myself, I smile. "Good morning," a soft laugh escapes me,

"You nearly scared me to death."

He swings his legs off the couch and stretches, shoulders rolling, posture loose and warm in a way Sebastian never is first thing in the morning. Or any time of day, really. "Sorry about that. You're up early," Jesse observes.

I shrug, "Couldn't sleep." Moving to the counter, I reach for a mug and the kettle to fill with water.

"Because Romeo disappeared again?" He asks teasingly. I pause for a beat, then huff a tiny, humorless breath. "Something like that." Jesse watches me with an expression that's far too perceptive for someone who looks like he slept a maximum of four hours on an uncomfortable couch. "He does that," he says. "Runs off before he can think too hard."

My head tilts at the accuracy of the statement. "He just...goes." I admit softly, voice barely audible over the sound of the kettle heating. "Leaves me wondering if he's okay. Or if I did something wrong." Part of me contemplates if these are things I should be admitting aloud. But the other part, the part that's much louder, is so tired of hiding.

"You didn't," Jesse says instantly, firm in a way that nearly knocks the breath out of me. "Trust me. If anything, he's the one screwing things up."

I bite my bottom lip, busying myself with plucking two coffee filters from the cabinet. Jesse joins me in the kitchen, leaning back against the counter. "You okay?" He asks, flicking a lighter to life to light the cigarette that hangs from his lips. The smell crinkles my nose, instantly turning my stomach.

"I'm fine," I lie, because that's easier than unraveling every hurt feeling in my chest.

"You're a terrible liar," he notes with a snort,

"Sebastian's rubbing off on you." That almost makes me laugh. *Almost.* "You have no idea what he was like before you," he adds after a moment, almost casually.

My breath hitches, head turning toward him. "What do you mean by that?"

Jesse's expression softens. "You think he's cold now? Trust me, this is practically angelic compared to the Sebastian I knew overseas." My ears perk. There's that word again. Overseas. "He never told me much," I mumble, turning my mug between my palms and letting the warmth seep into my fingertips until it stings. "About any of it."

"He wouldn't. Not unless he had no choice. And even then..." he shrugs, "he'd chew off his own arm before admitting the way he changed after everything." I swallow, nodding slowly, hesitation tangling the words on my tongue. Sebastian doesn't answer my questions—ever—so I've learned not to prod. But Jesse? Maybe he'd give me *something*. "What was he like? Before?"

Jesse crosses his ankles before him, as if he could relax any more, expression molding into equal parts nostalgia and something else that I can't place. "Hard," he says honestly, a puff of smoke bellowing from his lips and wrapping around answers I've been searching for. "Intense. The kind of guy who shouldered the weight for the whole team because he never trusted anyone else to carry it. Not because he thought we were incompetent but because he thought if anything happened to us, it'd be his fault." My chest tightens, eyes threatening to betray me with full understanding. "That's still him," I whisper.

"Yeah," Jesse agrees quietly. "But you...you made him human again. He's different around you, Sunshine. Hell, he actually did get some sleep last night. You don't know how rare that is." Warmth spreads in my stomach, completely uninvited, thawing a small slice through the hurt that still lives around my heart. I grip the mug tighter, pushing it back. "He barely talks to me now." My gaze drops to my hands.

"Because he's scared," Jesse says with a knowing smirk. "You scare the shit out of him."

I scoff at that, rolling my eyes even when the corner of my lips tug into the hint of a smile. "That's ridiculous. Nothing about me is scary."

Jesse taps a finger over his own heart. "He's afraid of this. Of you." That shouldn't make me feel as hopeful as it does. I shouldn't allow it to swell in my chest. But I do. So I dare another question, one Sebastian would never, ever answer. "What happened to him?" I ask quietly. "Before all of this, that made him change so much?"

Jesse goes still, gaze lifting to the window, remembering something far away and jagged. For a moment, he's silent. "That's not my story to tell," he finally says. "But I can tell you this. Whatever happened, it made him believe he wasn't allowed to want anything for himself."

I try to process that. The pieces are starting to come together, slowly. Why Sebastian is so reserved. Why he won't let me in. Why he always stops himself before things get too real. "And then you came along," Jesse adds gently. "And suddenly he wants something."

Heat pulses in my cheeks. I chew the side of my lip, preventing a ridiculous smile from overtaking my features. I know it's stupid to let my head swim with possibility, my heart bloom with hope, but when it concerns Sebastian...none of it was ever optional. "And that scares him worse than bullets," Jesse finishes, voice low with sincerity.

I exhale shakily, the truth landing in my chest with the

weight of a crushing stone. If Jesse is telling the truth, if I can believe him, Sebastian isn't indifferent. And maybe I did matter. Hope thrums through me with the beat of my heart treading dangerously close to forgiveness. But in the back of my mind, I can't help but prepare myself to be hurt again.

Jesse stands, stretching with a groan after he tabs out the cigarette. "Now that we've had our morning heart-to-heart," he says, flashing me a grin, "how about you tell me what you're making? Coffee smells too good to be for you alone." I laugh, genuinely this time, and pour him a mug.

I slide it over to him before settling across from him at the small table, curling my fingers around my own cup and letting my shoulders finally relax, even if only by an inch. He takes a sip, sighs like it might actually revive him, and kicks his feet up on a chair. It bewilders me how someone as casual as he carries himself ever got along with someone like Sebastian.

"Alright, Sunshine," he says, "what else do you want to know?" My brows lift. "You're just...offering information like that? Sebastian acts like every question I ask is classified." He grins deviously, "He just doesn't like to talk. Somebody's gotta compensate."

I snort into my cup. It feels good talking with him. Natural, easy. I'd almost forgotten what that felt like. "Okay," I say, leaning forward early. "Tell me something about him. Something he'd never tell me."

Jesse hums, pretending to ponder as he taps his index finger on his chin. "Something embarrassing? Or something that'll make you fall even harder for him?" Heat flares in my cheeks and I roll my eyes as if that will convince him that it isn't true. "Let's start with embarrassing."

He grins wickedly. "Excellent choice." He sets his mug

down and gestures broadly with his hands as he speaks. "Back in training," Jesse starts, "Big, scary, broody Sebastian? Your knight in tactical armor over here? His nickname was Boy Scout."

I raise a brow, crinkling my nose. "Why? Because nature is basically his second language?"

"Yeah right. Soldiers aren't that nice." Jesse shakes his head, shrugging one shoulder. "Because he refused to take short cuts, ever. Didn't matter how stupid the rules were, he did everything by the book."

I blink, then snort. "Some things never change, I guess."

"That's not all," he says, growing animated. "Couple guys used to make jokes. Mean, mostly hazing. They wrote it on his locker in red sharpie and everything," he shakes his head. "But when the jokes weren't aimed at him? Bash would get this look on his face. Looking at them like they disappointed him personally." I cover my mouth with my hand when my laugh fills the air. I know exactly the look. "Then his nickname became *Sergeant Boy Scout*. It drove him insane," he finishes.

I imagine it, Sebastian refusing to react, wearing that same unreadable expression like armor. A younger version of him that already knew what he wanted to stand for. "That's ridiculous. So where did Bash come from, then?"

"Oh, that?" Jesse snorts, waving a hand. "That's my personal nickname for him. Kinda literal, actually. Because he used to bash through everything, and I mean *everything*, that got in his way. People, walls, lockers. You name it."

I raise a brow, nodding as the memory of his bruised knuckles from the supply run comes to mind. "Now that one makes sense."

Jesse laughs, another memory clearly taking hold. "You ever play the Mario video games?" I grin as he throws his head back, laughing at his own joke. "Maybe I should've called him Bowser," he finishes once he catches his breath.

The sound of Jesse's laugh is easy, stretching a smile across my face. It's contagious, lifting the weight off my shoulders that's been living there for days easily when I find myself laughing so hard my stomach hurts in reply. Jesse beams like he's accomplished a mission when I swat a playful hand at his shoulder. "Alright," I say when I can breathe again, "give me another."

Jesse downs a sip of coffee, gathering himself. "Okay, this one's sweeter. Don't tell him I said that." I lean in, propping my chin on my hand. My eyes are wide with full attention, exhilarated by his stories.

"One winter," he says, "we got stuck in a remote outpost. Supplies were delayed for days. And there was this stray dog. Old, half-frozen, barely hanging on. I swear Bash acted like he didn't care, but the next morning the damn dog had a blanket, half a protein bar that no one could afford to give up, and a spot right next to his bunk."

My chest warms and I look down at my mug, tugging my lip between my teeth. "He didn't want anyone to know," Jesse adds. "But that dog followed him everywhere for months after."

"That sounds like something he would do," I whisper.

Jesse watches me closely, nodding. "Yeah. He's a hardass. But he's got the biggest damn heart." My throat tightens unexpectedly. "What about..." I pick at my nail, treading forward. I'm finally getting the answers I've wanted for weeks. Finally getting a glimpse into who Sebastian really is. "What about before all of this? Before his job?

Before…everything?" Jesse quirks an eyebrow, "You mean from his childhood?"

"Maybe." I shrug, shaking my head slightly as I lift my eyes to him again. "He won't tell me anything. Did he ever tell stories about it?"

"That tracks." Jesse smirks. "Well, let's see…from what I know, he grew up near the mountains. Quiet kid. Too serious. Always trying to protect people who didn't need protecting."

"So basically the same as always," I murmur, a breathless laugh leaving me.

"Pretty much," Jesse laughs. "But you should've seen the way girls used to look at him, even at basic."

My heart lurches, an unwelcomed pang of jealousy shooting through me. Yeah, I should have expected that. I never allowed myself to think about the girls that came before me. I'm not naive enough to think that there were none, just infatuated enough to hate the thought. "Oh?"

"Oh yeah," Jesse says, grinning into his cup. "Brooding, terrifying, mysterious? They loved that shit. He never noticed. Too busy cleaning guns or training or whatever."

I smile weakly, nodding, and let my eyes fall to my half drank coffee again, the warmth of it lost in conversation. "Still doesn't notice."

"Yeah," Jesse says softly, reaching over to place a knowing hand on my wrist, thumb brushing the skin in an attempt of comfort. "That's what scares him." Before I can respond, the door swings open. Heavy boots hit the porch, cold air surrounding us from all sides. And then, Sebastian steps inside. Snow dusts his shoulders and hair, but it's the look in his eyes that steals all the air from the room. Because he's staring straight at us. At me. At Jesse. Sitting together. Laughing. Talking. Jesse's hand pulling away from my wrist so quickly you'd think I shocked him. His jaw locks so tight I'm not sure he'll ever be able to open it.

My eyes dart to the floor, misplaced guilt constricting my throat. Jesse doesn't miss it. Of course he doesn't. He leans back casually, putting some space between us when he stretches his arms, and says in a too-loud, too-innocent voice, "Morning, Bash. You missed it. Savannah was just asking about your cryptic past. Turns out you've been terrifying since birth." Sebastian's eyes snap to me. Hard, hot, maybe even jealous. My heart slams against my ribs, cheeks flaming. I should've expected this.

He doesn't move at first. He just stands there in the doorway, snow melting off his shoulders, eyes locked on me with that distinctive look like he's trying to decide what to do with me. I straighten instinctively, fingers tightening around my mug. "Morning," I offer, too casually. His gaze flicks to Jesse, narrowing as it lingers. Jesse, of course, looks delighted. Sebastian exhales slowly through his nose, shrugging out of his coat. "I wasn't aware I authorized story time."

I snicker at the seriousness in his tone, earning me a scowl. I open my mouth, close it again, then try, "It was just coffee. Talking."

"Mm," he hums, stepping farther into the room. He takes the chair beside me instead of across the table, crowding my space so his thigh presses against mine again in a manner too deliberate, too possessive, but grounding, nonetheless. My pulse stutters at the contact. Jesse notices immediately and I think I might hate how perceptive he is. His grin turns sharper. "You know," Jesse says, swirling his coffee, "for a guy who insists there's nothing going on here, you're awful territorial."

Sebastian groans, running both hands down his face. "Don't start with that shit, Jesse."

"Oh, I'm just saying," Jesse continues lightly, "you don't usually sit that close to people you don't care about." I clear my throat, suddenly feeling defensive of Sebastian at Jesse's endless teasing.

"Okay, maybe we don't need to psychoanalyze him before breakfast," I shoot Jesse a warning look. Or at least, I try.

He chuckles, proving that it wasn't as sharp as I felt it was. "You're right. Wouldn't want to scare him off." Sebastian's gaze snaps to me. Something unreadable hides behind it. Hurt, maybe, or fear, disguised as irritation. "I'm *not* scared," he says flatly.

Jesse raises a brow, "Didn't say you were."

I hate it. Hate the way it feels like I'm standing between two worlds, tugged in opposite directions. Hate that Sebastian is shutting down again, retreating behind that wall I've been banging my fists against for weeks. "So," I say, forcing brightness into my voice, "Jesse was just telling me about your nicknames." Sebastian freezes just as Jesse loses it, nearly tipping back in his seat.

"Oh my God, you told her about training?" Sebastian snaps, incredulous. Jesse wheezes. "Can't believe you never told her the tale of *Sergeant Boy Scout*."

Sebastian shoots him a glare, gritting through his teeth, "Because it was ridiculous and irrelevant."

"Bash," Jesse says gently, "you haven't changed at all."

I bite my lip, trying, and failing, not to laugh. Sebastian turns to me, exasperated. "You're enjoying this."

"A little," I admit. Something in his expression softens despite himself. Just for a second. And then it's gone again, replaced by that familiar distance. Jesse watches the shift with sharp eyes, "You know," he says quietly, leaning back, "she's good for you."

Sebastian stiffens, his teeth grinding together once more. "Jesse."

"No," he presses. "You're different around her. Happier. And she—" He nods toward me. "She sees you. Even when you're trying like hell to disappear." My throat tightens and that stupid, hopeful flicker runs through me again. Because if Jesse, the only person on this planet who really knows Sebastian, I assume, can see it? Then maybe I'm not crazy, after all. Maybe I didn't make everything between us up in my head.

Sebastian's hand curls against his knee, voice almost strained when he speaks again. "This isn't—"

"—your call anymore?" Jesse cuts him off, "Because from where I'm standing, it stopped being just a mission a long time ago."

I feel Sebastian's thigh tense against mine and I catch his hand curling tighter, into a fist. His breathing changes subtly, but I notice. I always do. "God dammit, leave it alone," he breathes, defeated, his voice almost cracking over the words as his hand smacks against the table. The sharp noise makes me flinch away from him briefly before I can brush it off.

I turn to him, voice softer, letting the hurt at his dismissal roll off my shoulders. Hesitantly, I reach to rest my hand over his beneath the table. "Sebastian...you don't have to shut down every time things get hard. I'm not running and

I wish you wouldn't either."

He looks at me then and I can see the war behind his eyes, the one he's been fighting alone. "I have to," he says quietly. "Because if I don't, I'll make mistakes."

"Caring for me is a mistake?" I ask, and I think cabin fever must be a real thing because no way would I have had the guts to ask that a month ago. I just want to hear him say it. More than overhearing his conversation with Jesse when they thought I was asleep.

Jesse stands, stretching, clearly sensing the shift. "I'm gonna shower," he says lightly. "Try not to kill each other while I'm gone." He disappears into the hallway, still smirking.

Sebastian exhales, rubbing a hand over his face but leaving the other placed securely under mine. "You shouldn't be listening to him."

"I should be listening to *you*," I say gently. "But you don't talk." He looks away and I can feel the hope in my chest crashing again, dwindling as quickly as it appeared. *Please don't shut me out.* I don't have the courage to beg him out loud...again.

"I'm trying to keep you alive," he says. "That's all.

"And what about you, Sebastian?" I ask. "Who keeps you alive?"

His gaze returns reluctantly to mine. For a moment, it looks like he might say something. Something real. Instead, he pushes back from the table. "I need to finish my sweep." I release a slow, defeated sigh. He stands, already retreating, already rebuilding the wall brick by brick. "We'll talk later."

I nod, even though my chest aches. "Okay." My eyes are already blurring before he can leave the room. I busy my hands in his absence by wrapping them around my mug again, hoping what's left of the warmth can thaw out the ice that's beginning to take a permanent presence in my chest. He pauses at the door, just long enough to glance back at me.

His voice is rough when he adds, "Don't go anywhere." As if I could. The door shuts behind him, leaving me with cold coffee, unanswered questions, and the painful clarity that I never should have let myself fall for this man. From the bathroom, Jesse lets out a low whistle. "Yeah," he quips, "you've got him bad."

I roll my eyes, shaking my head, and wishing this cabin wasn't so damn small. "So does he," I grumble to myself.

41

Sebastian

The woods are quiet in that way that never feels accidental.
The cold should clear my head but it doesn't. Snow muffles
everything. My boots, the wind, the world itself. But my head
won't shut up. It replays images I don't want. Savannah
laughing. Jesse leaning back in his chair like he belongs
everywhere. The way her shoulders loosened at his comfort,
his hand on her wrist, *touching* her. The way she doesn't relax
with me anymore. I tell myself it shouldn't bother me. I made
this distance. I chose it. But knowing that doesn't make it
hurt less.

I pause at the edge of the tree line, scanning out of
habit more than necessity. Everything's clear. It always is
when my mind is the real battlefield. I drag a hand down my
face and exhale, watching the fog of my breath disappear into
the cold. She looked...lighter in there. That thought guts me.
The sound of her laughter echoes in my ears; not because it
was loud. But because it was small and surprising, like she'd
forgotten she still knew how. Jesse drew it out of her like it

297

was easy. I hate myself for noticing how easily she talked to him. For the way jealousy coils through my veins.

I should be glad. She deserves the ease. She deserves someone she can talk to without feeling like she's prying open a door with bleeding fingers. I built those doors because when I let people get too close, the world takes that as permission to punish them. So why do I feel like I'm being punched straight through the gut when she smiles at him? Jesse's harmless. I know that. He flirts with everyone the same way, like it's oxygen. He wouldn't do that to me, anyway. Even when I know that if it were a choice? I would lose.

My jaw tightens hard enough to ache and my fingers reach to readjust the knife at my hip just to have something to clutch. Jealousy is pathetic. It's a luxury that men like me don't get to indulge in. And yet, it crawls under my skin and up my throat, hot and ruthless. The way she looked at Jesse and offered him coffee. The way she flushed when he called her *darling*. The way she used that sweetness like a blade pushed straight through my heart. I deserved it. But that doesn't stop my blood from boiling. *Fucking hypocrite.* It shouldn't matter. Not after what I did. Not after I pulled away and pretended we were nothing more than circumstance. Not after I watched her crumble and told myself it was better that way. Better. *For who?*

I exhale into the cold and force my gaze outward again. The woods are still. My senses come online the way they always do. The wind shifts, whistling through the pine needles. Somewhere far off, a branch snaps under the weight of snow. Nothing that doesn't belong. The danger isn't here. Not right now. The danger is in the cabin, in the warm light, in the way Savannah's eyes have looked at me lately. Hurt, trying to be brave. Love trying to survive. *I did that.* I told myself distance was protection, but I can't pretend I don't know what it really was.

Fear. Fear of losing her. Fear of wanting her. Fear of becoming the kind of man who believes he's allowed to keep something good. I circle wider around the cabin, taking the long route to buy time. To let the cold numb the part of me that's too alive, too awake.

My mind drifts somewhere I don't let it go often. Afghanistan. The memory hits without warning, sharp and unwelcome. Heat instead of cold. Dust instead of snow. Sun so brutal it bleached the world around it until everything looked the same: tan, brown, blood-red. The air always smelled like diesel and smoke and something sour underneath. Days ran together. Nights weren't much different.

And in the middle of all of that, there was Ariana.

She showed up one morning like she belonged, head wrapped in a scarf, eyes bright, a sack balanced against her hip like it didn't weigh anything. She couldn't have been more than nineteen. Maybe younger. I was only twenty-two at the time. She brought little things that made a difference when you're down to rationing everything: food, water, medical supplies. Always smiling like the world wasn't falling apart around her.

I remember Jesse calling out to her once, half-joking, trying to scare her off, "You're gonna get yourself killed, you know that?" Ariana only laughed. It was a quick sound, light as air. She lifted her chin, said something in broken English I still hear sometimes when I'm trying to sleep. *If I am afraid, I do nothing. If I do nothing, I am already dead.*

We told her not to come but she never listened. She

reminds me of Savannah in ways I was too young to understand at the time. Brave without realizing it, kind in a way that felt dangerous. Selfless to a fault. She said helping us made her feel useful. Like she mattered. I wish I would have told her how much she did. The unit liked her. More importantly, trusted her. She made all of us feel human for a while. Like there was still a world outside the mission. Like it mattered whether we survived.

I told myself she was just a civilian. A variable. Not mine to protect. Not mine to think about once she walked away. But I watched her leave every time, shoulders disappearing into heat shimmer at the edge of the road, and something in my chest always went tight until she was gone. I didn't call it attachment. I didn't call it care. I called it responsibility. Awareness.

The day we got orders to move out, Ariana came anyway. She pressed a bundle into one of the guys' hands full of dried fruit, clean gauze, and a tiny carved charm she said was for luck. Jesse teased her about it. She looked at me that day too, longer than usual. "Sebastian," she said carefully, like she'd been practicing my name. I remember the way it landed in my chest. I nodded once, didn't speak—I was never good at speaking to people like her. People who weren't afraid to look at you like you were still worth something.

It was a short mission. In and out. Two days of hell. When we came back...there was nothing left. The town was rubble. Smoke. The kind of silence that wasn't peaceful; it was aftermath. I searched for her without admitting what I was doing. I told myself it was procedure. Accountability. But I knew. I always knew.

I never found Ariana. It wasn't just grief. It was a lesson carved into bone. If you let people matter, the world uses them against you. If you let yourself care, you don't just lose them. You lose the part of yourself that believed you could save everyone. So I stopped. I got colder. Sharper. Better. I learned how to keep my heart locked down so tight nothing could touch it, not even me. And it worked. Until Savannah.

The cabin comes into view through the trees, smoke curling lazily from the chimney when I stop walking. Light in the windows. Her silhouette, sitting at the table where I left her. My chest tightens with guilt. Savannah is different from Ariana in a hundred ways. Slightly older, a thousand times wiser. Stronger in ways Ariana never had the chance to become. But the core is the same, this impossible bravery wrapped in kindness, this refusal to fold even when fear is clawing at her throat.

She puts herself in danger because she hates feeling powerless. Because she wants to matter. Because she believes doing nothing is a kind of death. And I see Ariana in that. I see the way I failed then. The way I couldn't stop the world from taking someone so good. And now Savannah is here, inside my cabin, wearing my coat, laughing softly with my only friend, and my heart is doing that stupid, human thing it hasn't done in years. It's choosing.

I stare at the door for a long moment before I move. Because if I go inside, I have to be something other than a wall. If I tell her any of this, I can't take it back. I can't return to distance and pretend it's enough. But I can't keep watching her crumble either. Not after what she said in the hallway. *You broke up with me.* Like I took something from her and refused to admit it existed. I reach the porch and pause, gloved hand hovering near the latch. Through the window, I catch a glimpse of movement. Jesse's shadow moving through the living room, toward where Savannah remains at the table with her mug. Her posture tense, but not collapsed. Her face turns toward him like she's listening, like she's absorbing warmth from a conversation I keep refusing to have.

The sight makes jealousy flare hot in my chest again, sharp and humiliating. And immediately after, relief. Because she's smiling. Because she isn't alone. Because even if she never forgives me, she's still alive. I inhale slowly, forcing the emotion down until it sits heavy and contained. Then I open the door and step inside.

The smell of coffee and woodsmoke invades my senses, mingling with the faint scent of soap that still clings to Jesse even from across the room. She looks up. The smile she'd been wearing, small but real, vanishes so fast it's like it never existed. It shouldn't hurt. It does. "Did you find anything?" she asks, voice careful.

"No," I answer. "All clear." Her eyes hold mine, searching for something. Apology, maybe. Or proof I won't keep disappearing without a word.

Jesse glances between us, reads the room like he always has, and clears his throat. "I'm gonna—uh—check the radio." He grabs his jacket and shoots me a look on his way past that says *Don't screw this up.* The door clicks behind him and the room fills with a thick silence, the kind that hides inevitable truths.

Savannah stays seated at the table, but her shoulders are tight. Guarded. Like she expects me to retreat the second she speaks. I deserve that, too. I take one slow step closer, stopping where I can see her clearly. She looks tired. Not just physically but emotionally, like she's been carrying questions in her bones. I swallow, throat rough. "There's something I need to tell you," I say.

Her brows knit together, her lips puckering the way they do just slightly when she's curious. "Like what?"

I hesitate only for a moment. The words feel like glass in my mouth. I've spent years learning how not to speak about the past. How to tuck it away until it stops existing. But she deserves more than a wall. She deserves the truth.

"At my first deployment," I begin, keeping my voice low, steady, "there was a woman named Ariana." I move a step closer like I'm approaching something fragile. She doesn't interrupt but I catch the falter in her expression. I push forward anyway, hoping that maybe I can give her some sense of understanding.

"She lived near the outpost. She helped our unit. Brought supplies. Took risks she shouldn't have. She was always smiling, even when there was nothing to smile about." My voice sounds far away, even to my own ears. "We told her to stop but she never did. She believed helping was worth it. She wouldn't let us protect her because she thought other people deserved it more."

Savannah nods, listening patiently. Her gaze softens, but there's a tightness there too, like she already knows where this is going. "She was incredibly brave. Kind. Stubborn as hell...like you. Always smiling like the world hadn't chewed her up yet." My lips lift into a small grin. The words settle between us.

Savannah turns toward me slightly, like she can feel my heart reaching for her as I relive the pain over again. "And...what happened to her?"

"We got reassigned for a few days to help finish another mission and—" I clear my throat as my throat works around my words but I don't break her gaze. She deserves this vulnerability. "When we got back," I continue, voice rough, "she was gone. The town was gone. Everything. And there was nothing—*nothing*—I could do about it. I searched for her for weeks. It was pointless. I never found her." Savannah's eyes glisten and she blinks hard, quickly, fighting back the tears like its instinct. Her knuckles pale around her mug. "We never found anyone."

"I'm sorry..." the sympathy in her voice almost undoes me.

I shake my head, brows knitting together as I pierce her gaze with mine, quietly begging for her not just to listen but to *hear* me. "I see the same things in you," I admit. "Your kindness. Your stubbornness. The way you put yourself in danger without thinking twice and it feels like you always put everyone above yourself...." My voice cracks despite myself. "And I've been trying to keep you alive by becoming someone you can't get close to." I force my breath even. "I don't want to lose you," I admit, barely above a whisper. "And I don't trust myself not to if I let this, *us*, matter the way it already does. Caring doesn't make anyone safer. It makes you vulnerable."

She doesn't move right away. Doesn't touch me. Just looks at me like she's finally been handed a piece of the truth she's been aching for. Her voice is small when she speaks. "So that's why you pulled away."

"Yes." Whatever is left of my resolve crumbles around the honesty, chin dipping slightly.

She studies me, hurt and understanding warring on her face. "You think if you don't care, nothing can take me from you."

I flinch, because it's too close to the truth. "I think if I care," I correct, rough, "I'll make mistakes. And mistakes get people killed." Savannah's gaze holds mine. Steady, stubborn, warm in the way only she can be. "You don't get to punish me for something that happened before me."

The words catch me off guard and I shake my head, holding my palms up toward her as if in surrender. "I'm not trying to punish you."

"But you are," she says softly. "You shut me out and I'm the one left alone with it."

I take a small step closer. "I see her in you," I admit quietly. "Not exactly the same—" I shake my head. "But the way you throw yourself into danger for the sake of someone else. The way you insist you can handle it alone." My voice drops. "The way you refuse to be powerless." I see her jaw tighten at my honesty. Maybe because I'm right. Maybe because she doesn't want me to pull away again. "And it scares me," I whisper, the truth raw. "Because I've already watched the world take someone like that. Someone good. Someone brave."

She stands then, slowly, like she's not sure whether she's allowed to cross the distance between us. Her eyes shine, hands trembling at her sides. "I'm not Ariana," she says, voice gentle but firm.

"I know," I answer immediately.

"And I'm not going to disappear just because you're scared," she adds. "Not if you let me in." The words hang there. They're not an ultimatum or a plea, but a choice. My chest aches as my heart does that stupid human thing again, beats like it believes it's allowed to want. I nod, once, slow.

"I promise I will try not to shut you out like that," I say. "Not anymore." It's not a perfect promise. I don't know how to make those. But it's real and it's all I have to offer. Savannah's shoulders sag slightly, relief and exhaustion mixing in her expression. She takes a breath, and when she looks up at me, her voice is soft.

"I don't need you to be fearless," she says. "I need you to be honest." The truth is, I don't know if I can do that without breaking something in myself. But I look at her, standing there, brave even when her eyes are wet, stubborn even when her voice shakes, and I realize I don't want to keep surviving if it means losing her anyway.

I close the space between us and allow my hand to raise for the first time in days to graze across her cheek, slipping to curl around the back of her neck. My chest burns at the contact and I feel my lungs fill with fresh, crisp air being closer to her. "I'm trying," I whisper. "God, Savannah...I'm *trying*." It doesn't fix everything. But it's a start.

"That's all I need." Her words are soft as she wraps her arms around me and I feel her fingers curl into the fabric against my back like she's afraid I'll evaporate. And I can't blame her for that. But what I can do is wrap my arms around her and pull her close, show her that I won't retreat.

Because I've spent years letting moments die before they could matter. Because I'm tired of burying everything before it has a chance to breathe. Because this time, I'm not letting her go.

42

Savannah

I don't move when I hear the creak of the porch under the weight of Jesse's boots. I should. Part of me knows I probably look ridiculous. Weak, still tucked close to Sebastian, still resting in the space he hasn't taken back yet. But the moment feels too fragile to break just because someone else noticed it. "Well, *look at that*," Jesse says easily once he saunters into the kitchen. I feel Sebastian's breath change before I feel his body tense. "Guess you two kissed and made up."

Heat floods my face. Sebastian stiffens fully now, his arm dropping away like he's suddenly remembered himself. The space between us opens, cold and immediate. I swallow, fingers curling at my sides as if they don't know where to go without him there. My fingertips burn with the need to have him close again, the moment taken too quickly when I just got him back.

Jesse rubs his hands together as he looks between us, a mischievous smile spreading on his features. "Damn. I miss all the good stuff, don't I?" I glance up at Sebastian and he doesn't look amused. I don't either, not really, but there's something grounding in the way Jesse says it. Like affection is normal. Like closeness doesn't have to be something hidden or dangerous. Like it's okay to be vulnerable.

Then Jesse tilts his head, grin sharpening. "I'm guessing this isn't a celebration hug about our plan, huh, Bash?" The word hits me wrong and my eyes narrow in his direction so sharp they could cut glass.

"Plan?" I repeat slowly, turning toward Sebastian. "What plan?" His jaw tightens immediately, like I've stepped on a live wire. "There is *no* plan," he answers. Something inside me pulls taut and I feel a familiar prickle wash over me, the feeling that I'm missing something laid out directly in front of me. Jesse huffs, "Sure there is."

"I never agreed to anything," Sebastian snaps. I let my eyes drag over him. The tension in his shoulders, the way he's braced like this conversation is a threat he can physically block, his hands curled in on themselves and frame squared. Like if he keeps his stance firm enough, the truth won't make it past him. I step forward before I think better of it. My hands find my hips automatically, grounding me. Claiming space, demanding to be seen. "Sebastian," I press carefully, "*what plan?*"

He hesitates, mouth opening, closing again. His lips press into a firm line, and he looks at me like I'm fragile. *Again.* Like I can't handle whatever it is despite everything he just told me. That hurts more than if he'd lied.

"I just told you," he says, leveling his tone. "There isn't one." My chest tightens and I can feel the frustration building in my gut. I cross my arms over my chest, taking another step closer, but this one isn't hesitant. "You're lying," I call his bluff.

Jesse clears his throat behind us, clearly delighted, "I *love* her."

Sebastian shoots him a sharp look, an unspoken threat. "Not helping."

"No," Jesse agrees mildly, the same smirk stuck on his features. He leans back against the countertop casually enough that it has potential to melt all the tension hovering around the three of us. "But necessary."

I turn back to Sebastian. My pulse is loud in my ears now, but I don't let it rush me. I've spent too long reacting to everyone else's decisions and not giving myself enough time to stand behind my own. "You don't get to decide things for me anymore," I say quietly. "Not after everything you told me."

"You don't understand the risks," he says, dismissing me entirely.

I nod slowly, then shrug, mirroring Jesse's casual indifference. "Then explain them." Sebastian remains silent, stoic. As per usual. I realize then what this is really about. Not danger or even strategy. It's about him believing that if he keeps control, he can outrun grief. That if he decides everything himself, the world won't have a chance to surprise him again. But I am not a variable. I am not a mistake waiting to happen and I will not be treated like one. Not anymore. Not now that I know.

Jesse speaks gently this time, "She's already in it, Bash. We have to do something." My gaze never leaves Sebastian. "If something happens," I say softly, "it won't be because you trusted me. It'll be because someone already decided I mattered enough to come after me." He knows I'm right. He looks away, just for a second, but I see it. The fear he won't admit out loud.

Finally, Jesse sighs. "Look. Nobody's doing anything tonight." He glances between us. "But if we're gonna talk about this like adults, we should probably sit down." The suggestion feels strangely monumental. To finally be included. To finally be let out of the dark. After what seems like minutes, Sebastian nods, just once, lips pressed firmly together. "Fine," he says. "We'll talk."

The three of us move toward the table slowly, like none of us wants to be the first to break whatever this moment is. I take a seat, folding my hands together to keep them steady. My gaze jumps between the two men, waiting for this heavy truth that it seems like neither of them want to face, either. Jesse leans back in his chair, casual but alert. "Okay. Ground rules," he says. "This is hypothetical. Nobody's bait unless they say so themselves." *Bait?* My stomach flips at the word, but I hold his gaze.

I push down the acid I feel rising in my throat and nod, keeping my voice steady, "I want to hear it." Sebastian's head jerks toward me so quickly I hear a pop from his neck but I can see the desperation behind his gaze when we lock eyes. "Savannah—"

"I said I want to hear it," I repeat, firmer this time, "all of it. Whatever you guys are thinking, I deserve to be included." Jesse nods once and something close to respect washes over his expression.

"Alright," he agrees. The room is quiet now, weighed down by expectation. Whatever comes next will change things. And for the first time since I got dragged into this nightmare, I don't feel like it's happening *to* me. It's happening *with* me. I drop my hands to my lap to hide the nervous wringing of them, patiently waiting for them to speak. I keep my expression neutral, the same way I've seen Sebastian do too many times.

Jesse is the one who starts, because of course he is. He leans forward, forearms braced on the table, fingers laced together like this is just another briefing and not my life spread out between us. "Okay," he says calmly. "Here's what we know." Sebastian stays standing behind my chair, close enough that I can feel the heat of him at my back. Not looming, more like guarding, as if talking about this plan is a threat in itself. His presence is steady and comforting, even through trying to force myself to show no signs of weakness.

"They've been patient," Jesse continues. "Which tells me they're watching. They're not panicking so they already think they're ahead of us. That means they expect you to surface eventually." I nod slowly. That makes sense. "So the idea," Jesse goes on, "isn't to put you in danger. It's to make them think you're going back to something familiar."

My stomach drops like a pin and I swallow thickly, my voice small when I speak despite my best efforts to keep it level. "My house?" Sebastian's hand curls against the back of the chair. Jesse meets my gaze, "Your routine. Your neighborhood. Somewhere they already feel comfortable making a move."

"And you'd be watching?" I ask.

"Every second," Jesse answers without hesitation. "You wouldn't be alone. Not even for a minute."

Sebastian exhales sharply, "That's assuming everything goes right."

Jesse glances at him, nodding slowly, "That's why we plan for what happens when it doesn't." I tilt my head to look up at Sebastian. "Tell me what you're thinking?"

His fingers grip the back of my chair so tightly I hear

the wood creak under the pressure but he meets my eyes when he speaks and I finally see something behind them that's not fear. "The moment you're visible, they'll move faster. That's the risk. They upside is they'll be rushed, which will make them messy. They know you won't be alone if they got the gift I left for them at the supply cache."

Jesse chuckles from across the table. I'm not sure what he means by that, but then again, I'm not sure I want to know.

"And Mason?" I ask quietly. Both of them freeze like they hadn't considered my family at all. My heart drops at the realization. "What happens to him?"

Sebastian's voice treads carefully. "He won't be involved."

I shake my head, "He lives there," I point out, "you can't pretend he doesn't exist." I hear my voice start to falter and I clutch one hand harder around the other, every nerve tightening in my stomach. Jesse sighs quietly but he nods.

"She's right." Sebastian drags a hand over his face and I can feel the frustration rolling off his frame. "We can move him first if he's at risk of being implicated. Quietly. Somewhere safe."

I swallow, tongue running over my lips. My gaze drops to the table, head shaking slowly. "You're talking about uprooting my entire family." Even knowing that my father caused all of this, guilt floods through me.

"We're talking about keeping them alive," Sebastian says, sharper than he means to.

I flinch, then straighten. "I'm not saying no. I just— Mason has to be okay. These decisions don't affect just me." The room goes quiet for too long. Jesse leans back slightly, the groan of his chair the only sound for a moment, watching the exchange with something like approval. "She's not wrong, man," he notes.

Sebastian looks at me again, eyes dark and searching, "What would you change?"

The question surprises me. But then, so does having a voice in this at all. I take a breath, grounding myself. "I don't go in blind. I don't pretend I'm clueless or helpless. If something feels off, I don't go in. No heroics."

"Easy enough," Jesse says immediately. Sebastian nods once. "And," I add, pulse picking up, "I don't want to be used as a prop. If I'm doing this, I'm part of the plan. I need to know where you are. What the signals are. What I do if something goes wrong." Sebastian opens his mouth to object but stops himself before he speaks.

Jesse's smile grows broader. "Now you're thinking like a soldier, Sunshine." Sebastian's shoulders sag just a fraction, "I don't want you to have to think like that."

"I already do," I say gently, the hint of a humorless laugh escaping. "You trained me." That lands where I needed it to. He studies me for a long moment, like he's seeing the results of his own work for the first time. And I'm not sure that he approves, but he accepts it nonetheless. "Alright," he says finally. "You'll have a comm. Discreet. One tap means you're uncomfortable. Two means we pull you out immediately."

"And if I can't tap?" I ask.

His jaw tightens, unsettled by the idea. "Then we intervene anyway."

Jesse nods, "No hesitation."

I glance between them, my brows pulled together. "And you'll both be there?"

Sebastian hardly lets the words roll off my tongue before he answers, "Yes."

I feel my whole body relax at his reassurance. I lean back in my chair, exhaling slowly. "Then there's one more thing." Both of them look at me, waiting for my conditions. "If we're doing this," I say, steady now, "you don't get to shut me out again afterward. No disappearing. No pretending this was just a job. It's too far gone for that."

Sebastian stiffens like I've just caught him red-handed. "That's not fair," he says quietly. I feel the blood rush from my head. Is that really what he was planning? After everything? I scold myself internally for allowing myself to think otherwise. I hold his gaze, my tongue sharp when I speak. "Neither is making me trust you with my life and then acting like I don't matter." The words slice through the air like blades, meant to injure

Jesse clears his throat softly. "She's got a point."

Sebastian looks torn, a storm behind his eyes that I can't read. Finally, he nods once. "Okay," he says. "No shutting you out." It isn't a promise he makes lightly, I can tell. But it's real and that's enough for now. My hands finally unclasp and I brace my palms flat on the table, "Then we keep talking. Step by step."

Jesse pushes back from the table, "Good. Because if we're doing this, we do it clean." Finally, I don't feel like the thing everyone is circling around. I feel like part of the circle.

Whatever comes next, whether it's danger, fallout, or confrontation, I'm comfortable with one fact. I'm not facing it alone.

43

Sebastian

The perimeter is quiet when I finish my last sweep of the night. Too quiet, if I let old instincts have their way. I try to shake it off but my mind keeps drifting back inside. To Savannah. To the way she sat at the table earlier, spine straight, eyes clear, asking the kind of questions most people avoid because they're afraid of the answers. She didn't fold. She didn't try to bargain her way out of the truth. She leaned into it.

I stop at the edge of the clearing and stare at the cabin. Warm light glows faintly through the windows. Our temporary, fragile home. Everything in me still wants to shield her. To put myself between her and anything sharp, anything cruel, anything that might leave a mark. That part of me will never go quiet. But tonight, I understand something else too. She can handle herself. Not in the way I can. Not with weapons or tactics or blood on her hands. But intellectually. Emotionally. She sees the danger for what it is and still chooses to stand upright in it.

She's terrifyingly brave, but still worth protecting. I

exhale slowly, reaching for the door. I don't linger on the porch this time. I don't tell myself I'm giving her space or doing the noble thing by staying away. I promised her I wouldn't shut her out again. I promised her I would try. That promise starts now.

I make my way down the hall, pausing outside her door. I hesitate for half a second longer than necessary, then knock gently. "Yeah?" her voice comes, soft but alert. I open the door, peeking my head around the corner and offering a sheepish smile, hoping that after the way I've treated her—even with the best intentions in mind—she'll still accept me.

She sits on the edge of the bed, knees pulled up, arms wrapped loosely around herself as she stares out the window. Moonlight spills across her face, catching in her hair, outlining the curve of her cheek. She looks thoughtful. Awake in that way that means sleep is nowhere close. "Couldn't sleep either?" I ask, trying poorly to sound light.

"I hear it's contagious around here." She glances back at me, a faint smile tugging at her mouth. "A lot on your mind?" she asks.

"Something like that." I step inside and close the door behind me, leaning back against it instead of crossing the room. I don't want to crowd her. Don't want her to think I'm jumping in too quickly. Even when in this moment, knowing what awaits us in the morning, every part of me yearns for her. She watches me for a moment. Then, quietly, "Did you finish your sweep?"

"All clear," I say. "For now." She nods, gaze drifting back to the window. Snowflakes slide past the glass, slow and steady. I can see the thoughts moving behind her eyes. I push off the door and take a few steps closer. "You okay?"

She hums softly, shrugging a weak shoulder. "I think

so. Just…processing." Of course. Hell, I'm still processing too. I sit on the edge of the bed, leaving space between us. Close enough to feel her warmth, far enough not to overwhelm. "You handled yourself well earlier. Better than most people would've."

She lets out a small breath, almost a laugh. "That feels like a backhanded compliment."

"It's not," I say quickly. "I mean it."

She turns toward me then, eyes searching my face. "You really think this plan could work?"

"I think it's dangerous," I answer honestly, scrubbing a hand across the back of my neck. "I think it's risky and unpredictable and there are a dozen ways it could go sideways."

She nods, unsurprised, her teeth claiming her bottom lip in that familiar way. "But?"

"But," I continue, releasing a long breath. "I also think you understand what's at stake. And I think you're making the choice with your eyes open." Her shoulders ease just a fraction with my admission. "I'm not trying to scare you," I add. "Or talk you into anything. I just—" I pause, choosing my words carefully. "I need you to know what I'm worried about." She waits for me to finish, patient and steady, her gaze never breaking mine. "When you're visible again," I say, "they'll test boundaries. Watch reactions. They'll look for hesitation. For cracks. If anything feels wrong, we pull you out immediately. No debate."

"I know," she says softly.

"And if at any point you change your mind—"

"I'll tell you," she finishes for me. "I promise."

I nod in response, but my features don't tighten. Because I believe her. And because she has me. And Jesse.

After a moment, she draws a breath. "Sebastian?"

"Yeah?" My body answers, turning toward her slightly. She hesitates, fingers twisting together in her lap. "Do you think…you could stay with me tonight?"

The question lands gently, but it hits deep. My stomach turns and I don't know if it's from nerves or anticipation. "I don't think I'll get any sleep if I'm alone," she adds quietly. "Not with everything looming."

"Okay," I say, "yeah." Her shoulders sag with relief, and something in my chest loosens in response. I scoot back to rest against the headboard and she settles beside me without being asked. Familiar and easy in a way it shouldn't be. She tucks herself against my side, head resting against my shoulder. After a moment, I reach over and snuff out the candle she had lit on the nightstand. I stare at the ceiling, listening to her breathing slowly even out. "You're not weak for wanting company," I say quietly.

I feel her smile against my shoulder in response. "Good. Because I was about to argue if you said no."

A corner of my mouth lifts, "I figured."

We fall into silence again, the kind that doesn't demand to be filled. I feel the warmth of her body, the steady presence of her, and something inside me that's long been dormant relaxes its grip. I still want to protect her. I always will. But tonight, I don't feel like I'm guarding something fragile. I feel like I'm choosing someone strong.

Savannah shifts beside me, adjusting until she's comfortable, her knee brushing mine. I still at first, hyperaware of every point of contact. When she doesn't pull away, I let myself breathe. The dark gives us courage. It always has. "You ever notice that everything feels louder at night?" She asks quietly.

I huff a soft breath, "Yeah. That's when your brain decides to start listing everything you've ever done wrong."

She laughs under her breath, the sound warm against my shoulder. "You're not wrong there..." Her fingers fidget lightly with the hem of my shirt, grounding herself. The gesture does something unsteady to my chest.

"Are you scared?" I ask, not because I think she is, but because I want her to know she's allowed to be.

She's quiet for a moment before I feel her shrug. "I think... I'm scared of being brave and it not being enough."

That one lands. I turn my head slightly, resting it against the wall behind us as my eyes adjust to the darkness of the night and scan her features. "You don't have to be brave all the time."

She hums. "That's rich coming from you."

I smile faintly in the dark, "I'm good at pretending."

She shifts again, angling herself more toward me, her head tilting up toward mine. "Can I ask you something?"

"You usually do," I say, gently teasing. She pinches my side lightly, then settles. "When this is over...what happens to you?" The question is soft, but it carries weight. It's something I've tossed and turned in my head on countless nights since we first arrived. I stare into the darkness, considering the truth.

"I don't know," I admit. "Probably back to work. Different assignment. Different place."

She nods slowly, like she expected that. "And you're okay with that?"

I hesitate—not because I don't know the answer. Maybe because I've never considered it a choice. Protocol, orders, assignments. That's how my life has been organized since I was old enough to decide it's what I wanted. Before anything else mattered. "I've always been okay with it," I say carefully. She's quiet again, and I feel the shift in her breathing, the way she's absorbing what I didn't say.

"What about you?" I ask, turning it back on her. "What happens when this is done? Have you thought about it?"

There's a pause, like she's contemplating her words carefully. I feel her fingers tighten against the hem of my shirt again, her thumb grazing gently over my skin. "I don't think I can go back to who I was before."

Something in my chest tightens, feeling the words we've both left unspoken. "That's not a bad thing."

"No," she agrees softly. "It's just...scary. Choosing something new." Her hand slides into mine, fingers threading through without seeking permission. The warmth of her palm against mine settles me, my frame relaxing against hers. "You're allowed to choose yourself," I tell her. "No matter what that looks like."

She squeezes my hand, quiet for a moment before she speaks, her voice no louder than a whisper now. "Even if that means choosing you?"

The air pulls tight around us, pressing in on my chest. I don't answer right away. The truth feels too fragile. The truth is that I want her to. That I want to choose her, too. Hell, maybe I already have. Still, reality has a cruel sense of humor and we're only hours away from returning to the real world, away from the safe haven of this cabin. "I don't want you choosing me out of fear," I say quietly. "Or obligation. Or because you think I'm the safest option."

She tilts her head, resting it against my shoulder again. "What if I choose you because you make me feel seen?" *God*—That alone nearly undoes me. I swallow thickly, my fingers flexing against hers in response. "God, Savannah..." I breathe, "You make it hard to keep my walls up," I admit, voice rougher than I intend. "You know that?"

"Good," she chirps and even in the darkness shrouding us, I can see her smile.

I chuckle softly, shaking my head when I feel my lips tug into an easy smile. "You're trouble."

"I've been told," she muses. I feel her soft breaths against my neck and I allow myself this moment. The morning is inevitable but tonight? Tonight is a cruel dream that I know I'll have to wake up to even when I beg the minutes to stretch. Sharing this bed with her, holding her in my arms. I pull her in closer, letting my chin rest against the top of her head. I don't know when sleep finally finds her, only that at some point her weight settles fully against me.

I stay awake long after she drifts off, staring into the dark, memorizing the feel of her here—warm, real, and trusting. Tomorrow, I'll have to be sharp again. But tonight, I let myself stay. And this time, I don't regret it.

44

Savannah

The road looks smaller than I remember. Or maybe I've just grown. The tires hum softly beneath us, a steady sound that should be comforting but only makes my thoughts louder. Sebastian drives with one hand on the wheel, the other resting on my thigh like this is just another long night drive and not the moment my entire life shifts direction. Jesse sits behind us, silent. Neither of them have said much since we left the cabin. Just the essentials. Just enough to remind me I'm not alone.

I keep my eyes fixed on the road ahead of us. I don't want to see Sebastian's face right now because I know what I'll find there. Concern, tightly leashed. Readiness. The quiet kind of fear he never admits to. The same look that might convince me to back out of all of this. The closer we get, the more familiar everything feels. The curve in the road I used to take too fast. The old wooden sign I never noticed until now. But the air smells different here. It's heavier, laced with memories and thick with forgotten dreams. I try to breathe through it. *You chose this,* I remind myself. *You're not being led here.* Still, my stomach twists and knots.

I glance out the window as the car slows, easing off the main road and into a narrow side street. The houses thin and the trees crowd closer. Shadows stretch long and dark between the streetlights. Sebastian parks the car where the light doesn't quite reach, where the shadows gather thickest. Hidden in plain sight. Something about it makes my breathing shallow, an instinct I didn't have before. A whisper of awareness.

Sebastian shifts beside me once the car slides into park. "We're here," he says quietly, killing the engine. I swallow and nod once, inhaling a deep breath, fingers curling around his that still rests on my leg. "Okay." *Okay.* Such a small word for something this big. He turns toward me then, and I finally meet his eyes. They're steady, dark, searching my face like he's committing it to memory. He covers my hand with his. Firm and reassuring. "One last time," he says softly. "If you want out—"

I shake my head, pressing my lips together as if that will make my voice steadier. "I don't," I interrupt gently. He holds my gaze for a beat longer, then nods, acceptance and trust wrapped into the air around us. Jesse clears his throat, "Alright. Showtime." He leans forward in his seat, resting his hand on my shoulder before patting it twice. "You got this, sunshine."

I hold onto those words as I open the door, cold air rushing in and stealing my breath. The world outside feels sharper, louder, every sound amplified. Frozen leaves and remainders of snow crunch under my boots as I step out, the house looming ahead of us like it's been waiting. *My house.* The place that used to mean safety.

I stand there for a moment, staring at it, and all at once, it hits me. I'm not afraid of going back at all. I'm afraid of how much everything has changed. Behind me, the car door shuts quietly. Sebastian's presence settles at my back like a promise. Somewhere deep in the shadows, unseen, the past watches us return. I feel a chill creep up my spine. That feeling that someone is watching, waiting.

I press forward, practicing walking with my chest out the way Sebastian taught me. Through the feigned confidence, my fingers flex at my sides and my stomach turns with each step. I lift my chin slightly, attempting to ground myself with the sharp bite of the cold air brushing my cheeks.

The front door sticks the way it always has. I have to put my shoulder into it just a little, and the familiar resistance sends a strange ache through my chest. This door has known me my entire life, and yet stepping over the threshold feels like trespassing. Cold air follows me inside as I close it softly behind me. *Click.* The sound echoes louder than it should. I lost track of the days long ago but by the stillness of the house, it must be a Friday. My family is absent, all attending Mason's football game, or removed like Sebastian and Jesse promised.

Either way, the emptiness feels like they didn't even notice I was missing. Or maybe they did and didn't care enough to see if I'd turn back up. Maybe they were tired enough of my constant complaining that they were relieved. Happy, maybe, that they didn't have to watch over me anymore.

The house smells the same, though it's cleaner than it ever was when I lived here. Faintly lemony, like my mother's cleaning spray. The lights are off. Curtains drawn. Everything exactly as I left it. *Too* exactly. I slide my jacket off with caution that feels unnecessary. I hang it where I always did, on the hook that leans slightly to the left. I force myself to breathe normally, calming the rise and fall of my chest. *You're being watched,* I remind myself. *You're not alone.*

My hand brushes the small comm tucked securely beneath my sweater; a sense of safety. "Inside," I murmur, barely moving my lips. Sebastian's voice comes back immediately, low and steady in my ear. "We've got you." The sound of his voice alone releases a fraction of the tension in my shoulders. Jesse's follows, lighter but no less focused. "Cameras are clean. No movement on the perimeter." I nod even though they can't see me.

Moving deeper into the house, the living room opens around me, furniture cast in soft shadows, the streetlight filtering in through the curtains. The couch where my brother used to sprawl. The coffee table with the chipped corner. The bookshelf I never dusted. I flick on a single lamp, but the warm glow feels like a lie. I walk through the motions they told me to—normal, casual, unafraid. I drop my bag beside the couch. I move into the kitchen, open the fridge, stare inside without really seeing it. *Be visible.* I take a bottle of water out and twist the cap slowly, the crack of the plastic sounding obscene in the silence that consumes the rest of the house. My reflection in the dark window startles me and I gasp slightly. I look different now. Not quite older, but wiser. Stronger.

"Savannah," Sebastian's voice, again. Just my name. A check-in. A tether. "I'm okay," I whisper back. I carry the water into the living room and sit on the edge of the couch, like I used to when I didn't plan on staying long. My knee bounces and I glance back and forth, eyes sweeping the empty room the same way I've watched Sebastian's sweep the tree line. The air feels wrong. Disturbed, like a room someone else was just here. My gaze drifts toward the hallway, my heart beginning to thud louder in my ears. *It's nerves. That's all.*

I stand, forcing myself to move. "I'm going to check my room," I murmur. "Copy," Jesse says, "take it slow." I stand at the end of the hallway and hesitate for a moment. It feels longer than it ever did. Menacing and threatening, like my body already knows I shouldn't be here. Each step creaks softly under my weight, the sound familiar and yet suddenly unnerving.

My bedroom door is halfway open. I know I left it closed. My pulse spikes, ringing mercilessly in my ears. Maybe my family left it that way. Maybe they've been checking for any sign of my return or maybe they're waiting to notice something different, too. A sign of life or a sense of familiarity, something other than vacancy. I stop just short of the doorway, breath shallow. "Sebastian," I whisper, when I notice the faint, golden light sifting through the crack of the door, from the floor, like my lamp has been knocked over.

"I see it, I'm right outside," he says instantly. His voice is tight now. Focused. "Don't go in yet."

My eyes scan the narrow strip of my room I can see. The bedspread slightly rumpled, curtains pulled back farther than I remember. My closet door is shut now, not hanging open the way I left it when I rushed out. Nothing overtly wrong, but wrong enough. "I didn't leave it like this," I say, voice barely audible.

"I know," he replies. "Stand by."

I obey, lingering in the hallway far longer than I'm comfortable with. My mind spins with possibilities. What if they came here looking for me and hurt my family? What if my family left for their own safety? It's not like anyone could've told me. What if they've been taken, being used as bait for me to come out of the shadows? For a few long seconds, I spiral, nothing happens. A soft sound breaks the deafening silence around me. Not a footstep. Not a voice. The faintest scrape, like fabric brushing against wood. Inside my room.

My breath catches, every sense screaming at once. I press my lips tightly together to keep myself from gasping audibly and hug my arms around my torso, shielding myself pathetically from whatever is on the other side of that door. I'm frozen until I hear him. Sebastian's voice drops to something lethal. "Savannah. I need you to move. Now. Slowly. Back toward the front door."

I don't hesitate. I nod again, more to myself than anyone else. *You can do this*, I tell myself. *This is what he trained you for.* I step backward, careful not to make a sound, eyes never leaving the doorway. My heart is hammering so hard I'm sure they can hear it through the comms. One step, then another, slow and silent. The scrape comes again, closer this time.

"Go!" Sebastian says, voice borderline frantic. "*Now*." The urgency tells me he's seeing something that I'm not. My pulse rings through my ears and my fingers go numb with adrenaline. I turn and move, fear finally breaking loose in my chest as I head for the end of the hallway, for freedom. A shadow shifts at the end of the hall and I freeze. Someone is there. *Watching.*

"No," I whisper, brows threading together as I bolt toward the open end of the hallway. Not fast enough. Fingers close harshly around my wrist and I scream. *So much for staying calm.*

I'm whipped backward into the shadow before I can take another step, my shoulder colliding with the wall before I'm pressed into their torso. "We've been waiting for you," the intruder growls against my ear. The voice is different from the men that took me but carries the same Italian dialect. For a moment, I freeze, eyes going wide and vision blurring as tears well, a shiver running down my spine.

"*Savannah!*" I hear Sebastian's voice through the comms still connected in my ear and at once, it snaps me back to reality. "Fuck you!" I cry, wiggling my arm free enough to ram my elbow into the intruder's stomach. He groans, grip loosening enough that I'm able to free myself. "You bitch!" He calls but I'm already moving toward the open end of the hallway. *Distance, I need distance. Long enough for him to get to me.*

I'm jerked from my thoughts as I feel his grip around my ankle, collapsing to the floor when my foot is pulled from underneath me. Before I can react, my body is twisted and my back is pressed into the carpet. "You're not getting away so easily this time," he snarls, straddling my waist and pinning my arms to either side of my head.

"Get off of me!" I wail, turning my head to the side and closing my teeth around the wrist that secures my arm. He swears and I feel a blunt pressure to my temple when his fist connects with it. Blinking back the stun, my training takes over, the way Sebastian taught me to use my weight. And when his arm is pulled back, I plant my feet and push my hips up, bucking him to the ground beside me.

My hands move on instinct before I can doubt myself, reaching into the back of my waistband for the knife that I swept from Sebastian's nightstand earlier. A guttural scream echoes against the walls as I drive the blade into his neck. I'm instantly met with a sour, metallic smell, smothering every sense.

Warm, maroon liquid pools around my hands and sputters from his lips, his eyes wide beneath me as I press into the hilt with all my weight. His hands reach to grab at the knife but before they rise above his chest, they fall lifeless, his head lulling to the side. Blood slithers down his cheek and joins the growing puddle under his shoulders.

My chest rises and falls, breath heaving as I scramble backward, my hands shaking. My knees buckle when I try to stand and I crumble back down to the floor, scooting myself backward until I can feel the cool wall behind me, my palms sticky as I press them against it.

45

Sebastian

The moment her scream tears through the comms,
something primal detonates in my chest. The world narrows
to a single objective. *Savannah.* And everything else becomes
collateral. "Contact!" I bark, already sprinting toward the
house. Remnants of snow and ice explode beneath my boots
as I clear the distance between cover and the house in
seconds. Jesse's moving too. I hear him on my flank, feel the
shift in air as he matches my pace.

When I reach the front door, it doesn't stand a chance.
I shoulder through it, wood splintering under the force, the
sound sharp and violent. My weapon is already in my hand,
muscle memory taking over as I sweep the room. *Hallway.*
End of the hall. My legs move before I can think.

I see them and my vision goes red. The smell of iron
hits me immediately. Savannah is pressed against the wall, a
ball of emotion, her hands shaking behind her. And her gaze

is stuck across from her, where a lifeless body slowly bleeds out onto the floor. There's blood, so much blood. On the intruder's body, trailing across the floor, on her hands, splattered on her face.

I cross the hall in two swift strides, lowering myself in front of her. "Savannah, look at me." My hands move to her wrists, lifting her hands to inspect them, eyes trailing up her arms to her face. Carefully, I tilt her chin from side to side and even in the dark, I can see a bruise already blooming across her temple. "What happened?" I keep my voice steady in spite of the hot, merciless wrath I feel boiling inside of me.

Savannah's eyes stay trained on the body across from us and I crouch to move myself into her line of vision. "Hey, look at me." Slowly, green eyes lift to meet mine. "Are you okay?" I ask once I'm sure I have her attention.

"He—I—" she stutters, her hands still outstretched flat with palms held up between us. "I don't—" she tries again, head shaking slowly.

"It's okay," I cut in, leaning forward on one knee to pull her into my torso, running a hand down her back. "You're okay. I'm here." Her shoulders slump forward into my touch but her arms don't move, stuck in place like she's trying to fight her way out of a pool of tar. "You did good," I whisper, cradling the back of her head to my chest.

Before I can speak again, I hear a creak behind me. Foreign, quiet, weight pressuring floorboards. I'm on my feet before the sound can move any closer and I'm met eye to eye with another stranger, knife raised in his hand with every intention to strike. "*God dammit!*" I yell and the man turns just enough to register the action, enough to make his last mistake.

I close the distance in two strides and the knife is

already out of his hand before he understands what's happening. I slam my forearm into his throat, driving him back into the wall with a crack that vibrates through the hallway. "I've got you. You're good. Stay with me," Jesse's voice cuts through the noise as Savannah stumbles up from the floor, but she doesn't listen.

She twists violently in his grip, eyes wild, fighting to get back to me. Not thinking, but reacting. Like her body knows where safety is and refuses anything else. "Sebastian!" she gasps, reaching for me. Panic spikes sharp and hot in my chest.

"No!" I bark, harsher than I mean to. "Go with him!" Her head snaps toward me, stunned. Hurt flashes across her face for half a second but I can't hesitate long enough to swallow it. My eyes cut to Jesse, "Get her out of here!" I command. I need her away. I need her *safe*. "Move, Savannah! Now!" I yell, already stepping back into the threat.

The man lunges while my attention fractures, enough time for him to make his move. His fist connects hard with my ribs, knocking the breath from my lungs in a sharp, punishing burst. Pain flares under the impact, ribs throbbing immediately. I grunt, staggering back a step, teeth grinding as I absorb it. *Idiot.* One distraction. One mistake.

He steps forward again to go for a second blow, but I swipe my leg out, effectively taking him off his feet. Jesse hauls Savannah farther down the hall, her protests fading into panicked breaths as he shields her body with his and I silently remind myself that I owe him the biggest fucking favor. "Sebastian!" she cries when the man swings at me, and it cuts deeper than the hit ever could.

The intruder presses his advantage, scrambling to his feet and swinging again. He must've had another knife hidden because when I block this time, I feel my skin slice open. The impact reverberates up my arm, jarring but grounding. No more distractions. I drive forward, pure instinct now. Every movement is efficient, brutal. I slam his arm with my own, fingers gripping his wrist and crashing it into the wall, freeing the knife from his grip. I kick it away quickly. He swings at me again, movements desperate and sloppy, fear creeping into his eyes when he realizes I'm done playing defense. I brace his shoulders with both hands and plough him back into the wall again, skull cracking into the sheetrock. "Big fucking mistake, you piece of shit." I spit toward him, my knee coming up and connecting with his stomach. He doubles over, *weak*.

My grip on his shoulders slams him into the wall over again, then to the ground, and my boot finds his ribcage. He groans in pain and I almost laugh. I lower myself to his level, my knee hard pressing hard against his throat to restrict his breathing. "You will never win this. Consider this a message." I pull the knife from my side and the house goes still as I slice it cleanly across his throat, a sadistic smirk pulling onto my features as I watch him gasp for his last breaths.

I stand and listen for any sign of movement beyond the ringing of adrenaline pushing through my core. For the scrape of boots or the whisper of breath that means I wasn't thorough enough. For the quiet pressure of footsteps on the wooden flooring indicating that he wasn't alone. Nothing answers me except the sound of my own heavy breathing as my chest rises and falls hard and unevenly. The mantra of everything that almost went wrong. I don't call for cleanup. I leave him exactly where he fell. This isn't a mistake. It's a message. Intentional. Whoever finds the bodies needs to understand that they started this war, but I'm the one ending it.

I force my breathing to steady before I move. My instincts are still screaming, body on fire with adrenaline, but I move with caution, scanning every corner on my way out. I move through the house and into the cold night air, shutting the door behind me with care instead of force. The quiet feels wrong after the violence. Too soft, too fragile, but I let it settle anyway. I need my hands steady. I need my head clear. The porch light casts a dull glow across the front step and my eyes immediately find her.

Savannah is curled around herself on the porch step, knees drawn tight to her chest the way she always sits when she's overwhelmed, arms wrapped around herself like she's trying to keep from shattering. Her shoulders tremble with quiet sobs she's clearly been trying to swallow down. She's alone.

Rage surges hot and immediate, sharp enough to steal my breath. *Where the hell is Jesse?* I scan the dark instinctively, every muscle coiling again, ready to move. My fingers flex at my side and I swallow it. There's time for that later. Right now, there's only her. I cross the porch and drop down in front of her without thinking, my hands already on her and pulling her into me, the gash on my arm a forgotten thought. She makes a small, broken sound as she realizes it's me and she collapses fully, like whatever was holding her upright finally gives out.

"I've got you." It's a promise more than anything. I press my mouth to the top of her head, breathing her in like oxygen. "I've got you. You're safe." Her fingers clutch at my jacket, still sticky with blood. That's a conversation for later, once I know she's secure and the threat has been neutralized completely. She buries her face into my chest, her sobs deep and unrestrained now, and I hold her tighter, shielding her from the outside world with my arms locked around her. The girl I love. The girl I almost lost.

I don't move until I feel her breathing start to slow. Until I know she's okay. A throat clears behind us. I look up slowly, jaw ticking as I turn my glare on Jesse. "Where the *fuck* did you go?" I snarl, "Why would you leave her alone?"

Jesse lifts both hands in a placating gesture, but his expression is serious now. No jokes and free of his signature smirk. "Perimeter," he says. "And you're welcome, by the way. Took one out around the back."

My grip on Savannah tightens instinctively. Her head snaps up, eyes wide as panic reignites. "What?" Her voice cracks. "What does that mean? Are there more of them?" The words tumble over each other and I feel her body physically tremble.

I turn back to her immediately, blocking out everything else. My hands come up to cup her face, thumbs brushing the tear streaks under her eyes that muddle the specs of blood on her cheeks. I'm aware of the crusted blood staining my own wrist, but I don't pull away. "No," I say firmly, meeting her gaze and holding it. "It's over now. If there were more, they would've shown themselves already." Her breath stutters but she nods, giving me the trust that she always has. "It's done," I repeat, softer this time. "You're safe."

The house disappears in the rearview mirror and I don't bother looking back. If I do, I'm not sure what I'll feel. Relief, rage, or the delayed realization of how close I came to losing everything that matters. So I keep my eyes forward, fixed on the road Jesse is carving through the dark. My hand hasn't left Savannah's since we stepped off the porch. Her fingers are still trembling faintly but dried now. I hold on tighter than necessary, a promise I don't know how to say out loud yet. *She's alive.*

I repeat it to myself over and over, like a prayer I didn't know I believed in until tonight. Her weight presses into my side in the backseat, exhausted down to her bones. Not asleep, she's too keyed up for that, but quiet, eyes fixed on the window as the world blurs past. Every so often, her thumb moves against my knuckle like she's checking I'm still there.

Jesse clears his throat from the front seat. "I've been running it through my head," he says, tone more subdued than usual, the same calm voice he uses over the comms during late-night missions. "What we saw tonight? That was the tail end." I feel Savannah's grip tighten around my fingers and I pull her hand closer in my lap, letting my other fall over it. "They were desperate," he continues. "Scouts, not planners. No backup. No exit strategy. That usually means the bigger players already bailed." I nod once, even though he can't see me.

He's right. Logically, I know that. But emotionally? I'm still in fight-or-flight. My head pounds and my ribs ache from the earlier blow. My arm stings and my wrists are still caked with dried blood, but I'm not sure if it's mine or not. "And before you ask," Jesse adds, "I haven't heard a damn thing about local authorities yet. No chatter. No sirens. I'll keep checking, but...this stayed quiet." Good. Quiet means contained. Quiet means control

We drive the rest of the way without much else said. Jesse takes us deeper into Telluride, away from the familiar roads, toward the city safe house we stayed at before everything went to shit. It's strange being back here after weeks of trees and shadows. Streetlights, storefronts, and the muted glow of civilization slowly come into view. The normalcy feels surreal. The car slows, then stops. Another house. Another door. Another place meant to disappear into.

It hits me then, uninvited. This feels like the first night. Different house and different circumstances, but the same girl beside me, wrapped in borrowed warmth, trusting me with her life. Back then, I'd told myself it was just another assignment. That this was temporary. Now? I lace my fingers through hers as we step out into the cold and dare anyone to try and step between us.

Satisfaction settles in my chest when we move inside, the way it always does after a mission. Earned and laced with pride. We neutralized the threat. We completed the objective. She's alive. But this one came with a cost. She got blood on her hands that she never should've had to experience. I shouldn't have let her go in there alone. I should've moved faster.

I remember how I felt after my first kill. It was in a war zone, justified. But still traumatizing. I've grown numb to shedding the blood of others after twelve years but the first time...it's always stayed with me. And for Savannah—I'm not sure she can handle a scar that runs that deep. A memory that keeps you up at night, a face you can never forget no matter how hard you squeeze your eyes shut. My chest aches for her as I glance her way. She's still shaken and hasn't had time to process. I can only hope to find the words to comfort her when she does.

More than that, I know she'll have more questions now. I can already feel them circling my mind, relentless as ever.

What happens now? How long before the silence breaks? How would she fit into my world that's always changing, always threatening?

Jesse unlocks the door, glancing back at us. "We're good for the night. I'll take first watch before we can figure out what's happening with the unit." I nod my thanks and usher Savannah inside with a hand at her back. The drive to protect her hasn't shut off yet and I'm not sure it ever will. The door closes behind us and what should feel complete remains as unanswered as it ever has.

46

Savannah

The safe house is quiet in a way that feels unsettling. Not the mountain quiet I'd grown used to with the wind through trees and the creak of old wood, but this is something different entirely. Urban. The hum of electricity in the walls. Distant traffic muffled by the thin glass of the windowpane. I sit on the couch with my knees tucked up to my chest, curled into Sebastian's side like I've done a hundred times now without thinking about it. My head throbs and I can already feel a welt forming where I was hit. Blood still stains my hands but my legs are too weak to stand. Sebastian's arm rests along the back cushion behind me. "You should shower," he says quietly.

I shake my head in reply, "I don't want to be alone." It's the truth but deep in my chest, I just need *him* close. "Not right now." His arm shifts, settles around my shoulders, pulling me in just enough that my cheek brushes his chest. I almost feel my lips tug upward into a grin, if it weren't for the exhaustion settling into my bones.

"I know," he says, "But you'll feel better." I wrap my fingers around his arm, pulling myself closer. I know I'll feel better but I ignore it anyway. I feel him wince under my touch and my brows knit together as I turn to him. "It's nothing," he shakes his head, answering a question I didn't ask. "You're hurt," I reply. A fact he hides poorly. "Let me see," I don't give him room to argue.

Sebastian exhales a defeated breath but complies, pulling his arm from around me and straightening enough to slip off his jacket. My heart stumbles when I see the amount of blood staining his sleeve, another symbol of aftermath from tonight. "Sebastian," I breathe, closing the space between us. My fingers curl around his wrists and guide his arms closer, examining them. "Why didn't you say something?" My voice is frail, guilt pressing heavy on my chest as I stand, already rushing toward the kitchen in search of anything resembling first aid.

"Because I'm fine. It's nothing. And I'm more worried about *you*," he follows behind me, voice maddeningly casual.

"That," I point toward his arm, "is not nothing."

"And neither is that," he counters, closing the distance between us and brushing a gentle thumb over my temple. I hiss through my teeth, turning my head away and dropping my gaze. "Barely even feel it," I aim for nonchalant, but the words shake at the end.

"Savannah." His voice takes that stern tone and I glance up at him again, frown etched into my features. His hands graze down my arms, carefully wrapping around my wrists. "Let me take care of you for once."

I nod slowly, letting him guide me back toward the

bathroom. "Sit," he tells me, gesturing to the counter. I push myself onto it, exhaling a long breath as I let my head rest back against the mirror, eyes fluttering shut for the first time in what feels like hours. The sound of the bath running fills the room and shortly after, I feel steam sticking to my skin. "Come." I peek my eyes open at the sound of his voice and he stands before me with an outstretched hand that I take without protest.

His fingers graze my stomach as he lifts the hem of my shirt, pulling it over my head and discarding it to the floor. My breath catches in my throat when he unclasps my jeans, peeling them from my legs. Despite the steam, goosebumps rise on my skin at the exposure. Heat crawls up my neck as he carefully removes my bra and panties and I cross my arms over my chest, gaze dropping to the floor.

Sebastian lifts a hand to tilt my chin back up, eyes meeting mine. "I just want to help you," he murmurs, leaning forward to press his lips to my cheek. A flutter courses through my stomach at the contact.

"Okay," my voice is hardly above a whisper as he reaches for my hand, ushering me toward the bath.

I sink down into the water and release an audible sigh, the warmth of the bath melting away the tightness in my muscles. "I'm sorry about tonight," he breathes as he tugs his shirt over his head and lowers a washcloth into the water. My stomach sinks as the water tinges red, both from my hands and his arm. "This is all my fault," I murmur, eyes trained on the gash on his arm.

"Relax," he says gently as he catches my gaze, "I've had worse." *Is that supposed to be comforting?* "I shouldn't have sent you in there like that."

"I insisted," I retort, peering up at him. "If I had

listened to you, to Jesse…" I trail off, bringing my knees to my chest and wrapping my arms around them. I turn my head to peer up at him as he glides the washcloth over my shoulders and down my back. "I'm sorry."

Sebastian shakes his head, lips turning downward into a frown and brows pinching together as he runs the cloth along my arms. "Please stop apologizing to me, baby." My breath catches in my throat at the pet name, teeth gnawing at the inside of my cheek. I lift my eyes to his, searching for regret, or anger, *anything*. But there's nothing but understanding.

"You don't have to apologize to me. Ever." He lifts a hand to brush my hair from my face, tucking it behind my ear as his thumb caresses my cheek. "I will never put you in a situation like that ever again. I promise, Savannah. I'll never let anyone put their hands on you again." I'm not sure what that means for us, if whatever this is between us—if there's anything left at all—is anything more than temporary, but for now I let myself hold onto that and tuck it away into the depths of my heart that still cling to hope.

I let the silence stretch for a moment before I speak again. "You were right." He stiffens slightly, his brows laced when I glance up at him. He tilts his head in surprise, eyes narrowing slightly toward me. "About…all of it," I continue. "The danger. The watching. The way you kept saying I couldn't just exist without it touching me." I swallow. "I thought you were being paranoid. Or controlling. Or both. I never thought–" I pause, shaking my head, my gaze falling to inspect a hang nail on the edge of my thumb.

He raises the cloth again, running it slowly down my back, the water eating away at the tension left from the night. "You had every reason to think that."

"No," My head shakes again as I shift, turning my torso slightly to face him. "I didn't want to believe it. That's different." I press my forehead into his shoulder, grounding myself. "After tonight...I get it. I really get it." His hand moves instinctively, pulling me into him. "And it's always like that," I murmur after a beat. "The violence. The not-knowing if you're coming back."

"Yes," he answers quietly. No hesitation or sugarcoating. A shudder runs through me. I squeeze my eyes shut like it can hide the truth but all it does is flash images of tonight through my mind. The blood, the knife, Sebastian getting hit, Jesse pulling me away, the overwhelming anxiousness that followed. "I don't understand how you ever rest," I breathe. He's silent long enough that I lift my head to look at him.

His jaw is tight, eyes unfocused like he's looking through walls instead of at me. "I don't," he says finally.

My chest aches at that but I understand. Sebastian chose this life. He chooses danger every day. Walks into it with his head held high and his eyes wide open. "That's why you close off. It's why you build those walls so high, isn't it?" I pause. "Because if you didn't...it would destroy you."

His gaze drops to mine and I swear I see relief in it. I feel it in the way his shoulders ease. Because I finally understand. "Tonight scared you," he exhales.

"Yes," I admit. "But not in the way I thought it would." I take a breath. "I—" I stutter, pressing my lips together before I continue. My brain is exhausted but I push myself to find the right words. "Tonight was a lot. And I wish I could forget all of it. But it didn't make me want to run. It made me understand you more. And what you carry."

His brow furrows. "Sav—" The nickname rolls off his

tongue easily and my stomach flutters in response. It feels different from when other people use it. More...special.

"Let me finish," I hold a hand up, my voice gentle. "I saw you tonight. Really saw you. And I don't think anyone ever thanks you for that part." I feel heat rise to my cheeks as I peer up at him through my lashes. "So...thank you. For keeping me safe."

His features soften in reply. "That wasn't a question."

"I know," A soft sound leaves me, half-laugh, half-breath. "But I still needed to say it."

We sit like that for a moment, the weight of it settling between us. I don't think anyone has ever taken the time to thank him before. Not by the way his fingers curl around my shoulder and his eyes haven't left mine. I chew the inside of my cheek, the next question requiring a sense of bravery that I'm not sure I can muster up.

"What happens now?" I'm not sure I want to know the answer. He hesitates and finally drops his gaze. I'm not sure he *wants* to answer. I already know why.

"Now," he says, standing from where he was crouched by the tub to grab a towel off the counter, holding it out toward me. "You dry off and get some rest."

I scowl up at him as I stand, taking the towel and wrapping it around my torso. "You know what I meant. Are you going to be reassigned? Another mission? Another place?" His silence is telling enough. My chest sinks with unwarranted grief. It's the kind of grief you feel when you see something beautiful and fragile and know it can't stay untouched. I step out of the bath and he reaches for my hand, thumb brushing across my knuckles. Our fingers lace together, his palm warm against mine. "I know your work is...everything," I mutter. "It's not something you can just step away from. It's part of you."

He nods slowly, his eyes downcast to our hands. "Savannah..." He breathes, his voice tight, throat working around my name.

"I'm not asking you to choose," I say quickly. "I just...don't know where I fit in that world yet. Or *if* I fit in that world. And if I don't..." I don't add in the insecure part of me that wonders if he even wants me to. My voice drops, head shaking slowly. I quickly blink back the tears that threaten to brim, mind swimming with unanswered possibilities. "I don't know where I go from here. And that scares me."

He turns toward me then, fully, his attention absolute. I swallow thickly under the scrutiny. "We'll talk about that," he says, steady now. A promise that he can't make, left hanging in the air between us. "Not tonight. But we will. Let me get you some clothes."

He turns without another word, leaving me standing in the bathroom with no company but my reflection. I wipe my hand across the steam that clouds the mirror, tilting my head to eye the purple stain across my temple. I press a gentle hand to it, hissing through my teeth at the contact. The reflection that stares back at me is foreign, the image of a girl that feels a thousand lifetimes away from me now.

When I met Sebastian, I was weak. Naive, untouched by the worst parts of the world that live in corners and shadows. And I know that even if he chooses to leave me behind, I'm better for knowing him at all.

Before I can lose myself too far into my thoughts, the door cracks open again, and he returns with a pair of sweats and a tee shirt. "Thank you," I murmur as I take them. He nods once, "I'll be outside." I inhale a deep breath, letting the air fill my lungs as I tug on the clothes before I pad back into the living room. Sebastian is reclined on the couch, his body sinking into the cushion in the same manner as the first time I saw his face, drained and spent from the night's events. I move to the couch and crawl in next to him without waiting for his reaction, curling myself into his side.

For now, it's enough that he's beside me. For now, it's enough that I survived. And whatever comes next...missions, distance, choices neither of us are ready to name yet, I'm not the same girl he rescued from those awful men. And neither of us can pretend this didn't change everything.

I stay tucked against his side, but my body is heavier now. The adrenaline that's been holding me upright for hours finally starts to decline, leaving a deep, aching tiredness in its wake. My eyes burn and I blink more than I need to, lashes sticking together. My head dips slightly before I catch it again. I don't want to sleep yet.

I tilt my face up toward him, movement slow and tentative, like I'm afraid I might spook him if I move too fast. "Sebastian?" His name leaves me softly, uncertain, as if I'm testing whether he's still right here.

"Savannah?" he answers, and when I look at him, there's a softness in his expression that I don't see often. He still looks at me like I need protecting, but underneath that, I know he sees the part of me that's still standing.

My courage wavers just enough that I nearly let the moment pass. I chew at the inside of my cheek, brows knitting together as the question presses harder against my chest, demanding space. "Am I..." My voice trails off. I swallow, forcing the words back into order. "Am I still just the mission?" The question makes me feel like a child asking for validation. For a second, he doesn't say anything. But his body does.

The arm around my shoulders loosens subtly, like a reflex he didn't bother to stop. His gaze drops to my mouth, then back to my eyes, steady and intent in a way that makes my heart flutter. Whatever answer I'm bracing for, it's already slipping away. "No," he murmurs. Just one word. Quiet and full of all the meaning it needs. I stare at him for a heartbeat longer, searching his face for cracks or conditions or anything that might contradict it but there's nothing there. No distance. No walls snapping back into place.

"Okay." The word feels like relief on my tongue. My head tips forward before I can stop it, nestling against his shoulder. The world narrows, edges blurring as the exhaustion finally wins. My eyelids slide shut, my breathing evening out as the couch beneath me and the warmth beside me become the only things that matter. I don't fight it, not this time. Instead, I shift slightly, my arm falling across his lap as I settle against his chest. "Goodnight, Sebastian."

47

Sebastian

I wake up to the smell of bacon, the sizzle of the pan pulling me into consciousness. The smell tells me it's real bacon, not the barely edible strips Jesse once tried to pass off as food during a deployment. My first thought is that I'm dreaming. My second is that Savannah is still warm against my chest, her breath whispering against my collarbone. I don't dare move, staring at the ceiling, letting myself have this moment before the world remembers us again. Her head is tucked beneath my chin, one arm slung across my stomach like she claimed the place sometime in the night and never gave it back. I'd let her keep it forever if she wanted to.

From the kitchen comes the unmistakable sound of someone humming—badly, interrupted by a few hushed curses. Savannah stirs before I do, shifting slightly against my side. She lets out a soft sound that's half sigh, half yawn, and tilts her face just enough to peer toward the kitchen, one eye cracked open. "Good morning, Sunshine," Jesse's voice carries cheerfully. Too cheerful for this hour. Daylight has just started to creep in through the window, the moon not

351

fully retiring for the day yet.

"Morning," she mumbles, still thick with sleep.

I finally sit up a fraction, careful not to jostle her, and see Jesse, standing at the stove. Wearing a ridiculous apron. It's bright and loud and covered in cartoon mountains and the words *Kiss the Cook* printed across his chest like a personal insult. "Morning, Bash," he adds, voice falling completely flat as he looks at me.

I roll my eyes, one hand bracing behind me on the couch. "Where did you even get that?" I gesture my chin toward the apron, one brow raised in his direction.

He grins, unphased. "Borrowed it from the closet. Don't act like you didn't notice it was there." I shake my head, exhaling an exasperated breath. It's too early for...whatever this is. "I noticed," I mutter. "I just chose to ignore it."

Savannah laughs quietly, the sound warm and unguarded, and I feel myself relax beneath her. I glance down at her, catching the faint smile tugging at her lips, her eyes still heavy with sleep but brighter than they were last night.

I finally coax her fully awake with the promise of food, and she drifts toward the table with the blanket wrapped around her shoulders. Jesse sets a plate down in front of her with a flourish, like he's hosting brunch instead of debriefing after a violent night, and Savannah thanks him like this is normal. Like we're normal. "Bacon, eggs, and...whatever this is supposed to be," he says, gesturing vaguely at the toast, his smile far too wide. "I didn't burn it, so...Bone apple teeth, or whatever it is they say in *Paris*," he imitates a poor French accent. Savannah smiles at him, soft and genuine. "I appreciate the effort," she muses.

"That's all I ask for," he replies solemnly, "validation." I take a seat across from them, eyeing the spread before I shoot a pointed look in Jesse's direction. "You didn't poison it, did you?"

He scoffs in reply, "Please. If I wanted you dead, Bash, you'd never see it coming. Now drink your coffee and wipe off your resting murder face." Savannah's brows lift in his direction, fork pointed at him. "It's actually worse after coffee."

"Now that you mention it..." Jesse agrees, a laugh bellowing out of him. She snorts into her coffee, and I catch myself watching the way her shoulders relax as she laughs. It's subtle, but it's there, and the sight dissipates the remaining tension knotted in my back. She glances between us, curiosity flickering. "So, how long exactly have you two known each other? I never got that part of the story."

Jesse doesn't hesitate, "Too long."

"So...before he got all grumpy and broody, right?" She adds, stifling her giggle with a bite of her toast. The clear improvement in her mood and worth it, even at my expense.

Jesse shakes his head, "No way. He was always grumpy. Broody came later. Like a personality upgrade no one asked for." He pops a bite of bacon in his mouth, his grin lopsided in my direction. Savannah tilts her head, studying me. "You weren't always like this?"

I shrug. "Define *this*."

She gestures vaguely at me with her fork, "Emotionally unavailable. Mildly terrifying. Weirdly good at cooking eggs."

Jesse laughs outright. "Oh, yeah, no. He used to smile, I think."

I shoot him a look, my expression free of amusement, "Come on. You're exaggerating."

"Am I?" He turns to Savannah. "First time I met him, he told me to stop talking or he'd duct-tape my mouth shut."

Her eyes widen like it's far-fetched. "Well, did you?"

"Absolutely not," Jesse says, proud of himself. "I value my principles."

She shakes her head, smiling to herself. "I wish I'd known you guys back then," she says quietly. Equal parts ache and relief settle in me at that. "Trust me," I say quietly. "You're better off knowing us now." She looks at me for a moment longer than necessary, like a silent agreement she's afraid to make.

Jesse clears his throat and stands, clapping his hands together once. "Alright. As charming as domestic bliss is, I've got things to do." Savannah looks up at him, almost frowning. I roll my eyes involuntarily. "Things like...?" She tilts her head curiously.

"Loose ends," he says lightly, already shrugging into his jacket. "Phone calls. People who don't need names. Making sure last night stays last night."

I nod once in understanding, "Be careful."

He smirks, grabbing a piece of his bacon for the road. "Always am." He pauses at the door, glancing back between us with a knowing look and offering a wink. "Don't do anything I wouldn't do."

Savannah's lips twitch, "Wasn't planning on it."

Jesse grins, nodding once before he turns to the door and calls over his shoulder, "Good. I'll be back." The door shuts behind him, the sound echoing softly through the space.

I turn back to Savannah, the humor draining away, replaced by something quieter. More serious. Breakfast is over, Jesse is gone. And there's no more pretending we can avoid what comes next.

Savannah doesn't move from her seat at the table. She doesn't retreat, doesn't fidget. She just watches me, coffee untouched now, but her hands stay cradled around the mug like she needs something to hold on to, even with the blanket draped across her shoulders.

I draw a slow breath, my full lungs feeling like they're carrying me straight off a ledge I couldn't prepare myself for. "Now that you've slept," I start carefully, keeping my voice even. "And you've had something to eat...we should talk."

She blinks, nods once, waiting before she speaks. "Okay." A simple answer. One where I can't tell if it's because she wants to avoid the conversation or if she's gotten better at her poker face.

"I'm going to tell you everything," I lock my fingers together, bracing my forearms on the table. The instinct to withhold is still there, but she isn't just a civilian anymore. And she deserves this. "From the very beginning...not just pieces. All of it. You deserve to understand what you were standing in the middle of." My heart thuds in my neck and I'd be surprised if I didn't pop a vessel here at the table.

Her gaze drops to the table and I catch her hands tighten slightly around her mug. "Okay."

I take another deep breath and hesitate long enough to contemplate where I begin. I lean back in my chair, pulling my hands into my lap and force my vision to focus to the left of her shoulder. "I'm part of a special operations unit. Military, but...adjacent. The kind that doesn't exist on paper. We work *with* federal agencies, not under them. Our job isn't arrests or prosecution. We don't kick down doors unless it's the only option. It's long-term surveillance on subjects who've managed to evade traditional systems for long enough to become a problem."

She tilts her head slightly, leaning forward a fraction. "People who slip through the cracks," she notes.

"People who build lives in the cracks," I correct. "And make them profitable."

She nods slowly, ushering me forward. "Ten months ago," I continue, "my unit was assigned to your father's case." Her breath stutters, but she stays still. "He had connections to a cartel operating across the border. Logistics, transport routes, financial movement. He wasn't on the frontlines, but his involvement was significant. Valuable enough to catch the wrong person's attention. That's why it took so long." I watch her fingers curl slowly around the mug and release again. Her brows come together slightly, her expression reading that this is already a lot for her to take in. "My specific role," I add, after a beat, "was you."

"I figured." She exhales softly, her teeth capturing her lower lip.

"I was assigned to observe you," I explain. "From a distance. Learn your routine. Your habits. Your weak points. Not to interfere. Not to interact. Just...watch. Make sure you were never in the wrong place at the wrong time. And if something went sideways, I was the contingency."

"So you were...what," she asks quietly, "My keeper?"

"In theory," I chuckle quietly, my fingers wringing together in my lap as I speak. "In practice, no. The protection part almost never comes into play. Most targets keep their families out of it. It's cleaner that way. And your father made that expectation very clear. Through intercepted calls and meetings, we learned that he made it known that you and your brother were to remain off-limits and untouched."

Her brows lift in surprise and she leans forward like the truth takes her breath. "He did?"

"Yes." The word is clipped. I lean back slightly, exhaling through my nose and hating how her question has a hint of hope behind it.

She holds a hand up as if she can pause reality, eyes narrowing again. "But I was leveraged anyway?"

"You were *potential* leverage," I say gently. "Which is still dangerous. But it meant no one acted. Until someone broke the rules. You were never supposed to know I existed. I was meant to stay a shadow. That was the job. And until the night you were taken, everything was working." My head shakes, grinding my molars together. My knuckles crack when I clench my fists in my lap, the feeling of failure suffocating me all over again.

"When that happened," I continue, raking a hand through my hair just to have movement, "I knew immediately there was a breach. Someone inside my unit was feeding information out. I didn't know who yet. But I knew it meant you were no longer protected by my staying in the shadows."

She swallows but she doesn't ask any questions. I watch the way the vein in her neck pulses quickly, jumping with each heartbeat. I hesitate, then add, "The night I went to the cache and came back injured, that's when I confirmed it. The mole was dealt with." She doesn't ask how. Her eyes land on my knuckles anyway

"I was worried when Jesse showed up," I admit. "I thought maybe word had spread further. That maybe the breach went deeper than I realized."

"But it hadn't?" she asks, her voice wavering slightly

"No." I shake my head and I watch the tension release faintly from her shoulders. "Jesse was honoring what we'd agreed on after Afghanistan. Check-ins. Accountability. He didn't know he'd find you there because he wasn't supposed to. That's when I confirmed the threat was still active, but contained."

I pause, letting her absorb it all. The words hang heavy in the air between us, suffocatingly thick with truth. "And last night?" She finally asks. "Last night was the end of it," I assure her. "Loose ends. Desperation. No coordination left. I can't tell you more right now. I want to, please believe that." My voice falters and I tighten my fist in my lap again to steady myself.

"And once I get the clearance I need, I will." I pause, feeling pressured and disdain toward protocol all at once. I have to remind myself that I've already broken enough rules—and will have plenty of consequences to face for it when I get back to command. My hand aches to reach for hers but I restrain myself until I can form the rest of the words that need to be said

"I don't regret protecting you," I say firmly. "I don't regret keeping you in the dark while the threat existed. That wasn't about control or cruelty. It was about survival. It was necessary.

"I know. I get that now." She says softly, nodding slowly.

"But I do regret crossing boundaries," I push forward, my eyes dropping to the table. I feel my throat tighten around the confession. "I regret letting lines blur before I was ready to tell you the truth. I regret letting you care without giving you the full truth. It was too big of a risk." I keep my eyes trained downward, knowing I can't shoulder disappointing her more.

Her voice is quiet when she speaks. "Do you wish you

could take it back?”

I hesitate for a short second, long enough to know there’s no pulling back from this. “No,” I admit. “But I do wish it wasn’t so complicated.” Her breath audibly stutters but she doesn’t speak, like if she did, it would ruin the fragility of the moment.

“I care about you more than I should,” I admit, my hand scrubbing across my beard as I finally lift my eyes again, the truth leaving me feeling more exposed than if I were standing in the middle of a war zone. “More than is clean. More than is professional.” I exhale a heavy breath. “And that complicates everything.” I meet her eyes fully now. “You deserved the truth. All of it. And...now you have it.”

She pulls her hands away from her mug, gaze unwavering. It feels like she can see straight into my soul. “Why now?”

“Because the threat is neutralized,” I answer. “And because you needed to know before you had to decide anything else.” My brows lift a fraction when I add “Because I needed you to know.” And I did. Because if she chooses to walk away, I’ll have to live with that decision. But at least I can live with knowing that I had the strength to admit my feelings instead of hiding from them this time.

She studies me for a long moment before she speaks again. My stomach turns in the silence, my throat tightening again. “So, what happens now?” she asks.

I exhale slowly, shrugging one shoulder. “Now you get to choose.”

She blinks twice, her brows coming together again. “Choose what?”

“Whatever you want your next step to look like. Whether you want to stay,” I say quietly, the mere thought of the choice nearly enough to choke me. "Whether you want distance. Whether you want nothing to do with this world, or with me. It's your choice now, Sav."

Her voice is steady when she replies. "What about you?"

"I stay where I am," I say. "Until you decide."

48

Savannah

The truth sits heavy between us, but it doesn't crush me this time. It settles slowly, like a leaf following the current of a gentle stream. It clicks into place like a puzzle piece I've been holding upside down for months. I don't speak right away. Because for the first time, I don't feel like I'm scrambling to catch up.

I wrap my hands tighter around the mug, more out of habit than need. The warmth from the coffee has long since faded but having something tangible in my hands helps collect my thoughts. Sebastian watches me like he's bracing for impact, like any second I might bolt or break or demand something he can't give.

"I knew something was wrong," I say finally. "Back home. Before the cabin. Before any of this happened. Something always felt...off." I glance down at the table, tracing a faint knot in the wood with my thumb. "I never knew exactly what it was, I couldn't put a name to it."

He listens patiently, letting me speak, and through my

peripheral I can see him watching me carefully as if I'll bend or break under the weight of my own words. "I kept thinking I was being dramatic. Or paranoid. Maybe a little stir-crazy or something. Like I was always looking for something wrong because I didn't want to be there." A small, humorless smile tugs at my mouth. "I told myself I was imagining the weight of it. That if I stopped looking over my shoulder, it would go away." I lift my gaze to him then. "And you were there the whole time."

"Yes," he affirms, leaning back toward the table. Toward me. Like his body calls for mine when it senses something is off.

I nod once. "That explains a lot." The silence stretches as he offers me the space to decide what I want instead of telling me what to feel, like I've become accustomed to from every presence in my life before him. It gives me room to breathe. To process. "I don't love that you didn't tell me," I admit. "I don't love that I was watched without knowing." I inhale a calming breath, letting my lungs inflate entirely. "But I understand why."

My words seem to chip away at the tension he carries when his shoulders ease a fraction. "And I get why you close off," I continue. "Why you compartmentalize. Why you treat your life like something that has to be controlled or it'll explode. I don't *like* it, but I understand it." I swallow, the memory of last night flashing sharp and bright. "I lived it. Just for a few hours. And it scared the hell out of me. I still haven't really let myself sit and think about it...I might actually go crazy if I do." The confession makes me feel small. His features tighten at my admission like it causes him physical pain to know that I was afraid, to recall how he found me, the blood on my palms that didn't belong to me.

"It never stops," he breathes.

"I know," I say. "That's what scares me most." I shift in my seat, curling one leg beneath me. I study him for a moment, reading the lines etched into his face from years of fighting, of practiced vigilance.

I feel a pang in my chest, but I don't look away. I remember how I felt the day he went to the cache. When I was alone. When I thought he had left me, that he wasn't coming back. The memory sends a shiver through me. My head shakes in disbelief, unable to imagine the constant state of alertness, even when he makes it look so effortless. "I don't know how you've lived like this for so long..." I trail off.

His lips part, then press together, like he's searching for the answer that will satisfy me the most. "I guess you just adapt after a while." I reach for his hand without thinking, my fingers wrapping around his. He threads his fingers through mine in response, anchoring me. My thumb brushes the back of his knuckles, once again bruised, "Thank you, again. For last night. For all of it." My voice wobbles, feeling that familiar burn in the back of my throat. "For keeping me safe. I know that was never a question for you, that it was your job...but I need you to hear it anyway." He squeezes my hand once, firm and assuring.

"I would do it again," he insists. "Every time."

"I know." My voice is soft as I dip my chin, fixing my eyes on our connected hands. I give the moment time to settle before I speak again. The kitchen feels different in the daylight. Less like a bunker, more like a place where decisions actually happen. "So," I draw in a slow breath. "This is the part where I'm supposed to decide."

Sebastian doesn't look away and he doesn't pull his

hand from mine but his eyes seem to lose a small glimmer at that, the usual piercing blue shifting into something more worn down and ashen. "Yes. If you're ready to."

My eyes drift to the table briefly, trying to ease some of the weight from my chest. The faint scratch marks in the wood, the ripple in my coffee from my knee bouncing beneath the table. It's strange how normal everything looks, considering how much my life has cracked open. "You're not pushing me," I say, voicing my thoughts aloud, "Or telling me what I *should* do."

"No," His voice is even as his fingers tighten around mine. "I never would."

I nod, my lips tugging upward into a small grin. "You didn't give me a choice before."

"I couldn't," he says quietly and I feel the guilt behind it.

"I know," I sigh. It feels different this time. Less defensive, more resolved. "But you are now."

"Yes." His voice is rough, almost constricted, as if he's anticipating a crash before it happens. I guess I shouldn't expect otherwise. Sebastian never really has been the glass-half-full type.

I sit back slightly, crossing my arms to hold myself together while I think. "If I walk away," I say, choosing my words carefully, "You won't stop me."

I notice the way his jaw tightens when he shakes his head, catching the way his eyes shut for a few seconds too long to call it a blink. "No."

"And if I stay," I continue, arching a brow in his direction. "You won't...lie to me anymore. Not like before?" The word *lie* sits heavy on my tongue. I know that he omitted things for a reason. Still doesn't lessen the sting.

Sebastian shakes his head fervently, with what I think is the most urgency I've seen from him since we met. "No. No more keeping you in the dark."

I glance up at him, my tongue running over my lips. "Even when it's ugly?"

"Especially then."

That earns a small, crooked smile from me. "Figures." The truth is, I already know the shape of my answer. I've known it since the night in the cabin when I realized fear wasn't running my life anymore, knowledge was. "I don't want to pretend this didn't happen," I say. "I don't want to go back to not knowing. Not after all of this." He watches me closely, shoulders tight like he's afraid to breathe too loud.

"I'm not saying yes to your world," I clarify. "Not blindly. Not without questions. Questions that I expect you to answer," I tease. "But I'm not running from it, either." I pause for a beat, searching his gaze for the answer before I ask, "What are *you* choosing?"

"Savannah..." His eyes soften in a way that's honest and unafraid of what comes next. "It's not a choice for me anymore. It's you. And it has been since that first night in the cabin and I'm not going to pretend what I feel for you doesn't exist anymore." He pauses, just long enough for a flush to settle on my cheeks. "Even if it costs me everything." My heart swells and I tug my lesser lip between my teeth.

"Okay," I breathe, gathering myself from the quivering puddle of nerves in my stomach. "Then here's my choice." I reach across the table, resting my other hand over his and offering a soft, comforting squeeze. "I stay. For now. I learn, ask questions. I won't disappear just because things are complicated. I'm choosing this, Sebastian. *You. Us.*" His fingers curl around mine, firm and grounding. His lips curl upward slowly, like he's relieved and in disbelief all at once that someone could choose him at all.

The decision doesn't feel like a leap. It feels like planting my feet. He doesn't answer right away. Sebastian never does when something matters.

His thumb brushes once over the back of my hand, slow and deliberate, like he's grounding himself before he speaks. I watch his face as he looks down at where we're connected, our hands folded together on the table both fragile and intentional. "You don't have to decide everything today," he says quietly, as if there's any room left for doubt.

"I know," I nod. "I'm not trying to. But I know where I want to be."

The smallest huff of a breath leaves him. Not quite a laugh, but something close. "I just need you to know," I continue, "that I'm not here because I don't have anywhere else to go. I'm here because I *want* this."

He dips his chin once in understanding, even when I can still read the dull suspicion behind his eyes like he doesn't entirely believe it. "I've spent most of my life," he says slowly, like the words themselves are delicate and breakable, "assuming that wanting something was the fastest way to lose it."

I swallow the knot growing in my throat. "So you stopped wanting."

He shakes his head once, correcting me. "I stopped admitting it." I squeeze his hand, a silent beat of encouragement. "When you asked me if you were still the mission," he continues, eyes locking to mine where they were unfocused before, "that wasn't a difficult question." I feel my heart lurch in my chest. "The difficult part," he says, "was accepting that you haven't been that for a long time." The air between us feels charged—*alive*. I can feel my pulse in my fingertips where they rest against his skin.

"And now?" I ask.

He exhales slowly, lifting a single shoulder. "Now I'm here. Letting myself want something I know I can't control." His gaze doesn't waver. The words settle between us like a promise he isn't afraid of breaking.

I smile then, small and unguarded. "That's all I needed."

His thumb presses into my knuckle, firmer this time. "I'm not good at this," he adds.

"Trust me, I know," I say gently, a breathy laugh filling the air between us. "But you're trying." That finally pulls a real smile from him. Brief, crooked, gone almost as soon as it appears. "For what it's worth," he says, quieter now, "I don't see you as something fragile anymore, either."

I lift my brows, my own grin spreading. "You say that like it's a compliment."

"It is," he replies. "You're stronger than most people I've known. And braver than you realize."

Emotion swells in my throat, but it doesn't spill over. I just nod, leaning a little closer across the table until our joined hands are the only thing either of us is really focused on. "Then we'll figure this out," I say. "One step at a time, right?"

"Yes," he agrees. No hesitation this time. This time, the future doesn't feel like something rushing toward me. It feels like something I'm walking into, eyes open, with him beside me.

49

Sebastian

Jesse doesn't knock when he returns. He never does. The door closes behind him with a solid click that sounds final in a way I don't entirely trust. "It's contained," he says simply, shrugging out of his jacket. Snow melts into dark spots across the hardwood off his boots. "No active tails. No chatter. No movement. Checked in with command and whatever was left of it died with last night. Still want to talk to us, though." My shoulders loosen before I can stop them. Even with the looming threat of having to deal with superiors on my back, the hardest part of this all is past us now.

Savannah is the one who speaks next. "What about my family?"

Jesse's eyes shift to her. The easy grin he wears so naturally doesn't show up this time. His tone stays gentle, careful. "They're okay. Nobody saw anything. No one's hurt and as far as I know, they have no knowledge of anyone being there." I watch the tension leave her face in slow increments, her breath shaking lightly on the exhale

"But," Jesse continues, tongue running over his lips. "Your dad's on borrowed time. Feds are closing in fast now that the trail's lit up. It's not a matter of *if*—it's when." His arms cross over his chest, punctuating the finality of his statement. Internally, I'm relieved. The mission is over. Externally, I watch Savannah's brows come together and anxiousness cloud her features.

"I need to see him," she says, standing from the table. Her hand falls from mine and the emptiness presses in like walls caving under pressure. The words land like a misfire in my chest and I turn toward her immediately. "No," it's more forceful than I intended.

She doesn't flinch or argue. Just looks at me with that calm, infuriating steadiness she's earned over the last few weeks. "I need to close that door, Sebastian. I can't just...never see them again. Even if it seems like they've already moved past me." I catch a flicker of hurt pass through her eyes with the last of her sentence.

Every instinct in me screams against it. "I'll go with you," I offer, already running logistics in my mind, "we'll make sure it's safe."

She pauses for a short moment but shakes her head slowly. "No." Then, softer, "I *need* to do this on my own." My jaw tenses at the stubbornness that I can't help but admire from her and I release an exasperated breath through my nose. She reads me like a book, stepping closer to rest her hand on my chest as she tilts her face up toward me. "Can you just...wait for me? Be here when I get back?" I sense the uncertainty in her question and my stomach churns with regret. She thinks I'm going to disappear on her, again.

The room feels too small all of a sudden. I study her face, searching for fear, doubt, hesitation. I find none. Instead, it's full of trust. Raw and terrifying all the same. "I'll wait," I say at last, every syllable a surrender. "Right here." Her posture eases, breathing out a long breath full of relief

When she leaves, the door closes quietly behind her. And I lose my mind. I pace the length of the room like a caged animal. Check my gear. Then check it again, knowing damn well I won't follow. My foot taps. My hand curls and uncurls. I glance at the door every twenty seconds like it might disappear if I don't keep it in sight. This goes against everything I've ever been trained to do.

Every instinct inside of me is shouting, demanding that I act. But she asked me to wait—a request that feels impossible. I cross to the window, eyes scanning the street below, searching for movement that isn't there. When I return to the table, my gaze catches on her abandoned mug. I rake a hand through my hair, again and again, until my scalp aches.

Jesse watches me for a minute, leaning against the counter, coffee in hand. I almost forget that he's there and then he snorts. "Dude. Relax. She'll be okay this time." I glare at him, feeling the muscle in my jaw twitch. He raises his hands, palms out. "I'm serious. She fucking took that guy out last night. You think she can't handle herself?"

"I know she can," I hiss through clenched teeth. That's the *problem.* This time, I'm choosing not to intervene. Not to control the outcome. Not to protect by force. She didn't ask me to save her, she asked me to stay. And I am. Even if it drains every last bit of my sanity.

I plant myself in one of the kitchen chairs, gripping the edge of the table like it might anchor me in place. I force my lungs to work the way they're supposed to. In. Out. Slow, measured breaths. She's survived worse than this, I remind myself. She's already walked through the unthinkable and come out standing. *She'll come back. She has to.*

This time, the job isn't to intervene. It isn't to track or confront or neutralize. This time, the job is to wait. And it might be the hardest assignment I've ever taken.

The clock on the wall ticks, obnoxiously loud in the otherwise quiet house. I glance at Jesse, reclined on the couch like he doesn't have a care in the world. *Typical.* Each second stretches and drags. The minutes pile up until they feel indistinguishable from hours.

I replay every possible outcome in my head, every scenario I've trained myself to anticipate and prevent. I stop myself from reaching for my gear. Stop myself from standing. Stop myself from becoming the man who rushes in and takes control instead of trusting the woman who asked him not to.

I breathe again.

In.

Out.

I think about her steady voice. The way she looked at me when she asked me to wait. She wasn't afraid. Wasn't nervous. Nothing short of certain that this is what she needed. And I hold onto that because it's the only thing keeping me here.

50

Savannah

It's been so long since I've been behind the wheel of a car that I nearly forget which foot goes to which pedal. The roads are familiar in all the wrong ways. They haven't changed, but I have. When I pull into the driveway, the house feels smaller in the light. Not physically, nothing's changed there, but the air is tighter. Like everything inside is bracing for impact that it doesn't know is coming. My hand hovers at my side for a second before I finally let the door fall shut behind me. The sound echoes louder than it should.

My father stands in the living room, phone in one hand, papers scattered across the coffee table like he's been caught mid-scramble. He looks...shaken. Older. His hair is uncombed, eyes rimmed red and he moves restlessly. Not the composed man who used to command every room he walked into.

"Dad." The word leaves me before I can overthink it, falling flat into the space between us.

He spins around so fast he nearly drops the phone and

papers fly to the floor behind him. "Vannah?" His eyes go wide, disbelief flashing across his face before it melts into something frantic when my childhood nickname leaves him. He crosses the room in three long strides and pulls me into his arms. My arms remain starkly at my sides, lips curling back in disgust.

His grip tightens anyway, like he's afraid I'll vanish if he loosens it. "Where have you been?" he demands, hands sliding to my shoulders as he pulls back to look at me. His gaze darts over my face, my arms, my clothes. "Are you hurt? Did someone—" I step back, putting space between us. The movement is deliberate, drawing a clear line.

"Dad," I say again, every ounce of patience forced into keeping my voice calm, "I know."

I watch as the color drains from his face so quickly it's almost startling, his features morphing into something ghostly before he recovers. His mouth opens, then closes again, like he's recalculating. "What are you talking about, sweetheart?" The pet name twists in my stomach, any endearment I felt from it before quickly diminishing.

I shake my head once and lift a hand, squinting up at him. "Don't." He freezes, his nostrils flaring so minutely I almost miss it. "I know about everything," I continue, my voice steady despite the way my heart pounds against my chest like a drum searching for rhythm. "The drugs. The money. The people you've been working with. Don't try to lie to me about it." My arms cross over my chest, brows drawing together.

"You don't know what you're saying." His eyes dart across the room as if he's afraid someone might hear, like his world isn't actively collapsing beneath him. His teeth grind together despite his clear attempt to keep his composure. He inhales slowly through his nose, taking a cautious step forward. Instinctively, I take another back. "Vannah—"

"I've been gone for over a month," the bitterness drips from my words like poison. "A month! And you're standing here acting like I just stepped out for a long weekend." I scoff a humorless laugh, my hands gesturing viciously as I talk. "And you're still trying to act like everything is normal? Did you even wonder what the hell happened to me?"

His brows knit together and he grimaces, confusion flickering across his face. "That's not—Savannah, it's only been—" He fumbles over his search for excuses. "Mason said you left," he tries. "You're old enough now that I respected your decision."

"Bullshit!" I fume. "You're just covering your ass. *God*—" I feel my cheeks heat, my teeth grinding together. "All this time and you're still treating me like I'm fucking stupid!"

"Watch your language when you speak to me," he grumbles. His throat bobs as he swallows a thick lump, shoulders sagging like the weight he's been carrying finally has a name.

"Wow…" I mutter. "For a man that always acted so strong, you're looking weak these days, dad. What, you can't even defend yourself to your own daughter?"

"That's not fair," he snaps and I feel myself flinch at his tone, desperation bleeding through the anger now. "I've been losing my mind trying to find you."

My head shakes slowly, lips turning up in a grin that tastes sour. "No," I reply, shaking my head. "You've been losing *control*. There's a difference."

I watch his throat work as he swallows whatever lie he was about to conjure. "I know why they took me," I go on. "I know why I mattered. And I know you told yourself I was protected—as long as you followed the rules." His eyes flicker away. "I wasn't supposed to be part of this," I fire. "But you made me part of it the moment you decided money mattered more than your family."

"That's not true," he insists, voice cracking. His pupils dilate and he takes a step towards me. I take another away from him. "Everything I did—I did it for you. For Mason."

I point an accusing finger at his chest, rage burning hot in the pit of my stomach. All that I've been through and it's only earning me more excuses. "No, you didn't. You did it for yourself. And you told yourself it was for us so you could live with it."

My eyes flick to where his hands curl into fists at his sides. "You don't understand the position I was in," he tries.

"I understand more than you think," I snap. "I understand that you deliberately put me in danger and called it *necessary*. I understand that you decided what risks were acceptable without ever asking me." My voice wavers for the first time, but I don't stop. "I understand that I had to disappear for you to notice something was wrong."

He swallows hard, eyes glassy now as defeat washes over him. "Savannah... please."

I hold his gaze, every part of me aching. "I didn't come here expecting some sort of apology," I say, an uneven breath passing through my lips. "I came here to close this door. To tell you that whatever happens next—whatever choices you made—you don't get to make them for me anymore. I'm not your leverage anymore. And I'm not your blind spot. So this is goodbye, dad. I hope it was worth it."

"We're not done with this conversation," he starts as I push past him, leaving him standing in the wreckage of the world he created.

"Yes, we are," I call over my shoulder, storming through the room and leaving nothing but ruins of a life I once accepted behind me. His hand lifts like he might grab me, stop me, say something that matters but I'm already moving, already halfway up the stairs. Each step feels heavier than the last, not because I doubt myself, but because this house is filled with echoes. Old versions of me. Old fears. Flashbacks of the last night I was here flicker at the edges of my vision.

My room looks exactly the same, somehow, when I push open the door. Like that night never happened. Same pale walls. Same crooked picture frame above the dresser. Same dent in the carpet near the bed where I used to drop my backpack every day after school. It's like time paused here while I kept moving slowly, painfully forward.

I open the closet and grab clothes without thinking. Jeans. Sweaters. Things that feel like me *now*, not the girl I used to be. I fold them neatly, stacking them on the bed like I'm afraid if I rush, I'll lose my nerve. "Sav?" The voice stops me cold.

I turn as Mason steps into the doorway, his face pale, eyes rimmed red like he hasn't slept in days. His worry hits differently than our father's did. It isn't frantic or performative. It's quiet. Earnest.

"Oh my God," he breathes, crossing the room like the hallway is burning behind him. "Where have you been?" I don't get the chance to answer before his arms are around me, crushing and familiar and safe. I melt into him without hesitation, even with unanswered questions itching at the back of my throat. My face presses into his shoulder as everything I've been holding back finally loosens its grip.

I inhale a deep breath, his scent of citrus and musk

wrapping itself around me. He pulls back enough to look at me, hands braced on my shoulders the same way they always have been when he needed to make sure I was really there. "You scared the hell out of me," he croaks.

"I know." My throat tightens. "I'm sorry."

He shakes his head and releases a long breath, tightening his arms around me. For a moment, neither of us speaks. The silence between us isn't uncomfortable. It never has been. I allow myself to drink in the moment, knowing what comes next is going to ruin it in an instance.

"Did you know?" I ask when my courage finally returns, pulling back enough to gauge his expression. Mason may be able to conjure up a lie quicker than my father, but his eyes have never fooled me. And when they dart to the left, my heart sinks into the pit of my stomach.

His brows knit together, jaw slackening. "Know about what?" he asks, tone too close to casual to be genuine.

"You did..." My voice is no higher than a whisper as I take a step back, everything inside my chest shattering in an instant. Any idea I had of what trust was, the love I thought my brother had for me that I was never given by the rest of my family, the bond that we've shared since we were old enough to talk—all of it crumbles beneath me, a landslide of realization tumbling through me. My gaze drops to the floor, chin trembling with truth. "You knew the whole time, didn't you?"

When I glance back up at him, his eyes are examining me carefully, like he's debating if he can still try to convince me otherwise. "Vannah..." he mutters the same nickname as my father. "I couldn't tell you..."

I huff a quiet breath and the rest of my body deflates with my lungs when I clap a hand over my mouth to hide the soft whimper that follows. My head shakes quickly as I take another step away from him, turning my back to him to hide my devastation. He caused this, him and my father, but he doesn't deserve to see the aftermath. Betrayal wraps its violent hands around my heart and squeezes, my insides hollowing piece by piece. "Unbelievable," I whisper.

"I won't come back," I force my voice steady, pushing whatever strength I have left into it. "I'm not the same blinded little sister who left before and neither of you are going to drag me down with you." I shove my things more recklessly into my suitcase now, my feet aching to get away.

"Savannah, listen to me," he presses. When I feel his hand on my elbow, begging for my attention, I recoil from his touch like it scorches me.

"No!" I shout, whirling on him and pushing at his chest. "You lied to me! You were the one person—" my voice falters and I curl my hands inward, pushing my nails into my palms to ground myself. "I trusted you. I won't make the same mistake twice." When I turn to my suitcase again, I pause, my hands hovering over the clothes shakily. "Get out."

"You don't mean that—"

The sound of his voice pinches my last remaining nerve and I pick up the closest object my fingers can close around—the framed picture of us on my nightstand—turning and hurdling it past his shoulder in one swift motion. It shatters on the ground with a loud clash, knocking my jewelry trinket off the dresser in its path. "I said get out!"

Mason looks at me as if he's been struck, his features reading the same desolation as mine. But this isn't my fault. And I won't carry the guilt for it. Although hesitantly, he stalks toward the door. "When you decide it's time to come home," he rasps, "I'll be here waiting for you."

I don't answer. I wait until he disappears from the doorway to finish packing my things, my heart cracking an inch further with every move. And as I zip up the borrowed bag, standing in the room I grew up in, I feel the truth wash over me overwhelmingly. Leaving doesn't mean losing everything.

Sometimes, it just means choosing yourself.

51

Sebastian

Waiting is worse than any firefight I've ever walked into. There's no enemy to track, no angle to cover, no decisive action to take. Just *trust*. Trust that she'll be okay. That she'll come back. And for a man like me, trust has always felt more dangerous than jumping in front of a bullet.

Especially when it comes to relying on another person. I've always been self-sufficient. It's easier that way. No one to disappoint, no one to lose. But somewhere along the way…Savannah became more than the mission. It's dangerous. Incredibly irresponsible. And if I'm honest with myself? I don't know where we go from here. But I know that I want to find out. Because sitting here, waiting for her, is harder than letting her walk away.

The door opens and I'm on my feet before my brain catches up, heart slamming so hard it feels like it might crack my ribs. She steps inside, her movements steady, her expression calm in a way that tells me everything I need to know before she ever speaks. Pride swells in my chest, bursting through every seam. She didn't just survive. She took everything that meant to break her and turned it into strength.

My body reacts before I allow myself to think. I close the distance between us in two strides and stop just short of engulfing her in my arms. I lift one hand, tucking her hair neatly behind her ear, my thumb settling beneath her chin to tilt her face up to mine. "Are you okay?"

Her breath stutters under my touch but her lips curl into a small grin. She leans into my touch, delicate fingers curling around my wrist. "Yeah," she nods, "I'm okay."

I pull her into me, the restraint finally snapping, my arms wrapping around her like I've been holding my breath for weeks and only just remembered how to exhale. She fits against me easily, like she always has, like she always will. Her face presses into my chest, and I feel the last of the tension drain out of me in one long, shuddering sweep. I let my eyes fall shut, one hand cupping the back of her neck, the other settling across her lower back. Her arms slide around my waist effortlessly.

"Mason knew the whole time. About everything." she says quietly, her voice void of any emotion.

My eyes go wide, jaw falling slack. It isn't often that things find me off-guard, but when they do, it's enough to crash into my senses like a car moving headfirst into a wall. "I'm sorry," I murmur against her hair.

She pulls back enough to look at me, features set and filled with nothing short of determination. "I'm done running," she squares her shoulders. "And I'm done being managed. I'm making my own choices now."

My hands come up to frame her face, thumbs brushing along her jaw. "Yeah?" I lift a brow at her, my features relaxing into a soft grin, and my chest swelling with pride. If you had told me when I met Savannah Monroe that she'd become the strongest person I know, I would've wagered money against it. But now, with this version of her standing in front of me, I swallow every doubt and know with certainty that she can handle whatever might stand in her way next.

Her smile comes easily and mimics my own, like she's setting her past down and leaving it behind her, wrapped neatly in a box that's better left untouched. "I'm choosing where I stand now. And the only place I want to be is with you."

The world seems to narrow to the space between us. My breath stalls, chest expanding but refusing to release it, like my body doesn't know how to process what she's offering. It's sharp and overwhelming. My fingers tighten unconsciously into the fabric of her jacket.

With me. *Chosen.* Not out of fear, but want.

"Savannah…" Her name is a whisper when it leaves me and I drop my forehead to rest against hers. "I can't promise you an easy life," I admit. "Or a safe one. Even when I do everything in my power to protect you. There are parts of me that don't shut off. Parts that may never know how. But I can promise you that I'll try. And I can promise that you'll never have to doubt your worth again."

She lifts her arms, sliding them around my neck as she gazes up at me through half-lidded lashes. "I don't need easy," she shakes her head slowly. "I need honest. And I need someone who stands with me instead of in front of me. I don't want to go back, Sebastian. I can't."

I swallow hard. "Then I'm not going anywhere." I don't add conditions. I don't think about timelines or exit strategies or contingency plans. I choose her, fully, and everything that it means.

She exhales, something like relief softening her shoulders. "And Savannah?" My thumb trails along the fragile skin of her neck, feeling her pulse beneath my touch. I lift her chin gently, my lips meeting hers in an embrace I've been aching for. A silent confession of everything I've been unable to say. It ripples through my chest, slow and warm. When I finally pull away, my breath trembles slightly. "I want you to know that I love you."

Outside, the world keeps turning. Missions will come. Consequences will follow. Life will demand things from both of us that we don't fully understand yet. But when she whispers back "I love you, too," I know that I'm not a shadow anymore.

I'm a man standing beside the woman he loves. And for the first time in a long time, that feels like home.

52

Savannah

The remote slips through my fingers twice before I manage to catch it. Sebastian and Jesse left hours ago and the safe house has been uncomfortably quiet since. I'm surprised I haven't worn a path in the floor already from pacing. I've folded the blanket, unfolded it again because it didn't look right, and readjusted. I've stared at the same spot on the wall until the shape of it stopped making sense. Eventually, I reach for the remote again just to prove to myself I can still make something happen when I want it to.

The television clicks on and I don't even register the channel at first. There's a woman talking, all serious tone and perfect cadence. A chyron scrolls across the bottom of the screen. I glance down at it, half interested, half detached.

Then I see my last name. My breath catches so sharply that I choke on the air. There's an old photo on the screen now, cropped and slightly grainy. My father stands to the left of me, Mason and my mother flanking us. I was smiling there; happy and unaware. I looked like a girl who still believed the world made sense. The anchor keeps talking and I turn the volume up by a few notches.

"Tonight, federal authorities are confirming details in a multi-state investigation tied to an international narcotics operation with roots in Southwestern Colorado." The voice fades in one ear and out the other. Another image flashes on screen. My father, alone and older, shaking hands with someone who looks too important outside one of his offices.

"According to court documents released this afternoon, the investigation centers on a Telluride-based import-export company specializing in timber and raw materials. Officials allege the business was used to move illicit substances across state lines by concealing them with legitimate commercial shipments." My eyes are glued to the screen for so long they burn, the broadcaster flashing images of our house and our driveway in a way that feels explicit. Aerial footage shows trucks lined up at a loading dock that looks too familiar.

"The company's owner, Thomas Monroe, has long been considered a respected local figure and was identified by authorities as a primary distribution organizer for the operation." The words begin to blur together. My stomach sinks into the couch with my weight. The reporter says my father's name like it's a headline, like it belongs to the public now. Something people can pass around to dissect and argue over.

"Federal agents executed coordinated seizures earlier this week, freezing assets and shutting down multiple facilities connected to the business. Investigators emphasize that no evidence has been found linking Mr. Monroe's family members to the alleged crimes." A fleeting second of relief courses through me. Mason may not be innocent entirely, but he didn't start any of this, and he doesn't deserve to pay for my father's crimes.

They don't say my name, but they show my face. My heart thuds loud and uneven, a merciless tempo against my ribs. I can feel heat creeping up my neck, skin buzzing close to panic, but not quite reaching it. It's stranger than that— like my body is bracing for a blow that never lands.

"Officials say additional information will be released as charges are finalized." The front door clicks open, but I don't turn my head. My spine straightens without command, the result of instinct, memory. A lifetime of learning what footsteps mean.

I hear the familiar weight of his boots. The slow, careful way he closes the door behind him. The pause that always comes when he enters a room, like he's checking for safety before he takes up space in it. Sebastian steps into view, shoulders dusted with cold, hair damp from snow that's already melting. He looks tired, the kind that comes from finally setting down something heavy, not the exhaustion from violence or adrenaline that I'm used to seeing etched into his features.

The television keeps talking. I feel his presence shift, sharpen. My eyes finally drift to him, but his are locked on the screen. On my family's faces, on the life I didn't know was already being rewritten for the world to consume. He takes a cautious step toward me.

"Savannah..." he breathes, quiet enough to anchor me. He crosses the room to sit beside me, his hand a warm comfort when it lands on my thigh. It's real, solid, and says that I'm not as alone as I feel at this moment. "They moved fast," he offers gently. "I didn't think it would air this soon."

I nod, my eyes locking back on the screen. The

reporter keeps talking about contracts and shell companies, reach and logistics. About how trusted my father was. How no one suspected anything because there was nothing to suspect. That part cuts the deepest.

I inhale a breath through my nose and turn toward him, letting my leg brush against his. "How'd it go?" I ask, and I hate that my voice shakes on the last word. He exhales through his nose, leaning back against the couch. "Harris chewed my ass," he reaches to scrub a hand across the back of his neck. "Debriefing wasn't exactly pleasant."

I glance at him, my lips twitching up a fraction. "Harris?" I arch a brow at him. "Was it that bad?"

"Our field commander." He nods just once. "I've had worse, but not by much."

The TV cuts to another image. Paparazzi style, me, stepping out of a car months ago. Oblivious. My chest tightens.

"They never tell it right," Sebastian says quietly, softer this time. "They can't. They don't have all the details."

I let my eyes drift back to him again. His jaw is tight, I imagine in irritation, because the rest of his features are still collected. There's no calculation behind them, just presence. "If you have any questions," he continues, "I'll answer them for you."

I consider that for a moment. My insides still quiver with images flashing on the screen. But then I shake my head, reaching for the remote and turning off the TV. The room plunges into a silence so suddenly it almost rings. I place the remote carefully on the edge of the couch, releasing a long breath that feels like I'd been holding it for too long.

"No," I adjust to angle myself toward him. "I don't think I want to know." Sebastian watches me for a beat, letting me voice my thoughts without disappointment or judgement. He nods slowly in understanding. "My father was a bad man," I continue, swallowing the wobble in my voice. His hand closes around mine, steadying me. "And he did some evil things."

The truth of it doesn't fully settle. Even after everything, after the cabin and the news and the arrest. It still feels foreign in my mouth. But it doesn't feel like betrayal anymore. It feels like clarity. "But..." My voice catches. "He was still my dad."

Sebastian's gaze softens, his fingers slipping into the spaces of mine. I bring my other hand to rest on top of them. "I'd rather live in my truth of him. The parts that were real to me. The man that I knew..." I drop my eyes to our connected hands. "Not the version they're going to turn into a headline."

Silence passes between us for a moment. I draw in a slow breath. "Besides," I add, a small smile pulling at my lips despite it all. "I'm ready to leave this all behind, anyway."

Sebastian lifts a brow at me, his thumb brushing over my knuckles. "Yeah?"

I nod, meeting his eyes again. "I have something to look forward to now." His expression shifts, like he's finally allowing relief to run through him. "Okay," he says softly. "Then we leave it where it's at."

I lean into him, my head resting against his shoulder. "I love you." I feel his lips press to the top of my head in response. He doesn't have to say it back. I feel it in the way he wraps his arm around my shoulders, pulling me an inch closer. And in the way his cheek rests against the top of my head, the way I've never felt more at home than I do right now. And I know now, the future is no longer something I have to survive.

It's something we get to walk through. Together.

EPILOGUE

Savannah

The air is warm enough that I've abandoned sleeves entirely.
It still surprises me, sometimes, how easy it is to step outside
without bracing for cold, how the sun lingers instead of
vanishing behind mountains by mid-afternoon. I'm dressed in
shorts and an old tee that's already smudged with dust from
cardboard boxes, the windows of the townhouse thrown
open to let the city breathe its way inside

Boston is nothing like Telluride.

There are no hushed streets or familiar faces here. No
sense that everyone knows my name—or my father's. The
skyline cuts sharp against the sky, glass and steel instead of
pine and snow, and the noise never really stops. Cars, voices,
life. It's chaotic in a way that feels...right.

I balance on my toes, stretching to slide a box onto
the top shelf of the narrow living room built-in. It's lighter
than it looks, full of trinkets mostly, but my arms still strain
as I reach. Before I can adjust my grip, warm arms slide
around my waist, palms settling against the bare skin where

my shirt has ridden up. I don't startle. Instead, a lazy smile graces my features.

Sebastian presses in behind me, chin hovering near my shoulder. "You know," he sighs, voice low and thoughtful, "I think I'm going to like it here."

I breathe a soft laugh as I set the box down and let my heels drop back to the floor. "That almost sounds like optimism."

"Don't get used to it," he replies, but there's no real edge to it anymore. Just ease behind the smirk he's recently adopted.

"Hey," a familiar voice cuts in from the doorway. "Me too."

Sebastian groans on instinct, already annoyed, already resigned. Jesse stands there with his hands in his pockets, surveying the half-unpacked room. He grins wide, unbothered. "What? I'm allowed to have opinions." My smile widens as I turn in Sebastian's grip to face both of the men who have grown permanency in my heart.

"You're allowed to have fewer opinions," Sebastian grumbles.

I tilt my head to look up at him, slipping my fingers into the hair at the base of his neck. He still pretends not to like it, but he leans in anyway, his forehead brushing against my temple. "Don't be mean," I tease.

Jesse watches the exchange with open amusement, that low whistle preceding his words. "*Wow*. Domestic life looks good on you, Bash."

Sebastian shoots him a look over my head. "Go unpack something."

"I already did," Jesse says cheerfully. "Twice. You're welcome." I shake my head, laughter bubbling up before I can stop it. For a moment, I stand there, boxed in by half-built furniture, sunlight spilling across the floor, Sebastian's hands steady at my waist, and let the feeling settle. This is my life now. And I wouldn't trade it for anything.

I glance up at Sebastian again, my thumb idly tracing the line of his jaw. "Hey," I say casually, like my heart isn't thumping a little faster. "What would you think about me getting a job?"

He blinks down at me, caught off guard. "A job?"

"Yeah," I say, maintaining my smile, feigning innocence with a shrug. "Something normal, you know. Something mine."

Jesse's eyebrows shoot up and I assume he's sensing the rising tension in Sebastian's posture. "I love this idea," he snorts.

Sebastian exhales slowly, the corner of his mouth tugging upward despite the way I feel his jaw tighten beneath my touch. "You already decided, didn't you?"

"Maybe," I admit sheepishly. He studies me for a long moment, eyes narrowed slightly. Then his hands tighten at my waist, "I think," he says softly, "that you should do whatever makes you feel like this is home." I lean into him, with relief and excitement tangling together in my chest.

Because it doesn't feel like starting over. It feels like my life is just beginning.

DEAR READER,

395

Thank you so much for reading NOWHERE BUT HIM! I hope you enjoyed it.

If you loved Savannah and Sebastian's story, please consider leaving a review and sharing your thoughts with other readers.

Keep an eye out for my next novel to continue living in their world.

Jesse Pierce's story continues in NOTHING LIKE YOU—the second novel in the *Under Watch* series, featuring Devin Baker, a woman who is nothing like he expects.